ADVANCE FROM BROADWAY

ADVANCE FROM BROADWAY

19,000 MILES OF AMERICAN THEATRE

by Norris Houghton

HARCOURT, BRACE AND COMPANY   NEW YORK

PN
2266
H6

11-24-43 Coop 2.15

24145

TO

GRACE NORRIS HOUGHTON

Acknowledgment is made to the publishers for permission to quote from the following books: *Arena*, by Hallie Flanagan, reprinted with the permission of Duell, Sloan and Pearce, Inc.; *The Essence of Tragedy*, by Maxwell Anderson, reprinted with the permission of Anderson House; *Our Town* by Thornton Wilder, copyright 1938, 1939 by Coward-McCann, Inc.; and *New Theatres for Old*, copyright 1940 by Mordecai Gorelik, reprinted with the permission of the author and Samuel French.

Preface

THE ATTEMPT to relate the theatre of Broadway to the vast and complex field of dramatic activity which spreads out across the Untied States from Atlantic to Pacific took me during 1940 on a tour of approximately 19,000 miles. It might have been possible to remain in New York and assemble enough information to fill a book by sending out questionnaires and post-card inquiries, by studying the replies thereto and photographs of work done. It would have been impossible, however, to make any sort of evaluation of the work involved without seeing it at first-hand; impossible to grasp the meaning of the theatre to America without visiting its regions and its people; impossible, also, to gain any perspective on the New York stage without leaving Manhattan's turmoil for a time.

To evaluate, however, seemed to me of primary importance. We had heard for years of the work going on in college and university theatres, of the "little theatre movement." We all knew, through syndicated columnists and the stage periodicals, what was happening on Broadway. To collect and repeat this factual information, while no doubt useful, seemed to me less challenging than the attempt to discover why the theatre was functioning today in all these places, what significance it had for the present and the future. Especially interesting to me was the idea of tracing the relationships, if any existed, among all these elements of theatre.

One of the great difficulties involved in such an evaluation is the obvious one of lack of time. A few days in one place are insufficient to adequate understanding of all the factors involved in the apparent success or failure of a local enterprise. To help overcome this problem, I determined to base my study on as few different places as possible, while yet allowing for as broad geographical coverage as I could. Consequently I visited but about seventy stages along those thousands of miles. To each, however, I was able to devote much more time than would have been possible had I tried to observe the work of twice or three times that number. I know only too well, of course, that many of the places I omitted from my itinerary contain much that would have been of interest to me and of significance to this study. The loss of such material is regrettable but, as far as I can see, unavoidable. Also regrettable is the fact that a number of places I visited have no mention in this book; but the wealth of material with which I found myself encumbered when the survey was completed dictated further selectivity.

Another difficulty in evaluating the work in those places which I did visit was that it had to be done principally on the basis of what happened to be taking place at the moment I was there. Since every theatre has its high and its ebb tides which may follow one another with some regularity, it is possible that I have done an occasional injustice. If a judgment was to be made at all, however, I have felt that it must be made on the basis of what I actually saw, not of what I was told had occurred before I arrived or might take place after I left. And again I repeat, a judgment has seemed to me to be what was most needed.

This book makes no effort to trace the history of the American stage. My concern has been to catch the picture of the moment: to impress a few months of America's cultural life onto these pages—the momentous months of 1940 which may conceivably be the end of an era.

I have no right to claim all the conclusions of this study as my own. From hundreds of theatre workers in all fields and in all places I have gathered opinions as well as facts. The hopes and fears, the counsels and criticisms that go into these pages are a composite of their opinions, hopes and criticisms to which I count myself fortunate in having been able to be subjected. To such workers I make acknowledgment for these; to them I also offer my gratitude for hospitality and for enthusiastic assistance to me in my research. If in my effort to be honest, I appear to bite some of the hands that have fed me, I hope that I may be forgiven on the ground that I have sought their and the theatre's ultimate good.

My final and grateful acknowledgment is to the Division of Humanities of The Rockefeller Foundation, under a grant from which this book was made possible.

NORRIS HOUGHTON

Contents

ADVANCE

ASSIGNMENT

CHAPTER ONE

Vacation from Broadway

ON THE last day of January, 1940, I turned the key in my door, shoved my suitcases into a taxicab, headed toward the Pennsylvania Station in New York bound on a busman's holiday that would not return me to Manhattan for twelve months. I was setting out to seek the theatrical pattern of America.

It was growing dusk as the train drew out from the city. As I sat in the Pullman, I contemplated the scene I had left. The past three years had kept me busy about the theatre. Always, however, there had been that uncertainty as to what would happen next, which is part of the excitement of a theatrical career and part of its discouragement. This insecurity I had always assumed to be inevitable in an artistic life until I spent a winter in Moscow where I saw artists of the stage working together in theatre organizations that had a permanence out of which came consecutive growth. Since then I had been wondering whether our theatre would not be achieving greater artistry and perhaps a sounder economic structure if it could abandon the catch-as-catch-can procedure on which everyone, from producers to call-boys, operate. With co-

3

herent organization might there not be less frenzy, more creative thinking done by everyone, a chance to build co-operation out of which would be cast cut-throat competition and through which labor problems might find solutions? Even the high percentage of failure might be reduced. Could all this be accomplished, however, without some vast subsidy? Could it be accomplished without changing human nature? Might it be accomplished, perhaps, somewhere else than in New York under more felicitous circumstances? Or was it possible anywhere in the America we know today? Was this not, after all, Utopia of which I dreamt?

I know of no one around Broadway—except perhaps its youngest, naive, stage-struck novitiates—who is not impatient with the status quo in one way or another. We are impatient at Broadway's so frequent crass commercialism, which sometimes seems to pervade everyone who has anything to do with the theatre in any way. We are impatient at its waste of talent: at the vicious circle of employment it practices, and the unemployment for which it undertakes to find no solution. We are impatient at the lack of experimentation, at the rigid adherence to a pre-set style and technique, at the dearth of playwrights with something new to say or a new way to present old truths. We are impatient that our dreams so seldom come true.

Yet even as we are impatient of Broadway, we love it. It exercises a fascination, an hypnotic spell, so that even while counting my dissatisfactions as the train sped along, I could not refrain from wondering whether I had made a mistake in leaving it for a year. I thought of my friends in the theatre. Contrary to the assumption of some, Broadway contains a great many men and women of fine sensitivity, able intellectual capacity, fertile and eager imaginations, each with a strong love for the theatre. To be among these people is to draw refreshment and stimulation and the occasional rekindling of one's fiery dreams. The comradeship of persons who care about the same things, who talk the same language and whose capacities are a competitive challenge to assert the best that is in one —this comradeship is a fine thing and in spite of all the influences brought to bear to the contrary, it can be found on Broadway in as great degree as anywhere else in America.

I thought of the theatres of Broadway. With nostalgia I looked out across the fields shrouded in the dark of the winter night. What a contrast there was already between this blackness and the brilliant electric displays of Times Square: the flashing neons, the traffic signals, the rows of lights on and over the marquees, the taxis' headlights and the floodlit façades. At this hour cars would be drawing sleek men and women up to the playhouses throughout the West Forties; the sidewalks would be crowded with people hurrying along—on their way to see the glamorous Gertrude Lawrence or Tallulah Bankhead, to some comedy of Clare Boothe or George S. Kaufman. The musical show devotees would be crowding in to a Rodgers and Hart musical or pushing on to see Ethel Merman or William Gaxton and Victor Moore. The falling snow would be disrupting traffic and there would be a bedlam of taxi horns, policemen's whistles and shouting. Inside, however, the sophisticated chatter of playgoers to whom the theatre was a familiar experience would subside as the houselights dimmed, as late-comers hurried down the aisles, and the curtains rose up and down Broadway.

It was a sentimental picture I was painting for my own melancholy amusement. Although I was intending to thrust it behind me for a while, it was obvious that Broadway still clung close.

The next morning, however, Manhattan seemed a long way off. Now the challenge of exploration began to assert itself. As the train approached my first destination, my thoughts were striding ahead and beginning to examine the possibilities in this self-appointed exile from New York. There were so many things to be discovered and so many values to be weighed. I made a recapitulation of my purposes.

First of all I wanted to know what relationship this Broadway I had left bore to the rest of the country. Was it a self-contained organism that functioned without regard to the outside world or were there influences that emanated from it and that poured into it to bind it to some vaster environment? When people who cared for it used the word "theatre" in Virginia, or in Vermont or Iowa, did it mean the same thing to them that it did to us in New York? And, indeed, what did it mean to us in New York? I supposed that eventually I would have to define "theatre"—satisfactorily to myself if to no one else.

The difference between professional and non-professional theatre lay close to the heart of my problem. I wondered whether the difference was between being paid to do what you liked to do and doing it for nothing, so that the two were perhaps really one in the ends they sought; or whether they were moved by opposed philosophies and expressed in differing modes. Edith J. R. Isaacs had been using the phrase "tributary theatre" in *Theatre Arts* for a good many years to denote the work done outside of Manhattan. Was that activity a tide that flowed, as she seemed to imply, into a main stream somewhere else; was it perhaps the main stream itself; or was it possible that the current had reversed itself and the main stream was feeding the tributaries?

My first visit was to be to the campus of one of the state universities. I knew that there were young people there studying the theatre and professors teaching them about it. Why was this happening and what did it mean? All over the country in other colleges and universities students were receiving academic credit for theatrical studies; my itinerary included visits to some forty of them. I had heard of beautiful playhouses on some of the campuses, superior to anything on Broadway. The presence of buildings means that money has been spent. The stage, which until only recently had been frowned upon by institutions of learning as a waste of undergraduate time and possibly worse, was being included in their budgets. Certainly universities, always hard-pressed for funds, do not spend money for things in which they do not believe. What did this presage for the future of the theatre? I had a premonition that before I was through I would also have to be concerned with the philosophy of education, at least insofar as drama was affected by it in this new union.

My quest would also take me to the stage doors of community theatres, little theatres, civic theatres (those were the names under which they most frequently appeared in my itinerary—between thirty and forty of them that I was planning to visit). Kenneth Macgowan told in

Footlights Across America of that epidemic during the 1920s that had given rise to the little theatre movement. But his book was written a dozen years ago and this country changes fast. What of those theatres today? Barrett H. Clark, long an authority on the amateur theatre field, had told me that approximately five hundred thousand amateur groups were presenting plays in the United States every year—in grade schools and high schools and colleges, at Y.M.C.A.s and churches, in the halls of labor groups and granges, of women's clubs and 4-H Clubs, in little and community theatres. If, as it appeared, many more than a million people were acting in America each season, the stage could at any rate hardly be called dead! I had read in McCleery and Glick's *Curtains Going Up*, published in late 1939, that "the theatre of commerce, of the Max Gordons, of the Theatre Guild, of the Gilbert Millers, of all Broadway producers may have its woes and doubts, its moments of hesitation—but not the community theatres of America." Could this be true, I wondered; I was unable to imagine any theatre operating so happily and so surely, but perhaps it was happening. I could certainly not deny it without going to see.

Part and yet not part of this non-professional stage was the activity of the trade unions and other labor groups. The New Theatre League in New York claimed affiliates all across the country; its supporters were convinced that the real seeds of tomorrow's drama were in these "new theatres." I felt that I must attempt to discover the strength of this movement and where it was going.

There were other things I wanted to find out during my journey. What impress had the Federal Theatre left on the country, and what hope or desire did people have for that kind or some other kind of national theatre for America? I was interested in the fate of the stock companies that used to dot the land. Were they entirely a thing of the past or had they a contemporary counterpart? What had actually happened to the "road"? On one hand, I had heard reports that it was dying; on the other that it showed signs of rejuvenation. In 1937 the American Theatre Council's convention, which agreed about practically nothing else, was unanimous in its conviction that the future of the theatre lay in a healthy revival of the "road." Had that conviction been transformed into action? Were enough plays on tour out from Broadway to count as a significant part of the theatrical pattern?

As I posed these questions to which my travels were to find answers, I began to appreciate the complexity of my assignment. Yet the real theatrical pattern of America, I was convinced, would emerge only by connecting all these threads and I could afford to neglect no one of them.

A final problem which required consideration before proceeding further was the standard of judgment to be applied. Was there an absolute or must it all be relative? Could the frame of Broadway be the reference for Maine? I determined forthwith that there must be an absolute, and that it must be a theatrical absolute, since I was a theatre man and this was a theatrical study. I was unwilling, however, to call it the standard of either Broadway or Maine. It would not be important whether I saw anyone play *Biography* like Ina Claire, or Lincoln as Massey portrayed him. I was not going to care whether scenery looked as though it had been designed by Jo Mielziner and painted by Brad Ashworth. But I was going to demand that on the stage there should be something that rang true to itself. I was going to demand at least a seed of creativeness. I was going to demand that, when audiences were asked to come into playhouses, there should always be revealed to them something surprising—something better than they had hoped for.

Above and beyond this, however, and perhaps not properly a part of artistic criticism, lay another consideration which seemed to me of even greater moment. It was the necessity to consider the theatre in its every part and as a whole in its relation to the people, to our democracy. Maxwell Anderson once said: "A nation is not a nation until it has a culture which deserves and receives affection and reverence from the people themselves." He was thinking particularly of the theatre, I am sure. "The national conscience is the sum of personal conscience, the national culture the sum of personal culture—and the lack of conscience is an invitation to destruction, the lack of culture an assurance that we shall not even be remembered."

That was it. I was concerned with writing the story of an aspect of our national culture. That sounds perhaps pretentious; I say it, however, in great humility. Our obligation as members of a democracy imposes upon each one of us the necessity to take personal concern for the perpetuation and growth of our common culture and of those arts which form a part of it. The theatre is one such art. Those of us who care for the theatre must recognize its relationship to the life of our democracy, particularly in these times of stress when the forces of destruction ride high, when the flames of holocaust are licking at the national cultures of others and our own is none too secure. Without that relationship made clear and held firmly before us, our theatre must surely perish.

TRAVEL

CHAPTER TWO

1940 Barnstorming

Fifty years ago the professional theatre belonged to the whole of America. Every town of ten thousand or so had its "opera house" to which traveling troupes, swinging across the country, made constant visits. Vaudeville was at its peak. Larger towns had their local stock companies: luscious ingénues, mustachioed leading men, robust "heavies," each with his or her following of admirers. Theatre reached out with its glamour and its excitement into the lives of hundreds of thousands of men and women; and of boys and girls, too, who climbed to the peanut gallery and leaned over the rail for a glimpse into a magical world of song and dance, of raucous laughter and quick, hot tears. There was plenty of ham in the acting and sentimentality in the tale, but the living stuff of drama was there. Across the footlights in both directions it swept, as the heroine confided her heart's tremors to the sympathetic crowd, as that crowd, now galvanized to her support, hissed the villain, and as it roared response to the comedian's jokes thrown in its lap. The give-and-take of real theatrical experience was there.

This was the stage of the 1890s. Some people now performing and many in the audience today recall these "opera houses" and the life that was in them. Many of our current leading actors and producers were among the crowd of youngsters hanging over the rail in Seattle or Dubuque or Youngstown, getting their first taste of drama. To many of us it is only a story told by our elders, for this picture is not known to our generation. Gone are the opera houses with their roller curtains, the Cupids and plush and tassels; gone the stiff benches of the top gallery; gone the villains, the ingénues and their stage-door Johnnies.

In 1890 there were 5,000 legitimate professional theatres in the United States; in 1939 the number had dropped to 192, of which 44 were in the Times Square district of New York.

The causes of this decline of the professional theatre in America have been so often recited that only a rapid recapitulation seems necessary. The Theatrical Syndicate, which formed in the 1890s what amounted to a booking monopoly, started the standardized ball of commercialism rolling across the country. Messrs. Charles Frohman, Klaw, Erlanger, et al. were followed by Messrs. Shubert who bought up what playhouses the earlier syndicates had not taken. Against certain practices of these managers and others following in their wake, theatrical labor organized and unionism entered the picture. With labor costs skyrocketing and with a coincidental rise in railroad rates throughout the country which placed an additional financial burden on the traveling production, the "ten-twenty-thirty" shows were forced to assume a higher box-office scale or disappear. So the theatre went out of financial reach of the common people and the opera houses began to close their doors.

At this opportune time for the public and for itself the motion picture came upon the scene. Again in the towns and cities across America people could find release from the hard business of living in a magical world that flickered at first but which, as the years passed, grew steadier and more beautiful before their eyes; release, too, that was available for a dime or a quarter. True, this new entertainment had not the same robustness as the old drama and vaudeville. The give-and-take was gone, for there were no "flesh actors" there at all—only their shadow with whom one could scarcely enter into communal contact. Nevertheless, a new fabricated world opened before the boys and girls in Seattle and Dubuque and Youngstown—a world of Wild West romance and boudoir glamour, of exotic places and times, of Valentino and Theda Bara.

As the movie tide swept on and in, with sound added and then color, the theatre slipped farther away. Across America the movie industry bought up the opera houses and the stock company theatres and either tore them down or remade them into picture palaces. Cinema went into real estate on a vast scale, so that many times five thousand playhouses exist in America today, if the great motion picture circuits be considered; (indeed, many more playhouses than that industry can sustain for its economic and artistic welfare, as it is now discovering). By the mid-1930s the movies announced an average weekly attendance of 110 million.

Following close on the heels of the rising cinema, and jeopardizing both it and the theatre, came radio. Entering into almost every home to become a more constant and familiar experience than even the movies had been, radio offered the American public, with previously unheard-of immediacy of access, programs of entertainment and release, of education and information. It offered an easy aural substitute not only for theatre- and movie-going, but for concert-going, for newspaper-reading, for church attendance, for lecture-going—at a price within the reach of almost everyone.

But this is not a history book and the story of the decline of the theatre and the rise of the motion pictures and radio has been told again and again. This roving reporter's assignment is concerned with today and with only as few yesterdays as seem directly essential to our understanding of today.

2

"The theatre has its own self to blame for the sorry predicament it's in," said an intent young man with sharp, black eyes as he leaned across the table in a Pittsburgh sea-food house. Harold Cohen, dramatic critic of the *Post-Gazette*, continued: "The theatre has refused to tackle one after another of its problems; it has alienated its customers through bad public relations and box office discourtesy. By ignoring pleas to reduce prices—particularly in order to attract young people—and by not sending enough good shows on the road, the theatre has done all it could to commit suicide."

As I moved on across America, these complaints against the theatre were reiterated and reinforced. The high cost of the infrequent plays was regularly attacked. "If I could be allowed to sell second balcony seats at fifty cents so that high school students might come," said the manager of a large legitimate theatre in the Middle West, "I would be helping save the theatre's neck. But the touring companies won't let me."

The villain of the piece appears to be the manager of the touring company. He is willing to admit that the theatre should be able to compete with movies so that the people in cities throughout the country might see plays for a dollar and less. He says, however, that this is impossible as long as artist and labor union wages continue at their present scale and other costs prevail. To prove his point he offers a hypothetical budget of a week on the road with a company of fourteen actors, which is average size; with no star and with no individual actor receiving more than $250 a week. Let us suppose that he has grossed $10,000, which is a very fair week (there are exceptional weeks that are more successful, but without a star, this is a good intake). He leases the local theatre on the customary sharing basis, whereby he receives 65 per cent of the gross, the local manager receiving 35 per cent. On this basis he works out the following statement:

GROSS RECEIPTS $10,000.00

    Percentage to theatre $3,500.00

    Actors' salaries (*including stage manager*) 1,900.00

    Property man's salary (*union minimum*) 100.00

    Property rentals and miscellaneous   50.00

    Electrician's salary (*union minimum*) 100.00

Rental of electrical equipment, replacement of gelatines, bulbs, etc. 125.00

Carpenter's salary (*union minimum*) 100.00

Carpentry department maintenance (*repairs to settings*) 30.00

Press representative's salary (*required by union*) 175.00

Advertising and printing 1,000.00

Orchestra salaries (*whether music is played or not*)........... 250.00

Author's royalty (10% *when the gross exceeds* $7,000) 1,000.00

Director's royalty (2% *of the gross*) 200.00

Company manager's salary (*union minimum*) 125.00

Office expenses (*carrying charge leveled against all touring companies to support the New York office*) 150.00

Railroad transportation (*an average jump*) 600.00

Hauling (*from railroad to theatre and return*) 300.00

Taxes (*Federal and State, social security, co-labor, excise*) 95.00

Miscellaneous 35.00

TOTAL EXPENDITURES 9,835.00

PROFIT TO MANAGEMENT $165.00

These figures, while hypothetical, are a very fair estimate of production costs on the road. When a producer's profit on a $10,000 week is but $165, it is easy to see that he will not look with enthusiasm on suggested reforms that might tend to lower that gross and so reduce his returns to nothing. The general public is, of course, unaware of this problem. Understandably and properly it considers that the high cost of theatre-going should be reduced. How this can occur, however, as long as present costs obtain as indicated above, and as long as commercialism persists as the motive, I do not see.

There is another frequently voiced cry that rises from the mid-continent. "What does Broadway think we are out here?" they asked in Carolina and Minnesota and a dozen other places. "Does it think we have no taste at all that it gives us third- and fourth-rate productions and expects us to pay good money to see them? Does it think we don't know the difference?"

I suppose the honest answer is that Broadway often does not care. Whereas artistic motivations occasionally appear behind Times Square productions and a *succès d'estime* has a certain prestige value there, the only reason anyone would take to the road would be to make money. It is difficult to persuade some of the best artists to leave New York under any circumstances; and since the purpose of sending a play on the road in any case is to add to whatever gains it may have made in New York, if a less expensive cast and production can be assembled to replace the original, so much the better. When the public of the hinterland, being once bitten and twice shy, stays away, Broadway says the road is dead and that America has lost its interest in drama.

Most startling to the traveler from Manhattan is the complete absence over vast reaches of our land of any professional theatre, offering plays well-done or poorly, expensively or cheaply. Time and again across the United States I was told on the campuses of the State universities that ninety per cent of the college students up from small towns, farms, cities even, had never seen a professionally presented play in their lives. Time and again I went to places where there had been no such performance since *The Green Pastures* or *The Barretts of Wimpole Street*, nearly ten years before.

In spite of the bleakness of this outlook, I must record that an optimistic view persists in a number of spots. Let us return to the Pittsburgh critic. "Yes, the theatre is in a bad way," Mr. Cohen concluded, "but it can pull itself up by its own bootstraps and it must." Then he added: "But the professional theatre will have to do it." I had heard this statement before: I heard it often again. In fact, the newspaper dramatic critics and editors across America are pretty well in agreement on this point. In 1940 they were looking to the revival of the road, under a set of conditions that will assure its permanent progress, as the hope of the theatrical future.

Mr. Cohen admires the Lunts tremendously, and Ina Claire, and "Miss Cornell" as she is respectfully called. He and William McDermott in Cleveland and John Rosenfield in Dallas and a dozen other dramatic editors through the country will throw in their lot with these and other Broadway stars if ever it comes to a showdown. For the survival of the stage depends upon these top-flight talents, they believe, and the geographical extent of that survival depends upon the frequency and extent of their tours.

Those famous tours—triumphal processions they have

been—which Katharine Cornell and Helen Hayes and the Lunts (and almost no one else) have taken across the country during the past few years have given rise to the hope that the theatre is coming back to America. They have indeed been remarkable phenomena. Helen Hayes, they say, played *Victoria Regina* in Des Moines to a few hundred short of ten thousand people in one day. More than half of them had driven in from across the Iowa plains to the play. Katharine Cornell has had comparable experiences in Kansas and Montana and a score of states. People have ridden hundreds of miles to see her. The coming of Miss Hayes or Miss Cornell has been talked about for months in advance; their last appearance is still talked about years later.

What does this mean? Two different explanations were offered me. First, it does not mean that there is any real renaissance of enthusiasm for the theatre as a whole such as one might assume from the presence of such crowds to see these several actors and actresses. It is even suggested that if Miss Cornell and Miss Hayes were to return to some of these spots every three or four months, instead of every three or four years, they might attract increasingly smaller numbers. In other words, the novelty of the experience of theatre-going to see a great star has a great deal to do with it.

This explanation proceeds further by suggesting that the build-ups which these "first ladies" of the theatre have been given (Miss Cornell by the extremely able late Ray Henderson, Miss Hayes perhaps by her brief but brilliant movie career) have taken advantage of an increasing avidity on the part of the American people for "personal appearances." Various people told me that they believed much of the populace came to see what these great ladies looked like and sounded like so that they might say they had "seen Helen Hayes," "seen Katharine Cornell." Had Miss Hayes merely stood up and recited "The Boy Stood on the Burning Deck" in a rose-pink organdie dress or had Miss Cornell, gowned in green velvet, read "The Ancient Mariner," they would have been just as satisfied.

Such an ungracious explanation—in which there may, however, be a modicum of truth, which is why I repeat it—can be offset by other opinions and I hasten to present them. For I am also told that the real reason these two or three stars attract such crowds is because they guarantee a standard of excellence which no one else assures. "Everybody goes to see Katharine Cornell and Helen Hayes and the Lunts because he knows he will get his money's worth. Those names are an assurance that everyone in the company will be first-rate, that scenery and costumes will be the best to be had, and that to cap it all will be a star's performance of rare excellence. Cornell or Hayes would sell out if they demanded a five-dollar top, because we'd feel it was worth it to receive something so fine when we get it so seldom!"

The overwhelming success of Miss Hayes and Miss Cornell and the Lunts when they have brought the best that Broadway has to offer out to "the sticks" is reassuring to those who believe that the best will always pay and that nothing less is good enough for the rest of the country. It still, however, does not bear witness to a genuine, broad devotion to the theatre on the part of the American public. From Boston to San Francisco, from Minneapolis to Austin, Texas, drama editors reasserted that only the shows with the "big names" draw consistently well. "A beautiful play may come—but without a star it rarely will draw more than a handful. We can 'rave' in the press but it does no good." Again and again I was told "the public here will only support big names." That is not at all the same thing as supporting the theatre, I regret to say, and we must not be misled into thinking it is; although perhaps in time—who knows?

This mania for "big names" that has grasped America so firmly was undoubtedly growing before the movies came but they have given it a tremendous impetus. I suppose actually it is the doctrine of "rugged individualism" that has brought about this fascination for the successful personality. At any rate, conversely, any society based on collective endeavor rather than individualism tends to discourage such an attitude and will emphasize the accomplishment rather than the man. I saw this most clearly in the theatre of the Soviet Union, where never once during a season of constant attendance at the forty playhouses in Moscow did I see the name of a single performer up in lights over the doors. The public there went to see the work of the Moscow Art Theatre or the Vakhtangov Theatre or the Maly Theatre, or else they went to see *The Cherry Orchard* or *Intervention* or *The Storm*. The individual subordinated himself to the whole creation and the audience was expected to judge the results. But here— "only big names consistently fill the theatres." When the movies find their box offices slipping, they follow the same formula, bringing out a *Boom Town* with as many big names as they can afford: Clark Gable, Spencer Tracy, Hedy Lamarr, Claudette Colbert—all for the price of one. I walked down the street in Dallas and over the Adolphus Hotel was a sign: "Our new Ballroom season is about to open: Big Name Bands." Nowadays one will not even go dancing except to the swing of a big name.

This attitude seems to be the result of a wide-spread unwillingness, or incapacity, to make judgments for oneself. A big name is created in part by the public's will, but more largely by press agentry, syndicated columnists, radio personal appearances and references, illustrated papers and fan magazines. That big name is then automatically accepted as the epitome of excellence in any particular field and especially in entertainment, and the individual abdicates the exercise of his personal opinion to this artificially created mass judgment. The power of the New York critics over the fate of the theatre is largely the result of this public apathy and the inability of the individual to choose for himself. In this democracy of ours, a subtle but strict regimentation of taste is imposed upon an acquiescent citizenry. We may not be told by governmental decree how to think—but we are told just the same; at least in the fields of my interest we are.

3

Is the road really coming back? That was one of the things I went out to discover—one of the questions I was asked most often when I returned to New York. After a period of years during the height of the depression, when it was averred that the road was gone beyond recall, we heard more recent rumors that phoenix-like it was rising from the ashes; that other managers, heartened by the successes of Katharine Cornell and Helen Hayes and

of *The Green Pastures* and *Tobacco Road* were sending
out companies once more and that playhouses long dark
in cities like Indianapolis and Utica and St. Paul were re-
lighting their foyers and dusting off the seats. By 1940-41
the prospects of a real revival of the road seemed brighter
than ever, for a number of plays on tour with and without
big names had performed to larger houses than in any
season of the past ten years. Is the road then really re-
covered?

The answer, I believe, must be qualified, and is largely
dependent upon where you are. In Pittsburgh Harold
Cohen claimed that the season of 1939-40 was the best
in four or five years. "We have had thirty shows here
this year," he said. That was, however, an amazingly high
number for any city beyond a three-hundred mile radius
of New York. Boston has legitimate drama running in
three or four playhouses at once during much of the year,
having wrested from Philadelphia the reputation of being
the best place for producers to try out plays for Broadway;
in Washington the season at the National Theatre, to
which all road shows now come, is also about thirty weeks.
Paul Beisman in St. Louis was able to keep the American
Theatre open for twenty-three weeks in 1940-41.

In other cities, however, the picture is not so rosy.
The Twin Cities, Minneapolis and St. Paul, which used to
sustain a forty-week season as recently as 1920, now see
from six to ten shows a year. New Orleans in the past
couple of seasons has been lucky to get four or five plays.
(Its Municipal Auditorium seating five thousand people
is now the only place available to traveling companies
since the old Tulane was shut down by movie pressure.)
Shreveport, Louisiana, a city of about one hundred thou-

sand, was visited in 1939-40 by the Lunts in *The Taming of the Shrew* and by the road company of *Leave It to Me;* nothing more.

The geographical location of cities is today a factor in determining the number of plays they will receive. With railroad transportation tariffs so high, tours must be carefully planned so that the stops fall along the main rail arteries, particularly through the Middle West and the North and Southwest. Distances are vast; to go many hundred miles off the beaten East-West path for a one-night stand is now so costly that it is rarely attempted. This helps to account for the surprisingly slim fare of a city like Denver which receives under five plays a year; or of a little city like Charleston to which but one play may come in two years.

In an effort to generalize it might be possible to say that most cities in the United States with populations between one-quarter and one-half million have had from five to ten productions a year during the past three or four seasons. At mid-season 1940-41, *Variety,* theatrical trade journal, reported that there were thirteen dramatic productions on the road in the United States during the week of January 13. Of these, three were in Chicago, one trying out in Philadelphia before New York, one trying out in Washington, three playing in Boston and the other five playing split weeks and one-night stands in Michigan, Tennessee and Alabama, Minnesota and Iowa, California and Ohio.

No; you cannot say that the road is dead as long as the key cities receive one or two dozen plays a year. Neither can you say, on the other hand, that the road as a whole is particularly healthy or that its penetration is very widespread. What chances are there that the growing upswing of 1940-41 may continue?

Insofar as the road's success depends on the presence of stars, the number of them who will leave Broadway for the long period that a really comprehensive tour of the country requires will be a determinant. This, it must be admitted, will be largely influenced in turn by the chances for financial success. As long as costly union scales and high railroad rates persist, the assurance of large gains is reduced and the stars are not so enthusiastic. As for the companies going out without "big names," I am inclined to believe that their number will not increase in the next few seasons unless the hinterland public shows a greater inclination to support them than it has in the past.

If the motion picture industry, through its local house manager or its chain influence, continues antagonistic to the recovery of the road in medium-sized cities, as is now the case quite frequently, legitimate theatre will continue to have a slim chance for real recovery there. For in many such cities, the motion picture house is the only place where traveling legitimate shows may play; their managers, I am told, frequently dislike shifting their habitual movie schedule for one, two or three days when the profit to them seldom exceeds their usual intake from a picture.

In two or three large cities recent efforts to bolster the road have been made by the audience itself. Led by J. Howard Reber, an elderly lawyer with a passion for the theatre, Philadelphia citizens organized themselves a Philadelphia Theatregoers' Council. The purpose of the organization was to guarantee to commercial managers a sufficient audience lined up in advance for anything they

might bring to make it worth their while to come to Philadelphia. In the 1939-40 season, and again in 1940-41, the
Council had the support of five thousand people most of
whom paid two dollars for a general membership.

This was not a subscription audience in the sense that it
received a ticket price reduction for a specific number of
plays. Members did gain certain advantages in location
of seats which they could have for every production;
they were spared standing in line at the box office; but,
in the main, it was a semi-philanthropic effort to save the
professional theatre in Philadelphia.

In St. Louis theatre-lovers and business men who felt
that a living theatre was a good thing for their city banded
together to form The Playgoers, a similar organization
whose members get no other benefit than the opportunity
to see more professional plays in St. Louis. This organized
audience numbers about fifteen hundred. Cleveland, Kansas City and Cincinnati have recently adopted the scheme
and by the time these words reach the reader the movement may have spread. It is, I think, an interesting com-
mentary on the initiative of the commercial theatre that
the prospective consumers have had to organize themselves in order to persuade the tradesmen to sell to them!

The subscription idea applied to the commercial theatre
is not new. The New York Theatre Guild, in its heyday
in 1930-31, had 85,000 subscribers in thirteen cities and
promised to present them with six plays a year. This subscription list became that of the subsequent American
Theatre Society which included Guild plays and those by
other managers collaborating with the Guild. Now it is
again managed exclusively by the Guild, but the uncertain

merit of its output and the hard times of the past years have reduced the number of subscribers in 1940-41 to sixty thousand in eleven cities.

4

In spite of the uncertain picture which the road presents today, the demand for "flesh performers" continues. Even motion picture houses have had to offer "stage shows" to satisfy customers weary of being fed exclusively from tins. These "stage shows," usually with a dancing chorus or a jazz orchestra, occasional soloists and once in a while the "personal appearance" of a Hollywood celebrity, are familiar enough to all who attend the more de luxe cinema palaces of our larger cities so that I need not accord them much space in this volume. They should nevertheless be mentioned. Other efforts to meet the demand of the public for professional stage entertainment to augment the legitimate road also suggest themselves.

Stuffed into one side of a booth in a Dallas sandwich shop sat John Rosenfield. Drama and music critic for the Dallas *Morning News,* he has championed long and vigorously for the better things in art for Texas. "Have you thought," asked Mr. Rosenfield suddenly, "of including in your theatre report an account of night clubs?"

For the night club, Mr. Rosenfield pointed out, is the inheritor of the vaudeville tradition. In cities like Dallas and Houston, like Jacksonville and New Orleans and Atlanta, like San Francisco, Seattle, Portland and Omaha and St. Louis, in fact in almost every medium-sized city

and all the large cities of America, one no longer finds
vaudeville houses still operating. But in every such city
one or two or all of the big hotels have turned their largest dining rooms into night clubs. Usually they are not
the super-sophisticated spots that Manhattan's café society
means by night clubs nor that Hollywood portrays on
the screen. Often there is not even much drinking there.
They are rather places to which middle-class business men
take their wives and young clerks take their best girls.
Here for less than the six dollars a pair of good theatre
tickets would cost (if there were a good theatre around)
a couple will dine and dance and see a floor show. There
will always be an orchestra, but the floor show is our particular concern. It will vary, of course, from place to place
and time to time but there will be apt to be solo dancers,
or exhibition ballroom dancing couples, perhaps even a
dancing chorus; there may be several comedy acts: comic
dancers or singers or a funny *diseuse*; possibly you will
find a magician or a mind-reader or a young man who
makes strange sounds on a clarinet or who whistles; maybe
a juggler. In the hotel at which I stayed in Tucson, Arizona, they had given up half the floor to a rink for an ice-
skating ballet.

It is true that this is not exactly the theatre any more
than are the stage shows at the picture palaces, but it has
a good many of theatre's ingredients. Some of these same
performers would be in vaudeville if vaudeville existed,
and some of them would be in musical shows if there were
room there for all. (In fact there is a certain interchange
of talent between the two.) There is a strong sense of the
relationship between audience and performer that is accentuated by the frequent absence of a curtain and stage

and footlights, so the experience in a way is closer to theatre than the movies are. The performers in these floor
shows—which derive that name, I suppose, from this very
fact that they take place on the dance floor and not on a
stage—go on tour much as the old vaudeville troupes used
to do. They will stay a few weeks in one town—or if they
are important headliners they may make only a one-night
stand—and then on around the circuit they go to be followed by others.

I think Mr. Rosenfield was right in suggesting that this
kind of entertainment has a place in the theatrical pattern of America and must be considered when we are
thinking about the decline of the road and of what has
happened in consequence. The floor shows of these night
clubs bear witness to the fact that people must find an
escape from life in some medium of entertainment and
that the attraction of the living performer is still strong
even in this cinematic day. They bear witness, too, to the
fact that the singers and dancers and jugglers of an earlier
time persist in demanding a hearing and a crowd. The
two demands meet across America in the "Hawaiian
Rooms," the "Palm Courts" and the "Silver Terraces"
from Syracuse to Spokane.

Of course this night club aspect of the moment, like the
vaudeville that preceded it, is not concerned with the
heightening of living nor with ideas or emotions; it is
theatre simply as entertainment. Furthermore, unlike our
earlier vaudeville, it addresses itself to a public that has
at least one or two dollars to pay for that entertainment,
and it is available only in cities. Has the "ten-twent'-
thirt' " show any successor other than movies? In Abilene,
Texas, I found the answer to that question.

Abilene is a town of some twenty-five thousand inhabitants in the central part of western Texas. It was the first week in December but already red, and green, amber and blue lights were festooned across its downtown streets to remind that Christmas was on its way. As we drove in from the airport under this twinkling varicolored greeting, I saw that the sidewalks were filled with the regular crowd which comes in to such towns on a Saturday night all across the country. But its profusion of ten-gallon hats, its mud-caked cowboy boots and its rangy rolling gait made it seem a little different from other Saturday night crowds in Indiana or New Jersey or Vermont.

We went to Abilene's hotel to dine on some excellent Texas beef. In the middle of the meal, my guide and friend suggested rather tentatively that I might like to see a tent show. "It's been here for four days and this is its last. Of course it's not wonderful, and it may not have anything to do with the kind of theatre you're interested in," he continued, "but it's all most people have out here." "In that case," I replied, "I am certainly interested. Let's go."

December can be pretty raw and chill in western Texas so the Harvey Sadler Company had moved indoors. For those four nights it was installed in Abilene's City Auditorium which seats fifteen hundred people. However, through spring and summer and fall it sets up its tent in one of the open spaces that Texas can supply in abundance and offers the same shows it then was presenting inside. The plane had been late in arriving and the beef was too good to be eaten in haste, so it was almost nine o'clock by the time we reached the Auditorium. Since the show had begun at seven-thirty it was more than half through. I do not know the name of the play nor what it was about; the end of the second act is no time to arrive if you want to know that—but it did not matter. Even after we arrived people kept coming in and going out and it did not seem to matter to them either. You see, they had seen it before many times, for all these tent shows are alike and year after year the same company comes with the same sort of thing.

These performances are also called "Toby shows" because of the stock character of Toby who is in all of them. He is a kind of hill-billy *commedia dell'arte* comic with a flaming red wig and an equally roseate nose. In one part of the play he wears an antique Prince Albert or some similar approximation of formal attire; in the other part he dresses as a country bumpkin with generously patched overalls and bandanna. If the play contains no Toby, then he is written in and usually the principal actor plays him. He can be easily interpolated into any show for his actual dialogue is scant and is filled in with a good deal of Chaplinesque pantomime, frequent high giggles and some extemporaneous gags. At the end of the act when we came in, he was getting wound up in an exceedingly long telephone extension cord as he attempted to carry on what he supposed was a telephonic conversation with a character who, however, was standing just behind him and replying in normal tones. This was good for a number of laughs.

When the act was over there was only a momentary pause; an orchestra filed into the pit and a vigorous young man came out before the curtains and sang in a magenta spotlight; after a verse or two he broke into a tap dance. He was followed by a sextette of singing cowboys who

offered some traditional cowboy airs, accompanying themselves on guitars and an accordion. It was very effective.
When they had finished, the Toby came out and made a
speech. He was really Mr. Harvey Sadler, Manager, and
he thanked Abilene for giving such generous support,
made some sober references to the world situation, but
voiced the hope that they would be back together next
season, and wished them all a Merry Christmas. When
the lights went out and up again, the curtains parted and
the final act began.

This was laid outdoors, just where I am not sure. There
were wood wings of the 1905 vintage and a badly painted
backdrop showing a landscape. The unconvincing corner
of a very artificial bright pink brick porch jutted out from
one side. The lighting was a flat white. It was far from
fine art. What should one do—suspend one's judgment?
I don't think so; one could admit the presence of fearful
crudity and also be forced to say that it was a good show
by any unprejudiced standard. There was a liveliness that
is often lacking on better-lighted stages. The Toby was
really funny, the nostalgia of the cowboy singers was
moving, and there was an audience that entered into the
performance with zest; one could almost say they were
part of the show.

I looked about. The auditorium was packed to the
rafters: farm boys and girls without neckties or hats; men
with babies on their arms; little children ten or twelve
years old; aged leathery-skinned grandfathers—fifteen
hundred men, women and children sitting in solemn rows,
their faces pink in the reflected glow from the footlights.
They had paid ten cents apiece to get in. As we left, the
man at the door told us that the Auditorium had been

sold out at each of the four performances: six thousand people out of twenty-five thousand had been to the show within the last four days. If this is theatre, then the theatre is not dead in America.

There are some two hundred of these tent show companies still operating in the United States. Up in Iowa I heard of the Hila Morgan company and of Princess Pat and many others. In Dallas, along with the Hotel Adolphus' floor show and the Dallas Little Theatre (of which more later), the Madcap Players on the other side of town have been playing Toby shows for two or three years to a ten-cent audience (twenty-five cents for reserved seats). Up and down the country these tent shows go through the Middle West and the South particularly, playing in the towns and villages to thousands of farmers and drugstore clerks and the garage mechanics at the crossroads. Here is a "road" that most of Broadway does not know exists and most of its audience never heard of Broadway. It's a vast country, the United States.

CHAPTER THREE

Summer Stock and Winter "Rep"

IN THE SUMMER of 1928 Charles Leatherbee, then president of the Harvard Dramatic Club, and Bretaigne Windust, president of Princeton's Théâtre Intime, founded a stock company at Falmouth, Massachusetts, that boasted an ornate but not very stock-company-sounding name: The University Players Guild. It was a co-operative group of college boys and girls who wanted to act in the summer and felt that Cape Cod could provide them with a potential audience. Leatherbee brought some Harvard classmates, among them Kent Smith; Windust brought some fellow Princetonians, among them Joshua Logan. Several girls from Radcliffe and Vassar were invited to join. The boys lived on an unused yacht in Falmouth harbor; the girls lived on dry land. They rented the movie house for a couple of nights each week, put on plays directed, designed, built and acted by themselves.

Soon it seemed that the U.P.G., as its members called it, needed a home of its own, so borrowing some money they built themselves one on a beach by Buzzard's Bay. A good deal of the structure was the product of their own hands and all the subsequent landscaping the actors did themselves, planting trees and spreading manure. The walls were of celotex and every year were expected to fall apart; but the stage had a loft, a grid and a counter-weight system. To the other end were added a kitchen and a large room facing the bay which they quaintly called a "tearoom." This was primarily used to increase revenue by inveigling the audience to repair there after the play to be entertained at a kind of floor show presented by the indefatigable company who raced around from backstage to perform some more.

The company grew in wisdom and stature and in Cape Cod favor as the seasons passed. Everyone was quite young, for when the group began, the oldest member— the management included—could not have been more than twenty-one. Henry Fonda and Margaret Sullavan were early recruits and later from Princeton came Charles Arnt and Myron McCormick and myself and still later James Stewart. From hither and yon came Aleta Freel and Barbara O'Neil and later Mildred Natwick, Katherine Emery and a great many others. But always it was an informal collaboration in which nobody was thought of as "boss" (although Windust, Leatherbee and Logan did form a directorial triumvirate and tried to keep order), in which everyone was tremendously eager to grow into fine actors and directors and designers and worked exceedingly hard to that end, wherein nobody got rich or indeed thought about their salaries which frequently reached an irreducible minimum.

I tell the story of the early days of the University Players (they later dropped the "Guild") to illustrate the change that has come over the summer theatres of the Atlantic seaboard since that time. A dozen years ago, when this group began, summer stock existed in only a few places, mostly in New England. It was all rather informal and experimental. New plays were presented, young and untried actors were given a hearing (note that at its inception the University Players was composed entirely of people who had never been seen on Broadway), their budgets were small and the audiences uncertain. Some of them were a little more substantially organized than the West Falmouth company: notably the neighboring Cape Playhouse at Dennis, Skowhegan in Maine, the Berkshire Playhouse at Stockbridge. They were all looked upon as an invigorating influence on the theatre. Gradually the idea spread and grew. By 1940 Actors' Equity Association reported eighty-one summer stock companies employing its members, which means that this many had at least a nucleus of six professional actors.

In the process of expansion, however, the summer theatre idea has changed its complexion and now most of these stock companies may be regarded as extensions of Broadway, with Broadway's advantages and disadvantages. The change occurred primarily because summer stock was successful. The idea of theatre-going appealed to the public in the resort places where it had sprung up. People who felt that there was money in the idea were consequently attracted to it. Attracted also were Broadway's workers who so often eked out only a small living through the winter and were glad of the chance to play in the summer when Broadway offered nothing at all. The final stamp of approval came when stars began to take to the "straw-hat" stage: Ethel Barrymore, Jane Cowl, Helen Hayes, Ina Claire, Ruth Gordon, Nazimova, Laurette

Taylor, Katharine Hepburn, to mention but a few of them.

So it is that summer stock has become "big business." The competition that has developed when a number of playhouses have sprung up within relatively small areas has required them all to adopt much the same tactics. Experimentation with new scripts has become dangerous for the same reason that using unknown artists has become dangerous: money is at stake. Some stars have been paid one thousand dollars a week—a long jump from the room and board and five dollars with which Falmouth had lured eager-eyed undergraduates. Now if such young people apply to these places they are invited to join "apprentice groups" where they pay through the nose for a chance to help the star dress, drive a station wagon out after props or usher when the crowd gets too big for the regular house staff.

The repertory of these "straw-hats" rapidly has become a reiteration of Broadway's successes of the previous one or two seasons. When the stars have come they have repeated their last role as a rule, although occasionally it has happened that Helen Hayes would revive *Caesar and Cleopatra* or Ethel Barrymore would appear again in *The School for Scandal* or *Déclassé*. Stars have been unwilling to essay new roles partly because they could make as much money with scarcely any effort by playing in their latest Broadway successes; partly, be it said in justice to them, because they have considered the six days' rehearsal of summer stock inadequate to prepare a new part.

The next step in the summer theatre's commercialization has been developing in the past few seasons. For several years certain stars have toured the stock play-

houses, appearing in the same play in half a dozen places
—sometimes going alone, sometimes taking a supporting
company with them. So a little "road" of the summer
playhouses has developed and seems to be growing
stronger. A similar plan of interchanging productions will
also lead, it seems to me toward the eventual formation
of a circuit of the summer theatres as has in fact already
been proposed. The logical development of both schemes
will be that ten productions, for instance, will be prepared
in New York and taken on tour, with ten summer theatre
managers providing the houses and perhaps the scenery to
suit their varying sized stages. There is more money in
this for everyone concerned, and it can be much more
easily made than by the laborious method of preparing
and producing a new play every week in each place. Of
course fewer people will work this way—but that will be
desirable to the managers since it will mean fewer salaries
to be paid. If this final step is taken then the summer stock
picture will definitely fuse with the Broadway picture.
The next two or three seasons will decide.[1]

Away from the north Atlantic seaboard the "straw-hat"
theatres, perhaps because of their very distance from New
York, are much less extensions of Broadway. At any rate,
the Barter Theatre at Abingdon, Virginia, has managed
for a half-dozen years to maintain a complexion of its
own. Its original idea of accepting hams and other comesti-
bles at the box-office window in lieu of cash, has brought
it a good deal of publicity, but in spite of this, Robert

---

[1] In the spring of 1941 the so-called Association of Summer Theatre
Managers was formed to put such a plan into operation. The Council
of Actors' Equity Association opposed the project for this same reason:
that it would tend to reduce employment opportunities for actors.

Porterfield, its director, has managed to keep his theatre fresh and original by doing plays that were not exclusively Broadway fare, by taking companies out to an audience that was enthusiastic for more homely stuff, by employing a great deal of new young talent which had not yet had its chance to be seen on Broadway.

Westward across the Alleghenies the summer theatre idea has spread; during the past very few years in Western Pennsylvania and around the Great Lakes barn theatres have been jumping up like jack-in-the-boxes. Most of these are non-union and non-Equity groups although they are seeking to earn a living through the summer. The Erie Playhouse has moved its directorate and some of its staff and acting company out to Point Chautauqua on Lake Erie for the summer. In Ironton, Michigan; at the Coach House Theatre in Oconomowoc, Wisconsin, where new plays have been the special order of the day; farther west in the Log Cabin Theatre outside Minneapolis, and in a great many other places groups have assembled to offer summer stock. In St. Louis the Civic Theatre has presented its plays outdoors on a wooded hillside at the edge of the city and the Town Square Theatre has operated on the roof of a skyscraper with only the stars overhead.

There are occasional completely professional summer theatres west of the Hudson River. One such is the Elitch's Gardens Stock Company in Denver, whose story has often been told for it is an outpost of long standing. This company, whose members are outstanding actors brought out from New York or Hollywood, forms an unexpected Broadway island at the foot of the Rocky Mountains. Another professional stock company of actors drawn from New York and Chicago was set up in Indianapolis in the early summer of 1941 by Martin Burton and James Daggett. The Indiana capital proved to be disinterested, however, and the venture was summarily abandoned.

Perhaps the most significant aspect of warm-weather dramatics west of the Alleghenies lies in the fact that (except for Elitch's Gardens) young people have taken control. Like the University Players, students have risen to demand a hearing and to show what they can do. In western Pennsylvania students from the drama department of the Carnegie Institute of Technology with a couple of hundred dollars' capital have started a barn theatre which paid them back their investment and a little extra. At Lake Zurich, Wisconsin, young actors from the Goodman Theatre in Chicago have had a summer stock playhouse. These and other groups have been undertaken on student initiative.

Several of the universities themselves have appreciated that an opportunity for an extension of their work lay in the "straw-hat" theatres as laboratories for undergraduates. It is too soon to say whether, as the Eastern summer theatres have been remolded into the pattern of Broadway, the middle and farther Western summer stages will become extensions of the college drama departments, but there seems to be a trend in that direction. If it is accomplished the advantages and disadvantages of the academic theatre (to be discussed hereafter) will be imposed upon them just as the advantages and disadvantages of Broadway—quite different ones—have been imposed upon the Eastern barn playhouses.

In the spring and summer of 1940 the University of Iowa developed plans for a summer theatre at Lake

Okiboji in northern Iowa but the project did not materialize until 1941, when at its Lakeside Laboratory the University presented *The Winter's Tale*. Meanwhile on the Iowa campus the department has been running what amounts to another stock company; for, as part of a course called "Community Theatre Administration," it presented in 1941 six plays in seven weeks, with student actors, of course, and with Frederic McConnell of the Cleveland Playhouse and Thomas Wood Stevens as guest directors. In the new theatre at the University of Wisconsin a summer program of five plays in six weeks has been presented.

In 1941 Western Reserve University jumped on the summer theatre band-wagon. In the spacious stables of a beautiful country estate outside Cleveland, it set up a playhouse and presented two productions: an 1890 melodrama, *Love Rides the Rails,* directed by Lester Lang from Dallas; and an adaptation of Labiche's nineteenth century French farce, *The Italian Straw Hat,* directed by myself with John Cromwell as guest star.

The University of Michigan appears to be almost more interested in its summer theatrical activity than in its winter program. At Ann Arbor, the Michigan Repertory Players, composed of graduate students majoring in drama plus a professional guest star or two, have presented in stock six plays and one musical show during the summer. Outside professional directors have been imported (in 1940, David Itkin and Whitford Kane) and an outside designer, Alexander Wycoff. Northwestern University's Theatre has announced a summer "program of seventeen attractions": six University Theatre productions, five studio theatre productions, six special theatre lectures by visitors Elissa Landi, Mary Ward, Samuel Selden. Participation in plays has required enrollment in the summer school under the paid staff of thirty-eight.

Examples of the fusion of summer stock with the educational theatre in areas primarily beyond the East might be multiplied *ad nauseam*. Two more illustrations, one taking us back to New York State, the other drawing us farther afield, will suffice.

In 1941, for the first summer since 1935, the campus of Union College at Schenectady did not echo with the voices of actors rehearsing lines and the sawing and hammering of stage technicians. The Mohawk Drama Festival was suspended that year to allow the College to turn over all its facilities to training engineers for the defense program. For six years the Festival and Institute, founded by Dixon Ryan Fox, president of Union College, and Mr. and Mrs. Charles Coburn, had functioned as a non-profit enterprise under the auspices of the College.

"We desired to establish a school of the theatre," stated Dr. Fox, "in the midst of a professional theatre surrounded and penetrated by the traditions of a high intellectual and cultural aspiration appurtenant to an old and honorable American college." A professional company composed of able and often prominent actors presented seven plays in 1940 on the Festival's open-air stage. Additionally some thirty-five to fifty apprentices, drawn by no means exclusively from Union College, have been learning the craft of the theatre as members of the Institute. It is to be hoped that the Festival may be resumed when the period of national emergency has passed, for in this relationship between campus and Broadway both stand to gain.

Waco is a hot and dusty little city in the heart of Texas where the arts would not appear to find very fertile soil. The town is culturally dominated by a small southern Baptist University, Baylor. It has a great barn of a civic auditorium, Waco Hall, that holds 2,300 people—the only theatre around. In such unfelicitous surroundings Baylor's young professor of dramatics, Paul Baker, elected in 1940 to create the "Southwest Summer Theatre." From various colleges throughout Texas he assembled twenty-four boys and girls. To provide working capital for this summer group each member put up twenty-five dollars, for the theatre was no formal part of the University and could look to it for no subsidy.

Waco Hall was obviously too vast for this undertaking, but it was the only place possible, so they blithely built temporary high beaver-board screens around the center four hundred seats nearest the stage and stretched bright colored mosquito netting overhead. They cut down the sixty foot proscenium arch with an inner portal that brought it into their scale; effected an entrance through one of the forward side exit doors. They cooled the place with electric fans blown over ice water, and there they were with an intimate little summer playhouse built inside the large one! The company lived communally and in no elegance. Insofar as its purpose was not to make money, it succeeded. Nevertheless it managed to carry itself enthusiastically through a ten-week season giving six plays and in 1941 repeated the project.

In the East outdoor summer music festivals are becoming more frequent and finer. The Berkshire Festival led by Koussevitsky and the Boston Symphony Orchestra is pre-eminent, but one also calls to mind the Philadelphia Orchestra's seasons in Robin Hood Dell, the New York Philharmonic's Lewisohn Stadium concerts under the stars, the festivals at Silver Mine, Connecticut. In the Middle West instead of these outdoor music festivals we find outdoor opera and operetta companies.

Opera at Ravinia outside of Chicago was for many years an institution which attracted thousands; so also has the Opera in the Cincinnati Zoo. Since 1919 the Municipal Opera in Forest Park at St. Louis has been presenting light opera and musical comedies outdoors and in the past few seasons there have been smaller but comparable undertakings in Louisville, Dallas and Memphis. The St. Louis project will serve as illustration of this kind of summer theatre. By 1940 it was presenting in a thirteen-week season such old favorites as *The Great Waltz, The Chocolate Soldier, Rio Rita, Naughty Marietta,* as well as newer musicals like *Anything Goes, Babes in Arms* and *Knickerbocker Holiday.* In its outdoor theatre seating ten thousand, it played during the season to an audience of three-quarters of a million; its season's gross reached five hundred thousand dollars. It was importing stars and a staff from New York to supplement local choruses of ninety singers and dancers, and it had a fifty-piece orchestra. This was obviously summer stock raised to professional production level and truly a community, a people's theatre in its appeal to all ages and classes.

Its success is an interesting theatrical phenomenon and bears consideration. The first factor, I believe, is habit. Over more than twenty years—since long before the days of air-conditioning—St. Louisans have developed the habit of going to Forest Park to the Opera on summer

nights. It has become the thing to do. The theatre anywhere can only hope to belong to the people if it is able
to become an habitual experience. A second factor is civic
spirit. To maintain such a project over a long enough
period to foster the growth of this opera-going habit, it
has been necessary for it to have the moral and occasionally the material backing of the leading citizens. St.
Louis seems to be fortunate in having a number of public-
spirited men, who are able to couple in their minds the
cultural and commercial value to their city of such an
enterprise. A third factor is the economic. Although productions are lavishly staged with little expense spared, the
Opera is able to break even and yet sell five thousand seats
at twenty-five and fifty cents, five thousand at one dollar,
one dollar and a half, and two dollars, and provide seventeen hundred free seats available to anyone. This theatre
is consequently within the financial reach of every inhabi-
tant of St. Louis. The final factor is the performance itself.
The essence of theatre is in these musicals. Color and
dance and song, words to make laughter or tears: the
lowest common denominators of the stage at its gayest.
Like the old days of vaudeville, the audience is appealed
to directly and swept into the show—ten thousand strong.
When the performance fails to do this or provide enough
of these elements well done, the attendance drops. St.
Louis has its bad weeks too. But most of the time the
shows are good and the people are pleased. It has to be
so, for this is their theatre.

2

Summer stock is indubitably alive today in many forms and in many places; but what of the old regular commercial stock companies which flourished as well in the winter? Wherever I went in America I kept my eye open for them, but nowhere did I find any traces. When I got back to New York I was told at Actors' Equity Association the reason: as of January, 1941, there were only three playing in the United States (and I had been to none of those places): one was across the river in Montclair, New Jersey; one at Portland, Maine; one at Miami Beach, Florida. The one at Miami Beach I suppose should be classed with the summer theatres, since it was a seasonal group dependent upon a resort public through a brief period. Almost immediately after I received the report of its existence, having been buffeted about for thirty-seven weeks of stormy sailing, the Portland company, managed by Guy Palmerton, sank; the Montclair company lived but six weeks.[2]

It seems likely to me that stock, as it used to be known, has gone for good. But new ideas for stock or the replacement of stock have arisen and will arise discarding the old form. Let me present those I have come across.

[2] A note should be made of the stock company operated at Maplewood, New Jersey, by Cheryl Crawford in 1940 and again in 1941. Beginning as a summer enterprise, Miss Crawford was able to continue her program of plays with visiting stars for a twenty-two week season in 1940, thus taking her theatre out of the category of summer stock.

A plan which comes close to the old original stock scheme may be stated thus: if one town will not support its own local company six nights a week, four weeks a month, it might be possible to divide its support among six or eight towns; for each one might provide an audience three nights a month although it could not furnish one for twenty-four nights. This traveling stock idea is the one employed by the tent shows and it was the basis of a plan undertaken by Henry Adrian in Minnesota in the fall of 1940. Mr. Adrian formed the Minnesota Stock Company, with which he proposed to tour a half-dozen or more Minnesota towns where there had been scarcely any professional legitimate drama for a generation. Each month's tour would begin or end in Minneapolis and St. Paul. While the company was on tour, it could be preparing a second play thus allowing three or four weeks for rehearsal; in the second month it would be taken around the circuit. If the scheme prospered and all went well, at the end of the season his company would have worked thirty-two weeks, it would have brought eight plays to eight towns for three performances in each—a remarkable thing in a state like Minnesota—or in any state in these days.

The abandonment of the project after one production does not reflect on the basic soundness of the idea and appears not to have discouraged Mr. Adrian from contemplating an even more far-reaching program to embrace more than one Middle Western state in the future. Its closing in 1940 may rather be attributed to an unwisely planned repertory: *First Lady* by Kaufman and Dayton meant little to an audience of Scandinavian and German farmers in New Ulm; to a box office scaled too high: a

$1.65 top is more than can be demanded when there are no "big names" and people have not in any case that much money to spend on entertainment; to the lack of careful groundwork planning that would have eliminated both these errors in advance; to the inability to provide the "big names" that had been announced beforehand and to substitute for them artists of high enough caliber.

In the far West is a little bird that darts rapidly along the ground in desert land; it is called the roadrunner. It presents a funny picture—its neck reaching out in advance stream-line fashion and its tail stretched straight out behind, as it dashes by in a frenzy of haste. This bird has given its name to a California group called the "Roadrunners." It is a type of traveling stock company that is both very new and very old. Like the Minnesota organization, it is based on the idea of itinerant theatre. Like the former, it is also composed of young people—in this instance mostly recent graduates of Stanford University. Unlike Minnesota Stock, however, it carries its own theatre with it.

It was only a twenty-minute drive down from Palo Alto to San José, where I had heard that the "Roadrunners" had come to temporary roost. Some sleuthing revealed that in a vacant lot at the corner of Lincoln and Santa Clara Avenues I would find them; so down I went, and there they were. Drawn up in the middle of the field were two large van trucks. From broadside of one to broadside of the other stretched a sizeable tent whose pegs were just being driven into the ground by half a dozen young men in work-stained corduroys and sweaters. The burliest fellow around, a young man about twenty-five, was pointed out as J. P. Cahn, the producer. I managed to gain his ear and persuaded him to relinquish his foreman duties long enough to show me around and then to retire to a more secluded spot to tell me his story.

We entered one of the vans by a short ladder. Inside were five bunks (for the men of the company), a lavatory and shower bath; also the switchboard for the stage and house lights, their batteries under the floor boards; also storage space for the tent and for enough benches to seat 250 people. We dismounted from this truck, passed under the big canvas-top and there at the other end facing us broad-side was the second truck. The side wall of it was just being let down to form the floor of the stage, supported on its outer edges by portable piles driven into the ground. Inside were bunks for the girls, storage space for lights, scenery, costumes and props. Both vans had been equipped by the hand of Mr. Cahn and a friend and the ingenuity of the young men was breathtaking.

In June, 1940, the "Roadrunners" started out from their headquarters at Los Gatos, California, a company of eleven boys and girls; they had three or four plays in their repertory: *Yes, My Darling Daughter, Private Lives, The Late Christopher Bean.* Other plays were to be prepared as they went along. They had an itinerary in mind that would take them through much of California and perhaps across Nevada into Utah. This was abandoned, however, for the distances were too vast and the populace too apathetic; they concentrated instead on California, and went from town to town staying when possible three days in a place.

When the "Roadrunners" reached a city, having procured a license from the municipality, they would seek a large vacant lot like the one they were then occupying, preferably on a much-traveled thoroughfare. There they would set up their theatre, hang out their banners and hope for a crowd. A certain amount of advance publicity plus the novelty of their project were apt to bring them fair audiences. In Sacramento they had to get extra seats to supplement their own accommodations for 250. In other places they have played to as few as seventeen. By the time I caught up with the "Roadrunners" in November, they had played about seventy-five performances, which included some return engagements of which they were proud. Their plan, like Mr. Adrian's, included frequent returns to the same places.

Obviously this theatre, while able to operate on a shoe-string, represents a good-sized initial investment—close to ten thousand dollars, I imagine—and no doubt would have required twice that capital if Mr. Cahn and his friend had not been such good plumbers, electricians, engineers, metal workers and carpenters and had been incapable, like any normal artists, of building the whole thing themselves out of a couple of old chassis and some canvas. It will take the company some time to pay back the original costs; meanwhile they have taken their own unemployment problem in hand, along with the problem of finding adequate theatres and what to do about unions. They have provided drama to a great many little towns and to bigger ones too, where no good stage play comes, and have gained for themselves the opportunity to act and manage a theatre.

The "Roadrunners" have sought to align themselves on the side of what they considered good theatre. They have not wanted to go into competition with the old-fashioned kind of ten-cent tent show and they have sought a more sophisticated public; by charging fifty cents they have tried to discourage *hoi polloi* and attract a better class of patrons. It seems to me too bad that such an original idea and ingenious mechanical solution has not been coupled with more theatrical imagination. Noel Coward seems decidedly out of place in a van-and-tent theatre. Why have not these youngsters found some plays to suit their unique milieu, or else written some, and devised a new technique for presenting them? With such a start, it is too bad they have not carried through with some creative showmanship.[3]

3

Traveling theatres like the short-lived Minnesota Stock Company and the picturesque "Roadrunners" are one substitute for the old stock company. There are others, five of which I should like to discuss. In them lie the seeds of resident professional theatre, which is what the old stock companies really were, but each has noteworthy variations.

January 4th and 5th, 1941, I spent in Erie, Pennsylvania, an unprepossessing little city in the northwestern corner of the state. On that Saturday night I went to the Erie Playhouse to see its 2,871st performance; the play was *Madcap Mary*, the 308th play presented by this theatre during its twenty-five years of existence. On the following day, Monday, January 6th, Henry B. Vincent,

[3] Mr. Cahn and one or two of his colleagues were drafted into the army in 1941, so the "Roadrunners" have stopped running for the time being.

founder and director of the Erie Playhouse and the one man responsible for its long life and continuous activity, died. I consider it fortunate that I had so arranged my schedule that I did not go to Erie a week, or even a day later. I should not have wished to miss those hours I spent with the white-haired old man whom the papers said two days later was sixty-eight but whom everyone in Erie swore was nearer seventy-eight. It was not that he seemed in his seventies. The enthusiasm with which he told of his life's work—it was his valedictory he was delivering that snowy afternoon, although neither of us knew it— was the enthusiasm of a man at least forty years younger. The prosperous theatre he left behind bears witness to what may be accomplished when a leader devotes twenty-five years to sowing, cultivating and harvesting in one field.

The Erie Playhouse began in 1916 as a little theatre group led by Mr. Vincent who had come to Erie as a music teacher. In 1929 it moved into a new small play-house built by contributions from 475 individuals and or-ganizations of Erie. When I visited it twelve years later, the Playhouse had become a combination professional-community theatre. It had approximately five thousand subscribers upon whom it depended mainly for its support (although anyone might buy a ticket at the box office for one dollar). One became a subscriber, so its prospectus said, "by buying, at the beginning of the season for one dollar a book containing ten coupons. Each coupon is good for an admission at fifty cents. Coupons may be used in any number and at any time." Subscribers therefore paid sixty cents for a dollar seat and if they attended only three of the ten plays, they had received more than their original dollar's worth. These season subscriptions were sold by the townspeople of Erie in a great autumn drive. Townspeople also composed the board of directors.

At this point the similarity to a community theatre ends; for there is no community participation in the affairs on the stage. To all intents and purposes the Erie Playhouse is a stock company. Its actors form a permanent company of about ten who are engaged for the season and none of whom are natives of Erie. Some are old stock actors; most of them are young people out of university theatres eager for experience. On the whole they are a fairly talented group. The technical and business staff are also full-time paid employees. Of course the salary is small—less than Actors' Equity requires for its members —but one can live cheaply in Erie, apparently on less than one hundred dollars a month. Obviously, however, such a theatre must be only a steppingstone for the young artist whose capacities can command a greater return for him.

The Playhouse keeps its productions playing at least two weeks and if business prospers may extend it to a three- and occasionally to a four-week run. This allows longer rehearsal periods with a consequent improvement in results. The 1940-41 season expected to offer eleven productions: *Our Town, Skylark, The Guardsman, Love from a Stranger, Smilin' Through* were presented before Mr. Vincent's death, in addition to *Madcap Mary*. He had expected to round out the season with *Bachelor Born, Pygmalion, Craig's Wife, Call It a Day, The Petrified Forest*—a program obviously above what we used to consider the stock-company level.

The Saturday night I attended, the Playhouse was sold out to an audience of simple, pleasant-appearing middle-class Americans; a great many young people, I was glad to observe. The theatre was not dead in Erie, Pennsylvania.

Out in Rose Valley, south of Philadelphia on a winding, wooded suburban lane is Jasper Deeter's Hedgerow Theatre. A great deal has been written and told about Hedgerow, for it strikes a bizarre note in our monochromatic stage picture. It is hard to know whether to hail Deeter as a prophet crying in the wilderness, or as a fanatic carrying on in a world of his own creation. One is inclined to feel that if this theatre were artistically sound and essentially valid, the eighteen years since its inception would have brought it wider success or at least some general recognition of its greatness. Instead it still continues to be regarded as an eccentricity. It is certain, however, that it cannot be dismissed and my visit to Rose Valley impressed me with the seriousness of the project, the intelligence—the brilliance even—of its grasp on theatre, the rightness of most of its fundamental tenets, even as it disappointed me with the caliber of the particular performance I witnessed and disturbed me by its neuroticism.

The Hedgerow Theatre is, as far as I know, the only true repertory theatre in America (excepting, of course, the Opera companies). During the one month after my visit, for instance, Hedgerow in seven performances a week was presenting the following: *The Whiteheaded Boy*, *The Romantic Age*, *King Henry IV, Part I*, *Diff'rent*, a new play called *Chocolate*, *Macbeth*, *Arms and the Man*, *Beloved Leader*, *Ghosts*, *Inheritors*, *The Emperor Jones*. Indisputably any theatre with this current repertory (plus about thirty other plays prepared which could be substituted if desired) is significant. During April of each year it presents a Shakespeare Festival; in July, a Shaw festival (in 1940 *Man and Superman, Heartbreak House, Arms and the Man, Misalliance, Candida, Major Barbara*).

This program is presented by a company of between thirty and thirty-five people, mostly under thirty years of age, each of whom participates in all phases of production and maintenance: back stage, box office, parking lot, costume making and repair, scenery building, painting and shifting, business management and publicity, print shop (they turn out their own programs, posters and handbills), photography (they have their own dark room), dishwashing and acting. The company lives communally in two living houses and upstairs in the old mill where the shops are situated. It owns one of these houses and its theatre. The members are provided with room, board and cigarettes, but no salary. When necessary the individual member may draw small sums from the common treasury, for which he makes an accounting.

After an interview with the governing board of twelve, a new member is placed on probation for three months. Upon the successful completion of that period, he indicates how long he would like to work at Hedgerow: one year or three years, say, or five. Until that specified time has elapsed, he is obligated to remain with the group unless released. Such an arrangement seems necessary in a repertory theatre which depends for its operation on a more or less permanent company. The new member also indicates what are his particular aptitudes; on that basis he will assume responsibility for some special task in addition to acting (e.g., publicity, electrical management, etc.), and, when he leaves, must "teach his way out," that is, train a newcomer or another member to take over his responsibility. Only thus can continuity be maintained.

To operate a theatre in repertory, presenting never more than two consecutive performances of the same play, requires the most expert management of internal affairs and public relations. Advance planning is obviously necessary. The exact sequence of plays is laid out a month in advance. New productions are decided upon the previous year. In April, 1940, when I paid Hedgerow my visit, the designer was beginning his drawings for a production to open the following April. I saw rehearsals of *Major Barbara*, scheduled to open on Shaw's birthday, July 26—twelve weeks away.

Rehearsals are begun several months before the opening date, the director estimating the approximate number of rehearsal hours in advance. Readings for casting may occupy three or four afternoons a week for several weeks. It must be borne in mind that the company is operating its theatre and performing every night in repertory at the same time. Then the play is dropped for a month or so while work is done on another; for in this production scheme more than one play may be in preparation at once. During this time, however, the actors who have been selected are giving thought to their respective roles. Then the first play is taken up once more for a six to eight week period of rehearsals, again three or four times a week. During this period the chief work is done. After it comes the final stage when the technical aspects of production will be integrated into the whole—and Hedgerow has another bill to add to the 140 it has presented.

An analysis of Hedgerow's artistic accomplishments requires an analysis of Jasper Deeter, for he is the absolute director of the theatre, the undisputed arbiter in all questions of taste. The choice of plays is his and the style of performance is set by him. Unfortunately, however, Mr. Deeter, who was one of the members of the early Provincetown Theatre, very nearly defies analysis—at least by a passing observer, no matter how interested. One is apt to be startled by his appearance when at home. Lean and scrawny, with an unruly shock of rarely-cut gray hair, minus a tooth or two, his long fingers stained sepia by nicotine and with a six-day beard concealing most of his face, Deeter reminds one of a Cruikshank drawing of a Dickens character. But there is fire in the man and a kind of hypnotic force which manifests itself particularly in rehearsal. He may sit listlessly for a quarter of an hour; then when the scene starts to interest him, the fire begins to burn and the air blows hot through the rehearsal room. He claims to have no set method of approach and develops none in his actors. He appears to work primarily by intuition and by inspiration; the psychological is his particular preoccupation. Perhaps that is why *Twelfth Night*, which I saw, was only barely adequate and why crowds are always present to see *The Emperor Jones*, or any O'Neill play, for that matter. There is no doubt that he is a remarkably creative director when the play stimulates him; without that stimulus he is no better than average.

This inequality is present also in the company. Some of Deeter's actors are excellent, some only adequate. They all seem to live in a state of high nervous tension which can be felt at once by a sensitive visitor. The lack of any possible individual, private life, which such completely communal existence enforces—at least at Hedgerow—seems to lead to a partial drought of personality. This may account for the neurotic air of the place. The removal of the profit motive also seems a little unnatural to the average American and is responsible, I have no doubt, for the departure of some of Hedgerow's company from time to time, when they feel impelled eventually to want to receive money for their work.

Some of the reasons why the Hedgerow Theatre has not become the most significant producing group in America, in spite of its possibilities, are implicit in what I have just written. Two other inter-related factors remain. The first is that Hedgerow evinces little interest in economics and finance. It is all very well to believe that theatre is art, but, for better or worse, its growth is affected by its economy. This theatre has no professional business manager, no full-time press representative or public relations counsel. True, there are a number of committees of the members (their primary interest is in acting) who take care of various aspects of administration: ticket sales, repertory, budget, publicity, etc., but one gains the impression that this is handled with not too great efficiency. Its members state that a good deal of the time the company has been in debt. Notwithstanding, there are no subscribers, no endowment and Hedgerow abhors the idea of having either.

I have seen too many theatres with vigorous promotion machines and no product to sell to place emphasis on the absence of the promotional urge at Hedgerow, were it not that this is coupled with, and is perhaps the result of, a more serious attitude. This theatre does not really seem to care whether it has an audience or not. I do not believe that the theatre can operate in a vacuum, that it can disregard the people and grow. If it has nothing to offer, then it is another matter and it won't grow anyhow; but Hedgerow has at least great plays in its repertory, plays which most communities have only rare opportunities to see. The meager support which Philadelphia gives to its resident repertory theatre is only partly Philadelphia's fault. "We shall produce only what we like and as we like. If the public wants to find out about it and come, all well and good; if it doesn't, that is all right too." An independent spirit is as commendable as it is rare; at the same time there is definite inherent danger in it.

One June evening in 1937 as the sun was setting across Dartmoor, I paced the yew-hedged terrace of Dartington Hall in the southwest of England. Michael Chekhov, nephew of the great Anton, walking beside me outlined shyly and in halting English, but with sparkling eyes, assurance and the fire of great vision, his project for a permanent theatre studio. It would have its home there in Devon on the estate of Mr. and Mrs. Leonard Elmhirst, as part of their plan to join a cultural center to their reconstruction of rural life. It would be composed of a group of young people who would study with Mr. Chekhov for a three-year period and then go out on tours from which it would return to its Devonshire headquarters for sessions of creation much as the Jooss Ballet, also in residence at Dartington Hall, had been doing.

Only two years of the initial preparatory period had passed, however, when the shadow of Munich stretched across Dartmoor. The Trustees of Dartington Hall, sensing the imminence of international conflict and recognizing that a war-torn England would be no suitable haven for the arts, moved the theatre project to America in January, 1939, and set it up in the country outside Ridgefield, Connecticut. Since the majority of the company were Americans, this was the logical country to which to migrate.

In New England the young actors continued their study under Mr. Chekhov. His system was closer to his ex-colleague, Vakhtangov, than to his former master, Stanislavski, for he was more interested in theatrical form than in psychological representation. He was more of a mystic than Vakhtangov, however; and his theatricality became impregnated with the conceptions of anthroposophy and the creed of Rudolf Steiner. The infusion of an inner and an outer rhythm became for Chekhov the essence of stage production.

Unwisely the Chekhov Theatre Players abandoned their original plan of touring and determined to present themselves to Broadway. The selection of an incomprehensible dramatization of Dostoevski's *The Possessed* did not help the young players, who during their preparatory years had never had the experience of appearing before a public audience. They were a talented group but not possessed of any measure of the acting genius of their leader, one of the world's most remarkable artists. It appeared that they had poorly understood his meaning and had only caught his form, for their performance was lacking in any real richness, although remarkably sustained in style. Had this company sought American advice or even accustomed itself to the American public before facing Broadway's cold scrutiny, it might have avoided the charge of Russianism which rather deservedly was leveled against it.

After this initial failure in 1939 the Chekhov Theatre Players returned to Ridgefield and, sure of the ultimate validity of their endeavor, set to work on a production of *Twelfth Night* and a dramatization of *The Cricket on the Hearth*. Returning now to their original idea of a touring organization they designed their productions to be taken by truck out through the country. In 1940 the Players, led by Beatrice Straight, their founder, embarked on a three-month tour of one- and two-night stands which carried them as far afield as Oklahoma and Texas. They played principally in schools and colleges, community centers and art museums; everywhere they were received with enthusiasm, for these new productions had robustness and beauty, rich humor and fresh stylization. At the end of this tour they returned to their Connecticut headquarters and began preparations on a fairy-tale play for children and an ambitious staging of a Shakespearean tragedy which they hoped to take out in 1941-42.

It has been hard to assign a place to the Chekhov Theatre Players in the American theatrical pattern. As an itinerant organization, it should perhaps have been grouped with the "Roadrunners." Because it originated as a Studio and continues to operate a school from which new talent is enlisted into the company, its consideration should perhaps have been postponed to a later chapter. The continuity of its existence, however, suggests that it belongs alongside the Hedgerow Theatre. Like the Rose Valley group, its life depends upon one man. Like it also, the Chekhov disciples are in opposition to commercialism. Like Hedgerow furthermore there is a danger that as a result of its communal life this group may become ingrown and neurotic. Its artistic discipline is not equaled by its personal discipline which in the end may tend to cut down its power, particularly since its members are so young.

Unlike Jasper Deeter, however, Michael Chekhov does have a fixed belief in the kind of theatre he considers important, and he has worked out a method for its accomplishment. The value of training and technique is not overlooked by the Chekhov Studio. If it can avoid the tendency to grow in on itself, which every group working apart is so apt to do; if it can add new and perhaps maturer talent to its number; if it can infuse more American extroversion into its Slavism; if it can find some new native material to supplement the classics, then it has the chance of becoming one of our finest theatres. Three years is, after all, a very short time. The art of a Michael Chekhov is very long.

Three thousand miles west from Rose Valley and Ridgefield is the Seattle Repertory Playhouse. Like Hedgerow, it belongs in a consideration of the kinds of theatre which have replaced the old stock company by operating as permanent professional resident companies. Unlike Hedgerow—and this must be made clear at the start—it is a repertory company in name only. It produces but one play at a time, runs it for as long as it can be sustained, seldom revives a play, never within the same season. The Seattle Repertory Playhouse therefore resembles more nearly the Erie Playhouse and the old stock plan.

Hedgerow reflects the egocentric personality of Jasper Deeter; the Chekhov Theatre Players the genius of their Russian director; the Seattle Playhouse is the result of the labors of a middle-aged married couple, Mr. and Mrs. Burton James. Mr. James is a pleasant, paternal soul with an Irish wit and temper. Mrs. James shares his wit and temper and adds to it a driving energy; both have a hazy practicality. There is a nucleus acting group of about a dozen to whom the theatre guarantees a modest year-around salary of fifty dollars a month. In addition, however, and unlike the Erie, Hedgerow and Chekhov theatres, it supplements this group from play to play with what amateur recruits may be needed; in fact, even in its permanent nucleus are one or two unpaid non-professional members.

The Pacific Northwest is a wonderful part of America. Seattle, flanked by snow-capped mountains, glowing with a profusion of flowers and shrubs, breathing in the salt-tanged air of Puget Sound and the sea beyond, is a young and vibrant city. One expects pioneering here, and a clear-eyed view of things. It is not surprising, therefore, to observe actors and directors of the Repertory Playhouse sit down for a round-table discussion of their work (as they do once a week) in an effort to *understand* what they do, that they may make it better. This permanent company, like Chekhov's, recognizing in its very permanence the possibility for developing a common style and method of approach to the art of acting, is much preoccupied with welding itself into a group with a conscious artistic entity. Influenced chiefly by the Soviet director, Vakhtangov, they have come to believe that their talent is not subconscious, operating according to mysterious laws which it is better to leave alone. They insist, instead, that a conscious analysis of technique, of individual projection of emotion, of the line and meaning of a play, of its significance to contemporary life must be undertaken. They need to know all this if they are to make their own comment on the play, and to comment they believe is their duty.

It would be pleasant to recount that the results of the Seattle group's study made for a new and exhilarating experience to the beholder. I cannot honestly say that this happened to me, although *Tony Draws a Horse*, an inconsequential English drawing-room comedy, was hardly the ideal vehicle through which to convey their new-found power. Moreover, such an attack on theatre technique requires a long time to produce results of consequence. I should like to return to Seattle in another three or four years, for I believe that if the artists of the Repertory Playhouse can keep their number intact, they may by then have grown into a company with a forceful and incisive theatrical style. At least their studies are heading them in that direction.

The Repertory Playhouse calls itself "Seattle's Civic Theatre." It certainly has more right to this title than Hedgerow would have to call itself "Philadelphia's Civic Theatre." It has a Board of Trustees composed of Seattle citizens. Furthermore the Jameses are concerned that their theatre should relate to the lives of people around. Through this very concern, however, they have succeeded in placing the Playhouse in an anomolous position. Believing in a theatre of social comment , a few years ago they produced *Waiting for Lefty* and *Bury the Dead*. These plays antagonized one of the newspapers in labor-conscious Seattle to the point of forbidding any mention of the Playhouse thereafter in its pages. Many affluent supporters also deserted it. Faced with this ostracism, the Playhouse yet found itself unable to go over whole hog into the proletarian camp. It was not communist; it wanted to serve the whole city. It wanted to be able to follow *Tony Draws a Horse* with Irwin Shaw's *The Gentle People* if it pleased; and to follow that with *Peer Gynt* (three of its 1940-41 repertory). It wanted to be all things to all men, and in consequence was having a difficult time.

Like Hedgerow, the Repertory Playhouse lacks a firm business and public relations management. Also like Hedgerow, it has no season subscription plan, but depends on its door sales at fifty-five cents a ticket. It has, however, various schemes for balancing its budget. One is the practice of selling blocks of seats or the whole house for a single performance to some organization or club in a profit-sharing plan. In this way in the 1939-40 season, it disposed of nearly twenty thousand seats through one hundred and twenty-five clubs. It has also formed a school offering both full-time and part-time work in drama. The Junior Chamber of Commerce awards scholarships for full-time study to a dozen graduates of Seattle high schools. Through its school the Playhouse is training young people in its newly-developing methods of production, is consequently providing itself, like the Chekhov Theatre, with a source from which it can draw new talent for its acting company, and at the same time is increasing its meager revenue.

The Seattle Repertory Playhouse, like the Erie Playhouse and the Hedgerow Theatre, is making an attempt to provide a continuous season of professional dramatic fare to its community. It is paying actors a little—although not very much certainly—to come to and stay in Seattle, three thousand miles from Broadway; it offers them the opportunity to develop their artistic technique, and in so doing to contribute to a collective experiment toward creative theatre.

On a side street about half-way between the business center of Cleveland and its principal residential districts is the dark red brick Cleveland Play House. From its green paneled foyer one turns right into the Drury Theatre which seats about five hundred people; or crossing the outer lobby to the left, one may enter the little Brooks Theatre with room for only 160 and a small but well-equipped stage at the far end. A door from that stage leads into shops and dressing-rooms common to both theatres and from there one goes out onto the stage of the Drury Theatre. Here is equipment and working space equal to the best playhouses in New York when geared for production. This place has the air of being fully used and lived in. It pulses with activity; no pretentious palace half-filled with life. Combined with a patrician dignity which asserts itself, there is the smell of theatre here— of theatre functioning strong.

The Cleveland Play House is generally considered the outstanding product, along with the Pasadena Playhouse, of the "Little Theatre Movement." Although it began twenty-five years ago as part of that epidemic, it has long since outgrown the appellation. Occupying a plant that represents an investment of close to $400,000, attended by an annual audience purported to exceed 110,000 people, operating on an annual budget of $85,000, it is obviously no longer "little." Frederic McConnell, its director, says: "The Play House might closely be defined as a resident producing theatre, professionally organized, and operated not for profit and trusteed by a representative group of people drawn from the cultural, social and business life of the city of Cleveland." The Play House, according to this definition, can be grouped for consideration with its smaller sister playhouses in Erie and Seattle. It is hard to say whether it is the legitimate successor to the little theatre or to the stock company. The first part of the definition, "a resident producing theatre, professionally organized," connects it with stock; but the definition's modification, "operated not for profit and trusteed by a representative group," reveals its relationship to the noncommercial theatre.

"Professional" and "commercial" are two words often used interchangeably when referring to theatrical activity. I do not believe that they are synonymous. The Cleveland Play House is a professional but not a commercial theatre. By this I mean that it is directed and peopled by professionals: by artists whose sole source of income is through their work on its stages. However, as Mr. McConnell points out, his theatre is "operated not for profit." Neither he nor the trustees of whom he speaks, nor any other person, gains financially from its success. No capital is invested in this theatre which seeks a return that will increase itself. That, as I construe it, is what makes a theatre commercial. It is the angels, the backers, the managers, the real estate men of Broadway, or wherever they be, who invest in theatre (and so control it) with the idea of making money thereat—the capitalistic exploiters of the stage, it is they who make it commercial.

The Cleveland Play House in 1941 was employing the services of a company of thirty-eight, which included thirteen actors, nine technicians and an administrative and house staff. This company was engaged for the entire season in advance and a number of its members have worked together for fifteen or twenty years. Only three of them received above twenty-five hundred dollars for their eight months' work, but at that considerably more than one-half of the eighty-five thousand dollar budget went into salaries.

As a result of this professionalization, it has been possible to maintain a schedule of activity unequaled in any playhouse in America outside of Pasadena. Both its theatres are open between eight and nine months a year giving seven performances a week on each stage. Anywhere from twelve to fifteen productions are presented annually. In the large theatre one play may run from three to six weeks; in the small theatre the audience for a successful play may sustain it for as long as a ten- or twelve-week run.

The Play House maintains a school which numbers about forty students. It is conducted on the apprentice basis, with few classes and emphasis on the participation of the student in the active life of the theatre. "The student is not relegated to a distinct and separate functioning group," McConnell points out. "Instead he participates as a cognate personality in the intricate composite of stage production." In this way the theatre is able to increase the size of its acting company and at the same time give young stage aspirants the experience of actual performance.

The Play House considers itself a "community theatre" in the sense that it exists as a non-profit making institution to serve the city of Cleveland. Its subscribers number about five thousand. They pay ten dollars for fourteen tickets usable in any number for any performance.[4] In addition, anyone in Cleveland may purchase a seat at the box office for one dollar,[5] and student tickets are available for thirty-five cents. The Play House does not offer any general outlet to those in the community who desire to act (although it states that a few amateurs are used, "who through long association with the theatre have become a part of the Play House ensemble"). For those of the community who care to serve the theatre in other capacities, however, and to establish a liaison with the general public, the Play House has a women's committee numbering five hundred and a smaller men's committee, which are particularly useful in its promotion.

The Cleveland Play House is nevertheless not completely a community theatre. Although it talks of service to the city, Cleveland has a million inhabitants and five thousand subscribers are scarcely enough. The average citizen cannot afford fourteen dollars a year and a dollar top prevents thousands of persons from attending. Its audience is upper middle class and the Play House seems disinclined to include a greater cross-section of the city. If this theatre could reduce its admission, send out companies into underprivileged districts and schools, broaden the content of its repertory, it might become a broader cultural force in its community for its connections today with welfare agencies, schools and colleges although valuable do not suffice.

The Cleveland Play House nevertheless has been in a national sense, indeed in an international sense, one of the outstanding theatres of the past twenty years. The record

---

[4] Six dollars for twelve coupons usable at matinees only.
[5] One dollar and twenty-five cents on Saturday nights.

of its productions is as distinguished as that of any dramatic institution in the world. No single American stage, not even that of the New York Theatre Guild, can boast of a richer repertory: such plays as *The Sunken Bell*, *Antigone*, *The School for Scandal*, *Hinkemann*, *Dr. Faustus*, *The Fire in the Opera House*, *Anne Pedersdotter*, *The Brothers Karamazov*, *The Goat Song*, *The Jest*, *Peripherie*, as well as nine of the plays of Shaw, several by each of a list that would include Galsworthy, Ibsen, Chekhov, O'Neill, Pirandello, Shakespeare, O'Casey and modern comedies by Behrman, Barry, Kaufman, Sherwood, Maugham, Coward and many others. These have been staged with scenic investitures of great beauty and by a company that constantly maintained a standard of competence, and that occasionally in the performances of Russell Collins, Carl Benton Reid, Katherine Squire, K. Elmo Lowe, Byron McGrath and Dorothy Paxton has reached heights of splendor.

In 1941, however, the picture was changed—I hope only temporarily. In the small theatre in January an undistinguished mystery play, *Invitation to a Murder*, was on display and in the Drury Theatre *Tony Draws a Horse*, seeming more inconsequential than ever. On both stages there was a noticeable lack of good performances. *Tony Draws a Horse* was being harmed, if it could be, by hammy, muggy, overacting. The direction was dull and uninventive; the sets would have been improved upon in half a dozen summer stock theatres.

I shall undoubtedly be accused of unfairness: you must not judge the Play House by these two productions. I must admit that later in the season, on a return visit to Cleveland, I witnessed a performance of *Family Portrait* that was eloquent and moving, played in the high tradition of the Play House and testifying that this theatre is still capable of fine things. *Family Portrait* only served to strengthen the conviction which I had had when I left Cleveland earlier in the winter: that at no time can a first-class theatre afford to present third-class fare—unless, of course, it is willing to become a third-class theatre.

Reverting in conclusion from its momentary situation to a consideration of its career over these past twenty years, I can say that viewed as a whole it has the right, I believe, to command comparison with the Theatre Guild and the Group Theatre in New York, with the Abbey Theatre in Dublin, with perhaps even the Moscow Art Theatre. Placed in such company, it reveals, as one might expect, certain weaknesses. The first is that it has had no first-rate dramatists interested in it. All of those other theatres achieved their position very largely because they attracted playwrights: O'Neill, Odets, O'Casey and Synge, Chekhov and Gorki. The Cleveland Play House in nineteen years has done only sixteen full-length new plays. In the second place, it has not created a definitive theatrical style of its own as the Moscow Art, the Group, and to a lesser degree the Abbey Theatres have done. (This is perhaps not a matter to criticize, for its eclecticism may have been healthy: both the Group and the Moscow Art have been in some measure restricted by their self-imposed forms.) In the third place, the caliber of its artists, while high, has not been high enough to lift and sustain it in the absence of new playwrights. In the fourth place, like the Theatre Guild, it suffers from lack of new blood or from the need to refresh the blood that it has.

I have dissected the Cleveland Play House thus coldly

because I believe it is important to find out whether any great permanent theatre can be created in America outside of New York. It would seem that if it could be done, Cleveland has had the opportunity to do it. Its physical facilities are the equal of any of the four theatres with which I compare it. It has been removed from the commercial influences which smote so hard against the Guild and the Group and helped to bring about their undoing. It has been led by a directorate with strong belief in the best kind of theatre. It has had enlightened although perhaps limited civic support to sustain it. Most of its shortcomings when compared to those four other great theatres were the result of conditions outside its control. As long as the best American dramatists persist in marketing their best plays first in New York and are unwilling to have them tried out elsewhere, no theatre will have any greater success than the Cleveland Play House. As long as the best actors, designers and directors cling to Broadway, no theatre will have a better ensemble than the Play House. As long as American cities of a million inhabitants are not ready to support a permanent professional theatre of the caliber of their permanent professional orchestras: the Philadelphia, the Boston Symphony, the Minneapolis—which is to say, command as fine talent as is available in New York or anywhere—so long will there be no theatres in American cities any better than the Cleveland Play House.

CHAPTER FOUR

Tempests and Teacups

I WAS NOT born in a trunk. Neither of my parents were ever on the stage. Before I was nine years old I had seen only three plays that I can remember: *Pinafore,* Sothern and Marlowe in *The Taming of the Shrew* and *Chu Chin Chow.* At nine, nevertheless, I was certain that if I did not become a missionary or a doctor (my other ambitions) I would be in the theatre. At nine my chance came. The Little Theater of Indianapolis presented *Rackety Packety House* as a children's matinee. I played a small gnome dressed in green; I had twelve lines which I am told I delivered with considerable aplomb. That sealed my fate. The missionary and the doctor idea were dismissed. I am now in the theatre, and the little theatre movement is responsible.

Rackety Packety House was twenty-two years ago. We rehearsed it in an old carriage house both draughty and dirty, performed at the Masonic Temple, where the stage was twelve feet deep and forty feet wide. A great many ladies were involved in the production, I remember, and very few men. This may have been because it was a children's matinee; but I think it was largely a ladies' theatre anyhow.

Through the nineteen-twenties our little theatre grew out of its salad days. By 1925 it was able to build a playhouse of its own. In 1927 it changed its name to The Civic Theater of Indianapolis. Other little theatres were growing too. More and more men were becoming involved to make a better balance. In fact, there was a boom on in the amateur theatrical market. Then came the Wall Street crash in 1929. Even little theatres were affected. The weaker ones folded their tents and slipped away; the stronger ones, with buildings and equipment on their hands, retrenched. To the degree that any little theatre was a luxury and not a necessity, it suffered or died.

I have been considering thus far the state of the professional theatre in the United States beyond Broadway. Now we are entering a field where the stage rests on another base; where, except for paid leaders, people are participating with no thought of earning their living. The little theatre movement was brought into being by men and women who loved the stage and wished to express themselves in it without making it their profession; who were dissatisfied with the commercial fare of Broadway and wanted to experiment with the theatre as an art. Some of them also had social aspirations; others were motivated by a philanthropic desire to bring the stage closer to people from whom it was becoming far removed.

Those little theatres that weathered the depression to continue today and those which have arisen within the past eight or ten years differ in one respect from the amateur groups of the nineteen-twenties. The creative experimentation that animated the post-war little theatres has subsided. A good deal of that was phoney—a purple spotlight, a little chiffon, some unintelligible poetry. The loss of it has been a good thing. Some of it, however, was valid, and the loss of that is regrettable. In this the non-professional theatre offers an interesting parallel to the professional. It was just after the war that the creative impetus begun in 1914-17 came into flower. The Washington Square Players, the Neighborhood Playhouse, the Provincetown Playhouse; Robert Edmond Jones, Eugene O'Neill, Philip Moeller, Lee Simonson, Joseph Urban, Kenneth Macgowan and Arthur Hopkins—all these were effecting a creative theatrical renaissance in New York. At about the same time Frederic McConnell came to the Cleveland Play House, Gilmor Brown organized the Pasadena Community Playhouse Association, Sam Hume and Sheldon Cheney were at work at the Arts and Crafts Theatre in Detroit and Maurice Brown was directing in Chicago.

Whether these activities in New York and through the country were parallel developments or whether one was inspired by the other, it would be hard to say. The point is that pioneering was being done both by the professionals and by the non-professionals. In the last ten years, however, New York has seen less and less creative theatre and again the parallel appears: outside New York the amateur stage has exhibited a comparable artistic sterility. The only explanations I can offer are, first, that on Broadway and in the amateur theatres alike the economic struggle of the depression and post-depression years has operated to compel them both to give increasingly careful consideration to box office; in such times people seem to feel that the uncertainty of experiment is dangerous. Second, neither on Broadway nor off are there men and women with great creative talent to offer the theatre. The temporal coincidence of these periods of artistic expansion and contraction in the two fields is noteworthy. I shall have more to say about it hereafter.

It would perhaps be wise to halt such generalizations and get down to cases. In the composite picture drawn from twelve or fifteen average or better than average community, civic and little theatres, some idea should emerge of their contribution to the American theatre as a whole, of the degree of responsibility they are assuming in building a national culture.

2

Let us pay a return visit to the Civic Theater of Indianapolis. As I have said, since the day of my debut it has grown. Its new theatre, an attractive little playhouse, cost forty thousand dollars. It has now nearly fifteen hundred members. But the population of Indianapolis is over 350,000. That means that 99½ per cent of its citizens do *not* support this organization. Is it then truly a *civic* theatre? What right had it to change its name from "Little Theater"?

One reason, I feel sure, for its comparatively small membership is that subscriptions to its season of eight plays cost eight, fifteen and twenty-five dollars. Box office price for admission to a single production is $1.25—four or five times as much as a movie starring Greta Garbo, Paul Muni or anyone else. One can see Katharine Hepburn in person or Helen Hayes, Tallulah Bankhead or Gertrude Lawrence from a cheap seat in the commercial road house, English's Theatre, for less.

Of course, if the Civic Theater were offering quintessential dramas and a standard of production superior to the best that Hollywood or these visiting companies could offer to Indianapolis, it might be an excusable tariff—although even then my conception of a "civic" institution as one which makes its facilities available to all would forbid it the use of that name. But what was the Civic Theater's program for 1940-41? It announced the following: *Of Thee I Sing, The Petrified Forest* ("a Broadway success five years ago," as the prospectus said), *See My Lawyer, Two On an Island, Love from a Stranger, Private Lives, Mrs. Moonlight, Kiss the Boys Goodbye.*

This choice of plays might have some justification if Indianapolis were off the beaten path and no touring companies ever came to bring the city into touch with what Broadway was doing. But Indianapolis in the 1940-41 season was visited by: *Skylark, The Little Foxes, The Man Who Came to Dinner, The Philadelphia Story, There Shall Be No Night, The Time of Your Life, Dubarry Was a Lady, Tobacco Road, Hellzapoppin, Arsenic and Old Lace, Pins and Needles, Cabin in the Sky.* (The road is certainly not dead in Indianapolis.) Such a competition as the Civic Theater appears to enter into with Broadway fare seems foolish. What a wealth of plays it overlooks!

Furthermore, the standard of Civic Theater productions, while high, is surely not so much higher than these road companies that they can be sold to the public at prices more or less comparable to what it costs them to see Gertrude Lawrence, Tallulah Bankhead, Katharine Hepburn, Ethel Waters and their companies.

Before I stop biting the hand that once fed me, let me cite another Civic Theater situation that concerns me. The present director, Richard Hoover, assumed his post at the beginning of the 1940-41 season. His predecessor was Edward Steinmetz who served for two seasons; before him was Alfred Etcheverry who served for one; before him was Frederick Burleigh who served for three. I do not know the specific reasons for each change, but I believe it bodes no good for the Civic Theater as an institution which must develop continuity.

Indianapolis is only one among a number of community theatres where this occurs. Many of them seem to be at a perpetual Alice-in-Wonderland tea-party whereat the directors are always moving one place on. After a period of from two to five years, the director at Kalamazoo moves to Dallas; the director at Dallas moves to Charleston; the director at Indianapolis moves to Pittsburgh; the man in Omaha moves to Indianapolis; the man in Duluth moves to Shreveport; his predecessor there moves to Memphis; and so it goes, round and round in a circle.

This practice is so prevalent that it must be attributed to more than the roving spirit of an individual or the idiosyncrasy of any one little theatre. It seems to me that no doubt both director and theatre are responsible: the director, because he lacks either the desire or capacity to establish a permanent theatre on his own terms at any one spot; the theatre, whenever through the jealousy of its board of directors it will not encourage or allow any director to do so. If the argument be proffered that variety is an enlivener, that a frequent injection of new blood is stimulating, I should reply that a healthy organism grows without need for injections, that instability and impermanence are not conducive to increasing strength. I would cite the outstanding examples of the Cleveland Play

House and the Pasadena Playhouse as theatres which grew over a period of twenty years each under a single leader. (If new blood might enrich these theatres now, it does not follow that Frederic McConnell's or Gilmor Brown's usefulness is ended even after twenty years: these theatres might profit by fresh additions, not by replacement of their leaders.) Wherever community theatre administration continues in this state of flux, we shall have to wait there for really significant accomplishment.

On old St. Peter Street in the French quarter of New Orleans, under the shadow of the St. Louis Cathedral, stands Le Petit Théâtre du Vieux Carré. Beyond the flagstone loggia through which one enters lies a patio filled with oleanders and palms; jasmine and bougainvillea clamber over the railings; a pool in the center reflects the star-lit sky above. To the left of the foyer is a greenroom lounge; there an eighteenth-century crystal chandelier sheds a soft shimmer of light that is caught up in a gilt French mirror. To the right is the auditorium, with honey-color plaster walls; its dark polished wood trim glows in the reflection of lights from the stage.

To this spot I came to watch the dress rehearsal of *Kiss the Boys Goodbye*. In the gracious, old-world charm of this playhouse, Miss Boothe's brassy comedy struck a sharply discordant note. Nevertheless, since the theatre had elected to present it, they were doing a good job. Bernard Szold [1] had directed it to be played at a lively pace. The chief performers—the entire cast was amateur—

---

[1] Mr. Szold was succeeded in 1940-41 by Gerhardt Lindemulder, who had been Director of New Orleans' progressive New Group Theatre.

played with assurance and skill, although without much spontaneity. Most of them had been active members of Le Petit Théâtre for years and they knew what they were about. There seemed little doubt that the performance would be a very fair imitation of Broadway and that their public would be entertained and amused.

The audience at Le Petit Théâtre is composed exclusively of its members. There is no public box office sale; if one wishes to attend any of the eight plays, one must enroll at the beginning of the season and pay a ten dollar fee. The membership in 1939-40 totaled 2,314. It operated on an annual budget of about $25,000.

It can now perhaps be seen why I objected to the Indianapolis Civic Theater's claim to being a community playhouse. I was using it as but an example of a whole species of amateur theatres. Le Petit Théâtre belongs in the same class. Although its membership is almost twice as large as the Indianapolis theatre's, New Orleans is a much bigger city. Its membership does not by much exceed one-half of one per cent of the white population. In both cities, the high membership fee restricts play-going to the wealthier upper middle class. The New Orleans system of "closed membership" further limits attendance.

Both Le Petit Théâtre and the Indianapolis Civic Theater, however, open their doors to non-members who may wish to perform. Four hundred and twenty people came to the public tryouts at Le Petit Théâtre in 1938-39. Seventy-three members were cast, seventy-six who were not members performed. Any director like Mr. Szold who is concerned for the excellence of his product obviously cannot allow his casting to be limited to those who can pay ten dollars a year, as the fact that more than fifty per cent of his actors were not members bears witness.

The repertory of Le Petit Théâtre for the 1939-40 season was typical, I believe, of the catholicity of taste which this theatre exhibits: *Patience, The Dark Tower, Cyrano de Bergerac, Excursion, Shadow and Substance, Au Destin,* a new play by a New Orleans author, *R. U. R.* were presented in addition to *Kiss the Boys Goodbye.* Like many little theatres this one seeks to offer a "balanced fare"; having learned from Barnum that it can't hope to please all the people all of the time, it does its best to please some of the people with each bill.

Le Petit Théâtre du Vieux Carré is one of the outstanding pioneer amateur theatres. It was founded in 1919; its building was erected in 1922. By 1928 it had reached a membership of 3,500 which it maintained for two seasons. Then followed years when the loss of old members exceeded the gain of new ones. By 1935-36 Le Petit Théâtre had dropped from 3,500 to 1,613. In the seasons since 1935-36 there has been an upswing, although the theatre has not yet regained the support it had as recently as 1932.

Undoubtedly the depression has been largely responsible for this situation. It seems odd, however, that the organization did not readjust its economy to prevent some of this loss of support, that it did not take this opportunity to rebuild on a broader, more democratic base. Such was not the case, however. In 1940 Le Petit Théâtre appeared to lack that exuberance and zest which an amateur theatre must possess above all things. Its middle-aged and elderly Board of Governors seemed confused and weary; like gray-haired housekeepers they seemed to be forever engaged in dusting and tidying a house that was always already in order—for the children had grown up and left; their noise was only an echo and the house was growing quiet and old.[2]

I came to New Orleans from Florida where I had visited the Little Theatre of Jacksonville. This amateur group, in existence for some years, received a new lease on life in 1936 by the gift of a forty thousand dollar playhouse from Carl Swisher, wealthy local cigar manufacturer. Mr. Swisher built the playhouse for reasons best known to himself; the theatre could do no less than elect him its president, which office he was occupying in 1939-40. In consequence he controlled its policies both administrative and artistic.

The theatre is simple and attractive. Its auditorium seats 330; its stage is equipped with several shuttling wagons of great use in such elaborate productions as *The Women* which I saw. The settings for *The Women* were attractive, and the performance of a fourteen-year-old girl who played the daughter was excellent. The rest, however, played for the most part with a deliberateness of pace and lack of sophistication which would have caused Miss Boothe to shudder. Why, I inquired, did they undertake this play? Because Mr. Swisher had seen it in New York, I was told, where he enjoyed it very much and so thought his little theatre should do it too. He attended the same performance that I saw and seemed to be having as good a time as anyone could wish.

Under the direction of Edward Crowley the season of 1939-40 at the Little Theatre of Jacksonville began with a

---

[2] It is to be hoped that the regime of Mr. Lindemulder may infuse new life into Le Petit Théâtre.

six-week summer school of the theatre. For a three-dollar tuition 110 people were enrolled in the classes in acting, production, makeup, pantomime, dancing, diction, history of modern drama held nightly and on two afternoons a week. At the end of the summer *Yes, My Darling Daughter* was presented by the school as a pre-season opening bill. Then followed *Susan and God, The Silver Cord,* Sierra's *Holy Night* given free to the public at Christmas time, *The Women, Hedda Gabler* and *Candida*. In addition, a series of "workshop" productions were offered: *Brother Rat, Cock Robin, Hay Fever, There's Always Juliet,* to enable more members to participate and to permit local amateurs interested in direction to try their hands. There were also five Studio Nights at which informal programs and skits were presented. Few little theatres can equal Jacksonville's quantity of activity.

This theatre has a membership of over fourteen hundred. Like Le Petit Théâtre du Vieux Carré, attendance is limited to members who here purchase a season subscription for six dollars. No tickets are available for single performances. This "closed membership" policy is practiced a good deal among the community theatres of the Southeast in particular. In every case it was justified by the argument that when a product is hard to get, it becomes more desirable; most of the theatres using this plan pointed to enlarged memberships which they claimed were its result.

I find it hard to reconcile the "closed membership" scheme with any philosophy of community service. Insofar as these groups are dramatic clubs existing for the pleasurable profit of their members, such a plan is obviously their prerogative; in so doing, however, they make little

contribution to broadening the cultural base of our democracy. It must be borne in mind, however, that the
South retains an even stronger class-consciousness than is
met elsewhere. Not easily would New Orleans, Jacksonville or Charleston, which we shall hereafter visit, welcome any and every member of the community (even
though white) into their fraternity. One can condemn the
"closed membership" on principle, therefore, but at the
same time recognize those reasons strong in the background
and temper of this region which bring about its practice.

Upstairs over a store in downtown Salt Lake City is a
beguiling little theatre called "The Playbox." For three
years it has been in existence and if it retains the freshness and inventiveness it has displayed in its early days,
and does not become "arty," it should flourish for some
years to come. I describe it because it is typical of a number of the smaller amateur groups which form a part of
the little theatre movement, and because it is an example
to the students of our universities who are asking, "What
shall we do next?"

Robert Hyde Wilson graduated from the University of
Utah not very many years ago. He wanted to direct in
the theatre. Everyone discouraged him from going to New
York, so he decided to stay at home and start a theatre of
his own. He discovered that a number of the University's
graduates living in Salt Lake City longed to act, but like
him they had been discouraged from throwing themselves
on Broadway. From their various jobs, therefore, Mr.
Wilson assembled them, and in the evenings and over
weekends they rehearsed. But directing and rehearsing

plays is not of itself theatre; there must be an audience and a place where the audience may foregather. To build a playhouse is costly and the youthful Mr. Wilson had access to little cash. But following the pattern of Gilmor Brown's Playbox in Pasadena and of Glenn Hughes' Penthouse Theatre in Seattle, he rented the vacant second floor over the store and turned it into a theatre.

At the top of the stairs, I found myself in a small outer lobby which opened into a cheerful room where there were flowers on a table, photographs of productions and actors on the walls, a cozy glow from several lamps. This was a combination foyer and greenroom. Thence I passed into a long, narrow room where the play was to be given. Its walls were a deep dark blue. At one end about eighty chairs were arranged in ten rows set on stepped platforms that mounted rather steeply toward the back wall. At the other end of the room was the acting area. I cannot call it a stage, for there was no elevated platform, no curtain and no proscenium. That end was in semi-darkness, but I could see (it being after all only a few feet away) that it looked like the lounge of a ship. Its walls also dark blue merged almost imperceptibly into the wall beside my seat; but those portholes and that high-silled door were surely temporary and part of a setting.

When the audience had assembled—and I was interested to note that every seat was taken—the doors closed, the lights dimmed and music was heard. This mounted in volume. I sat in complete darkness for a moment. Then the light at the other end of the room came up, the music faded. Sunlight out through the cabin door shone on the deck beyond; from it came a young couple hand in hand and *Outward Bound* began. It was a moving performance.

In spite of traces of that pretentiousness which is sometimes a sign of inexperience, the values of the play were
projected with artistry combined with good showmanship.

According to Mr. Wilson, *Outward Bound* is a more
serious play than they usually present. Drawing-room
comedies like *Hay Fever* and *End of Summer* he feels
lend themselves more successfully to the intimacy of the
Playbox, where audience and actors are within arms' reach
of each other. The Playbox has an audience large enough
to compel it to present six or seven performances of each
of its four plays. Admission to the series costs $3.50. The
enterprise cannot have required an initial capital of much
more than two hundred dollars. Already it can count on an
income of two thousand dollars a year.

I suppose the Cleveland Play House or Le Petit
Théâtre du Vieux Carré and many another theatre must
have presented this same picture twenty years or so ago.
Today in dozens of other lofts groups are working like
this Playbox crowd. They may become the outstanding
non-professional theatres of tomorrow; granted unexpected success, they may even here or there turn into resident professional theatres; or they may continue along for
four or five years and then disband. That is happening all
the time, and those that fold are replaced by other groups
of eager young people with a similar desire to provide
themselves with a theatre and their friends with entertainment.

Shreveport, Louisiana, three or four hundred miles
northwest of New Orleans out near the Texas border, is
a little city of about one hundred thousand; as in most
Southern towns of that size, nearly forty thousand of these

are Negroes. It is a bustling place, more keyed to the life of Texas than to the sleepier deep South. Here is a little theatre that exudes a spirit of health, wealth and happiness. The director, John Wray Young and his wife, Mary Margaret Young who acts as an unsalaried technical director, beam with enthusiasm. Their theatre is housed in a thirty thousand dollar playhouse which is entirely paid for; its membership numbers seventeen hundred which is close to three per cent of the white population; it is able to provide seven plays for five dollars; Mrs. Young has 150 enthusiasts drawn from this membership to help her build and paint scenery and borrow props. Mr. Young has 160 enthusiastic members to act in his plays. Between him and his Board of Directors there is never a harsh word. The budget of ten thousand dollars is never exceeded. *Stage* magazine awarded it a palm. All concerned are as happy as larks.

Mr. Young and his Board believe that the primary purpose of the theatre is to entertain. Consequently their program is built on recent New York successes, mostly comedies. Occasionally something like *Jane Eyre*, which I saw in dress rehearsal, creeps in; but most of the time there is lightness and laughter. The 1938-39 season, for example, consisted of *Tovarich*, *The Star Wagon*, *Petticoat Fever*, *The Amazing Dr. Clitterhouse*, *The Distaff Side*, *Outward Bound* and *Our Town*. In the season of 1939-40 this little theatre presented *Kiss the Boys Goodbye*, *Journey's End*, *Susan and God*, *The Gentle People*, *Jane Eyre*, *What a Life* and *The Petrified Forest*. Mr. Young's argument in favor of these plays—apart from the fact that he likes them—is that they attracted theatre-goers in New

York, and "Why should people here not like what people there enjoy?"

The Little Theatre of Shreveport has a women's organization, "The Guild," which meets once a month on Friday afternoons and is open to all female members. "These informal gatherings," I read in a program, "have proven very popular in the past. At these meetings interesting speakers discuss topics of interest to all theatregoers. These discussions are followed by a social hour." I was not told how the men of the organization keep up with things, unless their wives pass on what they hear at the Guild. In this Little Theatre, as in many others, one hears a great deal about the social hour. Crew work regularly ends with hot chocolate. At the intermission of the monthly play-readings when tryouts are held and casts selected, all may repair to a refreshment table. At performances half a dozen local belles dispense coffee in the lobby during intermissions. Showmanship in Shreveport extends to more aspects than the presentation of plays; but after all, showmanship is essential in the theatre and it is a clever man who knows how to use it well.

Walter Sinclair, director of Denver's University Civic Theatre, is a gracious Canadian, of about the age and aspect of Walter Hampden. "It might amuse you to know," said he, "that two of my best actors are a hairdresser and a clerk at Sears, Roebuck." Mr. Sinclair recognizes that talent may lie in anyone and he is constantly on the lookout for it.

On the other side of the footlights, however, one suspects a less democratic atmosphere. The University Civic Theatre is neither university nor civic. Its only right to the former word is that the building in which it lives is on the campus of the University of Denver and is shared by its Speech Department; there is no liaison between student work and Mr. Sinclair's. It has no more right to the latter word than the Indianapolis Civic Theater had (in fact less so, for the Indianapolis organization makes a gesture toward civic welfare by presenting two dress rehearsals free to an audience obtained through settlement houses in co-operation with the city Park Board. One wonders in passing, however, how much an unemployed Polish laborer would enjoy *Susan and God!*)[3] The Denver Theatre has a closed regular membership costing six dollars a year which admits to six plays, and a patron membership costing twenty-five dollars a year for twelve admissions. Subscribers only may purchase Guest Tickets (single admissions) for $1.50. This season the members were treated to *Washington Jitters, What a Life, Through the Night, Brief Candle, Gas Light, Two on an Island.* In 1939-40 they saw *Family Portrait, Big-Hearted Herbert, Dear Octopus, The Good Hope, Art and Mrs. Bottle,* and *June Mad.*

Mr. Sinclair points out that much of his theatre's reputation for being a society group results from its treatment by Denver newspapers. Its publicity is always placed on the social page, and when the theatre requests attention in the amusement section, the newspapers reply that the amount of advertising the Civic Theatre carries does not warrant

[3] The Workshop of the Indianapolis Civic Theater has also co-operated with the City Recreation Department in an effort to establish seven community dramatic groups throughout the city. It also operates a Children's Theatre which gives sporadic performances. Perhaps the Indianapolis organization is swinging toward assumption of greater civic responsibility.

it. Such an attitude may be traced to the pressure of motion picture distributors, who point out that their two or three half-column advertisements daily, as opposed to the one-inch every couple of weeks that the Civic Theatre buys, should not allow the latter to receive news space which they would then be relinquishing. This situation is sufficiently widespread to require attention. It highlights both the relationship of the motion pictures to non-professional theatre, and the necessity for the co-operation of a public-spirited press in the success of any civic theatre. If newspaper publishers place a non-commercial theatre in the same category as the commercial films, the former can never afford to compete for space. On the other hand, of course, the little theatre can sometimes hardly be called "amusement." When, as in Denver, its public is restricted, one can also scarcely blame the newspapers for considering it a social activity and nothing more.

Tucson, Arizona seems a long way from anywhere. The vast desert and the strange varicolored mountains of the Southwest stretch away for miles in every direction. When you descend from the train, however, you find a little city humming cozily. Its climate has made it one of the country's most sought health centers; in consequence, there is a rather incongruous cosmopolitan air to its dusty streets and low unimpressive buildings.

To this town came young Edward Reveaux some years ago. At first he was mostly occupied with graduate work at the University of Arizona in Tucson. In 1937 he took over the Tucson Little Theatre. Its prospects were not bright. There was seventy dollars in the treasury; merchants and newspapers were antagonistic; townspeople apathetic. Reveaux's dynamic energy persuaded the Little Theatre, which had been getting along with haphazard direction and uncertain purpose, that it needed a trained professional leader. He offered himself for the job and agreed that he would accept as his salary fifty per cent of whatever season subscriptions the theatre could corral. Four seasons later the organization was operating on an annual budget of nine thousand dollars, there were three additional paid staff members, seventeen hundred people were attending each of the five plays offered that year. Tucson appeared to have ample proof that trained professional leadership could put across a theatre.

Mr. Reveaux began by taking the seventy dollars balance and dividing it among the theatre's creditor merchants in token payments—thereby establishing new credit. He enlisted the press in the idea of a community stage, dedicated the theatre to a program of entertaining drama, put on a high-pressure sales campaign, sold scrip books containing twenty-five cent coupons allowing a ten per cent reduction therefor. Books were available in three denominations: ten dollars, five dollars, and two dollars and fifty cents, each at ten per cent off. In addition, individual seats for any performance might be bought at the box office for from fifty cents to one dollar.

The Tucson Little Theatre also built up a working nucleus of people who wished to participate actively and constantly in the organization; it was called The Workshop. Any ticket-holding member who had devoted ninety hours to work in any phase of the theatre's activity was eligible. In 1940-41 there were about seventy-five members of this nucleus group. They constituted the voters of the organization, received a 16⅔ per cent reduction in purchase of scrip, had the exclusive right to appear in the three Studio productions a year, received special rates in the School of the Theatre, which offered ten courses to laymen interested in various aspects of the stage and drama.

During 1939-40 the program of major productions presented in the attractive and well-equipped playhouse of the Temple of Art and Music consisted of *The Star Wagon, The Gentle People, Kiss the Boys Goodbye, Texas Buckaroo, Tonight at 8:30.* In 1940-41 there were *Margin for Error, Here Today, St. Joan, Ladies in Retirement* and *George Washington Slept Here.*

Like many of the younger generation of community theatre directors, Reveaux is a combination of commercial manager and social service worker. He believes in a cooperative attitude between his theatre and the drama department at the University; he wishes it might be possible for a well-established theatre like Tucson's to assist struggling and amorphous groups in surrounding towns to get on their feet. He would like to establish for the Tucson Little Theatre a small group of full-time paid people, all of whom would participate in all phases of the theatre: publicity, crew work, secretarial duties, etc., and who would serve at the same time as a backlog in casting since all would be actors as well. These people, he believes, should be cast, however, only when no amateur talent as good as they was available to fill any role. He also thinks it might be a good idea once in a while to invite a star to appear in Tucson supported by a Little Theatre cast. The Southwest is hospitable to new ideas and Edward Reveaux has plenty of them to offer.

✦

Lester Lang, director of the Little Theatre of Dallas, agrees with Mr. Reveaux's visiting star idea and has put it into practice by inviting from Hollywood Margaret Tallichet to appear in *Accent on Youth* and Robert Paige to play in *Dollar Down*. He is, however, strongly opposed to the idea of a permanent nucleus. "You end with a kind of stock company which nobody wants," he claims. "Your public gets tired of seeing the same faces; the director has no opportunity to exercise that flexibility in casting that he can when there is the whole community from which to choose. A community theatre must always depend in the main on amateurs."

Dallas is one of the most beautiful and flourishing of America's medium-sized cities. An opening night at the Little Theatre there looks like an opening night in New York: the lobbies are crowded with handsomely groomed women in sables and silver fox, with men in white tie and tails; news photographers' camera bulbs flash; sophisticated chatter swells as people move through the Italianate foyer. Although at other nights later in the week there is a different audience, which comes less to see each other than the play; and although the Dallas Little Theatre would like to attract all types of people to its playhouse; the cameras click only at openings, so word goes out that only members may attend and only the elite may be members; the society tag therefore remains and at the later performances in the week the house is not so well filled. Only about two thousand people see any one production, a small representation from a city of 350,000.

The Little Theatre of Dallas has been a "big name" in the non-professional theatre world. In the pre-depression regime of Oliver Hinsdell, director from 1923 to 1931, this theatre built a $125,000 playhouse, grew to a membership of thirty-five hundred, three times won and permanently possessed the David Belasco trophy for amateur theatrical excellence and thereby gained a national reputation. After 1931 it began to decline, until in 1939 when Mr. Lang arrived, its membership had dropped to five hundred, its playhouse was mildew-stained and leaking. Internal disintegration is more to blame than the depression in this instance, for Dallas has never known the depression.

Applying in Dallas the formula that Edward Reveaux had applied in Tucson, that John Wray Young, Edward Crowley and Walter Sinclair had adopted in their theatres, namely, to provide entertainment based on a series of Broadway successes, Lester Lang offered in his first two seasons *Room Service, Our Town, Accent on Youth, Margin for Error,* and (in the footsteps of the Mercury Theatre in New York) a modern-dress scenery-less *Julius Caesar.*

Mr. Lang, however, has a strong belief that one of the functions of the theatre off Broadway should be to provide a hearing for new playwrights. (Looking back over this chapter on community theatres, I find this is the first time I have been able to report a director enunciating this theory; it is very nearly the last time.) Consequently, in his second season he and the Board of Directors decided to present world premières of three new plays: *Dollar Down,* a comedy by Margaret Sims; *Where the Dear Antelope Play,* a satire upon certain aspects of Texas society life by the Dallas writer and critic, John William Rogers; *We Are Besieged,* a moving historical drama of the battle of the Alamo by another Dallas newspaper man, Sam Acheson, which had crowds cheering at every performance. Mr. Lang was rewarded for his interest in new material by the fact that the Rogers play broke a five-year attendance record and *We Are Besieged* outstripped even that.

Kalamazoo, Michigan, lies about half-way between Detroit and Chicago. It is a little city of some sixty thousand inhabitants, with a pleasant air of well-being. Facing a downtown tree-lined square stands the Kalamazoo Civic Auditorium, valued at close to half a million dollars. It was erected by Dr. William Upjohn as a home for community enterprises and dedicated "to the happy use of leisure." The Civic Players dwell there, although they do not own the building. Through Dr. Upjohn's munificence they possess as fine a plant as any little theatre group in the country.

Kalamazoo has remarkable civic-mindedness and is enthusiastic in its support of the arts. Four or five road shows play there each year; in concert series Flagstad, Artur Rubenstein, Menuhin and others follow each other in rapid succession; in lyceum courses famous speakers turn up in Kalamazoo every few weeks; there are appearances of the local symphony orchestra; and there are the eight plays presented yearly by the Civic Players. Obviously all this is possible only because of wide community support.

When in March, 1938, the Players celebrated their one hundredth production, Norman Carver, business manager since its inception in 1929, wrote:

The use of the word "civic" as a part of the name of an organization is not meant to indicate any form of sponsorship or control by municipal government, but rather to signify the broad, all-inclusive community nature of the Kalamazoo Civic Players. Our activities are open to all without prejudice of race, creed, or color and the amazing extent to which the people of Kalamazoo have indulged their interest in the Players is a matter of record. To date over six hundred and fifty different actors have appeared.

Adding all those who have worked back-stage and on committees, Mr. Carver arrived at the "rather startling total of 936 individuals who have participated directly in the Civic Players' one hundred plays." By the time I reached Kalamazoo, nearly three years later, the number of participants had passed the one thousand mark.

At the time of that summing-up, the Civic Players estimated that admissions to these one hundred productions had exceeded 125,000. In 1940-41 the theatre had 1,220 subscribers: almost as many in this town of sixty thousand, as the Indianapolis Civic Theater could boast of in a city six times as large. A subscribing member pays four or six dollars for eight admissions.[4] Single tickets to any play may be bought at the box office at a cost of from twenty-five cents to one dollar. No doubt the size of the Civic Players' audience is partially due to this price scale that approximates the movie level.

The schedule of plays presented in 1940-41 consisted of *The Royal Family*, *Golden Boy*, *Knickerbocker Holiday*, *I Killed the Count*, *Prologue to Glory*, *See My Lawyer*,

---

[4] Kalamazoo has a useful scheme: a double subscription arrangement of sixteen admissions for seven or eleven dollars so that couples may save one dollar when they purchase a pair of season tickets.

Dear Brutus and *The Male Animal* ("if available—or one of the very latest releases" from current Broadway).

I saw *Knickerbocker Holiday* in Kalamazoo. Its scenery was its high point. It was gay and bright with a street unexpectedly paved in blue and white Dutch tiles, with cheerful little houses leaning out to gossip with each other. Parenthetically, Kalamazoo's Civic Players is one of the few community theatres where stage designing may be done by anyone in town. In most places, either the director himself or some person on the paid staff is responsible for the conception of the décor.

Throughout the community theatres—and the educational theatres too for that matter—I saw consistently acceptable scenic effects. In most instances they have been variations on established themes by Jones, Mielziner, Oenslager, or else derivative of their styles. Occasionally, however, there have been original spirits with something fresh to say, and even the variations of Jones have been handled with taste and refinement. It would be heartening indeed if the acting and direction were as good as the scenery, but this unfortunately is not always true.

"Karamu" in the Swahili language of Africa means "place of enjoyment"; in Cleveland, Ohio, it means the home of the Gilpin Players. Karamu House stands on the corner of East 38 Street and Central Avenue. That is the heart of Cleveland's Negro quarter. It used to be an abandoned pool room; that was before 1926. Now, in a broader sense than ever, it is a "place of enjoyment."

Shabby and dilapidated though it may be without, within the walls are bright with drawings and murals; the Negro loves color and he has splashed it liberally about the rooms where arts and crafts are studied; where young-sters fashion pottery and beads; work in metals; paint, etch, cut wood blocks and model in clay; where a group interested in dance experiments with original forms; where musicians gather; where club groups of various ages meet—everywhere there is color except in the theatre. To-day that part of the building is smoke-blackened and flame-scarred. In 1939 a fire swept through the flimsy frame structure and demolished the stage and part of the auditorium. Cleveland safety authorities would not allow the place to reopen. But Karamu House looks confidently toward a future in a new building that may have much more adequate facilities than before.

It deserves such a future for its past has been memora-ble. More than twenty years ago this Negro theatre was organized in Cleveland. It was in the midst of its third season, recalls Rowena Jelliffe, co-director of Karamu ac-tivities with her husband, Russell Jelliffe, that

Charles Gilpin, playing the title role of Eugene O'Neill's *Emperor Jones*, came to Cleveland. He came to see a rehearsal of one of our plays, left us a gift of fifty dollars (the only monetary gift the group has ever received), and gave us a deal of good practical advice. He said one thing which we took much to heart. "Learn to see the drama in your own lives," he said, "and some day the world will come to see you." That marked a milestone in our history. The following day we voted to take his name, which we now proudly bear. And we began to produce plays of Negro life, and to regard that field as a means of telling and interpreting to the community audience the Negro story in America. We see it also as a means of making our particular racial contribution to the growing American theatre.

The Gilpin Players are the outstanding Negro community theatre in America. Because of the unfortunate fire which left them homeless and dependent upon the hospitality of their neighbors, the Cleveland Play House and Western Reserve University, their production schedule in the last couple of seasons has had to be reduced to one or two plays. Consequently I was unable to see any of their performances myself; the record of their achievement, upon which I am regularly loath to rely in making a critical estimate, must in this instance suffice. That record, however, is impressive.

In the years since Charles Gilpin paid them his inspirational visit, the Players who took his name have presented about 140 different plays. About half of these are plays of Negro life. The other half are what Mrs. Jelliffe calls "white plays which have been adapted for our use, or in which the content honestly fitted into the experience and aptitude of the Negro actor." More than four hundred colored people have participated in these plays as actors or stage-crafters. At the moment there are some eighty-five active members.

Because of the varied activities of Karamu House (which is really a kind of Negro settlement house), the Gilpin Players are able to effect collaborations in several directions. Music and dance groups make their contribution to the productions; graphic arts classes help in stage design; the children's and adolescents' groups foster children's plays; so that actually many more colored people are involved in theatre than the membership of the Gilpin Players would indicate. This theatre is of course non-professional. Except for the Jelliffes, its personnel is all Negro. As a result of such newspaper encomiums as that by Wil-

liam McDermott, discerning drama critic of the Cleveland
Plain Dealer—"I believe the Karamu Theatre of the Gilpin
Players to be one of the most important institutions in
the United States in respect to its furtherance of education and allied arts in the community that it serves"—
the Gilpin Players have been able to draw excellent support and make some money. Both Negroes and white people are regularly in the audience. Out of their earnings
they have been able to make a gift of fifteen hundred dollars' worth of primitive African art and ethnological material to the Cleveland Museum of Art and the Cleveland
Museum of Natural History—the first instance that I
know of in this country where Negroes have presented to
civic institutions examples of their traditional art. With
other of their earnings they have set up a scholarship fund
of three thousand dollars to permit gifted young Negroes
to go to the Cleveland School of Art for training beyond
that which they can get at Karamu House.

The principal problem of the Gilpin Players—aside
from the paramount need to replace their burned playhouse—is the lack of good scripts. They are dependent today, they feel, "almost entirely upon the output and promise of four playwrights: Zora Neale Hurston, Shirley
Graham, Owen Dodson and Langston Hughes." The
Negro theatre everywhere is in the same condition; but
the awakening of their racial consciousness of the theatre is
so recent that one must not be impatient: the playwrights
will be forthcoming. Nevertheless all possible aid must be
given to encourage and develop potential Negro dramatists.

It is axiomatic to point out that the race problem in
America is inextricably bound up with the social system.

The searing indictment which Richard Wright's *Native Son* levels against us all is deserved. His communist solution has long been attractive to certain members of this minority group. The Karamu Theatre, however, has taken the opposite way: it has sought for social betterment for the Negro and an amelioration of racial strife within the framework of the existing capitalist system. However, a number of Negro theatres have sprung up which are concerned to present the left side of the picture. These, while not necessarily communist, nevertheless are interestd in fusing their racial problems with those other social and economic problems that are common to their white brothers of the proletariat. Upon such a platform stand the Chicago Negro People's Theatre, Philadelphia's New Negro Theatre, the Nashville Tennessee Negro Suitcase Theatre and newly-sprung groups in Los Angeles, Memphis, New Orleans. Most of these are affiliates of the New Theatre League and none of them are very strong.

By and large, the Negro community theatre movement is in so embryonic a state that little can be written of it. The signal success of the Gilpin Players indicates the possibilities, but lack elsewhere of such leadership as the Jelliffes have provided, plus pitiful lack of funds, accounts for Karamu's accomplishment being such a solitary example.

3

Two diverging lines of development—diverging philosophies of theatre, I might almost say—are already beginning to appear from the stories of these ten community

and little theatres. In the five that remain to be considered, these lines will grow sharper and the antagonism of
the two points of view will come into clearer focus. It
is that dualism which underlies the whole American theatre situation today.

There are certain little theatres which believe that their
principal purpose is to provide their communities with the
best theatrical fare possible. They maintain that since the
commercial theatre has been inadequate to the task, it must
be supplemented or succeeded (in cities and towns where
it no longer comes at all) by a local theatre that will assume the responsibility for providing drama to the people.
Only thus may the theatre as an artistic institution survive
in all places. Beginning as inexperienced amateurs, these
groups have aimed at constant improvement of their product. To accomplish this, they have employed a professional, trained director. As they have grown, they have
added more paid leaders, in order that other aspects of
their product might be improved. Finally they have
reached the point where, in order to provide an even balance between all the components of theatre, they have felt
it wise to supplement professional director, designer and
staff with professional actors. Either these actors have been
residents of the community who began as amateurs and
who have ended by devoting themselves full-time and for
a remuneration to their theatre; or the theatre has employed visiting professional stars or a professional company remaining in residence but secured from outside the
community. When this point has been reached, such groups
are in the category of the Cleveland Play House: "A resident producing theatre, professionally organized and oper-

ated not for profit"—in a sense a theatre of the people and for the people, but not by the people.

Certain other little theatres believe that their primary purpose is to provide always and only an outlet for self-expression to the members of the community. Basing their point of view on the recreational, therapeutic and adult educational value of participation in dramatics, they maintain that the chief virtue of the community theatre as opposed to the professional theatre lies in its availability to the individual desiring a spiritual or emotional outlet in creative activity related to the stage. These groups, also beginning as inexperienced amateurs, may proceed in the direction of professionalism only as far as to the employment of a trained leader. In their very amateurism is their strength, they believe. When a choice must be made, the quality of the product must be subordinated to the more sociological functions of the theatre. When this point has been reached, they are in the category of the Palo Alto Community Players, which is as completely of, for *and* by the people as any theatre in the country. Between these two extremes lie most of the non-professional community theatres of the United States.

With the Pittsburgh Playhouse we take a step toward professionalism. This theatre has no resident professional acting company, it is true; but it has occasionally imported a guest professional player and it does provide its actors with carfare; it also has a paid production and administrative staff of ten persons with a total salary roll of nearly eighteen thousand dollars a year. There was a period from 1935 to 1937 when the Playhouse, under the direction of Herbert Gellendré, was entirely professional, composed of a company of Equity actors and presenting experimental plays. This policy did not fare well. Under the regime of Frederick Burleigh who succeeded Gellendré, there was an increase in three years from twelve hundred to 4,170 members. Whether a change in type of play, method of production, kind of actor, or the installation of a club-house bar available at all times only to members was responsible for this 350 per cent expansion I cannot say; but the Playhouse is so content with its recent success that it would be loath to move soon again into the professional resident theatre category, unless such a company could grow out of its own membership.

The support of four thousand citizens is commendable for a city of Pittsburgh's size. In addition to these members, who buy seven coupon admissions for six dollars, the Playhouse can count on one or two thousand more people who will buy seats at the box office for a popular play. As a result of this support, the Playhouse can budget its expenditures to a total of thirty-five thousand dollars and still hope for a profit.

Pittsburgh theatre-goers' taste is apparently divided. Harold Cohen reports that Pittsburghers show a marked interest in the serious plays that come to the commercial house, the Nixon. He claimed that *Children's Hour, Of Mice and Men, Mamba's Daughters* had their best weeks on the road at the Nixon. On the other hand, Mr. Burleigh points out that the Playhouse is best supported in its lighter work. The greatest success of the 1938-39 season was *Tonight at 8:30;* its great failure a new play *And Niobe Wept.* In 1939-40 it presented *I Want a Policeman, The Ghost of Yankee Doodle, Private Lives, Thank Your Stars* (a new musical revue by Charles

Gaynor), *Our Town, Biography, The Road to Rome*. Of these the poorest business was done by *Our Town* and *The Ghost of Yankee Doodle*, both serious; the most popular were the musical, which ran for four weeks, and *Biography* which played to fifty-six hundred people. It is natural that Mr. Burleigh puts his stock in Broadway comedies with a high entertainment value. Experimental drama is not to be looked for here.

The Pittsburgh Playhouse appears to have no constructive policy of community service beyond providing entertainment at a reasonable price. It has had no program of plays for children, no educational or recreational group activity. Except for a radio program series, *Midnight Mysteries*, which it sponsored, it has devoted itself exclusively to its program of play production.

Charleston, South Carolina, gracious and aristocratic little city of camellias, cypresses and trailing moss, of walled gardens, Georgian brick and white side galleries; Charleston, patrician lady of the South, possesses a playhouse that is an adornment even to her. Historic pedigree is important there, but the Dock Street Theatre can obligingly trace its lineage back to 1736 when upon its present site, according to DuBose Heyward, was opened the first building designed for theatrical use in America. In 1937 at a cost of $350,000 the WPA completed reconstruction of this wood-paneled Georgian playhouse, added a modern stage and turned it over to the city.

Charleston, with a white population of only thirty-five thousand, is no longer a wealthy town; the maintenance of such a theatre was consequently a problem. There already existed an amateur dramatic group: the Footlight

Players, supported by seven hundred Charlestonians. An amalgamation with the Carolina Art Association which had four hundred members was effected and the latter took over Dock Street's operation. In 1938 the Rockefeller Foundation granted the theatre five thousand dollars and so it was possible to secure as director Charles H. Meredith.

Under Mr. Meredith's leadership the Dock Street Theatre rose in two years to a membership of twenty-six hundred, a remarkable number for a city of that size. There is a "closed membership" policy, except for an extra production during the brief tourist season, which is open to the general public. Annual membership costs five dollars; young people under twenty-one and students may become Junior members for three dollars.[5] One is entitled then to the privileges of both the Art Association and the Footlight Players: a season ticket to the six plays, admission to the Gibbes Art Gallery, half-price reduction to the motion picture series presented at the theatre, and various social privileges.

Mr. Meredith's choice of plays is determined by his own taste rather than by what he thinks the public may want. In 1938-39 the season consisted of *St. Joan*, *The Second Man*, *High Tor*, *The Beaux Stratagem*, three one-act plays, *First Lady*. In 1939-40 *Our Town*, *Johnny Johnson*, *Whiteoaks*, *My Heart's in the Highlands*, *The Contrast* and another bill of one-act plays were presented.

Mr. Meredith is also uncompromising in his contention that his theatre's first obligation is to that larger proportion of its membership whose only relation to it is as audience.

---

[5] There are also life memberships, annual patrons, sustaining and contributing memberships.

With this in mind he insists upon the use of the best people available, and if he finds no Charlestonian whom he considers capable of playing a specific role, he feels justified in importing an outsider. For the post-season production in the spring he has, in fact, invited a number of professional actors; Aline MacMahon, Rose Hobart, Irene Purcell, Kent Smith, Hiram Sherman are among those who have been guest performers on the Dock Street stage.

In adhering to such a policy, however, Mr. Meredith has brought down the wrath of many of the members of the Footlight Players. They contend that their organization came into existence to provide an opportunity for Charlestonians who wanted to act, and they object to the increasing professionalism that forces them off the stage and onto the sidelines. Even if the performances should not be so finished, they feel that they should represent native endeavor. Mr. Meredith, adopting an appeasement program in 1939-40, revived some workshop activity which he had abolished during his first season; classes in diction, body mechanics and make-up were resumed; play reading groups were reassembled—all this in order to allow more people to participate in activity around the playhouse.

It is easy to see that in the Dock Street Theatre we have the clash of the conflicting objectives I have previously described. Because of the intolerance of both camps there has arisen one of those internecine feuds that inevitably weaken the power of any theatre organization. This dispute became so fierce by the end of the 1940-41 season that the Art Association supporting Mr. Meredith and the Footlight Players completely severed their alliance. It seems unfortunate that with Mr. Meredith's intolerance of amateurs, he should have been attempting to work as their leader and servant. It is equally unfortunate that a compromise could not have been worked out to permit adequate opportunity for those wishing to participate without jeopardizing the excellence of the product offered to the large paying audience membership. A satisfactorily functioning community theatre should be able to do both.

Another community theatre which has faced this problem of whether to aim toward professionalism or to retain amateurism and which has sought a compromise is the Pasadena Playhouse Association. It must be accorded a place at the side of the Cleveland Play House as one of the most distinguished theatres in the United States.

I visited Pasadena in November, 1940.

In front of the Playhouse stood a row of sentinel palms. From the tower of the stage house its banner flew in the morning breeze. The autumn sun blazed in the outer patio as I crossed through it, past the splashing fountain, the plants and flowers set out in tubs, and entered under a Spanish arcade into the building itself. At first I thought I had made a mistake: this was a post office, for some two hundred mail boxes faced me. But no, I was told; this was the Playhouse and the boxes belonged to the 150 students of its school and to its staff. I walked along the corridor past vast general offices where typewriters, comptometers and stenographers were humming away; past a little office that said "Dean of Women" on the door; past another door through which I caught a glimpse of printing presses rolling. We emerged from the passage into a larger hall. "Now we are in the annex," my companion explained as we waited for the elevator to take us to the third floor.

There we emerged, passed a row of offices belonging to the eight or ten associate directors and the "production co-ordinator," and entered the lacquer-red-and-beige study of the Supervising Director, Gilmor Brown. The walls were lined with books and Chinese treasures that glowed in a soft light. Mr. Brown was charming and gracious in his welcome, but I felt like an uncouth ambassador calling on an oriental potentate; his visage was so calm, his smile so inscrutable; my voice sounded more Middle Western than usual. To heighten the effect, in the wall behind a hanging a sliding panel suddenly moved away and a minion silently entered the room. It turned out to be the Co-ordinator and he carried no dagger; he came simply to remark that it was well past lunch time. Thereupon Mr. Brown took me courteously by the arm, escorted me back to the elevator and up we went to the top floor.

In the staff dining room a dozen or fifteen men and women were already lunching. Everyone inclined his head attentively to listen to me try to justify my intrusion into their family circle. There was Mrs. Fairfax Proudfit Walkup, director of the School; there was a pleasant lean-faced, black-haired lady wearing two silk scarves of different colors whom everyone called simply "Mamzelle." (She taught languages in the School, I later discovered, and managed the Playbox for Mr. Brown.) There was Mr. Charles Prickett, the general manager, one of the best theatrical business administrators in the country; his brother Oliver, who directs the publicity department into which the Playhouse is said to pour something like ten per cent of its income. Ralph Urmy and Onslow Stevens came in—old friends of mine from New

York, then associate directors at the Playhouse. A number of others came and went, for the staff is large: about seventy-five people if one counts all the directors, instructors, technicians, stage crew, secretarial help, ushers, box-office attendants and building staff.

After luncheon Mr. Brown assigned the assistant to someone's assistant to take me on a tour of inspection. We started in the room next door—the "Canteen" where student lunches are served. Beyond was the student lounge. Outside was a large flat roof on which later I was to watch classes in eurythmics, fencing, theatre dance. I was told that on that roof some months before had been staged an experimental production of MacLeish's *Air Raid;* in that setting it had had unexpected impact, they said; for coincidentally on the night of performance a major movie première was occurring in Hollywood five miles away and arc searchlights restlessly combed the sky all evening—the perfect lighting background. As the play approached its climax an airplane droned across the horizon to set the final note.

From the roof we descended to the next two floors containing class and rehearsal rooms. I counted five different plays in rehearsal that afternoon in different halls, along with classes in voice training, make-up, history of literature. On these floors also were costume workshops and great storerooms containing the eight thousand costumes which the Playhouse values at $35,000; here too was the studio of Rita Glover, the Art Director; the property rooms; the library. On the second floor were the managers' offices, and the managers' secretaries' offices. Passing down a corridor we reached the small stage of the recital hall. This is a room that must seat about

150 with a platform at either end. For one platform there is a curtain and moveable scenery; on the other a permanent set arrangement. The laboratory plays are presented on one stage, the senior plays on the other. We returned to the patio and passed through heavy dark oak doors into the auditorium. The elaborate Spanish theatre seats 832. The stage is excellently equipped; adjoining it are large workshops and scene docks; beneath are dressing rooms. Under the lobby is a handsome greenroom with kitchens adjoining. This plant, the main part of which was built in 1925, the annex in 1936, is estimated to have cost in excess of six hundred thousand dollars. This is no "little" theatre.

At 8:30 that evening this mountain labored and brought forth a mouse. It was a pleasant little one: *Morning's at Seven,* and it was agreeably played in front of an attractive representation of two back porches. The audience found it more than passably amusing. I laughed a good deal myself, in spite of having seen it in two other places as well as on Broadway. Nevertheless it seemed rather inconsequential in these impressive surroundings, in this theatre which one associates with O'Neill's *Lazarus Laughed,* with Shakespearean cycles in which all his plays have been produced. Actually nowadays, however, except for the summer festival of eight weeks (in 1940 eight plays of James M. Barrie), a good deal of the repertory on the main stage consists of lighter contemporary works like *Morning's at Seven, Two on an Island, You Can't Take It with You, Kiss the Boys Goodbye,* interlarded with a few serious plays like *Of Mice and Men* (which was to follow the production I saw), two or three new plays a year and occasional classical revivals.

More experimental work is done elsewhere, however; for the Playhouse on its various stages presents a total of eighty-three different plays a year. This quantity is unparalleled by a single organization anywhere in America —anywhere in the world, I am tempted to say. On the main stage a new production opens every two weeks to play for eleven performances. In addition, there is the summer festival; the laboratory and senior stages (the latter using students exclusively) alternate with a different play every week from October to May. Furthermore, another series of eight plays are presented in the Playbox. All of this activity Mr. Brown supervises, choosing the plays, casting them and dropping in from time to time to watch a run-through.

The Playhouse probably presents more original plays than any other theatre in the country; for in addition to the two or three on the main stage, the Laboratory Theatre is devoted exclusively to the presentation of untried scripts, accounting for sixteen a year. In the Playbox, Mr. Brown will produce perhaps five or six more so that the Pasadena theatre gives a hearing to more than a score of new plays each season.

The Playbox has no formal legal connection with the Pasadena Playhouse. It is Gilmor Brown's personal toy. It is housed in a small building behind his residence; it is financed through separate channels: by its own subscribers who pay fifteen dollars a year. Its purpose is to provide a possible hearing to more esoteric dramas than the Playhouse can afford to offer the general public on its main stage; to allow Mr. Brown to present just whatever he pleases and as he pleases: such things as *The Great Galateo, The Sea Gull, The Tragedy of Nan, The Man with Red Hair,* and a great many new experimental plays. The new play I saw was a rather pseudo-intellectual fantasy drama by Jay Victor called *Tomorrow Is a Woman* which I hoped was not typical.

The Playbox holds but fifty people; it has no stage in the accustomed sense, no curtain, no footlights. Harriet Green describes it thus:

There is a central space with two floor levels; narrow spaces on three sides are raised still another step. On two sides there are fireplaces. The action of the play may take place in the center, on one side or on all sides. The chairs are arranged to suit the scheme of action, whatever it may be. . . . An elaborate overhead lighting system makes it possible to concentrate light wherever it is wanted. Dimmers, black-outs and bringing up the lights slowly prove effective substitutes for the act curtain. There is no scenery in the usual sense, but surprising transformations are sometimes wrought in the whole visible interior.

Like the Cleveland Play House, The Pasadena Playhouse Association is "big business." Its annual budget I am told approximates $175,000. The School brings in a yearly income of about sixty-five thousand dollars. Without this revenue it could not operate. I have already stated that its paid staff is nearly twice as large as the Cleveland Play House. Why then do I place it in a non-professional category and call Cleveland professional? I am not sure that I have a right to do so. The distinction on which I have made my decision is that at Cleveland actors are paid; at Pasadena although everyone else is paid, the actors are not.

Over this very point a dispute arose several years ago between the Pasadena Playhouse and Actors' Equity. A number of professional artists had played on the Pasadena stage without remuneration, glad for a vacation from the screen studios nearby or in order to be seen by those studios. Equity contended that if everyone else was being paid at Pasadena—including five stagehands receiving wages on the union stock scale—it was not just that the Playhouse should profit by the appearances of such people as Victor Jory, Douglass Montgomery and not remunerate them. The Playhouse contended that if it adopted the Equity salary scale for actors, it would have to go out of existence. Equity was unconvinced, placed the Playhouse on its blacklist, forbade professional actors to appear gratis in its plays. The Playhouse was forced to return to its original sources of talent: amateurs of the community who wanted to act.

This community, however, includes much more than Pasadena; it is the whole of greater Los Angeles which, as anyone who has been there knows, must embrace five hundred square miles. Throughout this area reign the almost hypnotic influence and power of Hollywood. Certainly within a fifty-mile radius of Hollywood anyone interested in acting cannot remain impervious to its spell. Consequently to the Playhouse tryouts, held every Sunday evening, come hundreds of people affected by this studio psychosis—who see in Pasadena a chance to act and perhaps to be seen and then perhaps to be caught up for movies. A number of these people have come West for that very purpose and they are good—better than the native inhabitants of Pasadena itself. So it has come to pass, I believe, that the Playhouse is scarcely any longer a community enterprise as far as Pasadena is concerned (in fact the word "Community" has been eliminated from its title: it is now the "Pasadena Playhouse Association"). It is not entirely a professional theatre, yet it is not strictly amateur. The only thing one can say with certainty is that it is non-commercial: it is incorporated as "an educational non-profit organization."

As an inspiring example to the non-commercial theatre of what can be accomplished in that field, the Pasadena Playhouse has been of great service. I cannot help feeling however that by 1940 it began to show the effects of its geographical situation. Except for Gilmor Brown himself and possibly one or two of his associates, the Playhouse turns its face more toward Hollywood than toward the world of theatre. It has ceased to become an end in itself (except to a nucleus of a scant half-dozen spirits) and has rather become a means to cinematic ends. I sensed this in numerous conversations with the Playhouse personnel, in observations of its students, and I find it reiterated in Playhouse statements. From its own literature I draw these excerpts:

While players who appear upon the Playhouse stages do so for the joy of it, participation in a Playhouse production frequently is not without great profit to the actor. The Playhouse ranks, as *Stage* magazine has expressed it, as "the leading showcase for ambitious talent in the neighborhood of the film studios." Talent scouts attend nearly every show, and many players have gone from parts in Playhouse shows to contracts leading to fame and fortune on the screen. In this way, the Playhouse has served many professionals as well as amateurs, who have found that the shortest road to Hollywood often lies through Pasadena.

Again, in a pamphlet to its members:

Present your card the next week and see a Senior Players' Production. Discover for yourself a new star for the stage or screen. Remember the long list of successful players that have gotten their start here at the Playhouse. Perhaps you will be among the first to discover one. Then it will be "I knew him when."

In literature addressed to prospective students:

As your talents develop, you will be given frequent opportunities to appear before the public. . . . When you are ready, you may try out for Main Stage parts, where your work may be seen by those who can offer you a professional opportunity. Many of our productions are attended by talent scouts. Situated as we are, we bring our students all the advantages of proximity to Hollywood, with none of the disadvantages. More players have gone from our stages to picture work than from any other single source of talent in the country.

And finally, from another brochure:

Among the most interested spectators at opening nights of Main Stage plays are regularly found talent and play scouts, representatives of Hollywood studios and Broadway producers, who are constantly in quest of new plays and players of outstanding talent.

One may say these are publicity blurbs and not to be taken too seriously. Nevertheless, I am of the opinion that Pasadena's preoccupation with motion pictures is too strong not to bear remarking. Whether or not this is a matter to criticize, I do not wish to say. I do think, however, that it must be borne in mind when thinking about the Playhouse.

It must still be recognized, however, that Pasadena is a first-class theatre. As a stage plant it is unsurpassed. As

testimony to the ability of one man to establish a permanent theatre it is impressive. If today it does not seem
overly preoccupied with meaningful service to the Pasadena community, one must remember that it is not really
a community theatre any more but an institution with a
professional responsibility to a wider area.

In Houston, Texas, is a young woman with a mop of
unruly close-cropped golden curls and twinkling blue eyes.
Her name is Margo Jones. The Community Players of
Houston is Miss Jones' creation. It is a rare example of a
community theatre in which are blended sociological and
artistic ingredients in close balance. The story starts with
Miss Jones' appointment to the Recreation Department
of the City of Houston in 1936. It was not long before she
managed to persuade someone to ask why the Recreation
Department did not present plays. She answered immediately by announcing in the newspapers that the Community Players was being formed and that tryouts for its
first play, *The Importance of Being Earnest* would be
held the following evening. She had chosen the Wilde
piece because, having no money at all, she needed a non-
royalty play, one in which she could stylize the décor and
so have next to no scenery, one with a small cast; there
are seven parts in that play. It was a fortunate choice,
for to the public tryouts came only seven persons, so each
one received a role. The city owned a recreation hall on
Buffalo Drive and the play was presented there. A few
hundred people attended. Miss Jones' salary being paid
by the municipality, the whole production cost twelve
dollars.

That first season the Community Players presented, in

addition to *The Importance of Being Earnest, Judgment Day, Hedda Gabler, Squaring the Circle, The Lay Figure,* a subsequent prize-winner in a Texas One-Act Play Tournament. Margo, as she is breezily known to everyone in Houston, decided it would be effective to present *Judgment Day* in a courtroom, since its subject is the Nazi Trial of the Reichstag Fire. (It would also be easier than to stage it on her inadequate platform, for it had a large cast and should have an imposing set.) She persuaded the local judiciary that they would like nothing better than to yield the bar to her, so the second production was done in the Court House.

Not until its second season did the Community Players have enough money to buy wood and canvas to build its first "flats." Margo was also able to postpone until the second season the production of a play in which she felt it necessary to dim the lights. She had no money even then to buy dimmers, so she called a local physicist who over the telephone told her how to make salt-water rheostats with a bit of copper and some Mason fruit jars. At once she did so and the theatre had a dimming system.

In the Community Playhouse during the seasons since 1936-37, Margo Jones and her confreres have presented *Merrily We Roll Along, Bury the Dead, The Long Christmas Dinner, Macbeth, Les Femmes Savantes, Blind Alley, Candle Light, High Tor,* three more new plays, *Pride and Prejudice, The Master Builder, The Taming of the Shrew, Our Town, My Heart's in the Highlands, The Torchbearers, Uncle Vanya, The Comedy of Errors, Family Portrait, Winterset, Two on an Island, Wild Decembers, As You Like It, The Devil Passes* and *Peer Gynt.* This is as sound and impressive a repertory as has been done by any young amateur group: in its first five seasons to include four plays of Shakespeare, three of Ibsen, two each of Rice, Anderson and Wilder, works of Molière and Chekhov, and four original manuscript plays is to establish at once that this theatre is no light-weight imitation of Broadway.

One of Margo's most provocative statements was: "My most successful box-office productions have been the classics. I always have to sell standing-room for Shakespeare, Ibsen or Chekhov." I have thought a good deal about this. Why should people in Houston support the classics when in places like Pittsburgh they are only eager for light modern comedies? Is there a difference in public taste between Texas and Pennsylvania or is it a difference in theatres? Margo considers that her productions of classics are her best work; photographs appear to support her contention. Is it perhaps that those dramas a director cares most for and in which he consequently outdoes himself, are those which the public most heartily enjoys? May it not be possible that the reason the classics are not supported in some places is because they are not well enough done, because *Margin for Error* and *What a Life* are given better productions than *Macbeth* or *The Master Builder?*

In the summer of 1939 Margo decided that Houston should have a summer theatre. The Playhouse was too hot, outdoors it was too hot; but the Lamar Hotel had an air-conditioned ballroom on the roof, so the Community Players leased this. There was no stage, no proscenium, but the intrepid director, undaunted, decided to capitalize on the novelty of a stage-less theatre, seated the audience of one hundred around an acting area in the center of the floor, brought characters in and out at the beginning and end of scenes during blackouts. The Intimate Theatre it was called and, it being summer time, Margo dedicated it to light drawing-room comedy. Pieces like *There's Always Juliet*, *The Second Man*, *The Circle*, *Springtime for Henry*, *Room Service*, *Art and Mrs. Bottle* have been done in this summer stock theatre which continued to play infrequently during the following fall and winter. Out of some of these productions Margo has built a repertory which is available and in wide demand for performances throughout the city and state; since no stage and scenery are required the plays can be presented practically anywhere.

By 1940-41 the Community Players had a membership of more than fifteen hundred; from those original seven actors her group of participants had grown large enough to cast fifty-one people in *Two on an Island*, handle its eleven sets with a backstage crew of twelve and run the theatre with a permanent staff of eighteen. None of these people are paid; Margo's own salary is still provided by the city which also still donates the hall. Under these circumstances the Community Players may spend from ten dollars to two hundred dollars on a production (exclusive of royalty). In consequence it is able to offer its season subscribers six plays for two dollars. This is a theatre for the people. It is by the people too, since it yearly attracts more than three hundred young men and women from every humble walk of life. This is no socialite group; if there is a debutante or a polo-player among them, that background is carefully concealed, for a completely democratic spirit prevails. To participate one pays no fees or dues, need not even be a subscriber. (Paradoxically, however, there is no Board of Directors, no Committees; Margo is sole head. The Community Players is simultaneously democratic and autocratic.)

In addition to its program of six plays and its season of Intimate Theatre, the Community Players has a radio producing group conducting a weekly radio program which in December, 1940, had been on the air for thirty-two weeks and had used the services of ninety people. It also holds Sunday afternoon play-readings with casts composed of members not currently rehearsing major productions; such plays as *The Wild Duck, Rosmersholm, Ghosts, The Silver Cord, She Stoops to Conquer, The Three Sisters, Time Is a Dream, Ethan Frome* have been read at these sessions to which the public is invited.

This theatre has a strong sense of community obligation. Various Players' groups present plays and programs at service club luncheons, women's clubs and sorority meetings throughout Houston. It organized a "Junior Community Players" for children between ten and sixteen interested in dramatics. This turned into an apprentice group having a twelve-week course for young people. It publishes a mimeographed news sheet: "The Community Players News." It holds a ten-week series of Saturday morning classes for teachers and club women at which "material to be given includes the fundamentals of direction, choosing plays for school use, for club meetings, special occasions, etc." There is beehive life on Buffalo Drive in Houston.

Particularly gratifying to me is the Community Players' combination of all these services with an insistence on maintaining and improving its standard of excellence. Margo hopes to build out of this broadly based community enterprise a really fine resident theatre. The performance of *Two on an Island* which I witnessed demonstrated that this theatre possessed artistic creativeness and imagination along with its social consciousness.

The Palo Alto Community Players is a theatre dedicated to community service and to the encouragement of participation on an ever-broadening base. In more than name does it resemble the Houston Community Players. Like the Houston theatre it came into existence through the Recreation Department of the municipality. As in Houston the building it occupies is owned by the city and its director is paid by the city. But in Houston the municipal tie stops there. In Palo Alto, California, the Community Players is truly a municipal theatre. Its Playhouse is a part of the city-owned and operated Palo Alto Community Center, which also contains a children's theatre, a library for children, social rooms and facilities for a number of organizations with a program of social service like the Boy and Girl Scouts, choruses and a light opera association.

The Players receive an annual subsidy of ten thousand dollars from the city treasury; out of that treasury the salaries of a business manager and a technical director are also paid. In return all the intake at the box office and from season tickets is turned back to the city. This amounts to about five thousand dollars a year, so the city is actually more than guaranteeing the theatre against possible loss. It is literally supporting the theatre to the extent of five thousand dollars, just as it supports its schools or its fire engines.

This has been going on for almost ten years, so the

city must feel that it is a worth-while burden. What or who is responsible for this success? Ralph Emerson Welles has been supervising director since 1932. If there is a "who" it is he. His policy is, I believe, directly responsible: this theatre must always be operated as a public service. Its doors must always be open to everyone who wishes to participate either on the stage, back-stage or in the audience. It must not be managed for the benefit of a few nor can its psychic gains go to a small number.

Palo Alto is not a large town: it has but sixteen thousand inhabitants. Approximately four hundred people annually participate in the work of the Players (they pay a one-dollar participating-member fee when they take part in any way and receive therefor voting power); over six hundred are subscribing members. That total one thousand out of sixteen thousand is impressive; but that is essential since this is a municipal theatre. Palo Alto has a rather homogeneous population: it is a college town, a wealthy suburb, really, of San Francisco. The level of culture is presumably high; there is an appreciation of the arts to begin with. Notwithstanding, the handsome playhouse and the teeming activity that goes on there are impressive. For twelve plays are presented a year, one each month; there is workshop activity besides, and a social program that includes a number of cast and workers' parties and outings. This theatre is within the financial reach of anyone in that community. A season subscription admitting to the twelve plays costs three dollars, which amounts to twenty-five cents for one show. Single admissions cost fifty cents.

Since this theatre is, after all, a recreational project it must be judged as such. Mr. Welles thinks of himself as a leader and a teacher almost more than as a stage director. His enthusiasm is for using the stage as a means to develop the personalities of his participants, to help them grow into better citizens and happier human beings. Through co-operative endeavor in the field of a creative art, he believes that inner and perhaps hidden wellsprings of the individual's spirit may be tapped. It is for this reason that the Community Players welcome everyone. "We use them all," writes Welles, "the brilliants, dims, rich and poor, the bores, the boors, the haves, the have-nots, the ins, the outs, the four hundred and the baker's dozen." It is for this reason that the emphasis swings away from the theatrical result and onto the process. "I am less interested," Welles will say, "in whether Susie's performance, perhaps as a result of high-pressure coaching, is 'as good as a professional' than I am in what happens to Susie during the production of the play. I think not so much about her finished performance as about the development of initiative and poise and sensitivity that I have observed in her over these past weeks."

Not only in the casts, but throughout the organization the doors are thrown open to all. The Executive Board consists of nine citizens—a sizeable and democratic group. A large play selection committee assists the director in choosing the repertory; a large casting committee does not actually select individuals for parts, but is useful in lining people up, encouraging city-wide participation and in conducting the tryouts.

With this emphasis on democratic principles and on participational values rather than on finished performances, one may question whether the audience derives its share of benefit. I was unfortunate in not being in Palo Alto for a performance so I can make no first-hand judgment. I can imagine that the excellence of any particular production will depend upon the chance amount of talent that happens to be participating. This may help to account for the varying size of the audience which ranges from eight hundred attendants to eighteen hundred.

The question that first arises in the mind of a visitor is to what extent a city-owned and operated theatre is affected by political interference or censorship. Mr. Welles is able to say that there is none; and he claims that the theatre's democratic policy is responsible. He points out that as long as its Board of nine tax-payers makes it its business to serve a thousand other tax-payers and puts their interests before any selfish personal ambitions, the city cannot curtail its activities, for it *is* the city. If one clique or class dominated the theatre it would be done for as a municipal enterprise, Welles contends (and incidentally suggests thereby why the average community theatre could not become a true civic theatre without a change of philosophy and personnel). Welles recalls that when an irate town commissioner complained about the presentation of *Reunion in Vienna* or some such play which he considered risqué, he was told that it was the choice of a majority of the tax-paying board, that it was a tremendous box-office success in Palo Alto, and so represented what the majority of taxpayers wanted to present and to see. Under such circumstances censorship would be a dangerous implement to the wielder if he wished to keep on good terms with the voters.

Palo Alto has the true community theatre. It is a comparatively new and certainly a rare phenomenon in this democratic land. It is one goal—if not the only goal—

toward which the theatre can aim; for it is of the people, by the people and for the people; it is concerned with broadening the base of culture and dedicated to the proposition that the theatre must belong to every man who seeks expression in it.

4

What responsibility are the community playhouses assuming for the maintenance and growth of the American theatre? That has been the question to which these fifteen illustrations should provide the answer. There are, of course, at least a hundred other theatres more or less like these; but I think the piling up of examples would still lead to the same conclusions.

The first thing to be affirmed is that these theatres are bringing drama to hundreds of thousands of persons throughout the country for whom it would otherwise become an infrequent and inconsequential experience. The possibility to see four, six, eight or a dozen plays a year is being provided by community theatres to regions that without them would be forced to depend upon one or two road shows or the high school play for their dramatic sustenance. This is no mean contribution. These theatres further provide opportunity to thousands of young and older people to enter into the experience of play production. Insofar as this experience is a creative enterprise, these men and women are in touch with those spiritual forces which are among man's most enlarging possessions. This too is no mean contribution. Insofar as it is a social enterprise (using the word in its broader sense), the participants in these community theatres gain those personal values which come through co-operative endeavor and recreational release.

The community theatre movement has passed from the first flush of its period of youthful idealism and dreams into a realistic phase of middle-age. It has built mansions for itself in a hundred spots: some magnificent, some humbler. It has grown in size and stability and has proved that it was no short-lived, flighty and fashionable phase of American culture, no mere momentary manifestation of post-war excessive Bohemianism. It is occasionally an institution that takes its place alongside of the art museum, the orchestra, the library, the school as one of the cornerstones of local culture.

These tributes must be paid to this kind of theatre. It would be useless and unfair, however, to let it go at that; for this movement has far from reached its goal—if, that is, its goal is the decentralization of the American stage, the creation of a real people's theatre. There are certain generalizations—obviously not universally applicable— which I feel bound to make. They are conclusions which the thoughtful reader may have also reached after studying the theatres I have described.

Already I have said that many of these theatres have lost their experimental character, their youthful idealism; I have said that today they appear middle-aged, realistic, quasi-commercial. The movement which started as an opposition force to Broadway and the road, voicing dissatisfaction at the fare offered by the commercial theatre, has swung pendulum-like toward more and more frequent imitations of Broadway. Using Broadway's own justification, that "this is what the public wants," the community theatres have clamored for the release of Broadway's latest hits; they have rarely had the patience to read its less successful plays with the thought that something New York did not fancy might yet be good; they have banished the classics from any important place in their repertories as old stuff and dull; they have lacked the courage to give new playwrights a hearing before the stamp of Manhattan approval was upon them. They are no longer artistic pioneers; they are now cautious followers in the ruts of Broadway.

It is reported that the most frequently presented play of the year 1940-41 in the little theatres has been *What a Life*. I have listed the offerings of most of the groups I have described in order that the reader might see for himself what a stereotyped pattern they were following. In February, 1940, I attended a meeting of the Southeastern Council of Community Theatres in Jacksonville, Florida. About a dozen little theatres were represented. I jotted down the list of plays which some of them were presenting or had done the previous season. At Columbia, South Carolina, there had been *Boy Meets Girl, The Second Man, Our Town, The Petrified Forest, What a Life*; Sarasota, Florida, reported *Night Must Fall, First Lady, The Pursuit of Happiness, You Can't Take It with You, Men Must Fight, The Dover Road*; Charlotte, North Carolina: *The Royal Family, Yellow Jack, What a Life, Tomorrow and Tomorrow, Kiss the Boys Goodbye*; Macon, Georgia: *The Bad Man, Candida, What a Life, Winterset*; Baton Rouge, Louisiana: *Mary's Other Husband, Square Crooks, The Night of January 16th, The Widow in Green, Pulling the Curtain*; Rock Hill, South Carolina: *Fresh Fields, Susan and God, Night Must Fall,*

Laburnum Grove; Aiken, South Carolina: *You Can't Take It with You, The Pursuit of Happiness;* Tampa, Florida: *You Can't Take It with You, The Servant in the House, The Man from Cairo, Our Town, Outward Bound, Tomorrow and Tomorrow.*

Almost all of these plays bear the stamp of Broadway approval; several among them, like *Tomorrow and Tomorrow, Yellow Jack, Candida, Our Town, Winterset* are certainly dramas that should be presented wherever there is a stage to bring them to an audience. Certainly, if one perhaps excepts the program at Baton Rouge, all these theatres are showing a certain amount of taste and discrimination: *Getting Gertie's Garter, Here Comes Charlie,* and the like are not on their lists. But what would have happened to them had the Broadway against which they inveighed suddenly gone out of existence or refused to allow them performances of any plays produced there in the past ten years? As these repertories reveal, most community theatres depend for more than ninety per cent of their offerings on Broadway's plays.

The result of this is a regimentation of the whole country—as far as little theatres are concerned—in the mold of New York. Among the twenty-two theatres mentioned in this survey, in the period from 1939 through 1941, my records reveal that outside of the Pasadena Playhouse only six original full-length plays have been given a major production. There is nothing in the program of any one of these community theatres to indicate whether it is living in South Carolina or Michigan, Arizona or Pennsylvania. All their repertories are practically interchangeable; they have no relation to the region of which their theatre is a part.

Another thing which a study of these repertories reveals is that the little theatre movement has cast its lot on the side of escapism, of drama as entertainment. I was constantly told that groups wished they might do more meaningful or more experimental plays but "the public wants entertainment." Since all these organizations depend for their existence upon their box offices or upon subscriptions they become necessarily as obsessed as Broadway's managers with "what the public wants." If the little theatres are going to seek justification for existence upon satisfying the public's demand for entertainment, then they must be prepared to stand comparison with the motion pictures and Broadway's theatres which exist for the same ends. In such a comparison the little theatres reveal their ineptitude. For the most part they do not give adequate return for one's money. The scenery and lighting may be as good as New York's, sometimes better; but in acting and direction their performances of *What a Life*, *Margin for Error*, *You Can't Take It with You*, et cetera, seldom equal the original Broadway production and rarely excel the acting and direction of the movie version.

I have been equally concerned by my discovery of the limited relationship the average little theatre bears to its community. Again an examination of the repertories of these groups reveals that they presuppose an upper middle class, more or less sophisticated audience. When one couples with this the high ticket scale that usually obtains, one sees to how few people in a community these community theatres really address themselves. I have already said that a playhouse from which ninety-nine per cent of the population stays away is no people's theatre. The fact that as far as I know to no little theatres, even in the

North, may a Negro belong; that to few little theatres may a ticket be bought for fifty cents or less, supports me in this contention: here is no people's theatre. We must look elsewhere for it, or else it remains to be created.

Insofar as the little theatres exist for the sake of their members, insofar as they are social or cultural clubs, they are justified in doing many of the things for which I have criticized them. There is no reason to compare their results with the professional stage from one point of view, and from the other no reason to condemn their exclusiveness. If they have come of age, however, and are laying claim to being the real American theatre today—the successor to the dying professional stage—then they must answer these charges. Why have they made so little effort to encourage and develop new playwrights to reflect the rich native pattern of American life from Atlantic to Pacific? Why have they usually been satisfied to imitate the commercial success of New York—why nothing new to say themselves about anything? Why have they been willing so frequently to be satisfied with mediocrity, to allow inner social or political machinations to interfere with excellence? Why have so few of them defined any artistic or ideational objectives through the pursuit of which the American theatre—if they have become it—might grow more creative and become a finer art?

On the other hand and finally, if their goal is not so much that of improving the theatre as an art, as of bringing it closer to the people—the democratization of theatre —then why have the little theatres been so self-contained? Why have they been satisfied to embrace but one or two persons out of one hundred? Why have they not lowered their prices? Why have they so seldom organized children's theatres and effected liaisons with the school and the church, the library and the settlement house? Why have they closed their eyes to the labor problems in their community and to social injustices? Why have they presented no plays for workers—not even a "living newspaper," which has something to say to all classes? Why have they not organized affiliate groups in factories and asylums and institutions? Why have so few of them held classes or social programs open to the underprivileged?

I believe in the community theatre movement; that may sound strange after such a salvo, but I do. I believe it has vast possibilities. Through these questions I have just posed, I have tried to reveal the resources which I believe this field potentially possesses. In a few places and on an occasional stage here and there I have been shown of what this movement is capable. An inspiring leader here and there has shown me the reach the little theatre might have into the remaking of American community life.

In 1941 the little theatre movement as a whole was about twenty years old; many individual theatres were much younger. By and large, up to 1941 they had not yet begun to live either independent or interrelated lives. Those theatres more than ten years old showed signs of vitiation. At the end of a decade they were already tired. The exciting theatres I seemed to find were almost invariably the young theatres: three, four, five years old. Would they, I wondered, in another five or six years be as uninspiring as today's veterans? I heard it often said that the life of the average little theatre is five to ten years and my observations seemed to corroborate it. Why is this so? I think I have an answer—not very original, in fact axiomatic; one that holds for Broadway as well or for any artist or group of artists working anywhere.

There must always be a goal, high and far away. If there is no goal, no objective, or if the goal is too easily attained and nothing lies beyond it, any theatre grows weak after a little time. That is what happens to these theatres. But if there is a purpose and if it is vital and valid enough to enlist the support of the succeeding generations that must be attracted to it and for which a place must be made, then at the end of ten years a theatre will be just beginning. The three-year-old theatre today will be just as young at thirty and just as creative, as much of a social force and more so. And that is what these theatres must be, if we are to say: here is the people's theatre; this is America's theatre for tomorrow.

CHAPTER FIVE

Collegiate Gothic

THE TWO most important developments of the American stage during the past decade have been the short-lived but significant Federal Theatre, and the expansion of dramatic activity in the field of education. Today in hundreds of colleges and universities, in more hundreds of high schools and professional schools, young people whose number reaches into the tens of thousands are supplementing their study of drama as literature with practical experience in the presentation of plays. This movement, which began no longer ago than the first decade of this century, when George Pierce Baker set up his "47 Workshop" at Harvard, has gained such momentum in the past ten years as to make one wonder whether the academic cart may not soon run away with the theatrical horse.

"Why has Cornell University a department of drama? Why is it paying salaries to professors and providing physical facilities for the study of theatre?" I asked Howard Babcock, then acting chairman of the Board of Trustees of Cornell. Mr. Babcock, no theatre man but an executive of the farm co-operative movement—a lean, alert agriculturist, replied (and I paraphrase): "If for no

other reason—although there *are* other reasons—than that
it creates in the university community an *awareness* of the
theatre's significance among the arts and in life. Through
the university's expenditure and academic recognition it
establishes indubitably that it believes the theatre is more
than a step-child of the movies. This awareness of theatre
is the first step to inquiry and then to appreciation."

Other explanations for the presence of theatre instruction in academic curricula are numerous. All of them are
predicated on the assumption that theatre practice may be
an art. Dr. George Reynolds, at the University of Colorado, points out that the reading of dramatic literature
must be supplemented by the visual and aural experience
of attending a produced play if the full impact and meaning of drama are to be comprehended. Use of theatre production as an aid to teaching dramatic literature is frequent.

There are those who say that greatest appreciation results from actual familiarity with technics; their doctrine
is: "learn through doing." The man who has himself tried
to apply oil to canvas can appreciate better the paintings
of a Turner or a Monet; he who has studied the violin
can more completely enjoy the playing of a Heifetz—
since through knowledge growing out of practice comes
the finest appreciation.

Dramatic instruction is also justified on sociological
grounds. Dean Paul Packer of the State University of
Iowa's College of Education asserted (again I paraphrase): "We believe in the importance of theatre at this
University because it prepares for co-operative living and
makes for a richer life." Hallie Flanagan quotes President
Henry N. McCracken of Vassar as saying: "I can always

tell at the Commencement Exercises which girls are drama majors when they come to the platform for their diplomas: it is not by any theatrical bearing or appearance; it is because in their eyes I see an awareness of the moment."

More specific statements of purposes of practical instruction in the dramatic arts are to be found in University bulletins and catalogues. The University of Texas, for example, lists the objectives for the College of Fine Arts (in which is the Department of Drama) as:

(1) to offer instruction in the fine arts accompanied by or based upon a broad and thorough general education; (2) to develop talent to the highest degree of artistic capability; (3) to train teachers of the arts; (4) to offer the opportunity for university students to develop discriminating standards of taste through courses about the arts, through art exhibitions, concerts, plays and through contact with artists of high rank in the several fields.

Through these cold and formal phrases, reiterated in a hundred college announcements, is revealed an awakening interest in the theatre as an art, as a social force, as a subject worthy of academic consideration. Let us now enter the campuses of a few of those universities and colleges that possess functioning theatre centers. We can begin with the liberal arts colleges where the picture is least complicated.

These colleges are primarily interested in presenting the theatre for its cultural value. Concerned with students on the undergraduate level, their primary desire is to inculcate an appreciation of drama to complement an appreciation of literature, painting, music. To the young man or woman who wishes self-expression in the theatre, they offer no particular encouragement and only a restricted amount of training; they seldom desire or are prepared to provide specialized professional instruction.

I crossed the snow-bound campus of Amherst College one frosty evening bound for the Kirby Memorial Theatre to see a performance of *Cyrano de Bergerac*. Out of the dark shone the lights of the Playhouse and as I approached the pink-brick structure with its white-columned Georgian portico, I reflected that here was the first of those beautiful new theatre plants [1] I had heard I would find in the colleges. I entered its severely modern auditorium which holds slightly more than four hundred people. It was filled with college boys and some professors and their wives. The laughter, when it came, was predominately male; *Cyrano* is an undergraduate favorite.

The performance was beautifully mounted according to designs by Charles Rogers, permanent member of the theatre staff. Complicated settings, beautifully lighted and standing out against a plaster dome of sky, were shifted with an ease and rapidity any Broadway stage manager would envy. Going backstage after the performance I discovered that the height, depth and side space of the stage made possible the use of multiple wagon stages running in tracks, as well as the flying of all sorts of complicated units. The lighting was controlled from a switchboard set in the orchestra pit where the electrician could observe the

---

[1] The Kirby Memorial Theatre was built in 1938 at a cost of approximately $250,000.

stage at all times. No wonder the performance reached such a high technical level.

The producers of this play were The Masquers, undergraduate extra-curricular dramatic club and under its banner four major productions are presented annually.[2] Professor Curtis Canfield of the English Department is their permanent director and he selects, casts and stages all the plays. The students act and build scenery; the actual creative work is done by Mr. Canfield and Mr. Rogers. A dozen of the boys, however, supplement their work in The Masquers by taking the one course the College offers in Dramatic Art. There during one year they study acting, directing, history of drama in its relation to theatre, production methods. It is to be presumed, however, that they can learn but a smattering about these things in such short time; just enough to give them a little better than average appreciation of them when they go to a play.

Dartmouth College also offers but one course in dramatic production. As at Amherst, the production program is under the aegis of the undergraduate dramatic club, the Dartmouth Players, directed by Warner Bentley, assisted by two permanent staff members. It offers, however, a more elaborate season: five major productions and five

[2] Ancient and modern classics predominate. In the last four seasons, The Masquers have presented such plays as: *Green Grow the Lilacs*, the one-act sea plays of O'Neill, *Murder in the Cathedral*, *The Late Christopher Bean*, *The Three Sisters*, *Henry IV, Part I*, *Juno and the Paycock*, *Peer Gynt* (the complete play presented in two parts), *Waiting for Lefty* and *Fashion*; also an original play by Amherst graduate, Dan Wickenden, *The Golden Dustman*. To open their new theatre they presented an all-Maxwell Anderson season: *High Tor*, *What Price Glory*, *Mary of Scotland*, *Winterset*.

experimental plays,[3] among which is a bill of three original student one-act plays, the best receiving the annual
one-hundred-dollar prize offered by the Players. These
one-acts are directed by undergraduates.

I wish I might have been at Dartmouth in the fall to
see the annual Interfraternity Play Contest. In many colleges the social system, represented by the fraternities,
looks askance at the artists in its midst. One would expect
this intensified at an aggressively masculine institution like
Dartmouth. But such an attitude is not to be found during
the week-end when the eighteen Greek-letter houses vie
for the Players' Cup. It may be their one and only appearance on the stage, but more than two hundred undergraduates eagerly perform in the one-act plays, adapta-
tions of short stories, scenes from classics, cut versions of
full-length plays, original playlets or musical skits offered
in the competition. And out of that number it is to be
hoped that some boys find their way to further participation or at least an increased interest in dramatics.

Dartmouth has no fine modern theatre. Until its projected million-dollar plant is built, it must present its
major plays in a convocation hall seating nearly a thousand people, lacking adequate stage facilities. The experimental plays are presented in a made-over lecture hall
with a hardly better stage.

Moving westward across the country I came in due time
to Cornell College in Iowa. About the size of Amherst,
Cornell, which is, however coeducational, has a surpris-

---

[3] In 1939-40 the former consisted of *What a Life, Our Town,
Twentieth Century, The Plough and the Stars* and *Golden Boy;* the
experimentals in addition to the one-act plays were *The Wild Duck,
My Heart's in the Highlands,* a Commedia dell'Arte, *Engaged.*

ingly New England air with its huge old elms, its red brick buildings, its commanding site on a hilltop with the hills and valleys of Iowa rolling out beneath it. A blind young man named Albert Johnson, assisted by his wife, is responsible for a dramatic program that involves between 130 and 140 undergraduates. Here a student may major in the dramatic and speech arts although the intention is not to provide training for professional careers so much as to develop individual personality and cultural appreciation.

This department presents six plays during the winter at its attractive little theatre in the new Hall of Fine Arts.[4] Notable among these have been experiments in original choric-dance dramas: *World Without End, Westward from Eden*—both religious in theme; also collaborations with the music department in presentations of *La Serva Padrona, A Kiss in Xanadu*, in addition to *Iolanthe* and *Trial by Jury*. In the summer of 1940 a refreshing production called *America Was Song and Laughter* was offered: an original variety show with music and dance-drama built out of nineteenth-century material, with an epilogue written by the Iowa poet, Paul Engle.

Farther west at the very foot of the Rocky Mountains at Colorado Springs is Colorado College. In the spring "Koshare," its extra-curricular dramatic club, piles its scenery and costumes and lights onto a truck and sets out on tour. Into four or five small Colorado towns the boys

---

[4] Since the new theatre's opening in 1938, the Cornell stage has seen performances of *As You Like It, Beyond the Horizon, Daughters of Atreus, Call It a Day, Candida, Hay Fever, Redemption, Mystery at Greenfingers, Mary Tudor, The Blue Bird, Iolanthe, Our Town, Private Lives, You Can't Take It with You, Penny Wise, Night Must Fall, Family Portrait* and *Macbeth*.

and girls go. In high school auditoriums or wherever is adequate space they set up their stage, hang their lights and put on their show. Usually it is a mystery play or a fairly unsophisticated comedy—but it is the only dramatic fare such places ever see, save for the local high school senior play. For "Koshare" members it is a theatrical experience fraught with novelty and excitement. They are "the road" for a brief season.

At home Colorado College, a coeducational school about the size of Amherst and Cornell colleges, is fortunate in having the use of the handsome modern theatre that is part of the Colorado Springs Fine Arts Center. Its curving walls are lined with fine-grained wood; its four hundred seats are upholstered in pearl velvet. From the great windows of its promenade, majestic snow-covered peaks stand visible. An ideal home for the arts is this and the theatre properly has its place there.

One-fourth of the student body at Colorado College are drawn into "Koshare" work which is led by Professor Arthur G. Sharp. Although there is one course in play production as at Amherst and Dartmouth, "Koshare" presents the plays, in 1940-41 *The Firebrand, The Christmas Carol, The Star Wagon* and *Twelfth Night*. All these are directed by Mr. Sharp who also designs the scenery, casts and guides the choice of plays. For this latter, however, and for the management of the program as a whole, an inner circle of "Koshare" is titularly responsible. Student initiative is encouraged up to a point: to a greater degree, in fact, than I observed at any of the colleges already mentioned.

The sky is blue overhead and the walls of Clytemnestra's palace are etched sharply against it. The wind sighs through the mourning eucalyptus trees. A chorus in dark robes weaves a moving pattern of highlights and shadows as the long rays of the sun strike the dancing figures. A tragic figure stands motionless before a great door. Majestic lines are spoken. This is the annual presentation of a Greek tragedy, this time *Electra* for example, which Dean Marian Stebbins produces in the outdoor theatre of Mills College, across the Bay and a few miles out from San Francisco. Mills is well known for its emphasis on the several arts. Here girls may major in speech and drama and about sixty-five do so. The core of the work is acting, with special emphasis on the students' voice and speech production.

Mrs. Stebbins, who is assisted by a staff of four, devotes three-quarters of her production schedule to the classics. Of the four plays presented each year, one is always a Greek drama; one is a Shakespearean play and a third is a classic of some other age. For Mrs. Stebbins believes in bringing up students on solid fare and in requiring them to test their powers in terms of the best that the theatre's library has to offer.

I could continue indefinitely with thumbnail sketches of theatrical activity in the smaller liberal arts colleges. At Smith College, at Tufts in Boston, at Allegheny in northwestern Pennsylvania, at Rollins in Florida, as well as at Vassar and Bennington, which I shall discuss hereafter, I observed dramatic programs. The list could be amplified a hundredfold. But in these five from New England to California a pattern has begun to take shape which most of the others will follow. Let us now turn to the universities, whose influence on the American theatre is perhaps more pronounced.

2

One of the pioneers in the academic theatre is Alexander M. Drummond who became director of the Cornell University Dramatic Club in 1912. He is the brain, the heart, the sinews of the present department. After nearly thirty years, this benevolent autocrat still reigns supreme, although failing health forbids his spending as many hours a day on the campus as he would wish. Nevertheless, white-haired and beetle-browed, he continues to preside over his course "66" on the esthetics of the theatre; chooses the plays for the Dramatic Club, casts and directs most of them; confers with the dozen master's degree candidates, cuffs the ten doctoral candidates when they do not behave to suit him, and manages to supervise half a dozen projects more or less related to his department.

Since 1912 Mr. Drummond has devoted himself to building a program at Cornell which now centers in "The Cornell University Theatre" and which consists of the Dramatic Club, The Cornell Summer Theatre, The Studio Theatre, The Laboratory Theatre, and undergraduate and graduate courses in drama. On the undergraduate level Cornell offers its students experience in the theatre for its educational and cultural value; on the graduate level its principal concern is in preparing teachers of drama. For undergraduates the work centers in the extra-curricular activity of the Dramatic Club whose active membership numbers about fifty. Over the years since 1909 when the Club was founded, there have been productions of two hundred long plays and of 736 one-acts, of which 127 were original Cornell plays (four of them full-length).[5] About three hundred students are involved in this production program that centers in the excellent small playhouse of Willard Straight Hall, the University Student Union. About a dozen of them are majoring in dramatic production for their A.B. degree, but obviously the majority are participating for their own enjoyment.

The Laboratory Theatre presents one or two plays a year and is the principal outlet for graduate work. The Summer Theatre is also chiefly composed of graduate students and of alumni invited back to participate. The Studio Theatre is now being devoted primarily to the work of the New York State Play Project.[6]

The chief problem which I feel Cornell's theatre faces is its relation to student life. On the Ithaca campus are some eight thousand students. I was told that not more than five hundred of them attend the average University Theatre production. The outside community forms the backbone of the audience at the two performances of each play. This is no problem unique to Cornell: it will have to be faced all across the country and it is a serious problem.

Another pioneer in the educational theatre is E. C. Mabie, under whose stimulus the State University of Iowa has become a prominent supporter of the drama.

---

[5] In 1940-41 the program included: *Music Hall Night, Springtime for Henry, The Star Wagon, My Heart's in the Highlands, George and Margaret,* four 1941 original Prize One-Act Plays on an American theme, *The Chief Thing,* a Spring revue and vaudeville, *The Male Animal, The Wild Hills,* a new play by Robert Gard of the University Theatre staff.

[6] See below, page 256.

Professor Mabie, Napoleonic in mien and dictatorial in tone, is as completely the autocrat of the Iowa stage as is Mr. Drummond at Cornell.

At Iowa the study of theatrical techniques is a part of the Department of Speech in the School of the Fine Arts. The work leads to a number of degrees: A.B., B.F.A., M.A,. M.F.A., Ph.D., and I am told Mr. Mabie plans further post-doctoral work![7] In the past twenty years Iowa has awarded three hundred Master's degrees and thirty Ph.D. degrees for work in dramatic art.

Although the department at Iowa began with emphasis on undergraduate work, that emphasis has gradually shifted to the graduate level. The undergraduate interested only casually and culturally in the theatre will work for an A.B.; the B.F.A., which leads to the M.F.A., is intended for those wishing to go into community theatre direction or into any dramatic career outside of teaching. The M.A. and Ph.D. are professional degrees designed to prepare students to teach drama. The primary interest here is in these latter which Mr. Mabie justifies by pointing out that of the 330 recipients of advanced degrees in the last twenty years, 92.8 per cent have gone into teaching.

John Jones, graduate student, cons the University catalogue and finds these courses from which to choose:

> Fundamentals of public speaking
> Advanced argumentation and debate
> Voice and phonetics
> Interpretative reading

[7] There are between sixty-five and eighty candidates for M.A. and M.F.A. degrees and eighteen Ph.D. candidates, although of course not all of these will be granted their degrees in any one year.

> Theory and technique of acting
> Interpretative reading recitals
> Technical practice in the theatre
> History and principles of scenic design
> Radio broadcasting
> The radio program: its planning and construction
> Theory and practice of stage lighting
> Dramatic activities in community life
> History of the theatre
> Acting
> Rehearsal and performance
> Methods and practice of stage direction
> Development of the American theatre
> Methods of teaching speech
> Teaching of speech: demonstration and observation
> Speech for the classroom teacher
> Experimental Theatre

He sees an additional nine courses in speech pathology, correctives, etc.

In addition to work in those courses which he has chosen from the above curriculum, what opportunities has John to practice all these things he hears preached? The University Theatre offers a "community series" of five plays. Perhaps he will be cast for a role in *Susan and God*, or in *The White Steed*, *Winterset*, *A Texas Steer* or in the new play *Middletown Mural* which is being tried out. In these he will be directed by Mr. Mabie or by one of the departmental assistants, Mr. Sellman or Mr. Morton. If he is not cast, he will doubtless work back-stage building, painting or shifting the settings designed by Professor Gillette, or on the switchboard or light crew executing the lighting designed by Professor Sellman.

But John is not being trained to be an actor; he does

not expect to be a stage hand. He is going to teach and in his teaching he will be required to direct plays. What experience can he have in this or in the other aspects of actual stage creation? The experimental productions are designed to give John this experience. There may be as many as eleven of these this year; they must be divided among seventy or eighty graduate students. John will be lucky if he is assigned one. It will not be surprising if he receives his M.A. without having had the experience of actually directing a single play himself. (There are other Johns at other universities up against this problem. It is not limited to Iowa.)

John's work has been in an excellent theatre plant. Its sizeable stage has a turntable and a shop so arranged that wagon stages may be shuttled in and out of it. The lighting equipment, designed by Professor Sellman, one of the country's experts in stage lighting, is more than adequate. Occasionally John wonders how he will get along in the school to which he will go, where there will be no revolving stage and elaborate switchboard to help him. But he is told that the student should come into contact with the best that is available so that he may get a glimpse of what can be done, may develop his own capacities as completely as material resources can aid him, have something to strive toward thereafter. These answers seem to make sense.

At Northwestern University on the shores of Lake Michigan, dramatics is administered as part of the vast School of Speech. Under Professor Theodore Fuchs, director of the theatre section, about two hundred students participate in the work of the University Theatre, approximately half of them enrolled as undergraduates, half as graduate students.[8] The emphasis at Northwestern is also on preparing people to become teachers of theatre; Mr. Fuchs estimates that about seventy-five per cent of the two hundred enrollees will go into that profession.

Northwestern's curriculum includes about twenty courses in all phases of theatrical production.[9] As at Iowa this work is implemented by a program of public productions: six major plays and eight Studio presentations.[10] Each major play is directed by a faculty member and is usually designed by Professor Lee Mitchell and lighted by Mr. Fuchs. In the Studio bills of one-act plays, student directors have the opportunity for practical experience. In a typical season twenty-one one-acts are presented; fifteen advanced students direct. These productions, however, provide no outlet for designers since they are presented in drapery setting with the order that "no new scenery will be built. Ordinary properties may be withdrawn from the University Theatre Storage. No costumes may be rented." In addition to these Studio productions, there is an opportunity for about twenty advanced students from courses in directing to gain experience by going to nearby public and private schools where they direct student one-act plays. It seems likely therefore that a student may go out from Northwestern with an M.A. under such a program and have directed one or two one-act plays; this is not guaranteed, however.

[8] Graduating with a B.S. in Speech specializing in drama are about twenty-five each year; eight M.A.'s and two Ph.D.'s is about an average for advanced studies.

[9] Courses in children's dramatics appear in Northwestern's curriculum, the first time they have been encountered in this study.

[10] The 1940-41 season of major production was *The Warrior's Husband*, Molière's *The Knavery of Scapin*, *The Romantic Young Lady*, *The Taming of the Shrew*, *The Three Sisters*, *Fashion*.

In addition to such practical work, the graduate student either carries out a program of theatre research or presents a production project. This latter, if elected,

shall be considered as embracing the planning for all phases of a dramatic production—the careful, detailed consideration and planning that should always precede the actual rehearsals and technical work of every production. The play chosen for such consideration on the part of the candidate is Henrick (sic) Ibsen's *The Lady from the Sea*. After the project has been submitted, the candidate shall present himself for an oral quiz on the project. . . . The completed project shall be submitted in six separately-bound parts corresponding to the parts enumerated below under "Contents": [11] Part one—Analysis of the play; Part two—Directing; Part three—Acting; Part four —Setting; Part five—Costuming; Part six—Lighting.[12]

Then follow eight pages of questions and four diagram sheets to be answered and filled in. All this is very interesting, but I am concerned at the degree to which it is removed from the actual experience of theatre—as any of these M.A. candidates would discover if he ever undertook actually to produce *The Lady from the Sea*. For the "consideration and planning that should always precede the actual rehearsals and technical work" is usually a long way removed from the finished product of an opening night.

Again, whatever criticism may be implicit in this exposition, is not leveled at Northwestern alone but at many other academic theatres offering advanced degrees. The

[11] It is to be understood that of course *The Lady from the Sea* is actually rehearsed and produced by no one.

[12] I quote from the 1939 statement concerning the "Comprehensive Examination for the Master's Degree."

actual creative experience too frequently is reserved by the faculty for itself; the student learns of theatre from the sidelines and by rote; the emphasis is on stagecraft, not on the living elements of the art. Young men and women go out to become directors in other colleges, in schools or in community theatres with but a "projected production" theoretically outlined and a couple of one-act plays practically produced as their background of experience. I consider this a grave situation.

The University of Minnesota is a three-ring circus; or perhaps it just seemed so to me because the activity of 150 undergraduate majors in theatre, twenty-six M.A. candidates and six potential Ph.D.'s, a staff of six, plus the dress rehearsals for *Peer Gynt* were all contained in the ground floor rooms and the stage on the floor above in the Music Building on the Minnesota campus. *Peer Gynt* in itself was a three-ring circus, employing forty-two student actors, a large stage crew to handle the twelve shifts on a special revolving stage built for this production; a student orchestra of twenty-two. Rehearsals were also under way for the first children's theatre performance, *The Emperor's New Clothes,* which was scheduled to open in about three weeks.

Professor C. Lowell Lees attempts to forestall the criticism that students have not opportunities for enough practical work by building a well-nigh back-breaking program to allow activity for everyone. There are six major productions which he or his faculty direct themselves.[18] The Chil-

---

[18] These in 1940-41 consisted in addition to *Peer Gynt* of: *The Merchant of Yonkers, Knickerbocker Holiday, Androcles and the Lion, Liliom* and *The Tempest.*

dren's Theatre program offers two plays; an experimental season consists of three old or unusual plays like *Martine*, *John Gabriel Borkman*, *Bury the Dead* of past seasons; there is a series of fifty one-act plays; a foreign language play series offering three productions of plays by such authors as Molière, Giraudoux, Benavente, Hauptmann in the original text (presented by language classes, but staged by the theatre staff).

The emphasis at Minnesota is on stage direction, for although the majority of students will become teachers, it is felt that their teaching will consist largely of directing students. An undergraduate major in drama must have served on the crew for major productions, have been the head of some one technical department for at least one production; he must have been both an assistant director and an assistant business manager for at least four one-act bills; he must have acted in at least four minor productions. Graduate students direct these fifty one-act and experimental plays; each one must have also directed somewhere a full-length play. By "somewhere" I mean in the churches, schools, clubs, lodges, etc. throughout the community to which these advanced people are sent to direct plays.

The University of Minnesota is the third largest institution of higher learning in the United States. It has a student body of fifteen thousand. It is also in a metropolitan area, situated practically on the line dividing the Twin Cities: Minneapolis and St. Paul. The handling of the audience for its public performances takes on more than usual importance under these circumstances. For the major series of eight plays, approximately five hundred student books costing $2.50 and three dollars are sold; guest mem-

berships cost five dollars, patron memberships ten dollars
—this latter giving twenty tickets to the season useable as
desired. About forty-five per cent of these patron books
are sold to the faculty, ten per cent to fraternities and
sororities who then dispense individual tickets to their
members, forty-five per cent to townspeople. Single seats
to individual performances are also available. The program
seems to be fairly well supported with perhaps one out
of ten of the student body attending the theatre. When
the new building which this department of drama badly
needs is erected, there will doubtless be an increasing support, provided, of course, that it is accompanied by continuing improvement in quality.

More literally a three-ring circus is the Department of
Drama at the University of Texas, for its activity occurs
in three different places: a major play series of four productions, a series of three plays in its "Theatre-in-the-
Round," and a series of three plays in its Experimental
Theatre. The major series is presented in Hogg Auditorium, the typical over-sized college theatre with just
barely satisfactory stage accessories. The Experimental
Theatre is really a lecture hall turned into an intimate
playhouse seating one or two hundred. The "Theatre-in-
the-Round," an adaptation of Gilmor Brown's Playbox,
possesses no stage or curtain; it is arranged like a prize-
ring, with the audience of 150 sitting in a circle around a
center acting area.

In the "Theatre-in-the-Round" series student talent is
supplemented by the use of ex-members of the department
still living in Austin: a step toward a combined university-
community group. The Hogg Auditorium series consisted

in 1940-41 of *Key Largo,* a new play by two Texas students: *Mañana Is Another Day, Twelfth Night* and an 1890 melodrama, the latter entirely produced by students. To them came about 2800 people and Professor James H. Parke, chairman of the department, estimates that about fifty per cent of the audience are students who pay seventy-five cents for the series.[14]

This triple-threat program is the joint presentation of the Department of Drama and the Curtain Club, undergraduate extracurricular organization. I was asked to attend one of the Club's weekly meetings. I went expecting to find a group of twenty or twenty-five devotees of the drama. I entered a room packed with 150 boys and girls —they were even perched in the window sills; for all I know there may have been an overflow listening by loud speaker in the basement! And this for a routine weekly business meeting.

In places like Northwestern and Cornell, students come from all parts of the country. At the University of Texas today almost all the seventy-five young people in the Department of Drama are Texans. This homogeneity is exciting; I suppose because Texas is exciting. There is something quite winning about Texan enthusiasm: these youngsters seem to feel that art was never created until they just now discovered it. They have all the excitement of a child with a new toy. They throw themselves wholeheartedly into every theatrical activity. They are eager to share with you their marvelous discovery.

The Department of Drama at Texas is quite young: it was only three years old in 1940-41. But then everything

---

[14] This is in addition to a "University Blanket Tax"—a student activity fee, part of which helps to support the dramatic program.

and everybody seems young in Texas. Because it has been so recently formed, many of this department's plans have yet to be realized. Mr. Parke wants to encourage native playwrights. He also believes in collaboration with the professional theatre. To serve both these ends he invited E. P. Conkle to join his staff as playwright in residence. (Mr. Conkle's *Johnny Appleseed* was given its première there in 1940.)

As the department grows Mr. Parke hopes to have a new building; to add a chair of history of the theatre, of radio drama; to offer courses in cinema, in public school dramatics. He would like to draw the Little Theatre of Austin into an affiliation with the department. He is enthusiastic about assistance to the recreational programs for the army camps—several of the larger of which are in Texas. Because the Music Department and the Department of Drama are both part of the College of Fine Arts Mr. Parke hopes for a closer tieup between music and drama than obtains in the average university and would like to present operas.

The sky appears to be the limit for Texas. The Department must be careful, as it expands its activities and organizes itself with such complexity, not to lose sight of the actual theatre. If its training in the theatre arts and crafts can be really superior; if it can develop a creative approach to supplement the historic approach to the stage, it can become as fine as any educational theatre center in the country.

3

Randolph Edmonds, recipient of a Rockefeller Fellowship at Yale, of a Rosenwald Fellowship to study in Europe, formerly a teacher at Morgan College and now a full professor at Dillard University, author of *Six Plays for a Negro Theatre,* is an outstanding representative of the Negro theatre's younger leadership. His name is known to all colored people who are working toward a stage for their people.

Dillard's attitude toward the arts is typical of all Negro educational philosophy: utilization of art for the service of the community. The position of their race in the American scene necessarily conditions the thinking and plans of all colored educators. The urgency of fulfilling their responsibility to their people, in view of the tremendous obstacles in the path and the great distance to be traversed, requires clear-eyed vision of the men and women in Negro schools. Among the ones I met I found no faltering and great enlightened zeal.

Self-realization of Negro art has come late. The Negro theatre is still a-borning. In fact as Mr. Edmonds has himself written, "The greatest achievement up to the present has been not a quantitive production of noteworthy plays written by young Negroes, but the realization on the part of many interested workers that something must be done to develop this important and virgin field." This realization most readily comes as a result of education and

that again is why the Negro campus is one of the genera-
tors of a colored stage.

The three fundamental problems of the Negro theatre
are the same three which face the theatre as a whole: the
need for playwrights, the need for trained, talented leadership, the need to develop an audience. In the case of the
first, the Negro stage is at a disadvantage, for whereas
our other playhouses have a great body of literature, domestic and foreign, on which to fall back and a Broadway
from which to draw at all times, the Negro has practically
no material of his own except as he develops it on the
spot. For most Negro theatrical leaders believe—and cor-
rectly, I am sure—that a strong Negro stage cannot depend upon the white tradition and the utilization of white
dramas indefinitely. Even those plays about the Negro
written by such white dramatists as Paul Green, Ridgely
Torrence, Eugene O'Neill, Paul Peters and George Sklar,
sympathetic and understanding though they may be, are
not an adequate substitute for a truly native Negro drama.

Whether or not this theatre can look to the universities
to provide it with plays, I am not sure. The stage has
seldom depended on the campus for that. But many of
the Negro colleges offer courses in playwriting and several of the foundations, notably the Julius Rosenwald and
the Rockefeller, have made it possible for talented colored
dramatists to study the technique of playwriting at places
like Yale and Iowa, so it seems likely that the colleges will
influence the rise of Negro drama.

More directly, however, are the universities tackling the
other two problems: that of providing leadership and of
developing an audience. At Dillard these two go hand in
hand, for this University looks upon itself as the cultural

fountainhead of the surrounding community. Mr. Edmonds' department is in close collaboration with three groups in New Orleans' colored section. There is the New Orleans Little Theatre Guild: a middle-class organization whose members are teachers or professional people, and which produces plays like *The Trial of Mary Dugan* and *Craig's Wife*. The New Orleans People's Theatre is truly proletarian and socially conscious: it presents such dramas as Langston Hughes' *Don't You Want to Be Free?* (a perennial favorite among Negro social theatres) and Edmonds' own *Land of Cotton*, a play about the sharecroppers; it is affiliated with the Negro Youth Congress. Finally, there is the Paul Robeson Children's Theatre, a group composed of youngsters between five and twelve years of age which works along the lines of classroom improvisations toward public performances of *Three Pills in a Bottle* and *Scrooge and the Christmas Fairy*.

On the one hand these organizations provide an opportunity for Dillard students majoring in drama to gain practical experience in community leadership and work with children (for undergraduates on NYA scholarships direct these groups). On the other hand, the programs of these theatres stimulate that interest in things theatrical which is the necessary concomitant anywhere for an expanding stage.

Dillard's influence in building up an awareness of theatre and an audience for it extends also into the secondary schools. The Interstate High School Drama Festival in which Negro children from Texas, Alabama, Mississippi and Louisiana participate is the result of Mr. Edmonds' organizational prowess, as is the high school drama section of the Louisiana Interscholastic Athletic and Literary Association, which fosters five regional festivals and a final festival on the New Orleans campus each year.

Mr. Edmonds has long believed in interscholastic and intercollegiate activity to stimulate interest in the stage. Pointing out the gain in interest for athletics by intercollegiatism, Edmonds more than ten years ago organized the Negro Intercollegiate Dramatic Association composed of dramatic clubs at Howard University, Hampton Institute, Morgan College, Virginia Union University and Virginia State College. Annual "meets" at which prizes were awarded for merit aroused so much enthusiasm among the colleges that when Mr. Edmonds went to Dillard from Morgan he founded "The Southern Association of Drama and Speech Arts" to enable the Negro colleges of the deep South to get together too. Outside the framework of this association the Dillard Players' Guild has arranged exchange productions with dramatic groups at other colleges; its own annual tour takes it to such places as Tuskeegee Institute, Fisk University, Wiley University, Tennessee State College, Alabama State College, Talladaga College (all Negro institutions), and in 1940 to the University of North Carolina.

The results of this collaboration among the colored drama leaders Mr. Edmonds summarized in a speech he delivered at the Carolina Regional Theatre Festival in April 1940:

First of all, these organizations have laid a firm foundation for the development of Negro drama. In the second place, there has resulted a changed attitude in respect to drama on the part of the Negro college presidents and administrators. Only a dozen years ago there was no teacher employed in the 120 odd Negro colleges who gave even a considerable part of his time to drama. Today over thirty colleges have at least one teacher giving a great deal of his time to the subject. In addition there is a growing demand for college and high school teachers with training in the arts and crafts of the theatre.

Still another result of these organized efforts is that much headway has been made in getting young Negroes to write plays depicting Negro life, and in breaking down the prejudice of Negro audiences against seeing them. It may seem strange no doubt that this prejudice ever existed. But when one considers that most of the character creations the Negro audience has seen to date have been the black-faced clown, Uncle Tom servants, crap shooters, over-sexed females, ignorant ministers, and such like it is not surprising that the intelligent would rather not see them at all than to see these types as the sole representatives of the racial group. This prejudice against Negro material is being broken down largely because the few plays that have been written, as crude in craftsmanship as they undoubtedly are, have attempted to portray human beings with human strengths and human weaknesses whose skins only incidentally happen to be black. In short they have presented real Negro People instead of black-faced stereoptypes.

The real pioneers of the Negro educational theatre were in the generation before Randolph Edmonds. Men like Alain Locke, Montgomery Gregory and Sterling Brown, all of Howard University, dreamed of a theatre that would truly express the poetry, the laughter, the tragedy and the problems of their race. In the realization of their early dreams, Edmonds is but one of a slowly-assembling collegiate phalanx. Anne Cook in Atlanta, who started the first Negro summer theatre I know of, is another. So is Fanning Belcher in West Virginia and James Butcher at Howard University who among other things organized a Repertory Players of twelve members in 1937. During a period of six months they gave performances of *The Dreamy Kid*, *The No 'Count Boy*, an original play by Butcher and Richardson, wherever anybody would listen to them in or around Washington and devoted their spring vacation to a tour that took them to Philadelphia, Bridgeport and New Haven.

4

Four universities commend themselves particularly because of their theatre architecture which is either so unique or so magnificent that they require separate consideration from the other academic centers.

The campus of the University of Washington at Seattle stretches down to the waterfront of Lake Union; there moored to a pier is a more or less accurate replica of an old showboat. Actually it is no vessel and actually it is not moored but constructed on a permanent foundation of concrete pilings. Inside, however, and on its decks one is transported to the showboat of an earlier time—whitewashed boarding, brass rails, swinging lanterns, flying pennants, red velvet swags. And then one goes behind the curtain. Here 1860 gives way to 1940. The small stage has a thirty-five foot stretch to the grid, a revolving stage twenty-seven feet in diameter, a modern switchboard and dressing rooms with private lavatories and showers. This bijou of a playhouse has but a twenty-foot proscenium and seats only 220. In it were presented in 1939-40: *Dinner at Eight*, *The Bishop Misbehaves*, *She Loves Me Not*, *Disraeli*, *Room Service*, *Pygmalion*, *What a Life*, *Night of January 16th, Kismet, Petticoat Fever.* This is a heavy schedule, but the Showboat is open fifty-two weeks in the year. Each play has a run approximating six weeks.

The University of Washington has a second theatre farther back on the campus. It is called the Penthouse. Both the Showboat and the Penthouse are staffed by students; all productions in both are directed by the faculty and acted by students. Both are under the executive direction of Professor Glenn Hughes, head of the Drama Division and an exceedingly able administrator.

The Penthouse theatre was built in 1940. The name derives from the fact that performances between 1932 and 1940 took place in a penthouse on a nearby hotel. The new building is a small but handsome white modern structure. Its auditorium seating about 125 is elliptical in shape, with a center circular acting area. There is a domed ceiling from which pin-point spots strike the performers; four entrances to the stage and auditorium divide the audience into equal segments; a lobby encircles the auditorium. The walls and ceiling are oyster white, the floor is heavily carpeted with taupe velour; the comfortable seats are upholstered in scarlet velvet.

I attended the opening performance of *The Perfect Alibi.* It was a hand-picked audience: the cream of Seattle's social and intellectual life. I was one of three persons not in evening dress. No students were present. I entered to find the center acting area already set with modern furniture, lamps and decorations. When the audience had assembled, the lights dimmed out; they came up in a few seconds to reveal actors seated and standing where a moment before had been no one. It was the most interesting piece of business of the evening and at the beginning and end of each act it was repeated—silently, swiftly, in absolute darkness the actors appeared and disappeared. As for the play itself, it was given a slick, smooth performance and the acting was competent.

The production idea back of this Penthouse theatre I believe to be of great importance. As I shall have occasion to say at some length hereafter, I believe that the theatre must face the problem of a redefinition of its form as a result of the advance of the motion pictures. Mr. Hughes is also aware of this and has written: "What the motion picture cannot give us is the living presence of the actor and the complete text of the play. That is what the legitimate theatre still has exclusive possession of and that is what the Penthouse style of production lays the emphasis upon."

I question, however, whether the Penthouse does lay any greater emphasis on the living presence of the actor than does any other style of stage production. Certainly the situation is eminently conducive to establishing a contact and direct relationship between living actor and audience; the technique of acting employed, however, works in the opposite direction. Hughes has set down elsewhere as one of the "important points to be remembered in connection with this method of production: actors must be taught to ignore the audience, even though they are always facing some portion of it, and are frequently within four or five feet of the front row." By ignoring the audience, however, by concentrating on forgetting its presence instead of capitalizing on it, the principal value of the Penthouse stage is lost. By his choice of plays, Mr. Hughes makes this inevitable: for *The Perfect Alibi*, *Hay Fever* which was to follow, *The Milky Way* which preceded, and such other plays done there as *Three Men on a Horse, Room Service, You Can't Take It with You* were all written for a realistic, picture-frame theatre. Created in the convention of representationalism, they demand that actors pretend there is no audience. I see no advantage, therefore, in giving them a Penthouse performance.

To carry the Penthouse idea to its logical and esthetically significant conclusion, Mr. Hughes should encourage the writing of plays for this kind of theatre. If there were no satisfactory results from that, he should adapt those plays written in the so-called "presentational" style, which takes conscious consideration of the presence of the audience and is predicated on a theatre theatrical. Such plays as *The Cradle Will Rock, Our Town, Waiting for Lefty*, almost any intimate musical play, and any classic written before the advent of Ibsen and of naturalism—particularly, for instance, the Commedia dell'Arte—belong in this theatre far more than *Room Service* and *Hay Fever*.

Mr. Hughes, however, is an eminently successful showman. In the year and a half preceding my visit to Washington (October, 1940) the Division of Drama made a profit of eight thousand dollars. He claims, in fact, that his aim is toward "the successful operation of public theatres." Mr. Hughes bases this policy on two considerations: first, that the University, as the cultural center of its community has an obligation to provide it with programs of the arts, among these the theatre; second, that the best means of training people for theatre work is to have them involved in the actual operation of playhouses to which an audience constantly comes.

I concur heartily with the second of these points: in a theatre where two plays are always in performance, two others always in rehearsal and where every play runs six weeks, the participants gain incomparable experience. As for the first point, I believe that Mr. Hughes is right in theory but mistaken in his application. He is giving the community very infrequent examples of the finest theatre; insignificant commercial entertainment like *Three Men on a Horse* and *The Bishop Misbehaves* is no greater contribution to the cultural life of Seattle than the local movie houses regularly make. In his definition of "community," Mr. Hughes also evinces a surprisingly blind spot where his own student body is concerned. Public performances are given in both theatres every Friday and Saturday evenings. One half of each house is reserved on Friday nights for students at a twenty-five cent rate. Monday, Tuesday, Wednesday and Thursday evenings the theatre is sold out to private performances for clubs and other Seattle organizations. Consequently, with no season subscription arrangement of any kind, only 375 students from the student body of ten thousand receive any special consideration at the Penthouse and but 660 at the Showboat. In fact, probably not a great many more students see the plays at all. I am bound to believe that the Division of Drama, although popular with the citizens of Seattle, has fallen down in its responsibility to that educational community to which it first belongs.

In 1937 Stanford University opened its new Memorial Hall as a home for the speech and drama division. It was a magnificent edifice costing between six and seven hundred thousand dollars. Passing through an imposing lobby I entered the large theatre (there are two in the building) seating 1,750. Looking out across a wide orchestra pit and forestage, I saw the stage itself, framed within a forty-foot proscenium, stretching back forty or fifty feet. Behind this I could make out scene shops and technical offices. Beneath the stage I went to see vast storage space and more shops; then to the little theatre that seats two hundred. Elsewhere I examined other offices, dressing rooms, classrooms.

Not until Hubert Heffner came in 1939 as executive director of the Division of Speech and Drama and undertook to organize a fully functioning department did Stanford make any real effort to put this plant to maximum use. When I was there in the autumn of 1940 the division was still too young to have gained character. In the theatre branch, Mr. Heffner had secured the services of F. Cowles Strickland as dramatic director, Charles Vance as Mr. Strickland's associate, retained Waldemar Johansen as technical director and designer and Helen Green as costume director. Eight productions were presented in 1940: *The Poor of New York, Of Thee I Sing, The Wild Duck, St. Joan, Rain from Heaven, The Bartered Bride* as a joint production with the Music Department, and *Accent on Youth*. In addition there was a repeated performance of *She Stoops to Conquer*, originally done in the summer time, and performances of a new play, *Mr. Congressman*, presented in the small theatre and repeated later at Oakland, California.

Again, as I have observed before, the direction, designing, lighting and costuming are in the hands of the faculty for all productions. Here the seventy undergraduate majors and the sixteen graduate students do not as yet have even any workshop program in which they may undertake any original creative activity. With benefit of such a theatre building, however, the Stanford program should go forward; whether it will move toward a more scholastic approach (already the Ph.D. is offered) or toward a closer alignment with practical, creative theatre it is too soon to say.

On October 9, 1939, the University of Wisconsin was host to a distinguished gathering of theatrical and academic celebrities; the occasion was the opening of the million-dollar Wisconsin Union Theatre. Alfred Lunt and Lynn Fontanne were there with their entire *Taming of the Shrew* company to give the gala opening night performance. Lee Simonson and Michael Hare were there too, the former as theatre consultant, the latter the project designer. I arrived a year later to find the excitement of the occasion persisting.

This theatre is a wing of the Memorial Union Building. Save for a grant of $266,000 from the PWA, and a few gifts, it will be paid for by the students of the University who as members of the Union are its owners. Lee Simonson says:

In an article on theatre building originally published in the *Architectural Forum* in 1932, I said, in part: "Throughout the country a theatre will presently be as necessary an adjunct to a completely equipped school or college as a science laboratory or a gymnasium is today. These theatre buildings cannot be wholly specialized. They are the center of all a community's cultural interests and must be flexible enough to be easily converted for concerts, choruses, moving pictures, public lectures, regional conventions, traveling or local art exhibitions." . . . The unique value of the theatre activities as incorporated in the present plan is that they are part of such a social and cultural center . . . part of a building of which all the major portions are capable of constant and multiple use.

The visitor is given ample testimony to the "constant and multiple use" of this building. As I went from the main Union building into this great wing, I passed the bowling alleys; cushioned by cork and blanketed with walls of insulation, no sound may escape from this room. I passed ping-pong courts and the outing club's rooms with big fireplaces and a kitchenette adjoining. I went through various storage and small rehearsal rooms: in one *Stage Door* was being prepared. I came out into the handsome lower lounge, modern in decoration as is the whole building. Here another cast was holding first readings for *The Concert*. I ascended a sweeping staircase to the main lobbies, everywhere heavily carpeted, their glass walls commanding an incomparable view of Lake Mendota on whose very shores the theatre is built. These lobbies are extended along one side of the auditorium to form a gallery that was currently housing an exhibition of etchings, lithographs and wood blocks. Thence I went into the auditorium, severely streamlined, warm in color, indirectly lighted, with a seating capacity of thirteen hundred persons; I was shown curtains which might be drawn across, however, to reduce the capacity when greater intimacy may be desired. The electrically-driven orchestra pit may rise and fall from basement to auditorium floor or stage level. At that moment it was being lifted to stage height to serve as a lecture platform in front of the house curtain for Marjorie Kinnan Rawlings, author of *The Yearling*, who was to speak there that evening.

Backstage I went next to be shown the excellent switchboard, the lofty stage house; no provisions for revolving stage or wagon stages, no built-in cyclorama or light-bridge, no extraordinary depth; nevertheless more than adequate space for an average production. Behind the stage was a medium-sized workshop, half of it two stories high, without any paint frame. Here undergraduate volunteers were at work on scenery for *Stage Door*. I moved on through dressing rooms and costume rooms and back to the main entrance from the Union building proper. Here were the doors to the laboratory theatre, seating about 180 and half surrounded by three connecting stages backed by a plaster dome. This theatre was intended to serve also as a small lecture hall, and to be used for radio broadcasts and motion pictures as well. Four experimental productions are presented here annually by student directors. In 1939-40 *The Spook Sonata, The Sunken Bell, My Heart's in the Highlands,* and an original play, *The World Waits* were offered. The tour was completed by visits to radio rooms, the camera club's quarters, rooms in which groups of students were gathered to listen to phonograph recordings, offices, the hobby shops maintained by the Union and a clubroom for small parties.

To indicate further the multiple uses to which this theatre is put, I should like to list the occupants of the large theatre during November, the first full month after its opening:

Wisconsin Hoofers program
Football forum (four evenings)
Sunday Music Hour: University Symphony Orchestra
Significant Living lecture
Friendship and Marriage series (three evenings)
Concert by Ezio Pinza

Performances of *The Witch* by the Wisconsin Players (three
    evenings and one matinee)
University Orchestra rehearsals (three evenings)
Fraternity Lecture
Ted Shawn Dancers
University Band rehearsal and concert
Sixth Wisconsin Salon of Art Awards
University Chorus Rehearsal
Wisconsin High School play rehearsal and performance (dur-
    ing University's Thanksgiving holiday)
Union Forum
French play rehearsal and performance
"Wiskits" dress rehearsal.

To Porter Butts, director of the Memorial Union, this
program of varied activities bears witness to the social and
recreational service to which this Union Theatre is hospitable. To J. Russell Lane, director of the Theatre, on
the other hand, I suspect that the situation is tantalizing:
here is a fine theatre so constantly in use that the theatrically minded—to wit, the Wisconsin Players—have the use
of the stage only for actual performances and one or
two evening dress rehearsals. It can be seen that the Wisconsin Union Theatre is consequently much more than a
theatre—just as it was intended it should be; but the stage
arts themselves find little opportunity to flourish creatively, hemmed in among concerts and lectures, forums
and meetings.

I remarked above that this theatre will be paid for by
the students. When it was decided to build a new wing
to the Union, a vote was taken in the student body of
twelve thousand to determine what it should house: additional hotel bedroom facilities, more dining rooms or

ballroom spaces, etc. Eighty-seven per cent voted for a theatre. Mr. Lane told me that the most popular production after the theatre's opening was *Our Town* which played to audiences totaling 7,800 people. Of them he estimated that approximately eight hundred were students. This seems inexplicable: that eighty-seven per cent of the students vote for a theatre to which barely seven per cent come to see a play. Mr. Lane does not believe the reason is financial. He points out that season tickets to the five shows cost $1.50, two dollars and $2.50; whereas 511 of the $2.50 books were sold in 1940-41, and 729 of the two dollar books, only 125 of the cheapest seats were bought in subscription. The cause may lie partly in the competition of so many campus activities bidding for student time. All the great universities feel this is one reason why they receive such inadequate support from their student bodies. Whatever may be the explanations, the situation is significant.

At the University of Indiana on March 22, 1941, a still larger, grander and more expensive theatre was dedicated.[15] It cost the taxpayers of Indiana and the Public Works Administration $1,170,000. The Lunts were again in attendance, this time in *There Shall Be No Night*.

At the end of a landscaped drive stands this building: an imposing mausoleum of Indiana limestone, modern in design but with occasional exterior and interior ornament vaguely Byzantine. We enter from an outer lobby through

[15] This plant would seem to be the theatre-to-end-all-college-theatres, were it not that Oberlin College is about to erect a building yet larger, grander and more expensive still. (It is reputed that it will cost a million and a half dollars.)

portals the size of St. Peter's in Rome into the first of two
inner foyers. Here up to a height of twelve or fifteen feet
the walls are of black marble; above this stretching another
twenty feet or more to the coffered ceiling are Thomas
Hart Benton murals. Two staircases of lighter marble
sweep to the balcony. Elaborate lighting sconces cap the
newels. At once we are aware that this is no ordinary playhouse: the scale is that of the Baths of Caracalla. From
the second lobby we pass into a third, heavily carpeted,
with mirrored niches at each end and elaborate pieces of
furniture lining the walls. Great piers rise at intervals to
support the ceiling above which is the upper part of the
steeply-ramped orchestra floor.

We emerge by vomitories into the auditorium of the Hall
of Music. Like a smaller edition of the Radio City Music
Hall it appears—and not so much smaller at that, for it
seats 3,800 persons. The curved contour of ceiling and side
walls is also reminiscent of Radio City. Like its Manhattan
predecessor, this Music Hall has an hydraulically-operated
orchestra platform that may sink to the basement or rise to
the stage level; it also has ramps running out from the sides
of the proscenium surmounted by stone fretwork grilles
behind which varicolored lights glow and change their
hue. Here is space for an organ chamber and console.
There is only one balcony but it is vast. An electrically-
driven curtain may shut it and a part of the parquet off
and reduce the hall to an intimate theatre seating 1,300.

After a brisk walk, we are down the aisle and up onto
the stage with its sixty-foot proscenium and its seventy-
foot sweep to the grid. This stage could comfortably contain any production which the Metropolitan Opera Company might bring to Bloomington, Indiana, and the dress-

ing room accommodations for some seventy people would be adequate for all its principals and chorus. For the principals there are shower baths adjoining their rooms. Downstairs in a maze of storage rooms are quarters and more shower baths for the orchestra. As at Wisconsin, the stage is equipped with no unique modern machinery; there is the usual counterweight flying system and an excellent switchboard. Its modest workshop does have space for a paint frame.

A passage leads from the stage of the Music Hall to another stage; we follow it to find ourselves in a second theatre. This one has a more normal-sized stage behind a twenty-eight foot proscenium. Its auditorium seats four hundred; there is no balcony. This theatre makes up for the excess of lobbies in the Music Hall by having none at all; inveterate smokers must don mackintoshes and stand outdoors if the night is wet. The walls of this theatre are also lined with Benton murals which the non-smokers may contemplate in the intermissions.

The rest of this great edifice is filled with offices for the staff, classrooms, a radio broadcasting studio and one rehearsal room on the top floor. There are none of the non-theatrical, recreational facilities to which much of the Wisconsin Union Theatre is devoted. The Hall of Music, I presume, will be used for concerts, opera and convocations appropriate to its size; not many plays will profit by performance in such a vast place. The little theatre will be the home for most undergraduate dramatic activity. In 1940-41 this consisted of a series of seven productions: *Outward Bound*, *What a Life*, a vaudeville-variety program, *Ah*, *Wilderness*, the Jordan River Revue (an all-campus musical show), *The Two Martyrs* (a new manuscript play), and *Family Portrait*. The rehearsal room will house the program of six workshop productions of original plays which are presented in connection with the speech courses.

Inhabiting this vastness will be the speech division of the English Department, headed by Professor Lee Norvelle, who becomes the impresario *in loco*. This speech work is divided into four fields: debating, drama, speech correction and radio; it attracts in all these fields a total of about fifty undergraduate majors and about twelve M.A. candidates. In the drama section Mr. Norvelle is assisted by a staff of two. Together they direct, design and produce the major plays.

It will be interesting to see to what use Indiana University puts this million-dollar plant. Since, as I have said, it presumably will serve principally as a hall for concerts and convocations, perhaps it should not properly receive consideration as a theatre at all. But since Mr. Norvelle claims it as one, it is to be hoped that the University is ready to increase appreciably the faculty in drama by adding a number of first-rate instructors and theatrical artists; to install a resident playwright or two; to invite other actors, directors, designers for short periods; to draw traveling companies of plays and operas to Bloomington; in other words to make this theatre a center for Middle Western theatrical activity. If it has not that intention, through lack of funds or of desire to develop such a program, then the University will be subject to the criticism that it has built a great palace and has nothing worthy to put into it. Indiana is assuming a great responsibility in erecting such a monument to the arts. She must see to it that her contribution to creative drama and to the American educational theatre field is great enough to justify this vast investment.

5

A long time ago, before the first World War—to be precise, on Shakespeare's birthday in 1914—the Carnegie Theatre of the Carnegie Institute of Technology was opened with a performance of *The Two Gentlemen of Verona* under the direction of Thomas Wood Stevens. Thus Carnegie Tech became a pioneer in the educational theatre, for excepting George Pierce Baker's "47 Workshop" course at Harvard, no institution of higher learning had taken significant steps toward welcoming the theatre into its midst.

In the years since 1914 Carnegie Tech has presented over five hundred different plays. There have been performances of twenty-six of Shakespeare's plays, nine Greek tragedies, from two to six each of plays by Molière, Racine, Ibsen, Chekhov, Dumas, Hauptmann, W. S. Gilbert, Pinero, Wilde, Yeats, Synge, Shaw, Rostand, Masefield, Galsworthy, Sheridan, Goldsmith, Dunsany, Maeterlinck, Pirandello and more than seventy plays written by students of the department.

Glendenning Keeble, Director of the School of Fine Arts, made the following statement on the occasion of the department's twenty-fifth anniversary in 1939:

The teaching of the drama department is governed by the following principles. The first is based on the conviction that in a profession which embraces as great a variety of activities as the theatre does, the most significant achievements are made by those who understand thoroughly its multiple aspects, who can use the allied arts in its service, and who have considered its place in the pattern of contemporary life. Consequently, whatever the major interest of the student—acting or directing, writing or designing—he must gain a working knowledge of every phase of the production of a play and the operation of a theatre. . . .

The second principle springs from the belief that only in performance on a stage, working with others before an audience, can the student complete the lesson begun in the studio and classroom. Fundamental theory may be taught and exercises practiced in classrooms, but not until the student can command and apply this material under the very special and exacting conditions of an actual performance has his training been complete and effective. For this reason the work of the department involves the regular production and frequent performance of plays chosen to encompass a variety of historic periods and styles.

This succinct statement of academic purpose and practice is applicable not only to Carnegie Tech but to any institution where serious work is being undertaken. It is not then in its adherence to such principles that this work is unique, but rather in two other characteristics. The first is that this is a professional school with the avowed purpose of preparing artists to pursue a theatrical career. The second is that the core of the work here is the training of the actor. Furthermore the major emphasis is on the undergraduate level where Carnegie offers a full four-year course in all of the arts of the theatre. To my knowledge this is the only place where such complete specialization is possible to candidates for the A.B. degree.

Through his freshman year the embryonic Barrymore is subjected to a number of fundamental courses in the various theatrical techniques. These are continued into his sophomore year when he becomes a member of the company from which all major and upper-class studio productions are cast and in which he will remain—if acting continues to be his forte—until he graduates. The eight major productions regularly have alternating casts which are usually rehearsed five weeks and have eight to twelve performances in the theatre. In addition, about forty short plays are produced annually in the studio theatre.

In his upper-class years the student chooses one major field of specialization: either acting, production or playwriting. In 1940 there were approximately one hundred students enrolled in the department of drama at Carnegie Tech of whom about half a dozen were specializing in playwriting. Production and acting attracted the remainder in about equal proportion. By the usual weeding-out process, about twenty students annually receive a degree. Of these approximately one-third go into the professional theatre, one-third go into teaching or other non-professional theatre work, one-third turn to other professions.

One of Carnegie Tech's recent policies appears to be the hospitable inclusion on its faculty of talent from the professional theatre. In 1939, to its staff of seven under the chairmanship of Henry Boettcher, the well-known actress Mary Morris was invited to bring her knowledge of the theatre and her technical skill. In 1940 Thomas Job, the playwright, came to the Pittsburgh campus to guide student dramatists. In 1941 the composer and conductor, Lehman Engel, was invited to stage a gay and unconventional production of *The Beggar's Opera* in the Carnegie

Theatre. Carnegie Tech seems once again to be pioneering in a new direction: toward the breakdown of that barrier which in so many places separates the professional from the non-professional theatre.

I have characterized the Department of Drama at the Carnegie Institute of Technology as a professional school built around the art of acting and functioning primarily on the undergraduate level. The Department of Drama of Yale University may be characterized as a professional school also, but built around the art of playwriting and functioning primarily at the graduate level.

If one man were singled out as the master of theatre in the world of American education, the late George Pierce Baker would be the inevitable choice. His work is so well-known that I need make only the briefest, albeit respectful, acknowledgment to his profound and unique contribution. The illustrious careers of such pupils of his as Philip Barry, Eugene O'Neill, Sidney Howard, Lee Simonson, Robert Edmond Jones, Robert E. Sherwood, John Mason Brown are sufficient testimony in themselves; the Yale University Theatre and its flourishing department bear further witness; and the whole expansion of the theatre through the colleges and universities is the final tribute to his life—for in half a hundred places his disciples and pupils have made it their work to perpetuate his high purposes, and educators on many campuses consciously or unconsciously have been influenced by him to accept the theatree into their academic households.

My concern here, as throughout this book, is to record my impressions of Yale based on its appearance today and not merely to repeat its illustrious history. There is no doubt that it occupies a position of pre-eminence in the educational theatre.

The Department of Drama offers one of the four professional courses of the School of the Fine Arts at Yale University. It takes its place by the side of instruction in architecture, painting and sculpture. As a result the theatre is taught as an art—not as an offshoot of public speaking or literature.

The staff of eleven, under the chairmanship of Allardyce Nicoll, includes several distinguished theatrical names: Walter Prichard Eaton, Donald Oenslager, Stanley McCandless, Frank Bevan, responsible respectively for instruction in playwriting, scene design, lighting and costume design. This department was founded, as I have already said, with the playwright as its core. To enable the playwright to see actual performances of his work, Professor Baker admitted directors, designers and technicians to the school. Gradually, however, these latter fields came to attract more students than the playwriting course, and threatened to dominate the picture. Out of 125 students in 1940, for example, only about thirty were specializing in playwriting; as for the rest, the chief interest of eight was in designing, ten in acting, five in costuming, five in lighting, six in technical work, six in historical scholarship, and about fifty in directing.

Mr. Nicoll points out, however, that because only about one-quarter of the department is specializing in playwriting it must not be construed that it receives that small proportion of importance. It must be borne in mind that to give productions to the work of thirty authors, many more than that number of interpretative artists are necessary. Nevertheless, I am bound to say that playwriting does not appear to have the significance here that it had in Mr. Baker's day: no outstanding literary accomplishments may be attributed to Yale in the last five to ten years.[16]

The program of activity at Yale is heavier than at any university drama department I visited. In addition to an elaborate schedule of courses, the department produces between seventy and eighty plays a year. There are regularly five major productions directed by the faculty. As many of these are original full-length plays by departmental students as are deemed worthy of such presentation. There are about twelve workshop productions—this number varying with the number of candidates for M.F.A. in direction each year.[17] These M.F.A. candidates are required in their third year (the course at Yale is three years) to produce either "a drama of any period previous to 1850, or an original long play" and the workshop series makes possible the meeting of this requirement. The second year students majoring in direction are required to present a one-act play each semester, which accounts for between fifty and sixty short plays. In addition, once every two or three years, a so-called "epic" production is presented: a classic directed, designed, lighted and costumed by the faculty.

With this production schedule the Yale student has his days packed with actual stage experience, for in the presentation of these plays each student director must depend on the other members of the department to participate

[16] It is true, however, that it may be ten years after college before a playwright is heard from, since dramaturgy is an art requiring maturity and literary sophistication.

[17] The M.F.A. and Ph.D. are the only degrees offered at Yale, the latter exclusively for "historical or critical study of the theatre."

in his production. Since "the aim of the faculty is to en-
sure that every student shall be acquainted with all aspects of theatrical art," playwrights and technicians must
take their turn at acting, just as authors and directors must
put in hours at crew work.

The three fields that have been built up to support
playwriting at Yale are direction, design and technical
production, scholarly research. Until 1940-41 there had
been no specialization in acting, and in a place where all
phases of stage production have been developed to such a
degree it seems surprising that training for the acting profession has not been offered. As this phase becomes more
developed under the leadership of Constance Welch, Yale
will have a better-rounded theatre and its potential playwrights a better chance to see in the hands of good performers the merit in their work.

In the field of historical and critical theatrical research
Yale has taken an increased interest under the chairmanship of Professor Nicoll. Mr. Nicoll, himself an eminent
British scholar, has attempted, without sacrificing the practical professional training which this department of drama
has always emphasized, to build a scholarly base. Pointing
out that this is not a vocational school but part of a university, he feels that through the historical and critical
approach to the stage this department may best justify itself as part of such an institution as Yale.

The growth of this academic approach has, however,
been complemented by a strengthening of the professional,
accomplished by inviting to Yale a number of guest experts of the professional theatre. In 1939-40 Otto Preminger took over a part of the direction work done by Alexander Dean who died in the summer of 1939. Dr. Premin-

ger came with a background of professional directorial experience in Vienna, Berlin, Hollywood and Broadway. In 1940-41 a series of six-week lectures was given by Harley Granville-Barker, Theodore Komisarjevsky, Arthur Sircom, Dr. Preminger and Elmer Rice; Mr. Komisarjevsky was also invited to stage one of the major productions, *The Cherry Orchard*, that was informed with the humor, social implications, nostalgic atmosphere of the old Russia with which Mr. Komisarjevsky is so thoroughly conversant. These frequent contacts of the students with directors as well as with designer Oenslager, costumer Bevan and lighting expert McCandless, all in touch with the professional theatre, have helped to keep Yale from becoming too academically didactic.

I have said that the Yale Department of Drama is a professional school. I mean this in the sense that it prepares for a career connected with the stage, but not necessarily in the professional theatre itself. That is to say, while perhaps one out of every four of its graduates may become a professional craftsman, the other three will become teachers of theatre or professional leaders of the nonprofessional stage.

The Yale Drama School, however, seems to believe that teachers and leaders of the non-professional theatre should receive the same kind and intensity of training as those intending to "go into the theatre" of Broadway. This is a sound point of view, but it is not sufficient. For the leader in the theatre outside of New York must be more than a trained technical specialist. He must be prepared, as Carl Glick, an outstanding writer and director in this field has pointed out, to devote fifty per cent of his energy to "community organization, business administration, promotion and publicity, social and recreational and cultural activities benefiting the theatre, making contacts with the community, teaching the arts of the theatre."

Yale, however, devotes a minimum of attention to the second fifty per cent of a director's duties; its graduates go out with exceptional training and skill in the technique of play production but with little or no consciousness of the administrative and broadly sociological problems involved. While at Yale they perceive no effort being made to relate the program of the Drama School to the university community or to the city of New Haven. Admission to all its public performances is by invitation only and most of the student work is witnessed only by the other departmental members. During their years of training they are part of a theatre that operates in a vacuum, or at least in disregard of the public around it.

The Yale Drama School appears to be strongly wedded to the theatrical status quo. All the research on which it prides itself is historic. I saw few signs of the development or even the encouragement of a creative approach to the stage, with the single exception of lighting technique. It may be that Mr. Oenslager would like his students to invent new theatrical forms, but the results are a sheaf of drawings by little Oenslagers.[18] Mr. Eaton may encourage playwrights to strike out in new directions, but he has produced no worth-while dramatists who do so. Frank McMullan, who succeeded to Alexander Dean's course for directors, may wish to stimulate creative direc-

---

[18] In all fairness it must be admitted that students under a strong master anywhere have a tendency to go through a period of imitation. It is perhaps not entirely Yale's fault if the period of imitation is infrequently passed beyond.

tion, but his students go forth with a knowledge of Dean's principles embodied in a syllabus which has become their Bible, because by rigid adherence to his admonitions even the most talentless can turn out a workmanlike job.

I am aware that a grounding in the past's accomplishments is an important part of the educative process in any field; but the translation of that grounding into creative endeavor must be concurrent—at least where a living art is concerned. Yale graduates, I have observed, exhibit an impatience with experiment, with any approach to theatre which is not compatible with the school of thought in which they were trained. Technical facility has become an end and not a means. After all, it is not the letter but the spirit which endures. Yale stands in danger of becoming absorbed by the letter.

As the work at Carnegie Tech centers around the art of the actor and at Yale around the pen of the dramatist, so at Western Reserve University in Cleveland the Department of Drama and Theatre, under the direction of Barclay Leathem, is focused upon the training of stage directors. In a comparatively few years Western Reserve has become one of the most prominent educational theatre centers in the country with 125 students registered in all courses. Mr. Leathem is a theatre administrator with an enviable flair for public relations and one of the most ardent and eloquent apostles of the non-professional theatre movement in America.

Probably the most interesting characteristic of Western Reserve's drama department is its relationship to its community—a matter of no concern to Yale. This school's recognition of the fact that it is training leaders for the non-professional theatre and its appreciation of the social implications in community service color all its activities. At every turn the students—particularly its ten candidates for the M.A. and its one Ph.D. candidate—are made aware of the problems of community enterprise. As at the University of Minnesota, student directors are frequently sent out to produce for an amateur group. Problems of non-professional theatre organization and management are frequently discussed, both abstractly and as they apply to various Cleveland groups in whom the University takes an interest. The department sponsors an annual Ohio High School Drama Festival; it issues a quarterly bulletin "Spotlight" devoted to news of and for Ohio school, college and community theatres; it operates a loan library of over twenty-five hundred plays available to these theatres. It maintains a close liaison with the Cleveland Play House; not infrequently its students appear in Play House productions and to the Play House all its graduate students go for courses and seminars in rehearsal methods, stage production, and children's theatre led by the Play House staff. It also operates a summer theatre.

Students at Western Reserve do not learn direction according to one set system. In 1940 Mr. Leathem invited Edwin Duerr, a brilliant young director from California, to be his associate in the department. Mr. Duerr's strong predilection for "presentational" style has provided a stimulating counter-irritant to Mr. Leathem's more psychological technique. Students exposed to both discover that there is no right-and-wrong in creativeness. Graduate students brought into contact with the Cleveland Play House staff are provided with still other and perhaps opposing approaches to theatre technique.

The production program at Western Reserve offers more variety than Yale's; perhaps because the lack of emphasis on playwriting releases space for other contemporary work; side by side with experimental productions of such plays as *The Spook Sonata* and *Murder in the Cathedral*, have been presented *The Merchant of Yonkers* by Thornton Wilder and *Thunder Rock* by Robert Ardrey, neither overly successful in New York but both decidedly worth further hearings. I saw an excellent performance of the latter with settings by Arch Lauterer of Bennington College who as guest designer-director also assisted in the staging. Western Reserve likes to enlist outside talent: Victor Schreckengost of the faculty of the Cleveland School of Art has designed several of the department's other productions; in the summer theatre Lester Lang of the Dallas Little Theatre and I have been guest directors.

As far as actual experience and thoroughness of training is concerned, Yale's students of theatre have a great advantage over Western Reserve's. There have been only six major productions a year at the latter—plus those few assignments to organizations off the campus—and all six have been staged by the faculty. The actual opportunities to direct have been limited on the graduate level to a Saturday morning series of scenes staged for no audience. Undergraduate third- and fourth-year students direct classroom scenes on which they have worked in class time for four weeks with casts of second-year students. Before undertaking this laboratory work they have received a six-week grounding in the principles of directing. This and a one-semester advanced course have been all the instruction offered in direction to undergraduates. (For graduates there have been a couple of seminars and the Play House rehearsal seminar.) The lack of adequate actual thorough training and a certain air of disorganization seem to be Western Reserve's chief weaknesses and ones it will need to remedy if it is to send out leaders whose enthusiasm and vision may be coupled with knowledge and authority.

At Syracuse in up-state New York the University of Syracuse stands on a hill overlooking the city of 175,000 inhabitants. The University's director of dramatics is Sawyer Falk, small, sandy-haired, taciturn. Under his leadership is one of the most stimulating dramatic programs conducted in any educational center in the country.

The first unusual circumstance the visitor to Syracuse notes is that the University's theatrical activity is centered not on the campus in any playhouse large or small, but in a downtown theatre—an ex-vaudeville house standing on a busy thoroughfare. On one corner is a motion picture house: Mickey Rooney's *Andy Hardy* is on view there. Across the street from it is a playhouse. Its marquee bears the legend: CIVIC UNIVERSITY THEATRE. The easel boards at the sides announce: "*Family Portrait* opening next Monday." Within is a long, narrow, rather dingy auditorium seating sixteen hundred persons; it stretches toward a stage, framed in an old-fashioned, gilt proscenium, with a vast apron but no great offstage or overhead space.

By leasing this theatre in 1936, the University, as Mr. Falk wrote:

took upon itself the custodianship of the drama in its particular community. Such a step was posited on the belief that the theatre is essentially communal and that a university drama department must step beyond its own campus and its strictly academic audience if it is to contribute to the development of a concept for an American theatre.[19] We believed that the nearer this new enterprise approached the conditions of the actual theatre, the more completely would it realize this concept, and we aimed as a true function of a university to establish a laboratory for the study, in an adult way, of a definite social institution.[20]

To accomplish this purpose, Mr. Falk worked out a five-point program which has materialized with varying success during the past five years. Its cornerstone has been the University productions: a series of eight plays a year chosen in line with a policy which Mr. Falk enunciates thus:

For our theatre we must select plays that establish the theatre in its own right, not plays that offer pallid substitutes for motion pictures, not merely domestic drama. The plays must be expansive and panoramic: plays of verbal beauty; with imagination. We must return to the theatre of Shakespeare and Sophocles, to the O'Neill of *Lazarus Laughed* rather than of *Beyond the Horizon;* to the Anderson of *High Tor* and *Sea Wife* rather than of *Saturday's Children. Three Men on a Horse* and *Personal Appearance* can be more satisfactorily done in the movies.

His list of recent productions consequently includes *Hedda Gabler, The Master Builder, Little Eyolf, Ghosts,*

[19] Glenn Hughes in Seattle has echoed this same point.
[20] It is in the breadth of his conception of theatre as a social institution that Falk outreaches Hughes.

Martine and *L'Invitation au Voyage* by Jean Jacques Bernard; *Tartuffe, Georges Dandin, L'Avare* by Molière; Galsworthy's *Loyalties;* O'Neill's *The Great God Brown;* Lynn Riggs' *The Cherokee Night* and *Big Lake;* Strindberg's *The Father; The Inspector-General* of Gogol and Dan Totheroh's *Distant Drums* and *Live Life Again!* These have been for the most part staged in styles that attempt to break away from sheer representationalism, and with a standard of excellence that judging from the *Family Portrait* performance I saw, is as high as any educational theatre I have observed.

Syracuse's interest in new playwrights, while by no means as significant as Yale's, is nevertheless noteworthy. Mr. Falk offers a course in playwriting, allows the substitution of a full-length play for the master's thesis. Totheroh's *Live Life Again!* was but one of a number of new plays by independent dramatists which have received pre-Broadway premières at Syracuse. Mr. Falk is also interested in the musical stage. Few, if any universities, he claims, "have attempted to encourage writers and composers to put together anything more than a 'college show' in the musico-dramatic field." Syracuse's recent original musical revues, *Life Goes to College* and *Bring on the Music,* have therefore been considered of as much importance as the dramatic plays.

The second in Mr. Falk's five-point program may be summarized in his own statement, "the word 'theatre' must, and without any condescension, be widened to include the cinema, for both financial and artistic reasons." In addition to courses in cinema technique and cinema appreciation, the Civic University Theatre presents a series of twelve motion pictures a year primarily devoted to unusual, foreign or "art" films.[21] Mr. Falk believes in a correlation of film and stage and to this end presented experimentally as a double bill the "living newspaper" *Power* and the documentary film *The River*. His desire was to place into juxtaposition the two mediums' handling of documentary material. The result was that part of the audience came primarily to see the picture, part to see the play; but each received both and the comparison and contrast must have been stimulating. Finally, the Dramatic Activities program in 1939 prepared its own documentary film—a presentation of the interests of the Community Chest of Syracuse. This provided an opportunity to the students to apply those cinematic theories they had been studying.

The third point in the Syracuse program relates to the establishment of a children's theatre. Under the direction of a graduate assistant an acting company of children between the ages of seven and seventeeen has been formed, varying in number between forty and 350. Usually two plays a year are presented to an audience of from six hundred to three thousand children who pay fifteen cents. Here, as in the Civic University Theatre proper, a performance may include a Mickey Mouse movie side by side with a play by living actors.

Community participation in drama Mr. Falk recognizes as a part of any broad theatre program looking toward the establishment of the stage as a strong social institution. So under the banner of Dramatic Activities of Syracuse

[21] Such a series of films, usually obtained from the Film Library of the Museum of Modern Art, New York, are presented in several other colleges and universities. I recall announcements of their showing at Amherst, Cornell, University of North Carolina and several other places.

University he has set up a community theatre organization. When I visited Syracuse in 1940 it had not yet any independent life of its own. It had presented only one play, *Excursion*, with Whitford Kane as guest director and star. In its production the University provided the theatre, production facilities; the crew and actors were composed of townspeople, a few faculty members, and some students whose homes were in Syracuse.

Such a theatre becomes not only of value to the community but is useful to the University as a laboratory for those students looking forward to a career of community theatre leadership. With this dual end in view, Mr. Falk looks forward to the establishment of other groups within the sphere of university influence. New low-priced housing projects recently set up in Syracuse offer a fertile field for such developments. The idea of establishing a Negro community theatre also appeals to Mr. Falk.

Finally, the Syracuse Dramatic Activities program would like to bring outside professional companies to the city to perform in its theatre. This has not yet been carried far: sponsoring Nazimova and her company in *Ghosts* has been its only successful undertaking. If and when this plan is realized and the children's and community theatre projects are further developed, the University of Syracuse will stand in the vanguard of educational theatres. Even today I do not begrudge it a place there.

I wish I had been in Waco, Texas, in April, 1940, when the Baylor-Civic Theatre presented *The American Way*. Waco had never seen anything like it, declared many in the audience of four thousand which crowded into Waco Hall to witness Kaufman and Hart's patriotic panorama.

There were 450 people on the stage: performers drawn from Waco High School, the Bachelor's Club, the drama group of the A.A.U.W., the Headquarters' Division of the 143rd Infantry, Baylor Chamber of Commerce, the Service League, Ars Nova (Baylor men's music organization), students of Baylor University's drama division, as well as many individuals affiliated with none of those organizations.

Paul Baker of Baylor University who engineered this mammoth collaboration of "town and gown" could say truly: "More people are working and acting in this play than have a chance to appear in an entire season in many little theatres." Mr. Baker considered this the first step in creating a combination university-community theatre. In 1940-41 the collaboration continued in a joint program of seven plays [22] in some of which townspeople performed with students, in others students appeared alone. A season ticket to these cost townspeople and students alike $1.25, the cheapest subscription rate offered by any theatre group recorded in this book.

Baylor's liaison with community enterprise does not end with this program. In 1939-40 the Drama Division took *Our Town* on tour through five Texas towns and presented it to audiences totaling three thousand people. Mr. Baker has elaborate plans for extension of this touring idea, which wait upon procurement of larger funds. Two large slum clearance Federal housing projects are under way in Waco, one for Negroes and one for whites. Like Sawyer Falk, Mr. Baker sees the assembly halls that each project

[22] *The Ghost of Yankee Doodle, The Merchant of Yonkers, Abe Lincoln in Illinois, Merry Wives of Windsor, Yellow Jack, Two on an Island* and *Margin for Error.*

will contain as ideal spots in which to foster community drama and provide a laboratory for Baylor students.

Dramatic activity at Baylor University is comparatively new. Working against a traditionally hostile Baptist prejudice, it is remarkable that any program at all has been set up. As it is, Mr. Baker has a long way to go. A plant in which to work is among the first necessities. The University has no theatre and Waco Hall, the only place available, is not only too vast, but is constantly used for state, county, city and university conventions so that even were it suitable, the theatre program would have far from exclusive use of it. Mr. Baker has prepared plans for a small theatre which will cost not many thousand dollars and will be highly flexible with stages on three sides of the audience, swivel seats for the spectators, a lighting system that will integrate auditorium lighting with stage effects, and other unique features. Baylor will be able to experiment along many lines of stage form. It is to be hoped that by the time this account is read the plans may have become an actuality.

In 1940-41 Mr. Baker was the sole instructor in drama; he was teaching four courses. As his faculty expands, he would like to add a technical director to work permanently; an acting coach, a designer and a playwright Mr. Baker would like to have on the staff for only one three-month term each year. In this way he feels that outstanding specialists, artists or exchange professors could be secured of a higher caliber than Baylor could afford to invite to join the staff permanently. Through this system of rotation Baylor students could have the stimulus of contact with a certain number of professional artists and gain a glimpse of a variety of theories and methods.

Mr. Baker also hopes to extend Baylor's theatrical service in the field of religious education. Believing there is need for a trained leadership in religious drama, and feeling that Baylor as an outstanding church school has obligations in this direction, he would seek to establish a center devoted to writing and to stimulating interest in church plays.

Western Reserve, Syracuse and Baylor Universities are outstanding in integrating their work with the needs of the surrounding community; Cornell and the Universities of Texas and Minnesota, as we have seen, are also aware of the possibilities of such a relationship; and there are others. The Department of Drama at the University of Utah has sent productions on tour during the entire Christmas vacation and several excursions with an individual play have occurred. *The Wingless Victory,* for instance, was recently taken out to Bingham, copper mining town near Salt Lake City, where it was presented in the employees' clubhouse of the mining company. Students frequently go out to direct plays in the Mormon churches which have active dramatic programs.[23] In the series of

[23] The Mormon Church has, since the days of Brigham Young, been concerned for the recreational life of its disciples. One of the first community theatres in the country was founded by the Latter Day Saints. Today the church has a noteworthy policy. It secures several plays annually from agencies by paying a blanket royalty running into four figures. These plays it then makes available to church dramatic groups at very reduced rates. Thus it stimulates production of superior plays at costs even the most struggling groups can afford. Robert Porterfield, in the report of a survey made in 1940 on the state of dramatics in the Commonwealth of Virginia, recommends that such a blanket royalty arrangement be instituted by state boards of education to encourage the improvement of standards of play selection among the high schools.

major campus productions [24] alumni of the Department of Drama living in Salt Lake City frequently participate. Perhaps as many as twenty a year will assume roles requiring more maturity than any undergraduate can bring. Joseph Smith and Wallace Goates, directors, believe that such a liaison is valuable, both to undergraduates, who gain by working with more experienced people, and to alumni who are thus able to continue their participation in theatre after leaving college.

The interrelation of community and educational drama is the cornerstone of the Studio Theatre School in Buffalo and of the theatre program connected with adult study centers in St. Louis and at San Mateo, California. Jane Keeler, director of the Buffalo Studio Theatre School, founded in 1927, is also director of the Players, a loosely affiliated organization which is in reality a little theatre presenting seven plays to a subscription membership paying ten dollars a year. It is natural that most of the players are present or former members of the school. But the school occupies the center of the picture. In the full-time course that is offered only seven young people were enrolled in 1941, but approximately one hundred children are enrolled in Saturday morning classes and another 125 in adult once-a-week courses in play production, playreading, public and choric speaking, dance, fencing, etc. Miss Keeler is more interested in offering these courses for their recreational, cultural and therapeutic value than with any thought of training these people for theatrical careers.

Similar motivation caused Harold Bassage to found in

---

[24] In 1940-41 the series included *Ethan Frome, Elizabeth the Queen, Room Service, Margin for Error, Rain from Heaven.*

1939 the St. Louis School of the Theatre, loosely affiliated with the Adult Study Center of Washington University and with the Little Theatre of St. Louis. Mr.
Bassage, with a background of professional theatre experience, believes, however, in the fusion of the amateur and
professional stage and contends that these recreational,
cultural and therapeutic aspects of dramatic activity can
be best served by adherence to professional standards and
by maintaining a professional outlook. He has written:

Artistic ideals, intellectual interests and zeal have characterized amateur thespians, as high standards of trained talent and
workmanship have typified the profession. I believe that play
production in America can reach a new high in artistry and
skill, beauty and truth, through the combination of the finest
amateur and professional tradition.[25]

In his two years' direction of the St. Louis School, Mr.
Bassage made considerable progress. Partially perhaps
because his enrollment fees were about one-half as great
as Miss Keeler's, partially because credit in some of the
courses could be applied toward a B.S. degree from
Washington University, partially because Mr. Bassage
placed more emphasis on full-time work to train for professional careers, the St. Louis School in its first year had
half again as many students as the Buffalo Studio Theatre
School had in its thirteenth year: twenty-one were enrolled in the professional course, 243 in once-a-week
classes and fifty-nine in courses offered for University
credit.

The school had its own series of nine productions in
1939-40, offered separately from the Little Theatre. In

[25] In the *Quarterly Bulletin* of the National Theatre Conference.

1940-41 outstanding was the production of a "living news-paper" written by Mr. Bassage, a reassertion of faith in democracy in relation to the problems of these times. It was entitled *For You to Live* and in addition to eight per-formances at the Adult Study Center, it was performed before more than a dozen schools, clubs and churches throughout St. Louis. In more ways than one this school was becoming a community enterprise.[26]

San Mateo is an outlying Peninsula suburb of San Fran-cisco. At the San Mateo Junior College another Adult Center offers evening classes in many fields. It is with the drama division's classes called "Little Theatre Workshop" and "Play Production" that we are concerned. They are conducted by a talented and enthusiastic young man named Robert Brauns in the conventional classrooms of the Junior College. These classes are actually rehearsals of the plays offered under the auspices of the San Mateo Little Theatre. In other words, the Little Theatre decides the policies, provides the equipment, and sells tickets for a series of plays [27] acted by the Adult Center's classes and directed by Mr. Brauns whose salary is paid by the Center —an interesting collaborative working arrangement. Here again educational and community activity find outlet in a common program.

[26] In the autumn of 1941 Mr. Bassage left St. Louis to accept a post at the University of California; at the time of this writing the future of the St. Louis School of the Theatre appears uncertain.

[27] Plays of the past few seasons have included *The Daughters of Atreus, The Masque of Kings, The Ghost of Yankee Doodle, Street Scene, Bury the Dead, Our Town, The Circle, Barchester Towers, The First Mrs. Fraser, Noah, Family Portrait, The Merchant of Yonkers.*

6

A vivacious little lady with an Irish wit and reddish hair, indomitable will and ambition, great administrative and artistic ability is Hallie Flanagan. After four hectic but exciting years as national director of the Federal Theatre Project, she returned to her post as Director of the Vassar Experimental Theatre. In January, 1941, she could be found in snow-bound Poughkeepsie.

Mrs. Flanagan has long championed new theatrical forms; she has been aware too of the need for fresh playwriting material that reflected in the theatre the contemporary scene. The Vassar Experimental Theatre has been built on these foundation stones. Ever since Mrs. Flanagan's widely publicized presentation a dozen or more years ago of Chekhov's one-act play *The Marriage Proposal* in three styles offered consecutively: realistic, expressionistic and constructivist, the Experimental Theatre has shown a constant right to the use of that name. Mrs. Flanagan and her students have explored every form that challenged their imagination in an effort to break away from representationalism. Classics have been treated to all sorts of novel performances but never has there been a hackneyed or a conventional mounting.

One of Vassar's recent experiments was a presentation of *Our Town* using a combination of scenes from the play and cuttings from the motion picture. With Vassar's President MacCracken in the role of Stage Manager, the performance began as a stage play; after a bit a screen was lowered and the action continued with film sequences. When a passage was reached which the stage version seemed able to handle more successfully, the screen was removed and living actors came on to take up the story. This alternation of media in close juxtaposition became not only a fascinating theatrical experience for the audience but was a stimulating experiment for students who could thus attempt an assessment of the resources of film and stage. This kind of experiment the commercial theatre obviously could not have made; if it is to be done anywhere, certainly the academic theatre is the place for it. But Vassar and Syracuse are the only colleges I know of which have actually attempted anything like this.

Although classics and plays of contemporary dramatists which have received no previous Broadway hearing—Ernst Toller's *No More Peace* for example—are frequent in the Experimental Theatre's repertory, it has been to the presentation of original plays by Vassar authors that Mrs. Flanagan has devoted most energy and enthusiasm; she has frequently collaborated with student playwrights. Many of these have been works that loosely deserve the appellation "socially significant." Mrs. Flanagan told her co-workers at the beginning of the Federal Theatre Project in 1935, as she had been telling her students at Vassar:

New days are upon us and the plays that we do and the ways that we do them should be informed by our consciousness of the art and economics of 1935. . . .

In an age of terrific implications as to wealth and poverty, as to the function of government, as to peace and war, as to the relation of the artist to all these forces, the theatre must grow up. The theatre must become conscious of the implications of the changing social order, or the changing social order will ignore, and rightly, the implications of the theatre.[28]

Vassar presents but three major productions a year. The preparation period for each occupies at least six weeks and often two or three months. What a marked contrast to the programs of so many educational theatres which include twice or three times as many offerings with a maximum of three to four weeks to prepare each one. Mrs. Flanagan's devotion to new plays and to a creative approach makes this long period of growth essential.

In any place where creativeness is a goal an entirely different schedule of work must be arranged. As at Vassar, and for the same reason, the Bennington College Drama Division presents but three productions a year (and in one of these faculty and townspeople participate, so that it cannot be considered as one of its typical college productions). Bennington, nestling at the foot of the Green Mountains in southern Vermont, is probably the outstanding example of "progressive education" on the college level.

Let us see how its principles operate when applied in the field of the theatre. The focus of work here is not on classroom activity but on the functioning stage. Each of the two annual productions, in preparation for ten or twelve weeks, becomes the hub around which the academic wheel turns. The plays are selected, therefore, "for their excellence as drama and for the light they throw on our own or past periods of civilization. The effort is rather to 'put over' good material by making the audience feel its

[28] *Arena*, by Hallie Flanagan, page 45.

perennial vitality than to find material which local or undergraduate taste has already accepted." This statement, made by the Drama Division as part of a "Prolegomena to an Evaluation Study" continues:

The theoretical possibilities of drama as the core of an education along the line of the Humanities seem clear enough. The plays of a Sophocles, an Ibsen, a Shakespeare, are in fact "abstract and brief chronicles of their times." Their comparative brevity makes them excellent focal centers, where the quality of the student's knowledge of many fields may be proved in many ways—in making and doing as well as verbally. The effort to understand a good play for production leads naturally to a study of the political habits and ideas and facts of the arts, the manners, the philosophy, the religion of its time and place. The effort to design an appropriate setting for it or to "bring its characters alive" in performance compels the student to utilize all her knowledge and understanding; and it brings home to her the all-important distinction between what she knows and what she only knows about. Ideally the student should always be bringing to her work in drama what she has "really learned" in other fields, and then returning to her other studies to increase her mastery and understanding of drama.

The plays which Bennington has used for this purpose have included *The Contrast, Electra,* Turgenyev's *Where It Is Thin, There It Will Break, Les Femmes Savantes* of Molière, *Of Thee I Sing, Six Characters in Search of an Author, Noah,* a dramatization of *The Bridge* by Hart Crane, Ibsen's *Lady from the Sea, Turandot.*

With such an approach to play production as Bennington has outlined above, it can readily be seen that a four-week rehearsal period is far from adequate and that a program of the *What a Life–Room Service* variety would have no point. Here, as at Vassar, the historic approach is coupled to the creative. Under the leadership of Arch Lauterer and Mr. and Mrs. Francis Fergusson, the search for new theatrical forms is constant. Aiding this is the close association existing between dance, music and drama. Except for the Turgenyev, Ibsen and Pirandello works, all the plays listed above have incorporated both music and dance in their presentations.

In addition to these major productions are four drama workshop evenings at which one-act plays or scenes from long plays are presented under student directors. These are drawn from the weekly drama workshop meetings in which the forty girls of the Drama Division try out their own ideas, develop their technique and apply what they have learned in acting sessions and in individual conferences. Throughout the work at Bennington there is a constant interrelation of the literary study of drama, work in acting and in design, direction and presentational methods.

The criticism most readily leveled at the Bennington theatre by those who have come into close contact with it or with its students or its faculty is that it has an unrealistic approach to the stage of today, that it leads an ivory-tower existence, out of touch with the theatre of the market place and the cross-roads, that its mountain retreat is shrouded in a kind of haze. Seeking to counteract this charge in every department of learning, Bennington has designed a winter period, extending from Christmas to Washington's Birthday, during which students work independently at projects connected with their field of major interest away from the College. During this two-month period, girls specializing in theatre, for instance, have the opportunity to observe and occasionally to participate in productions on Broadway, in some outstanding community theatre or in some other educational drama center.

While there is some justification for the criticism suggested above, it is more than offset in my mind by the constructive, creative approach which Bennington brings to the teaching of theatre; by its insistence on rejecting the tried-and-true formulas, the set patterns. If but one of Bennington's students in each generation brings into the theatre somewhere some of that creativeness instilled in her during school days, the college will have been justified in its approach.

Before leaving the college campuses I should like to speak briefly about those universities where dramatics has persisted only as an extra-curricular activity. I visited but three such campuses during my trip through the United States, but I know of many times three universities where drama has not yet received the academic benison. Nevertheless, the spread of theatrical training through the institutions of higher learning has been so sweeping, as the contents of this chapter have indicated [29] that those outstanding universities which have failed to swim with the current challenge our attention.

The second largest university in the United States, the University of California at Berkeley, had neither a depart-

[29] In addition to the colleges and universities discussed in this chapter, see discussions elsewhere in this book of work at the University of Delaware, University of North Carolina, North Dakota State Agricultural College. During my trip I also visited and observed interesting work at Allegheny College, University of Arizona, Catholic University, University of Colorado, DePaul University, Ithaca College, Louisiana State University, University of Oklahoma, Rollins College, Smith College, Tufts College, Tulane University.

ment of drama nor a playhouse (if its outdoor Greek
Theatre be excepted) when I visited its campus in 1940.
Its plays were presented in a completely inadequate lecture hall under a director employed not by the University
but by the student body itself. A department is being set
up in 1941-42, however, and plans for a playhouse are
being contemplated, so California must be removed from
this category. Two other outstanding universities remain
on the bank, however, unwilling to dive into the troubled
theatrical waters: Harvard and Princeton.

At both universities such dramatic programs as have
taken place have been initiated by undergraduates themselves.[30] At Harvard the Hasty Pudding Club presents annually an original musical comedy; at Princeton the Tri-
angle Club does the same in its handsome McCarter
Theatre. Harvard has its Dramatic Club and a series of
plays done by the Student Union; Princeton has its
Théâtre Intime. Both musical comedy organizations employ professional directors. The Harvard Dramatic Club,
which has no theatre of its own, regularly engages a professional director for each of its productions. The Princeton Théâtre Intime, which does have its own playhouse in
a converted small auditorium, has always prided itself on
keeping everything about the organization and its productions in student hands. Proud too is it of its outstanding
alumni who have entered the theatre with no other training: Bretaigne Windust, Joshua Logan, James Stewart,
José Ferrer, Myron McCormick.

At both Harvard and Princeton in dramatics as in athletics the supply of able men varies: there are good years

[30] At Harvard, that is, since the departure of Professor George
Pierce Baker.

and lean years. When exceptional talent is present, these student groups are good; when talent or initiative takes a drop, without a permanent and mature leader there is no way to maintain a standard and the campus must wait upon the arrival of new talent, which may take several years.

This situation bids fair to continue at Harvard until such time as the University may establish a College of Fine Arts, when it seems likely that the drama would be included. At Princeton the situation is changing slightly through amplification of its Creative Arts Program to include drama. This program, financed by a grant from the Carnegie Corporation, has provided for the residence in Princeton of practicing artists in the fields of music, painting, sculpture and writing. Work with them has accorded students in the main no academic credit, but their presence and their informal assistance to those men aspiring to express themselves in these fields has proved fairly satisfactory.

In 1941-42 this Creative Arts Program added a "Director of the Dramatics Program." [31] Working extra-curricularly he was to undertake to assist the existing dramatic organizations toward the more constant maintenance of a high standard of excellence, without stifling undergraduate initiative or jeopardizing their independence. There was to be no extension of academic credit to embrace this work and no thought of setting up a drama department. Whether the Director can accomplish anything in such an anomalous situation will remain to be seen.

Princeton's objections to the establishment of a depart-

---

[31] To this post Princeton University appointed myself.

ment of drama are significant. Apparently it is not that this University does not regard the theatre as an art. It has, however, a deep-seated dislike of establishing at Princeton anything that resembles vocational training. Furthermore it believes that creative accomplishment in the arts cannot be measured by academic standards; that when this is attempted, a level of mediocrity is induced. In fields that do not lend themselves to historical or systematic treatment Princeton disapproves of giving academic credit. Except to teach the appreciation of an art or its criticism, it believes the conventional educational system of today is not suited. The extension and dissemination of knowledge by rule and precept, by familiarity with past accomplishment, which is applicable to the exact sciences and in some degree to the humanities, breaks down when applied to creative arts, unless one deals with individuals of talent; and talent cannot be satisfactorily measured and regulated.

Princeton's stand, which I am inclined to believe is Harvard's also, is taken, therefore, not so much out of indifference to the art of the theatre, as on the grounds of high regard for the nature of the creative process on the one hand, of academic standards on the other; and of the conviction that the two are incompatible. Princeton would prefer to leave these arts to the initiative and talent of such students as possess them, or to encourage them by a plan like the Creative Arts Program. I am bound to say that such a point of view awakens my strong sympathy.

7

Into this chapter devoted to the educational theatre must go some consideration of those independent professional schools of the stage which award no academic degree and whose primary purpose is to train actors and occasionally a director or designer for a career on Broadway or the cinema. As would be expected, the outstanding schools of this type are to be found in New York, Chicago and Hollywood. The description of half a dozen of them should suffice.

New York possesses a number of schools of dramatic art and many individual dramatic coaches. The oldest and most famous of these schools is the American Academy of Dramatic Art, founded in 1884 by Franklin H. Sargent. Here over two hundred young stage aspirants are enrolled in a two-year course that includes instruction in the usual curriculum of stage graces. Perhaps the most interesting aspect of their training is the weekly performances in which students appear before anyone who wishes to drop in. The value of undertaking a number of roles is great, although with so many students enrolled, it is easy to see that the individual does not actually appear very frequently. In any case I am inclined to believe that the training is stereotyped to the Broadway tradition. After all there is every reason why it should be, since it is the Broadway scene these young people are being prepared to enter.

Existing for the same purpose but employing rather

different methods are the Neighborhood Playhouse School of the Theatre and Tamara Daykarhanova's School for the Stage. Each of these schools believes in a long period of preparation without an audience; only one major public performance is given annually to an invited audience and that by the advanced students of the two-year course. The Stanislavski system in various modifications is the basis of the approach to acting in both schools.

Youngest of New York's schools for the stage is the Dramatic Workshop of the New School for Social Research, founded in 1939 under the direction of Erwin Piscator, distinguished German régisseur. It proposes to train for the theatre not only actors but directors, designers, playwrights and critics. For this purpose it has assembled a distinguished faculty that included in addition to Mr. Piscator, the actress Stella Adler, John Gassner, Mordecai Gorelik, and a number of guest lecturers. It is hard to see how the Group Theatre's subjective approach, which I assume is Miss Adler's, can be fused with Piscator's objective style without creating utter confusion in all but the maturest students. It is stimulating to the observer, at any rate, however, to discover a spot where some specific approach to the theatre is made. Mr. Piscator's positive "epic" presentational style may be stiff fare for students to digest, and it may be unsuited to America's theatre today, but without debating its merits, it must be agreed that he offers a challenge to which few American teachers or theatre artists seem to make any constructive reply.

The characteristic of all these New York drama schools is that they are removed from the actual experience of operating theatres (for the American Academy's weekly

performances are little more than class exercises). Whatever value there is in playing to audiences and in observing
public reactions to theatre is lost to students in these professional schools in New York.

In Chicago, however, the School of the Kenneth Sawyer
Goodman Memorial Theatre offers not only professional
training, but experience as part of a functioning theatre,
and also the additional possibility, through its connection
with the Art Institute of Chicago, of working for a B.F.A.
or an M.F.A. degree.

The Goodman Theatre, a handsome and beautifully
equipped playhouse, which first served as the home of a
professional repertory group, is now one of the schools of
the Art Institute. It has two stages—one in its main theatre
seating about six hundred, one for its small Studio Theatre.
It offers a three-year course and in this surpasses the professional schools in New York and many of the college
drama departments. Mornings are spent in classes, afternoons are devoted to rehearsals; for the Goodman Theatre
presents a series of eight plays to the members of the Art
Institute, twelve plays in the Studio Theatre (also open to
members) and three children's plays. Actual production
thus becomes the focus of the work.

Each play in the members' series (which is also open
to the general public for one dollar) runs approximately
two weeks. Major roles in this series are played by third-
year students and by the two or three young people whom
the faculty invites to stay on for a fourth year at a small
salary. The children's series, in which Saturday matinees
of each play are given for seven or eight weeks, utilizes
second- and third-year students in major roles; in the

Studio Theatre series the second-year students are given their chance to play major parts.

This is essentially a school for actors and about ninety per cent of the 150 students specialize in acting. The advanced group consists of about twenty, which means that in the members' performance series these students should have the opportunity to play a number of parts, and always for a two-week run to a cosmopolitan Chicago audience in a downtown theatre. I was impressed with the caliber of Goodman Theatre productions: with the talent of its student actors, with the methods and artistic surety of its teacher-directors, Maurice Gnesin and David Itkin, with its scenic excellence for whose designs Spencer Davies and for whose execution Howard Wicks are regularly responsible.

I have already referred to the School of the Pasadena Playhouse. Among the quantity of studios and schools of acting adjacent to Hollywood it is the only one with a permanence and distinction worthy of mention.[32] It is approximately the same size as the Goodman Theatre School and it likewise has a three-year course (a fourth-year group was functioning as a separate little theatre in Santa Monica when I visited California in 1940-41). It is also primarily a school for actors—although only about two-thirds of its students aim at acting careers, I am told. First-year students appear in a series of classical plays presented privately; second-year actors are seen by such public as attends the "senior series" of the Playhouse; third-year actors appear occasionally on the main stage and in laboratory theatre and Playbox productions.

[32] An exception to this statement may be the Max Reinhardt school which I did not visit.

All of these professional schools are faced with the same problem if they are honest with themselves and their students: what is to become of their graduates? Are they not preparing for a profession which is practically non-existent? Pasadena replies by placing its hope in nearby Hollywood where there are employment possibilities. A solution for the Goodman Theatre School would appear to lie in the creation of a permanent theatre company on a professional level composed of graduates of the School. The presence of a superb plant, the Art Institute connection with its civic implications, a growing public numbering into the thousands already supporting this theatre are all factors of which the directors of the Art Institute should make use in providing Chicago with a real resident civic theatre combined with an academy.

None of these other schools, however, has such a solution to offer, and the only other possible opening I see for their graduates—outside of a career in radio—is for them to try to create theatres. The chief stumbling block lies in the fact that these youngsters are primarily actors and their training has included nothing to do with theatre management. Notwithstanding, occasional groups have banded together like the American Actors Company, composed of graduates of the Daykarhanova School in New York. Perhaps local resident theatres of the future will rise from such groups.

8

Inevitably the educational theatre invites comparison with community drama. Actually only a few comparisons can be validly made, for the background and conditioning circumstances of each are quite different. Certain of those criticisms leveled against the little theatres are not applicable to the college and university theatres; instead other new ones must be made.

The consciousness of the stage's social obligations and the relation of the playhouse to the people seems more often present and better understood on the campus than in the little theatre. The ideal of community service is more frequently voiced there and an effort to implement its practice with a program of co-operative usefulness is manifested again and again.

One criticism I made of the community theatres was of the shifting about of its professional directorate to such an extent that often no consistent and long-range program could be set up and executed. The university theatres, perhaps by their very nature, are not subject to this criticism. The careers of men like Professors Drummond, Mabie, Hughes, Koch, Arvold, Leathem, all of whom have devoted the better part of their lives to building up a theatre in one spot, bear witness to the strength that derives from permanence.

Kenneth Macgowan in 1929 wrote: "Radical experimentation in original and unconventional plays and in scenic production goes on much more in the universities than in the other local theatres, with the possible exception of the Pasadena Community Playhouse, the Goodman Theatre, the Cleveland Play House, and the Hedgerow Theatre of Rose Valley, Pennsylvania." In general, this statement still holds good twelve years later, although Mr. Macgowan's adjectives must be toned down. "Radical" and "unconventional" are too daring words to apply to all but a very little of what goes on in campus play-houses. Nevertheless, it is certainly true that more original plays are produced in the educational theatre and for the most part their repertories include many more ancient and modern classics than do the community theatres'. Experiments in form and technique, like an amusing Commedia dell'arte production presented in 1940 at the University of Texas, like Glenn Hughes' architectural innovations do occasionally occur.

That the universities follow the Broadway pattern less closely than the community theatres may be attributed in part to their educational obligations, in part to the fact that they are less dependent on their box offices. The average little theatre must be self-supporting; the college theatre regularly occupies a building on which it pays no mortgage and no rent, employs a staff whose salaries are paid by the institution. Only actual production costs must be met out of ticket sales and occasionally, as at Yale, Carnegie Tech and Vassar, even these are taken care of by endowment funds. So it can be seen that the campus theatres not only can lower their price scale, which, as we have seen, they regularly do, but can also devote themselves more readily to creating standards (which should after all be their function) than to satisfying pre-existent tastes.

The wonder then is that the educational theatre has not gone in more completely for creative dramatic technique. Except for the programs at Bennington, Vassar, Syracuse and occasional isolated work by an instructor like Edwin Duerr or a student at Yale, I found almost constant adherence to the traditional and historic approach to the theatre. The kind of creative research in the sciences that is conducted in the academic laboratories under a Millikan or a Compton finds no counterpart in the arts.

This may be laid partly at the doors of the institutions themselves who do not encourage such an approach. The art of the theatre is still suspect in almost every academic community, even where the greatest activity is taking place. In spite of much progress within but a couple of decades, the college theatre still has to fight its way. Tolerance for even the practice of the historic theatre in its accustomed molds continues to be rare. Educational theatre leaders everywhere receive only grudging recognition from their academic colleagues. So perhaps it is too early to expect a welcome for experiment. Furthermore, it takes time to be creative. Students with a dozen academic requirements in other fields to fulfill simultaneously are too busy. This lack of time leads to lack of adequate training. In almost every campus theatre only the high spots are hit. No solid groundwork technique can possibly be built in the short hours which most students can devote to a theatrical training. Added to this is the fact that in most colleges the creative opportunities are kept as faculty prerogatives; student initiative is rarely given free play.

In spite of the inadequacy of training or experience, however, hundreds of young people are being graduated from these academic theatres and the number is increasing. Departments of drama—like all other departments in a university—must maintain or enlarge their enrollments, turn out their quota of A.B.'s and M.A.'s and Ph.D.'s each year, or suffer the consequences of a reduced budget and administrative ire. Directors of college theatres who see the danger of this situation are powerless to challenge it.

The most disturbing discovery I made, and references to it have preceded, is that the academic theatre exhibits an increasing tendency to become inbred. Turning in on itself, it is devoting more and more attention to training teachers to teach teachers to teach. At University A a young instructor of English discovers that a drama department may soon be set up; appreciating that here is an expanding field, he hies himself to the well-known department of drama at University B, where he works for and is granted a Ph.D. under a professor who was originally also an English teacher and whose knowledge of the theatre came from the library. Back to University A goes our young Ph.D., now an associate professor whose actual theatre experience consists of the direction of two one-act plays at University B. He establishes his department at A, and in no time there are seventy-five students. A dozen of these will be candidates for an M.A. in drama. Whether they are talented or not, they will get their degrees if they show sufficient application and fulfill the requirement of directing their two one-act plays. Ten of the dozen will go into teaching. We follow one of them out to Teachers College C where he will take over dramatics courses and instruct high school teachers in the art of the theatre. He has thirty such students and they will scatter with their Bachelor of Science in Education throughout the state to become the local apostles of the drama. Here they will present the theatre as they learned it at College C from a man who learned about it at University A from a man who learned about it at University B from a man who got it out of a book.

Anyone can see that the product, not too close to the

source at the start, has become more and more watered down in this process, for the dissemination of learning and the conduct of a living theatre are two different things.

What effect does this inversion have upon the health of our theatre as a whole? From a positive and creative point of view it would appear that it tends to eliminate the academic theatre as a force. What would happen if ninety graduates of medical schools went back into the teaching of medicine for every ten who went out to practice?

The desire to find security in an academic refuge is one reflection of the professional theatre's breakdown; more significantly it is typical of a kind of paralysis of action from which the college generation appears to suffer today. Harold Ehrensperger places the blame for this back on the colleges when he pertinently remarks that "young people are being prepared to fill jobs not to make jobs." Everywhere across America students countered my exhortation to pioneer, to go out and create theatre with questions: "But how? Where? With what money?" Very exceptional is the person or group today which undertakes to do what the Provincetown Playhouse, the Neighborhood Playhouse or the Washington Square Players undertook to accomplish in their day against a Broadway quite as committed to commercialism and as antipathetic to experiment as it is today; or what McConnell and Brown and Hume did outside New York twenty-five years ago.

In justice, however, to these young people on college and university campuses, I must record that paradoxically existing side by side with this paralysis of action, side by side with their apparent cynicism—or perhaps I should call it their realistic outlook, there is enthusiasm for the theatre. They will defend it against the movies; they are posted on Broadway's life and on foreign movements; break down their protective crust and they are as stage-struck as any earlier generation. They are disillusioned but they persist in being idealistic. They are a healthy lot, too. Few among them are incipient long-haired esthetes. The academic theatres are no hot beds of Bohemianism; of that charge at least they are clear.

What conclusions are to be drawn finally concerning the activity in this field? First, that there are long-range possibilities in all this work whose recognition counsels patience. The educational theatre ministers to that hunger for drama which is but half-consciously recognized by the multitude. It creates awareness and interest and a degree of knowledge and appreciation. It may even finally call into being that general demand for theatre which must accompany any widespread cultural advance in this country.

The educational theatre must never think that it is an end in itself; that is its great danger. Becoming preoccupied with degrees and courses and credits, with increasing enrollments, with syllabi and reading lists, the educational theatre is apt to forget that it exists only as a means to an end; and that that end is the enlargement through individual culture of an American culture wherein the theatre may take its place among the arts for all the people. The proper and highly admirable purpose of this kind of theatre is to train leaders for such a movement. Regimentation and standardization and minimum requirements do not stimulate leadership; they retard it. These academic theatres must remember that the stage is unpredictable.

Its final essence cannot be explained and dissected. They must never forget that it is compounded of stuff that is at once tenuous and sturdy; that it is no abstraction like music, has no logic like science; that it is concerned with life, with men and women and dreams and realities.

CHAPTER SIX

Players in Pinafores

"I f you want to restore the theatre, begin with the children," writes George E. Sokolsky. I had thought I could omit children from my study. The educational theatre at the college and university level seemed so vast that I could not imagine investigating grade schools and high schools too. Community playhouses presented a complex enough picture without adding children's theatres.

I had not gone far in my travels before I began to have premonitions that I was making a mistake. I observed on college campuses that although the groups of students I met studying drama were very much excited about the theatre, thousands of young people there never came to see a play and gave it no thought. What conditioned this attitude, I wondered? Perhaps one had to go back into the earlier years of young people's education to find the reason why a boy at one university would be compelled to say, "My fraternity brothers will never come to see me act because they're afraid people will laugh at them. It brings a bad enough name on the House as it is that two of us are majoring in dramatics." Time and again student bodies revealed, if not hostility toward theatre, at least a frigid indifference.

Fundamentally I suppose this rises out of the rather widespread American disapproval and distrust of art and artists. Ironically on campuses as elsewhere culture is regarded with suspicion. This is gradually being broken down, but for that to be accomplished completely, we must, I think, wipe out the self-conscious attitude toward art which young people so generally have. This can be done only by making it a natural and habitual ingredient of life; that, I am well aware, is a task so enormous that its very mention appalls. Nevertheless I am convinced that if we are to create a demand for theatre—and a demand for an art can be created as we have witnessed in the past very few years in the case of music—it must begin in the elementary schools. "If you want to restore the theatre, begin with the children." Mr. Sokolsky is no theatre man, but he is right.

What theatre do children meet before college age? Although we have seen that from eighty to ninety per cent of the university dramatic students go into teaching and probably three-fourths of these into the elementary and secondary schools, it still remains that the theatre occurs on a low level there. For the penetration of these college-trained instructors into the school system has not gone far yet and in many places where they are at work, lack of co-operation and understanding prevents their accomplishing even as much as they might be capable of doing.

Drama in the average school frequently continues to be utilized today as a means to other ends. A play is put on to raise money for new band instruments, for new uniforms for the basketball team, to purchase books for the library; its educational, recreational and artistic values *per se* are seldom recognized. School principals and boards of education are stumbling blocks in the path of those who would like to make theatre-going and theatre participation a familiar and constant experience for young people. Funds are so seldom available, vast auditoriums and shallow stages with concrete floors and little or no offstage or overhead space are so often impossibly inadequate to satisfactory stage production, that it is small wonder secondary school dramatics look grim.

Nevertheless glowing exceptions occur—sometimes in a single classroom, sometimes in the schools of a whole city or town—so that again one is compelled to fall back on the old observation that wherever a man or woman with vision, leadership and ability is at work, the task can be and is being accomplished. The system crumbles before the enlightened onslaughts of the man who has something with which to replace it and the skill to convey his ideas to more prosaic minds.

Take the case of the Webster Groves High School, just outside St. Louis. For ten years Eugene Wood worked with students in courses open to juniors and seniors there, until discriminating people in St. Louis were able to agree that among the finest theatrical performances to be seen in that neighborhood were those given by the sixteen- and seventeen-year-old boys and girls in this suburban school. I saw *Our Town* and was held by the moving freshness of the students' performances. Equally interesting was it to see the crowds of youngsters who came out to see this kind of play. Mr. Wood never has compromised with what would be assumed to be student taste; as a result the level of taste has risen and his presentations of such mature and serious plays as *The Petrified Forest, Little Ol' Boy,*

Richard of Bordeaux have been enthusiastically supported by his high school audience.

Take another case: Glenville High School in Cleveland. Here Eugene Davis has conducted classes in drama from which come all the stage presentations of this school. Largely as a result of his work, I suspect, this school possessed in 1940 a handsome and workable theatre. Mr. Davis presents but three or four plays a year and each of these are in preparation for two or three months. *Abe Lincoln in Illinois* had been produced a few weeks before my visit to Cleveland, but Mr. Davis offered to repeat some scenes from it for my special benefit. Two classrooms thrown into one formed his workshop; at one end was a platform. There was no curtain, no stage lights; the gray afternoon twilight coming through schoolroom windows illumined the stage and audience equally. There were no props—a few golden-oak school benches and chairs; no one was in make-up or costume. A tall, awkward boy of sixteen, slightly stoop-shouldered, with a somber face and a straggling lock, went up onto the platform wearing a gray pull-over sweater. A short, bright-eyed little boy and a slight, dark-haired girl in a red-and-white jumper joined him. They moved the furniture about by themselves. There was a pause and then they began; scenes of Lincoln's youth and maturing years followed one another to culminate in the scene on his election night.

When it was over the young actors came down quite simply from the platform, seated themselves and stared at me. I was expected to say something. My voice, I discovered, was choked. "This has been as moving as anything I have seen in all the theatres I have visited since I left New York last year," I stammered. I meant it. "You have played with truth; you have lifted me out of this schoolroom and out of myself. I am grateful to you for a rare theatrical experience."

One bright October morning I rode out to the Shorewood High School on the outskirts of Milwaukee. Shorewood is an upper middle class suburb; its school contains a beautiful auditorium seating thirteen hundred, an adequate stage with good loft and a flexible lighting system.

I arrived about eleven o'clock as the school was starting its "activity hour." At this period students divide into groups according to their interest to work on the annual, dramatics, student council program, music, photography or the school paper. In this system the so-called extra-curricular interests are incorporated into daily school life. I was ushered into a room where Miss Lena Foley, head of the Speech department, was conferring with a group of students and other teachers on promotional and publicity plans for *Our Town*. At Shorewood the dramatic club gives three productions a year: in the fall a classic like *Romeo and Juliet, Bourgeois Gentil'homme* or a semi-classic like *The Admirable Crichton* or the forthcoming *Our Town;* in December a Christmas production; in the spring an operetta. To end the season the senior class presents a modern comedy.

Almost one-half of the entire student body are voluntarily involved each year in the Shorewood dramatic program: acting, building or painting scenery, designing and sewing costumes, applying make-up, making props and devising sound effects, handling business and publicity details. On *Romeo and Juliet* 175 boys and girls did some kind of work, gaining what Miss Foley claims is "one of the greatest contributions of high school dramatics—a realization of the significance of each individual's contribu-tion to a co-operative enterprise."

In addition to this major dramatic schedule there are weekly assemblies of the entire school at which programs by students are presented. These originate in class work, are planned and produced by pupils in assembly training and assembly production classes.

The next story begins in Washington, D. C., and ends a thousand miles away. I went one day to the vast and imposing office building of the Department of the Interior. I was in search of Miss Alice Barrows, Senior Specialist in School Building Problems in the United States Office of Education. She turned out to be a vivacious, penetrating little woman with short, close-cropped gray hair, sharp eyes and a frank enthusiasm for whatever she was dis-cussing. At the moment it was the schools of Gary, Indi-ana. "You must go there without fail and stay as long as you can," she said rapidly and emphatically. "You will find there the development of a program that began nearly thirty-five years ago and with which the rest of the country is just beginning to catch up. It's called the platoon school or the work-study-play plan. Today there are such schools in more than three hundred cities and a number of rural communities but it all began in Gary." As she talked she drew me across the office to look at a model of one of these Gary schools; she brought out of her files photo-graphs and pamphlets and publications of all sorts to illus-trate her story, which ran something like this:

"In some high schools the annual senior play is the only theatrical experience anyone has. In others this is supple-mented by a dramatic club where in after-school hours perhaps as many as fifty out of a school of five hundred or a thousand pupils will read, talk about or produce plays. In an exceptional school this is amplified by a course or two in the curriculum. This activity is sporadic and involves but a small percentage of the children.

"Most high schools have some kind of a meeting place. Most often it is a combination auditorium-gymnasium with a boxed-in stage at one end, a flat floor, portable seats. The dramatic and musical programs must compete with athletics for the right to its use. Some high schools, it is true, have a separate auditorium and in a few there may be a workable theatre plant. Customarily, however, this auditorium is used for an assembly program once a week; only rarely more often."

She paused and I agreed that so far she was right. "But in Gary," she said triumphantly, "every school has a theatre which is in use every hour of every day, five days a week from September to June. Furthermore, every child in the Gary schools, from the moment he enters at the age of six until he graduates at eighteen, spends one hour of every day throughout those twelve years in the theatre, either participating in some program or being a spectator. This hour is called the auditorium period and a great many other hours are necessarily spent in preparation for that period." She stopped and thrust into my hands a brochure entitled "The School Auditorium as a Theatre." In it I read about this program as it was working at Gary:

This auditorium period, in adult language, is nothing more nor less than a theatre period serving the child as the theatre has always served the adult—"A rest period in which he learns something." . . . The auditorium room, unhampered by classroom paraphernalia, creates an atmosphere not unlike that of the adult theatre. It is indeed a real theatre room with a real stage with curtains and screens, floodlights and spots, where one meets the real audience, not merely the fellows of one's own class, but members of two, three, or four classes— interesting, stimulating people, a bit younger and a bit older than one's most constant companions. . . .

In the child's life, this period is not extracurricular, not irregular, not a hit-or-miss experience, but is made an integral part of his program of living. . . . The situation is distinctly a social one. Here one works for one's fellows—not for himself, not for a teacher, not for a grade. Whatever one does he does because he believes he has something he can contribute to the group. He talks, sings, acts, paints, devises costumes and sets, adjusts curtains and controls lights because he believes the audience wants his contributions.

When Miss Barrows had finished her description I was ready to get on the next train for Gary, for the implications of such a program of education seemed to me important beyond compare. But it was two months before I was able to get there and see the work-study-play school in operation. There are auditoriums for different age-level groups. I started with the youngest. The hall was not large: it was filled with perhaps seventy-five or one hundred children from the first to the third grades. They were watching a performance of the dramatized story of the little Dutch boy who put his finger in the leak in the dyke and saved Holland. The dramatization had been made by the children themselves.

Like all these sessions, it was being conducted like a town meeting; when the play was over and the patter of childish applause had subsided, the cast came out and stood in a row before the curtain. The little tow-headed chairman rose and asked in a grave treble: "Are there any criticisms or suggestions?" Half a dozen children jumped up. Seven-year-old Eustace was recognized; he piped: "I liked the play but I thought the tempo was a little slow." I could hardly believe my ears. A seven-year-old talking about stage tempo! The teacher intervened: "That's interesting, Eustace," she said. "Where did you think the tempo was slow?" Eustace explained; he put his finger on a passage where the performers' attention had wandered a bit and, forgetting what they were about, the tempo had sagged. He knew, it appeared, the meaning of the term he was using. Here was critical appreciation of theatre being developed at the age of seven. Miss Barrows had been right; Gary was remarkable.

From this auditorium we went to a room where another group of slightly older children of the primary grades were preparing another play; then on to a still older group who were concerned with a choral dramatization of *Paul Revere's Ride*, with the scenic accompaniments for it and with an original prologue to relate it to the American history course. Many of these programs present in dramatic form the content of courses in various fields: history, civics, literature, geography, even science and mathematics. There are special "auditorium teachers" whose responsibility it is to assist the students in the transformation of such material into stage terms.

By the time the high school level is reached, students have lost all self-consciousness about appearing publicly; the play-acting of childhood has become habitual with them all. Audience participation through daily theatre-going—which is what it amounts to—has also become habitual. They listen attentively and naturally to any expression of opinion voiced from the floor, to any dramatic presentation they happen to witness. Typical high school roughnecks in football sweaters, who in other places would look upon such unfamiliar activity as a little sissy, here rise to say—as they have since they were seven—"I think the tempo of that scene was a little slow."

The Gary school auditoriums do not close when the school day is over. Until suppertime the high school dramatic club, to which belong those students who have been more caught by the stage than the crowd, remains rehearsing its special play. Then the lights are turned on; in a little while the building will be filled with adults come to participate in the evening recreational and educational program. Three out of ten grown-ups in Gary are going to school this way. The auditorium will be filled again—on the night I was there, to see a student vaudeville.

There is no last chapter to this story; it remains to be written. For outside theatre does not come to Gary. It is off the beaten path of the road; it is too close to Chicago to be a full-fledged stop and yet too far to make theatre-going into Chicago possible for slender purses. Local dramatic activity seems to end with the schools, for Gary possesses no wealthy citizens; nobody has money for artistic ventures. This is a mill-town. At night the sky is red and the sparks fly over the great steel plants on the flat land that stretches from the town out to nearby Lake Michigan. It has been the children of mill workers we have been watching; these children grown up, taking their places in the furnaces and smelters and rolling mills or in the kitchens of the simple homes to which their men return—these workers have not yet translated that school experience into a continuing theatre. When they do—and somehow I feel certain they inevitably will—Gary will have a community prepared to receive it and to participate in it as no other community anywhere.

2

Gary lies to the south and east of Chicago. Up the "North Shore" in the opposite direction is Evanston—an upper middle class community dwelling in substantial brick and frame houses, among lawns and trees; it is also the home of a university: Northwestern. Evanston has its own children's theatre, created by Winifred Ward, a slender, dynamic woman whose words fall over themselves in their eagerness to be uttered. The Children's Theatre of Evanston exists separately from the schools, but it works in close collaboration with them, with Parent-Teacher Associations, with women's clubs and with the University. It has its own Board of Directors composed of children: two from each school, who meet in not too solemn conclave to advise Miss Ward. It presents a series of four plays every year in the two Junior High Schools of Evanston. To the six performances of each play come three thousand children. Those who want to attend all four plays pay one dollar for a season ticket; those who come to but one or two pay thirty-five cents each time. Attendance is voluntary and plays, although presented in the schools, do not take place during school hours.

Miss Ward has found that children like best familiar plays or dramatizations of the old stories. The biggest hits are the perennial *Treasure Island, Robin Hood* (which has been repeated three times over the years), *Peter Pan* (repeated twice). Every generation loves and demands to see these old favorites. They are played by casts in which children's parts are played by children, the grown-up roles filled by students of Northwestern who are taking courses in children's theatre methods.

Although the Children's Theatre of Evanston is the center, there are creative dramatics classes in the schools themselves in the seventh, eighth and ninth grades. The purpose of these is to present drama as an art form, but the social value is not overlooked. Most of these classes spend most of their time with improvisations to draw out youthful creativeness and stimulate the imagination. By the ninth grade children are studying characterization through impromptu depiction of Shakespearean roles: Shakespeare's plays come alive for high school youngsters when improvisations based on scenes from *Julius Caesar* or *Romeo and Juliet* supplement what is usually uninspired conning of the text. Much of this class work is conducted by students of Northwestern who work in the schools for laboratory training. Out of their classes come most of the boys and girls who will appear in the Children's Theatre plays.

Miss Ward's influence has been spread far and wide by her disciples. At the University of Minnesota, for example, a comparable program is on the way toward development at the hand of Northwestern graduate Kenneth Graham, although he arrived to find that the ground had already been broken in Minneapolis. The University offers a creative dramatics course for teachers in the summer session, but in 1940-41, no winter term courses. The activity centers about the two children's plays (*The Emperor's*

New Clothes and *Seven Little Rebels* in 1940-41) and for older high school students special matinees of certain of the adult series which are suitable, such as *Romeo and Juliet, Peer Gynt, The Tempest.* Through the co-operation of the Minneapolis public school system pupils come to each of the four matinee performances from all the schools of one district in buses chartered by the Parent-Teacher Association. Each school will have its special block of seats, for a place in which each child will pay twenty-five cents. To these four matinees and a Saturday morning performance attended primarily by children from private schools will come some twenty-five hundred boys and girls. The special matinees of the adult classics are arranged for by the English Teachers Club.

The region around the lower end of Lake Michigan seems to be a focal point for children's dramatic activity. In addition to the work in Gary and Evanston, the Goodman Theatre in Chicago, as I have already said, has a program of plays for boys and girls under the direction of Charlotte Chorpenning. All through the fall, winter and spring children come to the Goodman Theatre on Saturday afternoons to see *Little Black Sambo, Cinderella, Robinson Crusoe, Little Women, Aladdin*—four different plays each year, given seven matinees apiece. At least half an hour before curtain time the tots begin to pour in, some in groups, some with parents, some older ones by themselves feeling very important. The little ones play tag up and down the aisles. As performance time approaches the babel rises in a crescendo until the footlights come up and the house lights start to dim when it reaches its peak in a burst of applause. The curtains part and there is a deathly hush.

Mrs. Chorpenning has herself written many of these plays presented in the Goodman series; she is probably the outstanding American author of plays for children. Stout, gray-haired, motherly, Mrs. Chorpenning knows by some sixth sense what children want, what they will laugh at, what will frighten them, what will thrill them most. She directs these productions herself and her inventive business is masterly. She insists on the best acting talent in the school for her casts and scenery and costumes as good as or better than those provided for productions in the adult member's series. She receives the enthusiastic support of the entire theatre, as well she might, for anyone would be gratified to play to the kind of audience that comes on Saturday afternoon: an audience that sits on the edge of its seat in breathless silence when the scene is tense, that rocks with laughter at comic situations, that claps and stamps and cheers when the play is good.

That was the kind of audience I observed watching *Aladdin.* No children act in these plays for children at the Goodman Theatre; one of the smaller young men students played Aladdin charmingly. Genii appeared mysteriously in the faces of rocks, distant palaces were wiped from the horizon by a puff of smoke and reappeared again as magically. There were dances and parades of people in wonderful oriental splendor, much to laugh at and moments of excitement too provided by the wicked magician who seeks throughout, as you will remember, by means of various disguises and wiles and tricks to destroy Aladdin and get the magic ring and lamp into his own hands. When the footlights came up before each act the round of applause was repeated and when the performance was over a long line formed at the door leading backstage where Aladdin and the princess appeared according to custom to autograph the programs of stage-struck ten-year-olds.

For more than twenty years the Chicago Drama League has conducted a children's theatre in the summer time on the Navy Pier that juts out into Lake Michigan. Boys and girls participate here themselves, more than three hundred of them during the eight-week season—some of them coming ten miles through the hot streets of the Middle Western metropolis to the waterfront. There amid the blare of barker's horns, the toots of lake boat whistles, the cries of jostling street crowds, the leaders of this stage attempt to conjure forth scenes of beauty and fun. Every week the bill changes: now scenes from *Midsummer Night's Dream,* now an operetta *Bon Voyage* or *In Old Vienna;* a play or dances: Swedish, Spanish, Indian; classic and modern ballet. A Mothers' Drama Club has been organized by the doting mammas who follow the children to the Pier. They help make costumes, enroll the boys and girls, act as stage doormen and even lend a hand with the scenery. Thoroughly democratic is this theatre: children from every walk of life and every kind of home work and play together here, their many accents and dialects mingling in the hot lake breeze.

In an earlier chapter I described the adult theatre of the Palo Alto Community Center. On the left as one enters the flower-banked courtyard is another playhouse: the home of the Children's Theatre, directed by Hazel G. Robertson, operating independently of the Palo Alto Community Players, although like it municipally owned and controlled.

That emphasis which Ralph Emerson Welles across the
patio places in his program on community participation,
Mrs. Robertson echoes on her stage. Unlike Miss Ward
and Mrs. Chorpenning, she believes that every part and
most of the backstage work should be done by the boys
and girls themselves. The Chicago stages exist primarily
for their audiences, and the leaders there believe that the
best possible performances—as closely akin to professional
as they can be—must be the goal, and that this can only
be achieved by experienced, trained and talented adults
playing for children. Here the emphasis is on the recreational, therapeutic and educational benefits gained by the
children through actual work and play around a theatre.
If the performances are a little unsteady and the scenery
childish, compared to the Goodman productions, and if the
audience does not behold as finished and artistic results,
Mrs. Robertson does not care, for her primary concern is
not so much for the audiences' reaction as for development
of the personalities of the eight hundred children who
work with her each year.

It must not be thought that at Palo Alto the audience
is altogether unimportant. It is certainly this theatre's
aim to present as well-done performances as possible.
Nearly two thousand of Palo Alto's three thousand school
children come to each play (a new one is presented every
month in the winter; in the summer when young hopefuls
are out of school eight are given in eight weeks). There
are regularly three performances of each play and admission is ten cents for children, twenty-five cents for
adults.

In an effort to determine what fare boys and girls enjoy on the stage, Mrs. Robertson consults the children's

library which is in another wing of this white-plaster and red-tile building. The books children read most avidly are the ones they like to see dramatized, Mrs. Robertson finds; the best-sellers—which are usually the oldest and most familiar stories, as Miss Ward and Mrs. Chorpenning have also discovered—become her material. *Peter Pan, Mary Poppins* are among the favorites.

Mrs. Robertson has two paid assistants; the rest of the backstage work is done by children—usually the older ones —who may number as many as twenty on one production. There is an amusing exception to this: Palo Alto women arrested for traffic violations may pay off their fines by sewing costumes for the children's theatre. Ladies ignoring red lights or parking too long where they shouldn't may be seen the next day in the workshops at the playhouse; every hour's sewing works off fifty cents of the fine!

All children pay a fifty-cent participational fee; if a youngster has not that much cash available he may earn it by working around the theatre. An indication of the effort this theatre makes to understand its youthful thespians' backgrounds, problems and needs so that it may minister most intelligently to them may be found in the questionnaire each one fills out when he applies for his chance to work at this children's theatre.[1] In the casts older children play adult roles, four- to six-year-olds are cast as rabbits, elves or little children. In rehearsal the boys

[1] In addition to giving his name, address, telephone, school, grade, age, and father's name, each applicant answers these questions: How long have you lived in Palo Alto? Where else have you lived? How many brothers and sisters? How many rooms in your house? Does anyone else live in the house? Average grades in school work? Father's education and employment? Mother's education and employment? Do you have a regular allowance? If so, how much? What church do

and girls are encouraged to be as imaginative as they can; few set forms, action or dialogue are imposed upon them. This is indeed the children's own theatre.

Several little and community theatres besides Palo Alto have a program of plays for children to supplement their adult series. Some of these follow Mrs. Chorpenning's practice and offer youthful audiences plays acted by grown-ups. Others like Palo Alto have casts composed of children. One such is Le Petit Théâtre du Vieux Carré in New Orleans, where three plays a year are presented by boys and girls from twelve to sixteen years old. Here no tie-up with the school system has been effected, although nearly twelve hundred children come with their fifteen cents clutched in their hands to see each play. Most successful at New Orleans has been a cycle of *Wizard of Oz* plays. The Indianapolis Civic Theater with a season of four plays for children is another example.

The "Curtain Pullers," which is the children's theatre of the Cleveland Play House, places its emphasis also on participation. It was organized in 1933 by Esther Mullin who invited each school in Greater Cleveland to send the two most talented children between the ages of seven and fourteen to Saturday morning classes in dramatics for which a one dollar registration fee was to be charged. More than one hundred boys and girls now meet in this group and present five or six plays a year to other school

you attend? How often? What magazines does your family take? What diseases have you had and when? Are you a member of the Children's Theatre? How many shows have you been in? What kind of books do you like to read? Your favorite book? Favorite play or plays seen? Activities? Hobbies? What play or plays would you like to see? Any suggestions?

children, about five thousand of whom attend each season. In addition, the adult company of the Play House regularly presents as the last production of its season a Shakespearean play which it offers in a limited number of performances to the members and which it presents in a series of fifteen to twenty special matinees for high school children.

In Cleveland there is another children's theatre deserving of mention: the Cleveland Theatre for Youth. It grew out of a Federal Theatre Project unit. Left high and dry when the Project was abolished, this group, led by Gordon Roberts and Wilson Brooks, decided it was unwilling to abandon the work it had been doing and struck out on its own. There was little, if any, financial backing, but there was the strong belief that the theatre must be allowed to bring "beauty, excitement and education" into the lives of children and that backing was not everything. As its name suggests, it is *for* youth, not *by* youth.

With the simplest kind of painted screens and improvised costumes, the Theatre for Youth tours the Cleveland schools bringing in 1940-41 *Hansel and Gretel, Beauty and the Beast, Pierre Patelin, Nathaniel's Witch.* In the average week it will visit six or eight schools; once it gave thirteen performances in one week—more than two a day. Its income is meager and it must be divided among the eleven young people who work full-time or part-time for the company. When children are charged admission the theatre gets fifty per cent of the gross with a minimum guarantee to the company of fifteen dollars; when children are admitted free, the school must pay the fifteen dollars for the performance. This is no get-rich-quick scheme; the chief reward is in hearing the clamor of enthusiasm as

children, in some cases for the first time, see a "real" play
with "round actors." [2]

There are a few other agencies working to bring plays
to children. In a number of cities the young women of the
Junior League have assumed this responsibility. The
Junior League has established a central clearing house
office in New York for the conduct of this work and employs a field secretary, Miss Gloria Chandler, to spread the
gospel. In most instances Junior Leaguers produce and act
in the plays themselves and their tie-up with the schools
is not always strong. Nevertheless, they have done notable pioneer work in many places.

There are two outstanding children's theatres touring
the road like the usual commercial company and employing adult professional actors. "Junior Programs" sends
out not only plays but little operas and ballets as well.
Clare Tree Major has more than one company presenting
dramas. Because these companies exist to make profit, the
box-office scale is in some instances so high as to allow only
the privileged few to attend. Nevertheless a number of
Mrs. Major's productions are charming and well worth
the price.

Probably the most significant work in children's dramatics, outside of those enlightened schools that have creative art programs, is being done in the settlement houses
of our big cities. In New York, for instance, one may go
any afternoon to one of a dozen or more centers and find
youngsters head over heels in play production.

Take the Children's Theatre of Greenwich House, for
example, or the W.A.O. Club of the Henry Street Set-

[2] Selective Service made an end also to this theatre in 1941 when
one of the directors and several of the company were drafted.

tlement, both in New York. W.A.O. stands for "we are one," and it is a group of high-school-age girls, white and colored, with names like Labiento, Alhofen, Guralnick, Grossman, along with Young and McNichols. I went down to Henry Street, which lies east of the Bowery, to see the W.A.O.'s present Molière's *Doctor in Spite of Himself!* A graduate of the Vassar Experimental Theatre had directed them and supervised the posteresque scenery that waved in the breeze of the recreational hall. The girls' costumes were reminiscent of the bits of faded finery and feathers that neighborhood children ransacked from attic trunks and chests in my childhood days to play "dress-up." In fact that was the clue to the whole performance. It was "dressing up," and the kids carried it off with the gusto of a game. They treated Molière none too sacredly; the dialogue was paraphrased in Lower East Side jargon and spoken with a Babel of accents; but it was abundantly clear to the audience of doting Italian and Polish and Russian Jewish papas and mammas, and of the adolescent Boweryites whom Henry Street's dramatic program makes stage-struck, that the girls were having fun. So everybody else had fun too—this doubting Thomas included. It was no performance to recommend to my friends, Mr. Atkinson or Mr. Brown of the Manhattan dailies; but the sociologists would have had a field day. On nights like that I am persuaded of the value the stage may have in that whole other realm that is tangent to the Broadway circle at no point.

"If you want to restore the theatre begin with the children." The Federal Theatre Project knew that; so it set up programs of plays for boys and girls in most of its centers. In some places, like Cleveland, these stages were the only successful ones on the project; the only ones, too, that have outlasted the project. Radiating out from the centers it sent circuses and puppet shows, jugglers and magicians; touring companies playing *Pinocchio* or *The Emperor's New Clothes* set up their platforms in parks and playgrounds, and thousands of children saw their first real performances by living actors. It was one of the great pieces of work done by Federal Theatre—one of the most important to the future life of the American stage. But Federal Theatre is no longer a part of the pattern. Its growing accomplishments in this field of theatre for youth were cut off.

Creating a demand for theatre, kindling an interest in it, a love for it in the young—this is one of the American stage's first problems if it is to survive the onslaughts of motion pictures with their ten cents cost and their omnipresence.

The stage has this great advantage: children instinctively like a show, like to be in one. The twin attractions of participation through play-acting and vicarious enjoyment through play-going must be capitalized upon. The first is perhaps the stronger in youth; the second grows out of the first. Non-professional theatre must minister to the former; professional and amateur theatres must join hands in ministering to the latter. Schools and settlement houses seem best equipped to do the participational job; they also seem to be facing up to it better than other agencies. In some places, but not often enough, community theatres take over for everyone the task of giving children an outlet for self-expression.

As for bringing boys and girls up to be members of a theatrical audience—the only relationship ninety per cent of them will have to the theatre later in life—the surface has just been scratched. There are woefully few plays for high school children to see after their interest in drama has been aroused through participation in the school or the community center. The commercial theatre has remained blinder than usual to its obligations to the audience of tomorrow.

One step, which should have occurred years ago, is being undertaken in New York. A plan worked out by Alfred Harding of Actors' Equity Association will enable school children to attend special matinees of plays selected by their English teachers. On the epoch-making afternoon of Decoration Day, 1941, fourteen hundred high school children—two-thirds of whom had never seen a play before—poured into the Shubert Theatre in Times Square to see Katharine Cornell, Raymond Massey and the current Broadway cast play a matinee performance of Shaw's *The Doctor's Dilemma*. Each youngster paid *five cents!* The Shubert's doorman was reported to have opined that it was "our best audience since a medical association was here." (That profession being the subject of the play, the compliment was a high one.)

In its early stages the plan will enable only a very few of New York's vast army of school children to become theatre-goers. The audience for *The Doctor's Dilemma*, for instance, came from but thirty-five vocational and senior high schools chosen by lot at the Board of Education. At these schools the faculty selected those forty seniors who would best appreciate the play or who would otherwise have the least opportunity for theatre-going.

From these small beginnings it is to be hoped that something permanent may emerge on a wider scale. To be sure, a Broadway season contains few plays which an English teacher could conscientiously recommend as valuable enough to young people to serve as a substitute for school hours; but the scheme with all its limitations should be hailed as a definite step forward. It has been accomplished at all only because the theatrical unions have agreed to waive usual labor costs—in itself a hopeful sign.

What happens in New York can conceivably be repeated in other cities except, of course, in the one-night-stand towns where the commercial theatre can scarcely afford to co-operate. Looking at the problem as a whole, I wonder whether this great field can ever really be touched without large-scale theatre subsidies. Until national, state, municipal or other grants make it possible for children everywhere to come into regular contact with as fine artists as the American stage possesses, so that they may come to know its highest excitement and its strongest impact, I cannot feel that the theatre will be able really to become a people's art.

CHAPTER SEVEN

Drama at Our Crossroads

So far the story has kept close to the beaten path: the key cities and their professional theatres; the well-known community theatre centers—Cleveland, Pasadena, New Orleans and a dozen more; the campuses of Yale, Stanford, the big state universities; all of them familiar ground to the surveyors of every field. But what about the "et ceteras and the and-so-forths, the nobody who's everybody"? What about the real people's theatre?

Out across the table-land of west Texas, where the gray-green mesquite sprawls along the earth and the arc of sky seems to fill out much more than its half of the circle, out thirty miles from Abilene lies Albany. Around it stretch ranch lands. Settled against the side of those promontories that rise and fall away again without rhyme or reason in the vast expanse of landscape stands a ranch house; its corrals are close by. Twenty miles to the west or the east is another one. This is cattle country. Here and there is a black oasis; this is also oil country—but mostly cattle.

In Albany live two thousand people. There is a court-house with a broad expanse of gray-green grass and dirt that stands in the center of town. Along a wide dusty street a couple of blocks of sand-color two-story buildings face the court-house. On the ground floors are stores; upstairs in one is a law office, in another a real-estate office; in a third is Albany's dentist. On the far corner is the bank. Half way down the block is a movie house. Beyond and partly behind it is the school with a big sports field spread out in the rear; space is plentiful.

Away from the center a little, set among simple frame houses, are two churches. On the edge of town to the west are the oil company's derricks and engines and sheds; to the east are the houses where its workers live. On the other side of town is a railroad station. It is closed, for no trains come through Albany these days—except once in a while a night freight. Instead a big blue-and-silver Greyhound bus twice a day sweeps along the broad high-way bound for El Paso or Fort Worth. At night great vans occasionally lumber in at one end of town and out at the other in chugging caravans.

The oil company and some of the cattle land are responsible for this story—at least for my knowing it. Together they put money into the pockets of one or two of Albany's families. In one was a serious lad who liked to study and seemed born for another kind of life than the ranch or the oil field. He was sent away—up north and east to a big preparatory school and on to Princeton. There the theatre attracted him; modestly and quietly he worked backstage in his first two years, for he was not much of an actor. In his upper class days he began to assume control, to be appreciated. He directed; he became president of Princeton's Théâtre Intime; he began to write plays. One, *Time of Their Lives*, was the undergraduate prize play in 1933; it was a drama of Princeton life and because it has been unequaled for its humorous, compassionate, richly-drawn portrayal of student days, it has been revived by every undergraduate generation since.

By the time this young man graduated, with a Phi Beta Kappa key on his watch-chain, he knew he wanted to work in the theatre. But he did not go to Broadway, or to the Yale Drama School. Instead he turned back to the Southwest and for a few years directed a little theatre in one of Texas' prosperous cities. But he was an honest young man and he did not like the pretentiousness of the people in the little theatre, who were self-consciously striving for culture for the sake of appearances, as it seemed to him; so back he went to Albany. Several years later a couple of Broadway directors, always searching for new material and having read or seen a revival of *Time of Their Lives* at Princeton, sent a letter to the young Texan, asked him to write some plays again; they thought they could guarantee him Broadway productions. He replied that he was grateful for their interest but much too busy to pen any plays for Broadway.

What was keeping the young man so busy, out in the middle of west Texas? As my train dragged across the hundreds of miles of treeless range from El Paso east to San Antonio, I looked out of the window and thought of Robert Nail—for that was the young man's name—and wondered what could so busily occupy anyone like him in this desolate no-man's land. I decided then was my chance to find out; so when I got to Dallas, I took a plane and flew out to pay him a call.

It all began with and now centers around the "Fandangle." That part of Texas, like all the Southwest, is rich in native lore. The vivid history of Texas—Indians, Mexicans, soldiers, settlers with their long-horn steers, the first oil prospectors—all this was only yesterday. The story of it is the stuff of which drama is made. Out of this the young man fashioned a kind of poetic historical epic of the country and christened it a Fandangle. The first one was given in the summer of 1938; in 1939 he wrote another, and in 1940 a third was produced. He would like to do five of them; by that time he thinks the idea and the material relating to that immediate locale will be exhausted.

A Fandangle takes months of preparation, for not only must it be written; there are dances to be arranged, parades organized—all a part of the show—parts to be rehearsed, music adapted, costumes, scenery and properties devised, lighting equipment to be secured and set up. Two hundred and fifty people perform in the Fandangle: boys and girls from the high school, townspeople of every age, cowboys in off the ranches. As we walked down the street, a couple of ranch hands were leaning against a street lamp, their rolled cowboy sombreros tilted back to reveal their bronzed leathery faces.

"Hi-ya, Bob!" they called friendlily.

"They rode in the last two Fandangles," the young man said to me after we had passed.

"Who trains the dancers in these polkas and schottisches?" I asked, as we looked at photographs of last year's performance.

"I do," the young man replied.

"I didn't know you knew how to do that."

"I didn't, but I learned. It's really easy and lots of fun."

"Who makes the costumes?" I inquired.

"I do," he answered, "with some of the women to help. It's funny how you can do all sorts of things you never thought you could when you have an incentive like this."

The Fandangle takes place outdoors in the athletic field behind the school. Great boughs of mesquite and cottonwood are hauled in off the range to be set up as a background. There are covered wagons and horses galore, pioneers with broad-brimmed hats and sunbonnets, Indians in paint and feathers. Flowing through it all come the words of the young author's vibrant verse.

There is only one performance and the bleachers are filled to capacity with eighteen hundred people, some of them having driven in for miles across the plains. The young man tells of an old settler now eighty-five years old. He had known many of the characters in the play himself—had come out to the Southwest with them. He started out for the school field before it was dark because he walked slowly. As he came near it began to rain. In disappointment he turned around and went home. He was just getting into bed when he heard the music of the Fandangle coming across the town on the evening breeze. It had stopped raining and the show was about to begin after all. Getting out of bed, the old man dressed again with trembling fingers and hurried once more to the field. There the glowing days of his youth and of the youth of the country unfolded before him.

The Fandangle is only one of the things that keeps the young man too busy to write plays for Broadway. At Christmas time in the larger of the churches he produces a Nativity play which he also writes himself. I say the larger church, but it only seats two hundred; so ten performances are given in order that everyone in Albany and from the surrounding ranches who wishes may have a chance to attend. Tickets are distributed free so that the capacity will not be exceeded on any one evening. But word of the Nativity play has spread widely. It rained a good deal last Christmas time; nevertheless every night a crowd stood outside on the church steps for an hour or more in the drizzle, hoping that some of those who held tickets would not show up and they might get in after all to hear the old story unfolded by these simple Texans repeating the Bible words and the young man's verse in their rangy drawl.

The Fandangle is in June, but preparations begin in March; work on the Nativity play is started before Thanksgiving. Between times the young man writes a one-act play or two for the high school to enter in the state-wide drama tournament of which I shall tell you later. These he may lend a hand in directing. Then there are book reviews—*How Green Was My Valley* or *For Whom The Bell Tolls*—which he delivers from time to time to a crowd that packs the movie theatre on an odd afternoon to learn from him what people are reading and what it means.

"I don't know what we'd do here if Bob ever went away again," said the superintendent of schools to me; "but I guess you can see that for yourself."

Nick Ray worked for the Resettlement Administration. Part of his job was to help people put on plays. One day while he was working in Alabama a letter came from the students in the white high school of a little town about forty miles south of Birmingham. It asked him to come down and help them put on a play. He replied that he would come as soon as he could. When he got there he found himself in the heart of the Alabama coal-mines— the toughest mining region in the country, where they try out the strikes to be pulled later at Harlan, Kentucky and places like that. The high school class had all ages lumped together. He looked at them dubiously.

"What kind of a show do you want to do?" he asked.

"Well," they replied, "We don't rightly know. We never did have one before."

"Have you looked at the catalogues?" Nick inquired.

"Yes, but the stuff they talk about there sounds pretty silly. We had an idea maybe we could write our own— if you'd help us."

"O.K. What do you want to make a play about?"

"We've been talking, and it seems like most of us'd like to have a show that would tell about some of the troubles of the Negroes hereabouts."

That set Nick back on his heels: a white high school in the deep South wanting to write a play about the problems of the Negro! But if that was what they wanted— swell. They set to work and composed a sort of scenario; around it they improvised dialogue. It lacked all literary quality, but it rang true. Together they worked for several weeks. The time came for the performance.

Into the little hall were packed a crowd of tough, burly miners and their wives; little boys and girls darted in and out. Most of them, young and old alike, had never seen a play before. A sleazy curtain hung across one end to separate them from the stage. The problem of make-up had bothered the boys and girls: they didn't want to black their faces and anyhow they hadn't the money for make-up.

When the audience had assembled, one little boy came before the curtains to explain this.

"Everybody in the show is supposed to be black except the judge. Since you won't have any trouble telling which he is, and since everybody else is a Negro, we aren't any of us going to be black. Only you must remember that we're all supposed to be."

Then the show began. It lasted for an hour. When the final curtains closed, there was a heavy pause. Then someone clapped. Soon the long, low room jammed with hot humanity was reverberating to applause, cheers, whistles. Suddenly someone yelled: "We want to see it again!" Nick went back to the youngsters.

"Do you want to do it again?" he asked.

"Sure!" they said. In ten minutes the performance was repeated. No one had left the hall.

2

Concern for this real people's theatre, for the men, women and children off the beaten path of culture, has prompted several state universities and certain other organizations to undertake the dissemination of drama to gatherings from the hamlets and the crossroads and the solitary farms. Almost all of these have social rather than artistic goals. Appreciating the value that comes through self-expression on the stage, the development of character arising from co-operative community enterprise, the release and joy that recreation such as play-making gives to monotonous and uneventful lives, leaders in rural sociology have carried the theatre far and wide. Most of these leaders are attached to universities, but they regularly function through co-operation with other organizations like the Grange or the 4-H Clubs which come into closer direct contact with the people.

Into the office of the University of Wisconsin's beautiful theatre came Marie Kellogg to tell me the story of that University's work out through that state. Mrs. Kellogg is one of the few full-time drama specialists in the country attached to an agricultural college; for we are no longer dealing with a drama department, but with the Department of Rural Sociology in the College of Agriculture.

The story goes back fifteen years. Even before that time the University was holding farm group meetings to discuss cattle breeding, dairy methods, soil enrichment and allied agricultural problems. But it was in 1926 that playlets began to be introduced into these conference programs. Most of this took place during Farm and Home Week sponsored by the Agricultural College at Madison. A little later, as interest and enthusiasm in dramatics grew, Ethel G. Rockwell of the University Extension Division was pressed into service to help train people and to arrange a state-wide program of activity. Miss Rockwell has now retired and the work has reverted to the Rural Sociology people.

This theatrical program is carried on through three organizations: the Farm Bureau, the Farmers' Equity Union and the state Grange. Working through the County Agricultural Agents, Mrs. Kellogg and her colleagues reach into Homemakers' Clubs, Community Clubs, 4-H Clubs and churches to bring the glad tidings of Thespis. The

County Agents set up one-day institutes for Mrs. Kellogg in court-houses, normal schools, church basements: in any place large enough to hold the group of from fifteen to fifty who come to learn to be dramatic leaders. These institutes are repeated in the same spot every month or six weeks so that in the course of a season there is time to bring up a number of subjects: choice of plays (this is a real problem throughout this field where the maximum royalty that can be afforded is five dollars), casting, direction and principles of stage movement, make-up, stage equipment and scenery.

From these institutes the farm people (most of them women) go back to their clubs. As the days grow shorter and colder in the Wisconsin autumn and as the evenings grow longer, groups of boys and girls, men and women gather in grange halls and schoolrooms and farm kitchens to make plans and rehearse for the state one-act play tournament. Approximately ninety plays are offered all over the state in county contests and the best are brought to Madison for Farm and Home Week in January.

The gala opening of the Wisconsin Union Theatre was in October, 1939. In January it was opened in a sense for the second time; this time to the people of Wisconsin. To celebrate the occasion the people gave a "pastorale of Wisconsin rural life"—a play with music: a chorus of sixty and two hundred others participated in . . . *Of Folks and Fields*. The program notes that "this play seeks to demonstrate what rural people can create out of their own history and express for their own entertainment. Each of the three acts is played by rural community groups from different counties, yet preserving the continuity of 'the Chester family,' " whose life on Wisconsin's farm land through three generations became the theme of the play: "the farm family, 1895; the community, 1928; youth, 1940." Music and dance was provided by a Yuba band, Bohemian Folk Dancers, a student orchestra, the Cottage Grove P.T.A. Chorus, Sauk County Male Chorus, Dane County Farm Bureau Chorus.

A very different performance this must have been from that opening night three months earlier: Alfred Lunt and Lynn Fontanne and the glittering Theatre Guild cast of *The Taming of the Shrew,* playing to a stiff-bosom-shirt crowd that had paid a five dollar top for its seats. The theatre for . . . *Of Folks and Fields* was filled with apple-cheeked boys and girls flushed with excitement of competitions just completed in stock raising or fruit growing and preserving; with clear-eyed, raw-boned men and women taking recreation from the dairy world of butter and cheese to watch men and women like themselves sing and dance and tell the familiar story of their own lives.

I do not suggest that the theatre is more concerned with . . . *Of Folks and Fields* than with *The Taming of the Shrew.* It is clear to me, however, that this rural drama is a part of America's theatrical pattern. It is new and young and halting; it stands unsteadily on spindling legs. To minds set upon Broadway and to tastes whetted by the Lunts it seems unfamiliar and easily shrugged off. I should not be surprised, however, if the theatre that rises from . . . *Of Folks and Fields* may in another ten years be as familiar an ingredient of American culture as adroit Theatre Guild productions. We cannot do without the Lunts; neither can we do without these spontaneous folk expressions of the people.

At about the same time that Wisconsin was beginning

to insinuate a few playlets into its Farm and Home Week program to pep things up, the same thing was happening in upper New York state. The high-sounding Rural Social Organization Office in the Extension Bureau of the State College of Agriculture at Ithaca was responsible, and Miss Mary Eva Duthie was the person who put it across —who is still putting it across.

The story of Cornell's rural extension work in drama parallels Wisconsin's: there is the same emphasis on the sociological values derived from adult education; there is the same co-operation through 4-H Clubs, Farm and Home Bureaus and occasionally the Grange; there are comparable institutes—except that Miss Duthie's are three-day affairs and sometimes as many as two hundred leaders attend: school teachers, ministers, farm wives; there are extension libraries and play lists sent out as at Wisconsin. At Cornell, too, the dramatic program for these rural groups comes to a head during Farm and Home Week and during the 4-H Congress. The four best plays among the adult community drama groups of fifteen counties are presented; out of 250 4-H Clubs from thirty counties, the three best are presented.

This is not the end of Cornell's services in behalf of the rural people's theatre. Professor Drummond, from his post in the College of Arts and Sciences, also had concern, even before the Agricultural College began its work, for the country people of up-state New York. As early as 1919, Mr. Drummond was taking the Cornell Dramatic Club to the State Fair at Syracuse to give performances, in the hope that by that example rural communities might be stimulated to produce plays themselves. The Cornell University Theatre has continued its interest over the years in regional drama and has attempted to supplement the services of the Agricultural College to rural New York.

Mr. Drummond has been a stickler for excellence. The choice of plays of many of these groups has displeased him. When *Who Gets the Car Tonight?*, *Orville's Big Date*, *Aunt Jerushy on the War Path*, *When Paw Has a Fit* and plays of that ilk were repeated year after year, Mr. Drummond felt that something should be done. The most desirable procedure, he felt, would be to persuade up-state New Yorkers to make use of their own rich native material and of the folk-lore indigenous to the mountains and valleys of the Empire State. But such material did not exist in dramatic form. To encourage its creation, the New York State Play Project was established under a grant from the Rockefeller Foundation.

For the past three years a young playwright, Robert E. Gard, has worked on this project under Mr. Drummond's supervision to collect a body of original material drawn from the people themselves which might be distributed among the dramatic groups of the state. A number of short plays Mr. Gard has written himself or in collaboration with Mr. Drummond; the full-length *The Cardiff Giant* has been the most pretentious and successful of their collaborations. A number of plays have been submitted to the Project, the products of the pens of various amateur dramatists inspired to the task by Mr. Gard's field trips and his own kind of "institutes." These plays Mr. Gard has edited or revised or simply passed out in the form he received them.

Some idea of the results of the theatrical pioneering of Miss Duthie and Mr. Drummond among rural people may be gained from a survey conducted for three years by H. Darkes Albright at Cornell. For the purposes of his survey, Mr. Albright concentrated on "small communities," which he defined as "a village or hamlet of less than five thousand population." At the end of his research in 1939 he was able to report that

there are in New York State's small communities a minimum of 2,300 producing units yearly, and that they publicly present between four and five thousand plays. These figures include high school, church, grange, 4-H, community, club and little theatre groups, as well as other community units more or less sporadically presenting plays from year to year. . . . The number of active workers (that is to say, actors as well as production assistants) involved in these productions has, in recent years, approached thirty thousand annually. This, of course, takes no account of dramatic interest and activity in New York State communities of more than five thousand population.

Delaware is a tiny state; yet here in 1939 eight amateur theatre groups produced forty-five full-length plays and fifty one-act plays to an audience of thirty thousand; more than fifteen hundred persons took part. For much of this dramatic activity the University of Delaware at Newark is responsible. Through its Dramatic Center, set up by a slight, energetic young man, Professor C. R. Kase, it ministers to the needs of high school and community groups in the surrounding Delaware hills. The Center encouraged the formation of a Delaware Dramatic Association and holds a dramatic conference in the winter and a play festival in the spring. To the former more than 225 delegates come, to learn through demonstrations and exchange of ideas how better to carry out their dramatic-recreational exercises.

Mr. Kase's Center has a play-lending library, issues news and service bulletins, offers consultation on theatre problems to district school teachers and distraught directors. Kase himself teaches a Saturday morning extension class for drama instructors. He is also in constant demand to judge plays in contests held by the state grange which is theatrically active on its own in Delaware.

This kind of organization of people's theatre by the state university center is not restricted to Wisconsin, Cornell and Delaware. In many other states the drama of the crossroads receives its stimulus from the campus. At the Universities of Iowa, Indiana, Maine, Washington, Oklahoma state-wide play festivals are encouraged and play-lending-libraries and consultation services are offered as at Delaware. Players with pitchforks are not forgotten.

It's a long jump geographically from tiny Delaware to vast Texas. Everything in the Lone Star State is on a big scale. Notwithstanding I was startled to learn that in 1940 668 high schools competed in a state-wide one-act play contest, one of many competitions in various fields conducted by the University Interscholastic League (again the state university is the pivot) under the leadership of F. C. Winship, Director of Speech Activities. All over Texas these schools meet annually to present their plays. Judges select the eight best which are brought to Austin; out of them a state winner is determined. Mr. Winship claims that as a result of this contest the production of plays in Texas high schools becomes an end in itself and does not, as often happens in other states, serve as a money-maker for some other cause.

Although it may be true, as critics of the contest idea claim, that the competition takes the emphasis off the values of play production and places it all on the idea of winnings; nevertheless, under whatever circumstances 668 schools are producing plays in any one state, more people are becoming aware of the stage, the living actor, the drama, than would otherwise be the case, and one is bound to believe that from such vast animation some revelations of the meaning of culture will be unfolded.

3

The real pioneers in this movement to bring drama to the crossroads, the two men whose names are enrolled at the head of that band of missionaries who have devoted their lives to the cause of a true people's theatre are Alfred G. Arvold and Frederick H. Koch. A consideration of their work forms a fitting conclusion to this study of rural and regional drama.

The plains of the Dakotas have almost the same spaciousness as Texas. As in the Southwest, the sky here seems to dominate the earth. But in Dakota it is rich black earth; this is farm country, not cattle land. This, too, is a solitary world: great sweeping spaces separate one little group of farm buildings from another. There are no cities, few towns. Into this country Alfred G. Arvold has chosen to bring theatre. It is hard to imagine less suitable terrain.

Mr. Arvold's headquarters are in Fargo at the North Dakota State Agricultural College. Upstairs in a Victorian brick-and-stone college building is The Little Country Theater. From an unprepossessing institutionalized entrance one enters the simple hall: three stained-glass windows, gifts to the Theater, are its only relief; the stage is poor and its equipment outmoded. Upstairs are several rooms fashioned to look like a log cabin; they are the workshops and social rooms of The Little Country Theater. The walls and shelves are filled with souvenirs and curios, also gifts to the Theater. Downstairs in a big golden-oak room is the Theater's loan library containing thousands of plays.

This rather shabby spot Mr. Arvold looks upon with indulgent eyes as a thing of beauty. On its stage he recalls performances of plays like the Icelandic classic, *Eyvind of the Hills,* by young farm lads and girls who came to Fargo, as ninety-five per cent of his students do, never having seen a play at all. In the auditorium his mind's eye conjures up the rows of men and women in off the prairies to see his plays—rough peasant folk, mostly blue-eyed and fair, with the names of that region: Peterson, Severson, Henrikson, Opgaard, Bjornhai, Skonnard. In the rooms above he remembers the informal community gatherings before the fire when he has told a circle of these same farmers what possibilities and impulses for drama lie in themselves.

The "package library" is not for him just a collection of books to be loaned out. Each copy brings back from its wanderings some story familiar to Arvold—of a little gathering of Scandinavians in the New World plains arranging a home talent show to present in a grange hall or church. Arvold recalls these gatherings so vividly because he has participated in hundreds of them, has been directly responsible for many. All year round he is off in his car to some outpost or other to hold a one-, two- or four-day drama institute. By day the women come, in the evening the men join them to hear Arvold read plays aloud to them, to have him tell them how to produce these plays, to listen to his encouragement of indigenous drama.

Sometimes Mr. Arvold stages the production himself. Shortly before I came to Fargo he had presented *Peer Gynt* at Fort Ransom, North Dakota, in a cow pasture, which he euphemistically called in the program "The Hall of the Mountain King—a natural outdoor theatre." There were fifty participants and more than a thousand people assembled in the pasture to see the two performances. Neighboring farmers blew out the stumps that cropped up in the pasture where audience and actors needed flat ground.

Mr. Arvold is an arch pageant-master. Harvest festivals, May-Day celebrations (the non-political kind), lilac pageants, historical and patriotic programs chase each other around his calendar every year. These are a wise brand to sell, for they require no individual excellence—just hundreds of willing people, big splashes of color, wide spaces and a simple message as familiar with repetition as "O, Beautiful for Spacious Skies."

With Salvation Army enthusiasm Mr. Arvold believes in the country and country people. He has written:

When the people who live in the small community and the country awaken to the possibilities which lie hidden in themselves through the impulse of a vitalized drama, they will not only be less eager to move to centers of population but will also be a force in attracting city folks to dwell in the country. The monotony of country existence will change into a newer, a more beautiful and a broader life.

There is one thing about the story of The Little Country Theater that disturbs me. Kenneth Macgowan wrote twelve years ago his account of it in *Footlights Across America*. Now more than a decade later I find nothing new to add to his story. Mr. Arvold is doing in 1941 just what he was doing in 1929. The missionary zeal and the dedicated faith with which he was serving the students at Fargo and the country people of North Dakota then is as strong today and it is a wonderful thing to behold. But I see no signs of progress. Perhaps that is too much to expect in this situation, where one man works single-handed in such a vast area and where there is such a dearth of developed talent; or perhaps I was too much influenced by the comments of a middle-aged rough-knuckled Norwegian artist-farmer, who had come into Fargo the day I was there to hear Kirsten Flagstad sing. I admit he sounded like one of Job's comforters.

"Arvold is a fine fellow," he murmured, "and when he's around everybody is glad to do as he says. But he can't be everywhere at once, and when he's gone, nobody seems to be up to carrying on the kind of thing he says we ought to do to make ourselves happier."

He paused and sighed. "It's the young people," he said, looking at me apologetically. "They don't seem to like the old-fashioned get-togethers any more. Instead of having home talent shows and such, like Mr. Arvold talks about, they're always running off in two's and three's in cars or going ten miles to the nearest movie. They don't speak Norwegian much any more either; and the choirs in which we all used to take such pride in these parts—singing our folk tunes and Scandinavian airs—

they've gone to pieces too because the young people don't care about singing together either."

To restore the discouraged spirit of the reader and of Mr. Arvold should he read this, I must record that I sat next to this Norse Jeremiah at Flagstad's concert that night. He was hearing her for the first time. When it was over, he turned to me sadly and said, "It's too bad she hasn't a better voice."

Little, gray-haired, pipe-smoking Frederick H. Koch is such a master of publicity that the story of his "Carolina Playmakers" manages to work its way into every account of the American non-professional theatre. I am consequently loath to reiterate its history and recount the usual anecdotes about "Proff" Koch and his Playmaker colleagues during their twenty-year missionary campaign to bring the theatre to the natives of the North Carolina brush. To be sure, tribute must be paid to Mr. Koch's work; at the same time a critical comment on the present situation at the University where Mr. Koch is chairman of the Drama Department may make a refreshing contrast to the usual panegyrics.

There is no doubt that the Carolina Playmakers, like The Little Country Theater at Fargo, have had a profound effect on the lives of many untutored folk who would otherwise have never seen a play. Koch's attack has differed from Arvold's in several respects. In the first place, the Dakota leader has gone out into the field to produce plays with the people themselves. Mr. Koch has instead usually put his whole company of Playmakers into a truck and taken the show to the people. Probably the chief difference, however, lies in the disregard Arvold has had, either through lack of personal inclination or talent, for stimulating regional writing, as contrasted with Koch's almost fanatical obsession over original play material.

Mr. Koch believes firmly that "anyone can write a play." His corollary is, "everyone should write a play." This obviously menacing point of view Koch has promulgated wherever he has gone. The result has been a plethora of exceedingly bad stuff—vast fields of weeds. Nevertheless such enthusiasm—and Koch's is matchless—has resulted in widespread awareness of theatre throughout the area in which he has worked. The Carolina Dramatic Association in 1940 included ninety-two member organizations, thirty-five of them directed by Koch graduates, and undoubtedly all of them called into being by his example and propulsion. That is a sizeable output even after twenty-one years of tillage, for North Carolina is not a heavily populated state. That tillage has also resulted in basketloads of original plays, most of them one-act, to which the long, published series of "Carolina Folk Plays" bears testimony.

Mr. Koch's approach to playwriting is fundamentally sound and is the only possible basis on which any native drama can be built: "Write of what you know." His constant preaching of this dictum and his long insistence on "folk" material has earned him the right to be considered the arch prophet of regional drama in this country: a drama devoted to portrayal of the warp and woof of simple human experiences in whatever humble environment they occur.

The pivot around which the work at the University of North Carolina revolves is, as might be expected, playwriting. The courses in acting, directing, technical production, historical background are neither numerous nor remarkable; the Playmakers' theatre is not above the average. Samuel Selden, who appears to be the power behind the Carolina throne, makes a stab at inculcating some standards of excellence, but the soft-scented breezes of Chapel Hill and the aroma of "Proff" Koch's placid pipe combine to work a critical lethargy for which there are but two antidotes.

The first of these is the presence at Chapel Hill of Paul Green. Most noted Playmaker alumnus, this ex-professor of philosophy, Pulitzer Prize dramatist, ex-Hollywood scenarist is now on the faculty of the Drama Department to lead seminars in play and radio writing. Among all the artists of the theatre with whom I talked throughout the country, none had greater vision or wisdom than Paul Green. His playwriting is the epitome of all that Koch seeks in the theatre. To young people trying to follow Koch's precepts and in Green's footsteps to write of what they know in the simple folk tradition, the counsel and encouragement of such a master must be very precious.

The second valuable possession of the Carolina Playmakers has already been referred to: Mr. Koch's personal enthusiasm which is pervasive and indomitable. After twenty-one years at Chapel Hill he retains a buoyancy and relish for the task that must be as great as the day he arrived on that previously benighted shoal, clutching in one hand the bible of folk drama and waving aloft with the other the banner of "Playmakers."

Koch's enthusiasm is a match for Arvold's missionary zeal. In each case, however, it is combined with a joyous disregard for any kind of standard—a situation which I regard as too serious to be overlooked. The Carolina Playmakers have occasionally been compared with Ireland's Abbey Theatre. Insofar as each has been concerned with the authenticity of folk expression and the stimulation of appreciation for native lore they are comparable. Each revealed to its countrymen the untapped resources of drama and poetry in the lives of the simple people among them. Beyond this the Abbey playwrights soared because they had the wings of genius. Except for Paul Green, the Carolina dramatists have remained on the ground, scratching in the earth in search of substitutes for poetry.

Is it simply dearth of genius which has prevented the Carolina Playmakers from releasing the contents of the Pandora's box they discovered? The constant reiteration of the fact of discovery is not enough. Perhaps there are other reasons why in their actual work Koch and his disciples have been unable to realize the folk-play dream adequately. Mr. Koch's own apparent lack of critical acumen, to which I have already alluded, stands in the way, I feel sure. Artistic discipline is rarely practiced at Chapel Hill. William Peery, in an informal but penetrating portrait of Carolina playmaking,[1] puts his finger on several other weaknesses which seem to me to be present.

In the first place [he wrote], an attempt to preserve the past—not as history but as a living anachronism—may be in practice an attempt to block progress, to deny contemporary life. Carolina folk drama has been too largely an escapist drama. . . . Professor Koch's student of the second generation no longer comes from the world portrayed in the first Carolina folk plays. He is a product of the consolidated school,

---

[1] *Carolina Playmaking* won the Gray Essay Award of the Dramatists' Alliance at Stanford University in 1939.

a son of the radio and cinema. He can quote the batting average of every player in the American League. When Paul Green wrote his first play, it is reported, he had never seen a play performed. The present crop of student authors has been acting in plays since childhood. The Playmakers cannot for twenty years take their theatre, as they do in their annual tours, into the isolated hamlets of the state and expect those hamlets to remain dramatically inexperienced. North Carolina has been drama conscious for more than ten years—at the expense of the naive wonder which made the early Carolina folk play so effective. "Write what you know," Professor Koch repeats, and I doubt that anyone will disagree with this part of his doctrine. But recent student authors do not know at first hand, and they are not a part of, the life with which Playmaker plays most commonly deal. They will have to face problems typical of today or lose that creative power of native materials which largely accounts for the success of folk movements in the past. . . .

Like other arts, drama is at its best a happy marriage of form with content. This delicate balance between manner and matter the writer of folk plays can hardly be expected to attain. Subscribing to a creed which emphasizes content, the Playmaker author either "created fresh dramatic forms" as Professor Koch says or perhaps was careless of form altogether. Many early Playmaker efforts . . . through their strange beautiful dialect, their eccentricity of character, their antiquarianism, and the earnestness with which they were first acted, appealed strongly to audiences weary of superficial drama —without ever having to meet high standards of dramatic effectiveness.

Now, however, there remain few uninitiated audiences in North Carolina. . . . Playmaker audiences have seen many a comedy of mountain life, of preachers leaning too heavily on their jugs of corn liquor, of still operators "het up t' git them revenooers"—comedies very close to farce because of exaggeration in speech and such character traits as punctuating one's sentences by spitting tobacco. Since Harold Williamson wrote *Peggy,* that ancestor of *Tobacco Road,* they have seen many a tragedy of the tenant farmer whose women-folks "crave purties" and whose children cry for "a tech o' fat-back" to eat with their hominy. Shorn of his novelty, the typical folk character is no longer so interesting; the young author may no longer use him for a crutch to a play lacking structural backbone.

Mr. Peery's criticisms of the playwriting fostered at the University of North Carolina suggest the pitfalls into which regional folk drama everywhere has a tendency to drop. These pitfalls are not inevitable and they can be avoided. Elsewhere in his essay, Mr. Peery speaks of the "confusion of life with art which has been characteristic of the Playmakers and of other folk writers. At Chapel Hill the stock rebuttal of any criticism of authenticity or motivation is: 'But I used to know that man. He *did* do just that!'" This confusion is chronic among our recorders of folk-ways for the stage. But Synge and O'Casey never suffered from it.

My chief criticism of much regional drama is that it exploits the idiosyncrasies of a locality without attempting to examine or express their causes. The value of regionalism in the art of a vast country like ours lies in its ability to interpret one part of our people to the rest of us. Most folk drama makes no effort at all to interpret; it is content to portray the superficial oddities of local behavior and to revel in its quaintness. Mr. Koch is right in challenging his disciples to look about them and find

the ingredients of drama in their own experience and surroundings. He is wrong in thinking that any formless
projection of those ingredients on the stage automatically
makes a play.

North Carolina is rich in native materials, as is almost
every other part of the United States. Each region can
yield abundant treasure to the artist who digs there. Poets
of the stage like Paul Green, Lynn Riggs and E. P.
Conkle have shown us by their spadework how close to
the surface and how rich the vein is. But everywhere that
material must be worked and sifted and weighed and
rubbed before it can be called a work of art.

The rich material for drama in Carolina or in New
Hampshire, Arizona or Oregon is not only in the story
that is ended. Folk dramatists live too much in the past;
old tales spun out by the fire are more attractive to them
than the news of the present. But yesterday is important
to us only insofar as it illumines our understanding and
appreciation of today and fortifies our hope for tomorrow. And today each region of our land faces its own
problems—some rooted in the past, some new: dust or
drought, hunger or strikes; farm troubles, town troubles,
factory troubles, class troubles. Each region has its own
triumphs too, and they as well as the problems are food
for our stage.

I do not seek to dampen the ardor of the regionalists
or to shake a disapproving head at their purposes. I believe it is exceedingly important—and I repeat what I
have said before—that the pattern of fashionable Broadway playmaking should not forever be imposed on the
country as a whole. But it will persist thus until dramatists

arise all over the land who will replace the Broadway patter with strong native speech that is meaningful; until dramatists arise to sing of today as well as the day gone by. The folk writer must make the tie between past and present, just as he must make the tie between his region and ours, if he is to command our ears.

CHAPTER EIGHT

Players in Overalls

THERE IS ANOTHER people's theatre in America beside the one of Frederick Koch and Alfred Arvold. It is found less often in country schools and grange halls than in the lofts and union headquarters on city side-streets. It is the stage of the workers; the proletarian, trade-union theatre; in the centers of industry we must seek it most frequently. This theatre has no mention in *Footlights Across America*, for in 1929 it was just beginning to stir; it is not talked about in *Curtains Going Up*, for by 1939 it took special sleuthing to uncover its hibernating retreats. It exists, however, and it commands a place in any study of theatrical patterns.

It is too bad that this chapter could not have been written five years ago, or that it cannot be postponed to five years hence; for this people's theatre belongs more to yesterday and tomorrow than it does to today. In the 1930s it sprang into being, struggled and began to march. In 1935 when Ben Blake, one of the founders of the "new theatre movement," wrote *The Awakening of the American Theatre*, this people's stage was shaking the foundations of Broadway, and observers were beginning to say that the long-awaited revitalization of our dramatic art was on its way in from the left.

Mr. Blake was able to report in that peak year of the movement the success of the Theatre Union on Fourteenth Street in New York, where *Peace on Earth, Sailors of Cattaro* and *Stevedore* were attracting large crowds and increasingly favorable attention from the "capitalist press." He was able to tell of the rise in New York of the Theatre of Action out of the amateur Workers Laboratory Theatre and of their production of *The Young Go First*.

In 1935 the Artef Theatre, also in Manhattan, came into prominence with its brilliant performance in Yiddish of *Recruits*. This semi-professional group under Benno Schneider's direction was composed of Jewish workers who devoted their days to bread-and-butter trades and in the evenings came together to study, rehearse and produce. By 1935 the socially-conscious Group Theatre was beginning to be hailed by many as the outstanding theatre organization in New York. That was the year it produced three plays by one of its young actors: *Waiting for Lefty, Awake and Sing, Till the Day I Die;* Clifford Odets became the leading playwright of the "new theatre movement" and the Group his distinguished mouthpiece.

It was also in 1935 that the so-called League of Workers Theatres became the New Theatre League, which at that time summarized its purposes thus: "For a mass development of the American theatre to its highest artistic and social level; for a theatre dedicated to the struggle against war, fascism and censorship." It welcomed men and women of all nationalities, races and creeds within America, so long as they believed in its program. Its member organizations included groups, some professional and

semi-professional, some amateur in New York, Philadelphia, Chicago, Boston, Los Angeles, Cleveland, New
Haven, Newark, Pittsburgh, Detroit. Its magazine *New
Theatre* claimed a circulation of over eighteen thousand
by the end of 1935; its contributors included such persons
as Lincoln Kirstein, Archibald MacLeish, John Howard
Lawson, Alfred Saxe, Lee Strasberg, King Vidor, Richard
Watts Jr., Tamiris, Herbert Kline and a great many
others.

All this was occurring in 1935. Now I write six years
later and the world is very different. So is the theatre.
Most of the activity I have described centered in New
York. Today that city contains no strong workers' theatre. The Theatre Union did not survive; the Theatre of
Action came to an end. So did the Theatre Collective and
the Actors Repertory Theatre, organizations for which
there seemed some hope immediately after 1935. The
Artef Theatre ceased to produce and at last in 1940 the
Group Theatre disintegrated, the last to fall. *New Theatre* no longer appears on the newsstands. What is the
story behind this decline and fall? To what extent is it
a fall?

We are concerned here, even more than hitherto, with
the social forces of the American scene. In the mid-1930s
liberalism was flowering with unprecedented vigor. The
impetus of the New Deal and the overwhelming approval
of its program at the polls the next year were part of the
cause-and-effect of a revitalized social outlook. The news
from the Soviet Union was particularly encouraging in
those days. The ranks of the "fellow travelers" were
swelled by many of the country's intellectual leaders.
Labor made tremendous gains in the mid-thirties as hun-

dreds of thousands of workers were organized for their own benefit and progress.

Between 1935 and 1940 came the rise and fall of the Federal Theatre Project. Its popular-priced playhouses absorbed most of the labor theatre's potential audience and onto its rolls were added many of the artists of the Theatre of Action and of the other workers' stages that had served that audience. A real people's theatre appeared to be in the making and one that, standing in opposition to commercial Broadway, was devoted artistically, ideologically and economically to the creation of a "new theatre." This then helps to explain the disappearance of many of the independent "new theatres," especially in New York; with government support Federal Theatre was better able than they to minister to the workingman.

Federal Theatre's very preoccupation with this workers' audience and its policy of devoting much of its energies to plays that would be especially meaningful to such a public were among the causes of its downfall. But when it went, the labor theatre it had supplanted did not come back. The abolition of Federal Theatre would have been the signal for a new spurt by the labor stage to take over the newly-created low-price audience, had not the world suddenly begun to change with even greater rapidity than ever.

The strongly "interventionist" Roosevelt administration seemed to many labor leaders to be swinging away from its early liberalism. Our involvement in the new World War, they considered, would wreak irreparable damage to all labor's hard-fought gains, even as it would restrict freedom and call a halt to cultural progress. By 1940 the "fellow-travelers" had lost from among their company most of the middle-class intelligentsia, the erstwhile pinks; for the defeat of Loyalist Spain had disheartened them, and the German-Soviet pact and the Finnish war had further disillusioned them and turned them against the Soviet Union. The loss of these middle-class patrons of workers' stages cut down their financial resources. The growing war sentiment and the powerful aid-to-Britain propaganda were exceedingly hard on a labor theatre militantly dedicated to peace. The Theatre Arts Committee, formed to arouse stage workers to the cause of the Popular Front against fascism abroad and at home, which published TAC Magazine and led the theatre in a rousing program in support of Loyalist Spain, finally succumbed at the end of 1940.

By 1941, therefore, the labor theatre was finding a reorientation necessary; this process is still going on. The New Theatre League early in that year decided to decentralize. The national office was abolished and in its place five regional centers were established in Los Angeles, Chicago, Nashville, Philadelphia and New York. At each of these centers there was to be an operating theatre; in addition a school was to be set up in each center and a service bureau for the surrounding region whose primary purpose would be the publication and dissemination of indigenous play material. Three of these five theatres I visited in 1940 before the new organization was effected, and a fourth I visited in 1941; a description of them may illustrate the characteristics of the workers' theatres generally.

2

The scene was a remodeled old church in Philadelphia's near north side, not far beyond the Broad Street Station, where the streets are narrow and the buildings low. It was the New Theatre of Philadelphia. That night they were opening a new play, *Medicine*. It was a "living news-paper," an edition based on material collected by the Federal Theatre before its demise, which was being used at about the same time as the basis of a play for Broadway, *Medicine Show*. In Philadelphia it was offered in a slightly different version under Lem Ward's direction on a very different stage to an opening night audience not very reminiscent of Broadway's: no one in evening dress, of course; a great many young people; much serious attention to what was to be seen on the stage.

A piano thundered some startling chords, the lights flashed out, a loudspeaker voice from the back of the house cried out some challenging words, the curtains parted and the play was on. Against a background of projected light forms the story of man's struggle against disease was unfolded. A reviewer wrote next morning:

Medicine is a plea or rather a demand for socialized medi-cine. It states that every year 500,000 people in the United States—most of them in the lower income brackets—die before their time from ailments which could have been cured. It states that this needless loss costs the nation $10,000,000 annually. . . . It presents the paradoxical situation of young doctors seeking in vain for practices while thousands of patients seek in vain for doctors and it implores governmental aid in the situation.

It was an exciting evening: the tense, taut drama drove fast and steadily to its conclusions. Its searing indictment was convincing, its demand for action challenging. No great actors paced the boards, no visions of loveliness were unfolded, but the cast of twenty-nine was sincere and forceful and the staging dynamic. As I descended the stairs from the drab hall, I had to say to myself: "This is the most vivid and valuable evening I have spent in the theatre since I left New York three months ago."

I was taken backstage but there was little to see. Real drama had been evoked without benefit of modern lighting equipment or a grid; actors were crowded into a couple of inadequate dressing rooms; props spilled over into work-rooms that also served as classrooms, for there was no off-stage space behind the flimsy black curtains.

When the cast had doffed their costumes and make-up they took me off to the apartment of one of their number where we sat on the floor and they talked about their work. The Philadelphia New Theatre, like most labor theatres, is non-professional. Its organization differs from the usual little theatre wherein the Board of Directors is the ultimate authority. Here the active membership, numbering about eighty (of whom fifty are actors), votes on all important issues, even including final choice of plays. To handle emergencies and to regulate the day-to-day activity of the theatre are a Production Council, responsible only for matters actually relating to production, and an Executive Committee which integrates the business management with the Council's work.

The repertory for 1939-40 consisted of Paul Horgan's *To Every Goliath*, an original revue entitled *We Beg to Differ*, a revival of *Bury the Dead*, in addition to *Medicine*. These plays are presented only on Friday and Saturday nights during a five- or six-week period. A workers' audience is a week-end crowd. It includes several hundred "club members" of New Theatre who for one dollar receive a twenty per cent discount on all tickets they buy.

Equally important to the New Theatre—and to all new theatres everywhere—is its mobile work. Out through the city and large parts of eastern Pennsylvania go its units to present one-act plays or brief vaudeville programs with a social content at union meetings and to groups of strikers. Several nights a week groups of these indefatigable young people pile into automobiles and set out for a rally in some steel town or tough suburb of Philadelphia. The shows they stage are rudimentary dialogues inflamed with passion and speaking out in childishly simple terms for peace or labor unity. But they suit the audience at which they are directed.

Material for these constantly presented programs of skits and even for the major production schedule is scarce. In the hope of encouraging some one of their number to develop hidden talent and become its Odets, the New Theatre sponsors a playwriting group in which twelve of its members are at work; it also sponsors annually a one-act play contest.

Even before it became one of the regional centers of the New Theatre League, the Philadelphia affiliate conducted a school. Adult classes were being held in 1940, five hours a day, five days a week during a ten-week semester. Equally important were its classes for children. Aaron Spiegel, acting Executive Secretary, described their organization thus: "We sent to the principals of all public and parochial schools in the city asking for nominees to the New Theatre Free Children's School. One hundred and fifty names were submitted. We gave auditions to the entire group. Of these 150, forty were selected and given scholarships for a two-year course." There was a class for youngsters ten to twelve years old, another for high school age boys and girls. To this school members donated time for instruction, but in 1940-41 the strain of this became too great; an unsuccessful attempt was made to subsidize this activity; although adult education continued, children's classes had to be abandoned.

Moving on across America to Lake Michigan, I met the Chicago Repertory Group, another collection of butchers, bakers, candlestick-makers and truck-drivers, waitresses, stenographers with an urge to act and something they considered important to say. Occupying a grimy two floors on Balbo Street, the Repertory Group were in the throes of rehearsing an original musical revue. It was called *The Lady Is Right* and it was being directed by Donald Murray who had come on from the West Coast to be production head of the Group.

The show was in that embryonic state any musical is in up to the day before it opens, so it was hard to tell what impact it would have. Its material was fresh, new labor stuff; the staging was becomingly fast and vigorous. There seemed to be no great talent in evidence, however; most of the book was pretty obvious and the music was not remarkable. One gathered that the production's merit would be in its topical allusions, its timeliness, in the gusto, enthusiasm and sincerity of its performers.

The rehearsal began at seven o'clock or as soon thereafter as the participants could get away from their factories, packing houses or stores, get a bite of supper and be at the theatre. By ten o'clock it was over, for a mobile group of about a dozen of the key people had to be off to provide entertainment at a dinner that some striking furniture workers were holding. All "new theatre" activity seems to take place on the second floor. This dinner to which I was taken was upstairs too, over a café in a part of town far away from Lake Shore Drive. The program was light but informed with a social message. It seemed to me that the performers were more enthusiastic over their work than the audience was; perhaps this was because cabaret was unfamiliar to many of these striking workers. By the time everyone had joined in singing "Solidarity," things were a little easier.

The Chicago Repertory Group resembles the Philadelphia New Theatre not only in its attention to mobile work, but also in having a playwrights' group that meets once a week and works to provide topical material for both mobile and major production schedules. It likewise has a studio school with courses in acting, voice training and body movement. Like the Philadelphia group this Chicago theatre also depends in large measure for its audience on organized group bookings by trade unions or other progressive units. In Chicago they claim that by this system 1,460 of their three thousand seats for the run of an average play are sold three weeks in advance. The Chicago Repertory Group had about sixty members in 1940. A governing board of twenty-four, to whom an executive committee is responsible, is the final authority. In 1940-41 it had no permanent director but divided his work among veteran volunteers.

These first two representatives of this social new theatre movement have been amateur, even more amateur than the little theatres; for whereas most of the latter have paid leaders or assistants numbering from one or two as at Houston or Jacksonville to seventy-five as at Pasadena, these labor groups have no salary list at all. Every full-time worker (and Philadelphia, for instance, has three) is a volunteer.

On the West Coast, however, is a professional "new theatre," as far as I know the only one in the movement today. It is the Hollywood Theatre Alliance with whose sharp and gay musical revue, *Meet the People*, Los Angeles, San Francisco, Chicago, New York and a few other road towns are familiar. *Meet the People* was its first production; it opened on Christmas night, 1939, and was immediately a tumultuous success. Few theatres—no progressive labor groups—have found their initial effort so rewarded. The Alliance deserved this success for it had fashioned a bright, trenchant, amusing revue; had peopled the stage with attractive new faces and personalities; had put into their mouths strong social satire which was not afraid to talk plainly against war and class injustice; had put the Bill of Rights to music and made it into a stirring clarion-call to remind of democracy's meaning. In short, *Meet the People* showed everyone that a talented social theatre could be as clever and entertaining, as provocative and stimulating as any other theatre—perhaps more so!

The Hollywood Theatre Alliance is professional in its

participating membership, commercial in its practice, community and social in its spirit. In its program its policy is stated as "the presentation of contemporary material in which, as Ibsen says, 'a dramatist's business is not to answer questions, merely to ask them.' Let the theatre be provocative and stimulating and the answers will come."

The Alliance is a collective theatre. Its membership numbers about three hundred, three-fourths of whom are professionals; the remainder are from the audience. Payment of five dollars a year allows these members ticket reductions, a vote in elections to the Executive Board and the opportunity to serve on committees. There is also an audience membership costing one dollar a year.[1]

The Executive Board of thirteen members, whose chairman in 1940-41 was J. Edward Bromberg, is responsible for the theatre's maintenance. It employs a managing director, a casting and repertory director, a craft director. There is also an accountant and a publicity and public relations manager. Responsible to the Board are five committees:

(1) Financial. It might be well to point out that the Alliance sees no reason why it should not pay actors to work in a social theatre if it can be afforded. Consequently Equity salaries are paid to all.

(2) The Future Productions committee is composed primarily of professional playwrights, men like John Howard Lawson, Michael Blankfort, George Sklar, some of them at work in Hollywood studios but interested in

---

[1] This audience membership offers ten per cent reduction of two seats for each show, fifty per cent reduction on two tickets to each theatre forum, the privilege of voting for an audience Council to represent its interests in the Alliance.

this theatre. The committee works collectively on script revisions, determines the approach to the play; a sub-committee becomes the Production committee when the show is finally put into work; it recommends a director and designer, supervises casting (which seeks to take advantage of the great amount of professional talent available in Hollywood, although the Alliance is not averse to importing artists from Broadway when necessary).

(3) A Children's Theatre committee hopes to develop a program of plays for youngsters performed by adults; to establish a children's workshop where boys and girls will learn to make and work puppets, make improvisations which will develop out of dance work, finally write and present plays for themselves to supplement the program of children's plays performed by grown-up actors.

(4) A Negro Theatre committee is attempting to establish collaboration with a Negro group which in 1940 was preparing a colored revue and which hopes eventually to set up its own stage.

(5) The Mobile Theatre committee, with whose work the reader is familiar elsewhere, has not functioned very successfully in Hollywood.

In all this description of the Alliance's program, it must be borne in mind that I visited it less than a year after its inception. Its future plans are consequently more significant than its accomplishments. It aims to create a unified approach on the part of all workers in the Alliance toward a truly new theatre. This requires the foundation of a definitive dialectical and esthetic point of departure; the search for it occupies the Theatre Alliance today. I would err if I sought here to make its definition for it. From the artistic standpoint the establishment of an actors' council, which is contemplated, would lead to a laboratory work-shop where explorations toward a unified approach to act-ing would be made and out of which a whole production method might be devised. From the ideological stand-point, this unity of approach would lead toward further clarification of the Alliance's credo:

The theatre still remains a place to cry out our hopes and doubts in an effort to solve our common problems. Under democracy it turns a searching spotlight on the most telling aspects of contemporary life and vividly illuminates man against his background. In this way only can an audience be moved to light-hearted courageous laughter, purposeful indignation or clearsighted action.

The establishment of its fourth center in Nashville bears witness to the New Theatre League's concern for the South. I did not visit Nashville nor did I come across any workers' theatres in this region. Nevertheless the annals of the League are full of reports from Southern states and I am tempted to quote a passage from one of them.

The South is not industrial and to reach the workers at whom this movement aims—tenant farmers, sharecrop-pers, Negro and white—one must leave the small cities and penetrate into the back country. Most "new theatre" activity in this area has consequently been mobile. The Red Dust Players of Oklahoma City are a typical exam-ple. Dorothy Schmidt wrote to the New Theatre League in May, 1940:

I wish every one of you could have been with us on our last Tuesday's booking for the Oklahoma Tenant Farmers Union up in Creek County. It's sharecroppers part of the state, rolling hills covered with red sand. What hasn't been bled out by the oil wells has been blown away by the wind. We were off the highway, some ten miles from the nearest town, in a little Negro church, playing by light of five oil lanterns that the audience had brought with them. Our audience came from twenty miles away in all directions; some of them we had to fetch in ourselves. The admission was ten cents, children under six, free—but we felt we should have paid them for the pleasure of performing. One old man toted a sack of flour into town and sold it to raise the admission for himself and kids, and one family mortgaged their old sow. One woman said she would've stayed up all night seeing it over and over, and one woman said it'd been ten years—maybe longer—she'd forgot just when—since she'd "clupped her hands together" last. But they clupped and they laughed way down deep, Negro and white together, and scraped their feet on the floor, and said, Yes, sir, that's the truth; that's the way it is; and sang "We Shall Not Be Moved."

Six months later I was in Oklahoma City. I tried to call on the Red Dust Players, but they were no more. I talked on the telephone to a young man who I was told had been connected with them, but Peter-like he thrice denied them. You see, Oklahoma's criminal syndicalism law has been freshly invoked; it has become a treasonous act to suggest to sharecroppers or tenant farmers that their lot may be bettered. The Red Dust Players' meager quarters were raided; all their scripts and material were seized; its leaders found it necessary to disband and abandon the theatrical work Miss Schmidt described in her letter.

On my return to New York I found the reorganization of the New Theatre League just being effected. An independent theatre unit was being set up and *Zero Hour* by Sklar and Maltz, which had been given its première

by the Hollywood Theatre Alliance, was to be revived as
the first production of the Manhattan Center in May,
1941. Donald Murray, transferred from Chicago, was the
director.

For several years the New Theatre League has been
conducting a school in New York, not only training leaders
for the labor theatre but preparing actors to practice their
art on Broadway or wherever they could gain a hearing.
In 1941 the School decided, however, to offer only evening sessions and to concentrate on instruction for potential leaders of workers' and trade union theatres.

Throughout the country the "new theatre movement"
has decided to look to the trade unions for its outlet and
its support. I have already suggested that in the 1930s
organized labor pushed forward at a tremendous pace. In
those years the unions were so busy organizing that there
was no time to build an educational or cultural program for
their members. In the 1940s the prospect for such activity
looked hopeful to the New Theatre League (provided, of
course, war did not put an end to all labor's plans for self-
betterment). It accordingly urged its affiliates to encourage
and assist in all possible ways theatrical expression in trade
union locals everywhere. In the spring of 1941 the New
Theatre Center in New York was able to report that dramatic groups were active in Manhattan's Fur Workers'
Union, Hotel and Restaurant Employees' Alliance and
its Waitresses' Local, United Wholesale and Warehouse
Employees Local 65, the American Communications Association (employees of Western Union, Postal Tele-
graph, etc.), Teachers' Union Local 5, Department Store
Workers (Hearn's, Bloomingdale's, Macy's organizations
—one is inclined to believe this should be one of the finest

theatre groups in America, when one considers the number of talented unemployed actors clerking in these stores), United Office and Professional Workers, Furniture Workers' Union, Cafeteria Employees' Union, Amalgamated Drug Clerks, Union of State, County and Municipal Workers, United Electrical Radio Machine Workers; units were about to be set up in the Transport Workers' Union and the Newspaper Guild (drama critics to become actors, one wonders).

One unseasonably hot Sunday night in May I elbowed my way into the assembly hall of the Fur Workers' Union in New York. It was jammed with more than six hundred perspiring young people who comprised the audience at the second annual New York Trade Union Drama Tournament. The United Office and Professional Workers offered an original one-act play about an office workers' strike, which was based on their actual experience. The Furriers presented a condensation of *Bury the Dead,* doubly moving today, I found. (One of the soldiers who refused to be buried was being played by a young man off to the draft army the following week.) The hit of the evening was the Wholesale and Warehouse Employees' short original musical show. It was possessed of a gaiety and militant trade union loyalty that swept everything before it. The audience clapped and cheered and whistled and stamped on the floor; the heat was forgotten.

The general public has become aware in the last few years of what can be accomplished in a trade union theatre, by the success of the International Ladies' Garment Workers' Union's Labor Stage which produced *Pins and Needles.* The ILGWU has long been one of the wealthiest and most powerful units in organized labor. Back in the NRA days when the Union's rolls expanded from forty thousand to two hundred thousand members and when through the institution of the thirty-five hour week there arose a leisure-time problem for workers, this progressive organization set up an educational and cultural program.[2] Athletics, music, dance and drama became familiar ingredients of a new life for thousands of garment workers in Greater New York. After several years of class instruction in the stage arts under Lee Strasberg, S. Syrjala and others, ILGWU decided to start actual play production; after a couple of amorphous beginnings *Pins and Needles* finally emerged, and in its various editions it played more performances in the succeeding three seasons than any musical show on Broadway.

Labor Stage was housed in a tiny remodeled playhouse on the fringe of the Times Square district. Its severely streamlined walls painted with strong flat color, its hard seats, the affirmative chords of the two pianos, but above all, the enthusiastic rapport between working-class actors and a working-class audience reminded me of workers' theatres in Moscow. There was a positive and passionate exuberance to be felt in this little playhouse during the early days of the *Pins and Needles* run, before the "carriage trade" began to patronize it, an exuberance that was unparalleled in any other New York theatre. Labor Stage showed that the workers could laugh and make fun, could discover among their number plenty of vivacious young talent; could, in short, meet and beat the Broadway managers at their own game. Its success at popular prices showed too that the economic problems of New York production are not insuperable.

[2] Many other progressive trade unions have comparable programs.

Unfortunately it must be recorded that Labor Stage has not as yet fulfilled its early promise. For *Pins and Needles* opened in the season of 1937-38 and nothing else has followed it (save a mammoth labor pageant in which the whole union participated). Lack of worth-while plays is purported to be the reason. Whatever the cause, it is regrettable that in 1941 Labor Stage had nothing to offer New York. Regrettable too are intimations that this organization has become somewhat commercialized. Labor Stage has done so much to set the standard for trade union dramatics that it must not allow itself either artistically or socially to sit back on its laurels and become in any way reactionary.

3

The social theatre has fewer friends today than it has ever had. The increasing unpopularity of the leftist point of view—particularly among the powerful middle class—as the lines of the present world conflict become more sharply drawn makes sympathetic attention to the cause of the labor stage increasingly hard to command. It is not the purpose of this book to argue politics or economic and social theories. Any effort at an impartial appraisal of the American theatre, however, must give the "new theatre movement" its due.

The greatest strength of the social theatre is that it has something to say. Whether you agree with what it says or not, you must admit that this gives it an element of affirmation which those who have nothing to say lack. The fact that it has a message and is fired with the importance of delivering it, elevates it above those little theatres whose sole *raison d'être* is the egocentric self-expression of a few people. Almost no community theatre has the "mobile" units which the poorest "new theatre" operates. Almost no community theatre has a school in connection with it. Almost no community theatre would continue to exist at all if it were faced with the lack of newspaper co-operation, the antagonism of local government and the poverty which are the almost constant accompaniments of workers' theatres.

Poverty is probably this movement's greatest handicap. Its members are all low wage-earners; there are no angels in a mood to endow it these days; it can get no support from foundations or educational institutions or city treasuries; it cannot support itself at its box office either, for it is committed to serving a public as poor as itself and so its price range must be low. Without money, however, it cannot easily improve its situation: cannot build playhouses, cannot hire enough trained leaders, cannot endow playwrights to write for it, or offer them high royalties if they do.

Since the workers' theatre is for the most part amateur, it is subject to the same uncertainties as regards talent as face other non-professional theatres. Some of its artists may be good; others eager but ungifted. Its most serious handicap artistically is its lack of experienced direction. Because of its poverty it cannot afford to invite the graduates of good drama schools to lead it, nor hope to lure professionals to come to its aid.

Not only is the labor theatre lacking in first-rate artistic leadership; it is also devoid of adequate organizational management. Finally, it is woefully lacking in playwrights.

There is plentiful material for such stages but not enough skilled dramatists to weld it into cogent theatrical form. So these groups fall back on a handful of tried favorites which they revive repeatedly: *Waiting for Lefty*, *Bury the Dead*, *Plant in the Sun*, *Let Freedom Ring*, *The Cradle Will Rock*.

The labor theatres, however, are trying to meet these problems more directly than are the little theatres. They are presenting new plays: living newspapers, musical revues, serious dramas; as we have seen in every theatre I have mentioned. Although these may not have been good enough, their performances have encouraged others to write and shown the authors themselves how to improve. Furthermore, labor theatres are holding playwriting classes and seminars which few community theatres do. In their schools they are attacking the problem of leadership and are trying to train people realistically in organizational methods and business management which many non-labor schools so comfortably omit.

Because they have a common purpose—the cause of labor—the affiliates of the New Theatre League have effected greater co-operation with one another than have the variously tried confederacies of little theatres. For in all workers' theatres there is the subordination of individualism to the collective spirit and a common cause, which also holds in the relations among the theatre groups.

The material of which labor stages make use strikes some observers as being exceedingly crude and naive, its humor frequently heavy-handed, its pathos obvious and its conclusions over-simplified. This is a just criticism. It must be recalled, however, that many of the audience to which these stages address themselves are simple folk, on whom nuances and fine points may be lost at this early stage of their theatrical sophistication. Even while admitting this, however, it must also be admitted that the labor theatres have been less loath to experiment with dramatic forms than the bourgeois little theatres and on their stages (and the people's Federal Theatre) more stimulating, new, fresh mediums of expression have been seen than anywhere else in the last ten years.

Enthusiasm and conviction of purpose are no substitutes for talent. Nevertheless, they can accomplish wonders when allied with intelligence and informed with something to say. I have less fear for the future of the labor theatre than I have for that of the little or so-called community theatres. No one knows today what kind of an America we shall find when the smoke of this present war blows away, but I am willing to hazard a guess—I would even like to state it as a conviction—that the theatre of tomorrow will be a people's theatre. Whichever has the most to contribute to that—the college or the community playhouse, Broadway or this labor stage—will be the leader of the American theatre of the future.

RETURN

CHAPTER NINE

Broadway Revisited

IN MID-JANUARY of 1941, I returned to New York after eleven months of checkerboard jumps across the United States; back from nineteen thousand miles traversed on streamlined specials, jittery locals, buses, automobiles and an occasional flight by plane; back from America to Broadway, my search for this country's theatrical pattern done.

The year had made little change in that neighborhood. Forty-fifth Street New Yorkers know as the "street of hits"; most managers try to install their shows in one of the theatres that line it or are as near it as possible. The second week in January, crowds were pressing down it about 8:30 each night bound for the comparatively newly-arrived play of John Van Druten, *Old Acquaintance* (although most of them were going to see Jane Cowl and Peggy Wood who appeared in it), for *The Man Who Came to Dinner*, still holding forth next door after more than a year; or on down to the Imperial to Irving Berlin's *Louisiana Purchase* where they might worship at the feet of Gaxton, Zorina and Victor Moore; Ethel Waters' devotees kept on across Eighth Avenue to the Martin Beck where she was starred in *Cabin in the Sky*. Cutting left through "Shubert Alley" into Forty-Fourth Street, one found Messrs. Al Jolson and Ed Wynn ensconced side by side, the one in *Hold On to Your Hats*, the other in *Boys and Girls Together*. Across the street the Theatre Guild and Gilbert Miller had jointly leased the St. James to present Helen Hayes and Maurice Evans in *Twelfth Night*. On Forty-Sixth Street *Arsenic and Old Lace* had just opened and was proving an affluent neighbor to Ethel Merman, holding court in *Panama Hattie*. A little farther away crowds were still heading to *Hellzapoppin*, *Life with Father*, *Tobacco Road* (announcing its "last weeks" after seven years) and the newer *My Sister Eileen*, *Pal Joey* at the Ethel Barrymore, and Ethel Barrymore at the National in *The Corn Is Green*, *Charley's Aunt*, which surprisingly resurrected itself with eminent success, and Elmer Rice's *Flight to the West*. Across the street from this last the Alvin was being prepared to welcome Gertrude Lawrence in *Lady in the Dark*, accompanied by four revolving stages, music by Kurt Weill, book by Moss Hart, lyrics by Ira Gershwin and an ecstatic press. At the Center, Norman Bel Geddes had brought real ice into the theatre and had created *It Happens on Ice*.

This—offered the reader because Broadway changes raiment so fast that no one can remember offhand what was playing when—was the panorama of Broadway activity at the height of the 1940-41 season. That second week in January there were a total of twenty-eight productions in the Times Square district. The ones which I have singled out for mention were those considered noteworthy by most or all of the drama critics and consequently those which the public was paying most money to see.

No, the year had made little change in Broadway. Although the world had taken a long step toward self-annihilation in those months, the New York stage, now the center of the only great free theatre in the world, reflected none of this—unless the addition of a few more musical shows than usual and an insistence on laughing at nothing was a reflection. The only stage in the world where intellectual freedom persisted had apparently nothing to say.

The returning wanderer contemplated the scene. One's gratification at it depended upon what one was seeking. If theatre is escape from reality, then its function was being fulfilled. With the exception of *Flight to the West* and in a slightly different way *The Corn Is Green,* there was nothing here that had even the remotest relationship to the problems of the world, of society or of the individual in these troubled times.[1] If theatre is also entertainment, there was in it plenty of laughter—somewhat hysterical, to be sure, but yet a titillation for tired business men; none of that "thoughtful laughter" which is high comedy; but then *Arsenic and Old Lace, My Sister Eileen* or *Charley's Aunt* made no pretense of being high comedy. If glamour is the theatre's index of success, this was a good season, for it was abundantly present in the luminous personalities of Ethel Barrymore, Gertrude Lawrence, Jane Cowl, Peggy Wood, Helen Hayes, Ethel Waters and

---

[1] I must remind the reader that I am subjecting Broadway, as seems only fair, to the same treatment that I have accorded the rest of the country. Everywhere my judgments have necessarily been based on the picture presented at the moment of my inspection. So with Broadway. However, I must add that later in the 1940-41 season Hellman's *Watch on the Rhine,* Green and Wright's *Native Son,* Barry's short-lived *Liberty Jones* would have had to be added to *Flight to the West* as exceptions to the above.

Ethel Merman (all women, be it noted; Maurice Evans might have a little as Malvolio, but Monty Woolley and José Ferrer, Ed Wynn and Olsen and Johnson hardly seem to qualify. Glamour in our theatre now seems to be feminine—no John Drews and Edwin Booths in our day). But if the theatre be thought of as standing among the arts; if, in consequence, it can be expected to address itself to the mind and heart, to effect a "catharsis of the emotions," to challenge one's thoughts and amplify one's reason, to arrest one's attention with fiery eloquence, to uplift and ennoble and cause one's spirit to rejoice: if theatre is concerned with any of these, Broadway in January of 1941 denied it. Turning its head resolutely away from greatness, the New York theatre had plunged with the enthusiasm of an ostrich into the sands of pettiness and nonsense.

Broadway's justification is obvious, and it has gained conviction through reiteration over the years: pettiness and nonsense and the perfume of glamour are what the public want just now. In effect, says Broadway, in the gargantuan turmoil of the world today, man wants to shut his eyes and close his ears; he does not want to be moved; he does not want to think; he does not want to feel. He has no desire to come into contact with those things upon which he has built his culture; he sees no occasion to reflect on the possibility of greatness in the human spirit; he is done for the time being with what Maxwell Anderson calls "the dream of the race," which is "that it may make itself better and wiser than it is."

If Broadway is right, then the American people are finished. But Broadway is right in only one respect. The men and women who compose the New York theatre audience *are* being moved today and are thinking and feeling more sharply and deeply than they have in some years. Thought is being challenged and soul-searching is being demanded. Out of a period of great confusion a new certainty and a renewed faith are emerging. But Broadway speaks truly when it says that it is not to the theatre that people come to find this. To serious radio commentators and newspaper columnists, to thoughtful books and periodicals this same public turns with alert eyes and eager ears. To churches they return, filled now with greater crowds than in easier times; to concerts they go in unprecedented numbers, seeking in the abstraction of music to find some clue to the half-lost "dream of the race." But not to the theatre: for it has come to the point that they do not expect it there, do not demand it, and so Broadway has nothing to offer; nothing, that is, but a wisecrack, an occasional sentimental tear, a shapely leg and a husky voice. Broadway fiddles while Rome burns because having forgotten how to do anything else, it feels itself inadequate to cope with the conflagration of life today.

Certainly the theatre has always contained the wisecrack; laughter undoubtedly belongs there alongside of discussions and tears and nobility. Our humor is something of which we Americans are properly proud. It is right that in times of strain we should have a place to go to find release in laughter. The Greeks had their Aristophanes and Satyr plays as well as their Euripides; Elizabethans had Falstaff as well as Lear. But there was always some kind of a balance. Theatre was compounded of laughter plus tears, excitement and elation. Today Broadway is selling principally giggles and guffaws.

Broadway's common rejoinder is that dramatists are writing only commonplaces and froth. One cannot produce a great play if none is being written. A glance at the plays running at the peak of the 1940-41 season reveals the only distinguished American authorships represented to be Elmer Rice's and George Kaufman's; nothing by O'Neill, Anderson, Sherwood, Odets, Barry, Saroyan, Green, Wilder, Behrman.[2] Furthermore, no new writing talent has appeared to replace these or to fortify the scene.

That is a matter of the utmost concern to all who care for the health of our stage. "Where are the playwrights?" all Broadway producers cry; and to no one is the answer vouchsafed. There is, to be sure, the economic explanation: the writing talent goes to Hollywood, into radio, into advertising, where remuneration is more certain. The theatre consequently faces the first of many vicious circles. Dramatists cannot afford to write for a contracting market; but as long as they do not, the market continues to contract.

But the economic explanation is not the final answer, I fear. The real truth is that we seem to be experiencing a drought of playwriting talent. It may be symptomatic of the general decrepitude of the theatre, of the uncertainty of the times; one thing may cause another. I have no answer that satisfies me. But I know, along with everyone else, that the theatre must find dramatists or lose all significance.

At such a moment, with contemporary productivity so slight, one might expect a surge of revivals. Have the

[2] It is true that before the end of the season Broadway saw undistinguished samples of Behrman's and Barry's work, a Paul Green collaboration and Saroyan's *The Beautiful People;* but the first of these did not reach Broadway until February.

classics no relieving laughter or no words pertinent to
these times or that would bear rehearing for their own
sake? *Twelfth Night* was the only one to be seen [3] and it
in a production that did scant justice to either the lyricism
or the gustiness of Shakespearean comedy.

Paul Green only a month or so earlier had pointed out:

> For the first time in the 350 years of our history, the cul-
> tural and spiritual leadership of the earth is in our care. Art,
> literature, music, drama, true science, philosophy and all the
> noblest creations of man's genius are dislodged and beaten
> almost beyond surviving there in Europe and Asia—where
> once was their dwelling place, their haven and their home.
> Then we must provide them a new home, a fane for their
> worship, a sheltering cathedral over them. [4]

To the responsibility of maintaining the continuity of
the world's dramatic heritage in living terms, however,
New York shrugged its shoulders. As the repertory playhouses across Europe closed their doors in the face of holocaust, the great plays disappeared into libraries, nowhere
produced in these days except on a university stage or a
local playhouse somewhere beyond Broadway.

2

The theatre draws life from many sources. My criticism
of Broadway has been leveled against the narrow confines
of its content and my concern has been for its lack of

---

[3] Later Katharine Cornell revived *The Doctor's Dilemma*, making a
total of two important revivals for 1940-41.

[4] National Theatre Conference *Quarterly Bulletin.*

dramatists. But there are other ingredients of theatre. What of Broadway's acting, its direction, its scenic accouterments: lighting, costumes, scenery? What of music in the theatre and of dance?

When I returned five years ago from Moscow after my last twelve-month sojourn away from Broadway, I remarked:

Were three New York producers presenting the same play at once, it might be very possible to see the first act in one theatre, the second in another and the third in a third and still receive a fairly unified impression of the play, for the idiom of the New York theatre is on the whole a common one.[5]

What could be said then must be reiterated today. A fixed style has imposed itself upon Broadway from which it is next to impossible to escape. This style is one based on representation. It is not naturalistic, certainly, for there is in it a self-consciousness and trace of theatricality incompatible with naturalism. Nevertheless, it assumes that the theatre's concern is essentially to reproduce life, subjected to a refining selectivity and the product delivered at a breath-taking speed. This selectivity has no rational basis, but is the result (as Mordecai Gorelik points out in his provocative *New Theatres for Old*) of individual intuition applied according to no external artistic or ideological laws. Speed has so grasped hold of the Broadway theatre that any performance keyed for any reason to a slower pace inevitably seems to the spectator to drag and be boresome.

With the exception of a few first-line performers, acting

[5] *Moscow Rehearsals*, p. 251.

has become, through long years of type-casting the projection of individual personality. Actors are cast, as Stark
Young once remarked, "in parts for which they are fitted
congenitally, photographically." Managers exert all their
energy "to find a blue-eyed boy for the blue-eyed role,
sweets for the sweet, and fat for the fat." Real acting
in consequence is seldom to be seen on Broadway. In its
place has developed a convention of personality convey-
ance which is matchless. On top of this has been built a
surface theatrical technique that is slick, sure and service-
able, and for which we are primarily indebted to George
Kaufman and George Abbott.

One of the curious things about this contemporary
theatrical technique in acting is that it has been learned
and applied half-unconsciously. Few young actors, or
seasoned ones either, can tell one their method, can define
this technique they use. They have picked it out of the
air, it seems, for the air is full of it. Newcomers to Broadway quickly acquire it through exposure: by watching each
others' performances; by the experience, if they are fortunate enough to be cast, of playing on the stage with actors
who have already caught it. So the technique spreads and
results, as a discerning theatre artist recently pointed out,
in everybody of one age, sex and general appearance
giving the same impression: the same pattern of movement, same tone of voice, same method of entrance and
exit, same speech rhythms, same emotional responses.

These matters are perhaps superficial, but beneath them
there is too often nothing else on which to lay hold. Stark
Young was again quite right when he said [6] that "at

---

[6] *Theatre Practice*, p. 24.

present there is no way to tell just how much talent there is because of the lack of training by which that talent might be developed and exhibited. . . . We have mostly crowds of actors who never take the trouble to learn their business. The details of acting they pass by; they merely go on the stage." Most actors have not had the time to build a groundwork upon which to apply a technique. The speed with which any role is assumed (except in the case of stars who occasionally spend several months studying a projected role before going into actual rehearsals) makes it essential that the actor have technical resources available for immediate use. There is never time for him to explore deeper into his art, unless, during periods of unemployment and without outside stimulus, he works toward a fundamental approach than can be brought to bear on whatever role he may subsequently undertake.

The notable exception on Broadway in the recent past was the individual and collective work in acting carried on by the Group Theatre. Here there was a conscious effort to discover and apply some artistic rules in dramatic presentation. That by mid-season of 1940-41 the Group seemed to have dissolved was highly regrettable. Not until another unit of artists with equal seriousness of purpose and talent band together to create collectively, will Broadway be likely to see such ably orchestrated ensemble performances and such grasp of the fundamentals of acting as divorced from personality projection and superficial technique.

In examining Broadway direction, it is inevitable that the observations made upon the state of acting should be extended to include it also. For directors are responsible for the product and directors determine the style and the speed and the values which the play will assume. I have already suggested that two of New York's most successful directors, Mr. Kaufman and Mr. Abbott, have left their imprint on acting. That the former is one of Broadway's most successful playwrights makes the circle complete. In virtuoso directing of any other kind, Broadway seems to be woefully lacking at this time. Most of our good directors today are like able locomotive engineers, whose first job is to keep the train on the tracks and whose second is to bring it in on time, or ahead of time if conditions allow.

Many of Broadway's directors, like Broadway's actors, depend in their staging upon a set of tricks acquired from a common grab-bag. A conscious style or philosophy pervades the work of not more than a handful. Arthur Hopkins is the only director I can think of who has set down in writing any statement of his credo.[7]

Guthrie McClintic remains a master of the school of direction by intuition with the faults and virtues that such a method embraces. Lee Strasberg remains leader of the transplanted Vakhtangov method. Margaret Webster has cornered the classical market. Jed Harris, perhaps as close to a virtuoso director as we have left this side of Hollywood, is inactive much of the time, *Our Town*, in 1938, being his last notable representation. Herman Shumlin's productions, like *The Corn Is Green, The Little Foxes, Watch on the Rhine*, bear the stamp of thoughtful artistry; but among the older generation, one is at a loss to find further examples of consistent high accomplishment. Among younger directors, Joshua Logan, Bretaigne

[7] *How's Your Second Act?* New York, 1918.

Windust, Elia Kazan and Robert Lewis monopolize the field once shared with Orson Welles, Garson Kanin and Robert Sinclair, now all cozily nesting in Hollywood.[8]

None of these directors, young or old, with the possible exception of Orson Welles, whose career on Broadway has been too brief to be conclusive, has had the strength, however, to break any of the molds received from his predecessors. Broadway in the past twenty-five years has had no Reinhardt or Meierhold, no Stanislavski or Craig, no Belasco even, to refashion the theatre, or any part of it, in his own image. The maintenance of the representational style has been our directors' concern and to that style they have added little to make Broadway direction of 1940 different from that of 1920.

In the field of stage design Broadway has hewn close to the line established by Robert Edmond Jones, Lee Simonson and Norman Bel Geddes fifteen to twenty years ago. New impetus has been provided from time to time by the arrival of contributions like Jo Mielziner's and Donald Oenslager's poetic variations, like Mordecai Gorelik's and Howard Bay's strong and observant social comment, like Stewart Cheney's, Raoul Pene du Bois' and Albert Johnson's decorative styles. By 1940-41 Broadway's scenic investiture had maintained for so many seasons an excellence in not a few instances far in advance of the dramas for which it was provided, that it was coming to be taken for granted. With increasingly flexible instruments, particularly electrical, at its disposal, the craftsmanship of production was at its Broadway highest.

This technical facility, however, and this general "excel-

[8] Welles did come East briefly in 1941 to stage *Native Son*.

lence" seemed to be leading nowhere in particular. Young designers (the author included), like young actors, were satisfied to imitate the form and spirit of their predecessors; little Joneses, Oenslagers and Mielziners were entering Broadway as fast as the scenic artists' union would accept them. To be sure, the imitation of good masters is better than the imitation of bad ones, but the appearance of widespread imitative processes in art at any time is a danger signal. I believe that Gorelik was right when he contended in 1941 that

In general, a certain amount of simplification, agreeable color schemes, tasteful furnishings and pleasant lighting were almost all that remained to tell the story of the hard-fought struggle to pass beyond the naturalism of Belasco. American scene design was losing the lessons it had learned in the school of Robert Edmond Jones. Few of that school had Jones' restless, poetic spirit; fewer still seemed destined to create new schools of their own.[9]

Musical comedy, which so dominated Broadway in January, 1941, reveals more creativeness than the stages that shelter spoken drama. Its technique of acting is, it is true, the apex of personality projection, and its direction is dedicated to that end. But here there seems justification, for musical comedy character is built out of personality and trimmed to fit it.

In top-notch Broadway musicals, there is a synthesis of the stage arts that exceeds anything done elsewhere in our theatre. These musicals draw forth the greatest inventiveness and imagination of which our scene and costume designers and our lighting experts are capable. They are not

[9] *New Theatres for Old*, p. 309.

afraid of entering the dangerous realm of fantasy, as in *Cabin in the Sky*. They call into the theatre the services of composers like Richard Rodgers and Kurt Weill, of dancers like Charles Weidman, Doris Humphrey, Katherine Dunham and their confreres. They strike out toward new media, as in the Geddes' ice show and toward new combinations of music and dance with drama as in *Lady in the Dark* and *Liberty Jones;* frequently they essay, as in *Meet the People* and part of *Louisiana Purchase*, to make comment on the contemporary scene. They are the peculiar product of America, and it is consequently, perhaps, not remarkable that when the average man comes to New York for a few days and wishes to go to the theatre, he will first turn his steps toward a musical show; instinctively he recognizes its validity.

3

The most frequently-leveled charge against Broadway is aimed at its commercialism: "The New York theatre is not an art; it is a business," one hears on every side. "It is dedicated not to beauty, but to money." Certainly it is difficult to deny this charge. Of course, occasionally some experiment of high worth appears and refutes the proposition that the temples of Mammon cannot bring forth an artistic masterpiece. *My Heart's in the Highlands* and more remotely *The Green Pastures* come to mind, and the Arthur Hopkins-Robert Edmond Jones-John Barrymore productions of *The Jest, Richard III, Hamlet*. Plays of O'Neill and Shaw, Anderson, O'Casey and many another superior artist have had their first American performance amid the money-grubbers, proving that such a charge must be qualified.

It is dangerous for any critic-reporter to attempt rigid classifications in the hope of making his work easier and his conclusions more obvious. Commercialism, entertainment, art; professional, amateur; these tags are so handy, so ready for use, so easy to apply and thus end the matter. But in the theatre, as everywhere else, the exception often seems so much more significant than the rule. Just when something has been proved impossible, it occurs. Then the rules must be altered to fit. One must be careful, therefore, in use of over-comfortable generalizations. (Already exceptions to earlier statements in this chapter about playwrights, actors, directors, designers occur to me as they have undoubtedly occurred to the reader.) Nevertheless, some generalizations have to be made.

There is no doubt that too often Broadway's commercialism stands in the way of its art. There is no doubt that the economic structure of the New York theatre is responsible, in some measure, for the conditions that have been described as typical of its artistic life. When the purpose of stage production is to make money, the box office is obviously the determinant which affects all that transpires on the stage: choice of play, choice of cast, even style of performance. I do not believe that the majority of Broadway people are in the theatre to make money, that is, big money. If they were, nine-tenths of them would have given up long ago. In order to produce at all, however, there must be capital and the theatre depends in large measure on non-Broadway sources for that. These sources provide money in order to make money; these sources own theatres as real estate in order to make money. When domestic times are bad or world conditions serious, then dollars are harder to get; the assurance of a return on the investment more necessary. Risks are more unwillingly taken. What has happened in consequence?

In each of the peak seasons of modern Broadway, 1926-27 and 1927-28, 302 productions were presented. In the season of 1940-41 the number had dropped to seventy-one. Every year from 1928 to 1941 (with the exception of 1934-35, when there was a slight upswing) the number has steadily decreased: three hundred to two hundred to one hundred, and on down. Even in the first season of the depression, 1929-30, there were 286 Broadway productions. I spoke above of the prevalence of musical shows today. In 1927-28, there were sixty-nine; in 1940-41, seventeen.

It would be reassuring to believe that such a diminishing quantity was compensated for by an improvement in quality, reassuring to be able to say that although 1926-27 and 1927-28 saw more than four times as many plays, those of 1940-41 were much better. The reader may decide this for himself if he compares the summary of best plays running in January, 1941, as described above, with Burns Mantle's selection of the ten best for 1926-27: *Broadway* (Dunning and Abbott), *Saturday's Children* (Anderson), *Chicago* (Watkins), *The Constant Wife* (Maugham), *The Play's the Thing* (Molnar), *The Road to Rome* (Sherwood), *The Silver Cord* (Howard), *The Cradle Song* (Sierra), *Daisy Mayme* (Kelly), *In Abraham's Bosom* (Green). In 1927-28, he chose *Strange*

Interlude (O'Neill), *The Royal Family* (Ferber and Kaufman), *Burlesque* (Watters and Hopkins), *Coquette* (Abbott and Bridges), *Behold the Bridegroom* (Kelly), *Porgy* (Heyward), *Paris Bound* (Barry), *Escape* (Galsworthy), *The Racket* (Cormack), *The Plough and the Stars* (O'Casey). The durability of the last two or three seasons' best plays can obviously not be determined today and certainly many of them are as good as many on the 1926, 1927 and 1928 lists; nevertheless, it would be hard to make a strong case for the claim that fewer plays mean better plays.

The increasing difficulty in getting financial backing for the theatre is partly the result of the mounting cost of production which in itself helps to increase the risk and completes a vicious circle. Whereas in 1919 and 1920 Arthur Hopkins could produce the elaborate *The Jest* for not much more than $14,000 and *Richard III* for less than $30,000, those productions would cost at least three times as much today. Nowadays, a manager seldom undertakes to produce even the simplest play without at least $15,000 in the bank and $100,000 productions are not uncommon. Brooks Atkinson, writing in the New York *Times,* has said:

The amount of money that must be spent before a play and a performance can have a public showing is all out of proportion to the culture, art, amusement or intellect involved. A publisher can give an author a public hearing for a thousand dollars or less. A producer cannot give an author a public hearing without a preliminary expenditure of ten thousand dollars, more likely twenty or twenty-five thousand and perhaps thirty-five thousand. The Ernest Hemingway *The Fifth Column* represented a preliminary investment of about fifty-five thousand dollars.

When such sums are involved one must be as reasonably sure as is possible in the theatre that one will get one's money back. In consequence, it is no wonder that the box office becomes the all-important factor.

Seeking to find the reason for the tremendous cost of theatrical production today, we come to the labor union situation. Everyone concerned in the professional stage and many a layman is aware of the problem that it presents. Theatre workers organizing originally to protect themselves against abuse have found in organization a powerful weapon which today they are, in many instances, using destructively. It is generally admitted that unionism in itself is a good thing; it is its practices which are matters of concern to everyone who cares about the theatre's health.

When in May, 1940, *Theatre Arts* conducted a symposium on the stage's economic ills, thirty-six of Broadway's leaders discussed labor problems from many points of view. Rowland Stebbins sounded what proved to be the keynote when he wrote that he believed that "certain producers and managers took unfair advantage of their employees and were directly responsible for the existence of these unions today. I think the pendulum has swung the other way now and that production is hampered and made unnecessarily costly by some of the union regulations."

Illustrating Mr. Stebbins' contention, Clare Boothe wrote:

What I object to, emphatically, is having to pay for work that is *not* done, simply because of the economic fact that there are more builders, painters, stagehands and musicians today than the industry can possibly absorb. This last is a serious economic problem, I realize. But it should not be solved at the expense of those for whom there still is work to do. That is often the unhappy result. In this matter the union seems to have made of a *predicament* a policy.

To cite a specific instance: In *Margin for Error* there is a brief moment when a gramophone recording is played offstage to supply music which is heard on the radio before Hitler's speech is broadcast. For that half-minute of recorded music, we were told by the musicians' union that we had to hire four musicians to sit backstage and do nothing at a cost of three hundred dollars a week. At the moment when I write, the show is still making healthy grosses, so the producers can actually afford to pay the disproportionately heavy cost. *But,* when the gross dwindles, that extra three hundred dollars a week may well make the difference between the show being in the red or the black. A show in the red is the danger signal that *all* the actors and stagehands will soon be out of work. . . .

In two of my shows, the stage crews were getting more pay at the end of the run than the actors. Had they been as able as I am sure they were willing to take cuts with everyone else (including the author) the shows might have continued for weeks longer than they did.

Margaret Webster continued the attack with a summary statement:

Unions, from Equity to Local 1 of the I.A.T.S.E. (stage hands union): the trouble is not the minimum wage clauses and similar necessary safeguards, but the way in which these safeguards are made to work in every case to the detriment of the production in which all are equally concerned, without being of the slightest benefit to the members of the union.

Repeating Miss Boothe's illustration, Miss Webster continued:

You may not have recorded or radio music played off-stage without employing at least four, and often more, musicians, to play craps in the basement. This simply means that producers eliminate music from their shows, unless it is absolutely impossible to avoid its use. The play is the poorer—I believe that music is of the utmost value to almost every play—and no musician is one cent the richer. . . .

Again, let me quote. After a dress-rehearsal I dismissed the crew, sent the actors out for an hour, and then called them back for notes. The last act set was left standing on the stage, since it was to be used in the morning. I was rehearsing some "noises off" which occurred in a different scene, when the rehearsal was stopped by a union delegate who informed me that as the set was still standing I should be required to pay the crew double-time from the time they left the theatre until the time I eventually dismissed the actors, if I continued my rehearsal. . . . Obviously, I dismissed the rehearsal; no one was any the better, and the production was slightly the worse.

Unions have maintained the prohibitive wage scales and regulations they established in Broadway's palmier days because they contend there are so few opportunities for employment and such uncertainty about the length of employment. In so doing, however, they insure the continuance of the conditions against which they are protecting themselves and will perhaps effect the eventual collapse of the whole structure with themselves caught beneath it. Until the stage unions clean their houses (or have them cleaned for them by Federal investigations), and until some form of co-operative solution of the whole labor problem is arrived at, we shall find Broadway bending lower and lower under the load.

From one vicious circle, let us move to another. Because of the costs of production and operation today it is necessary for managements to be sure of an income of from five to twenty-five thousand dollars a week. The seating capacity of the average New York theatre dictates that to achieve this at least a three-dollar top must be charged (in the case of musicals, often four dollars), and in most instances, a minimum of one dollar. With box office prices so high, the public which can afford to pay for the theatre is reduced in quantity. Although the success of Federal Theatre productions at a fifty-five cent top indicated the presence of a vast low-price audience for plays in New York, Broadway seems unable to take the risk of lowering its prices and hope to make up the difference in extension of run. The fact is that the "hit" shows do not need to and the others cannot afford to. However that may be, it is obvious that the Broadway public that kept 302 productions going for an average length run of eighty-eight performances in 1927-28 is much reduced in size when in 1939-40 it supported only ninety-seven for an average length run of eighty performances. The seriousness of the situation lies in the fact that it is fast moving from a temporary doldrum into a continuously accelerating downhill roll. The bottom cannot be far away.

One of the gravest results of the contraction of Broadway Brooks Atkinson has also pointed out:

The tragic thing is the waste of potential ability. Within a radius of two miles from this office, any number of intelligent theatre people are frittering away their time. Any number of trained actors whom everyone would be glad to see upon a stage behind the footlights are wasting their knowledge of the stage. Some of the best scene designers in the world are either doing nothing or working at things that do not vitally interest them. Several play directors whose heads are full of creative ideas have nothing to go to work on.

To this picture should be added the actors, designers and directors with something to offer the theatre that is fresh and young and new but of whose work Atkinson, from his opening night seat, has not yet seen more than a glimpse—if that—for they still await their initial "break." "The theatre is devotedly loved by thousands of people whose love is not returned," says he and he is right, at least insofar as Broadway is concerned.

Actors' Equity Association, to which all performers in plays on Broadway must belong, reported in January, 1941, that it had approximately 4,500 paid-up members.[10] The week that I returned to New York, in January, 1941, 279 of them were playing in the Times Square district (exclusive of those in musical productions, many of whose participants are instead members of Chorus Equity). There were five plays in rehearsal which probably employed another fifty or sixty. On the road, that week, were thirteen dramatic productions involving perhaps 175 more actors. Five hundred actors at work in mid-season with more than four thousand unemployed—a tragic waste indeed.

The waste is not among actors alone. The directing field is unorganized and so it is impossible to estimate that situation, but in designing, the problem is equally acute. In the 1939-40 season, only six men out of approximately one hundred designer members of the United Scenic Artists were commissioned to do more than four produc-

---

[10] To this number should probably be added another 1,500 members who were not paid up.

tions. This means that only six designers on Broadway were able to earn at their profession more than two or three thousand dollars that year. Even the most sought-after and high-priced designers like Jo Mielziner cannot afford to meet the costs of studio up-keep out of their theatre earnings and must seek employment in other fields to supplement Broadway's meager allowance.

The New York theatre has not been unaware of this situation, but it has been slow at making any efforts to come to grips with it. An organization calling itself the American Theatre Council sought several years ago to tackle the problem of uncovering new acting talent; it auditioned several thousand young people. Without any particular power of its own, however, the Council failed to be of great constructive value.

Frequently actors undertake to give themselves the hearing that Broadway denies them. Groups of young people spring up along the periphery of Times Square; they work together for a time; lease, when they can afford to, the old Provincetown Playhouse or auditoriums like ones in the Barbizon-Plaza Hotel or the Roerich Museum to show themselves. Usually under economic pressure or a gradual weakening of incentive they disintegrate.

For several seasons theatre leaders who appreciated the seriousness of the artistic and economic impasse toward which Broadway was marching cast about for ways to break the rigidity of the bonds which prevented experimentation there and which held talent back from the continuous exercise it must have in order to grow. The stumbling block lay in the apparent inability of the organizations to which these various artists belonged to agree to a plan that would be acceptable to them all in safeguarding the interests of the artists themselves.

Finally, after months of discussion, the Experimental Theatre, Inc., was set up in November, 1940, by the Dramatists' Guild and Actors' Equity Association under the devoted and unselfish leadership of Antoinette Perry, who had long pioneered for the idea. With a small grant from the National Theatre and Academy, it presented three plays during the spring of 1941. Between the Experimental Theatre and complete success, however, lay a dearth of plays worth doing; a somewhat bureaucratic set-up that kept the control in the hands of the people already on the top of the Broadway pile; a financial crisis which could again be laid at the unions' doors. (Miss Perry claimed that $1,400 of the $2,000 grant went to labor costs, and that office charges had to be paid from her own pocket.)

Although The Experimental Theatre seems miles away from tackling the heart of the problem, it represents a tiny step in a good direction and one may hope for results that will encourage more serious and far-reaching attacks that strike beyond the fringe. The cancer of commercialism, however, requires far more drastic surgery.

4

As an industry, it seems fairly easy to diagnose Broadway as a failure. Any other commercial enterprise operated with the disregard which Broadway evidences for even the simplest principles of economics, operated year after year with from a sixty-eight to an eighty-three percentage of failure, would quickly fold up. As a creative art, the theatre's condition is more difficult to diagnose. I cannot fall back on facts and figures. I can only undertake the same kind of intuitive personal criticism to which the theatre is from day to day subjected, criticism without dialectical foundation, with nothing more than "I know what I like" as a criterion.

As a matter of fact, it might be interesting to consider the state of dramatic criticism in its relation to the problems of Broadway. At more or less stated intervals, wrathful producers and playwrights fulminate against the critics. The butts of their attack are regularly the reviewers for the daily Manhattan newspapers. The reason is that the critics, as everyone on Broadway knows, have accumulated tremendous power in determining the commercial success of productions. When this power is turned against anyone, as he feels, unjustly, the victim naturally seeks to strike back. (The managers or authors of "smash hits," one notes, seldom write articles damning the critics.) How the daily reviewers have acquired this power would be hard to say; [11] the fact remains that if they all agree a play is bad, it has barely a Chinaman's chance of survival. If they return a split verdict, the average play, unless graced with an actor of box-office "draw" has slight opportunity for success. If they greet a new piece with salvos of enthusiasm, it is almost equally impossible for it to fail, whether it be good or not.

The average man, accustomed to attending a dozen plays a year, will doubtless see the twelve best; he is not

---

[11] I have, however, suggested one explanation in Chapter Two, above.

aware of the abysses into which the theatre drops about seventy-five per cent of the time. Since the only condition laid down to determine whether anyone in this country may be a Broadway producer is that he have money; and if he has, there being nothing to prevent him from offering the public any play written by anybody, it is obvious that someone must be delegated to wield a sharp ax.

The question is, then, on what basis is the critic to operate against this laissez-faire system of production. What will be his touchstone to determine excellence? My analysis may oversimplify. To the worker behind the footlights, the Broadway reviewers in their aisle seats appear frequently to be, first, newspaper men and, second, theatre men. That is to say, their primary obligation seems to be to their papers on whose staffs they are and by whom they are paid; after that appears to come their obligation to the stage and its artists. From this, the outsider concludes that since a newspaper's first obligation is to its readers, the drama critics are necessarily concerned primarily with the public, secondarily with the art of the theatre. Since the public and the box office are the same thing, as far as Broadway is concerned, the critics appear consequently to become an integral part of the commercial structure of the theatre with the satisfaction of the public taste as their principal concern.

Now I am not assuming the point of view that the theatre is not concerned with its audience and the satisfying of it. That is the primary purpose of its existence. I do not believe, however, that in matters of art, the people (for whom, if this viewpoint obtains, the critics are the mouthpieces) predetermine the creative process. The artist contains this within himself; it cannot be otherwise. If he is great, then his creation is inevitably acceptable to the people; in proportion as he removes from greatness, the inevitability of this diminishes. Always, however, he must be free. If, in search for success, he relinquishes his freedom by attempting to coincide with what he considers to be a pre-existent public taste, he foregoes the prerogative of his own creativeness.

The artist of the theatre must lift the beholders of his play into a region of thought and beauty, laughter and tears that is beyond their anticipation. Lynn Riggs has written that "the theatre is the place in which to enlarge and illumine life." The spectator comes bringing his experience of life; he must go out with that experience expanded or clarified or illuminated, else the theatre has fallen short. Wherefore, it is clear that the spectator must follow, not lead. Broadway and its newspaper-men critics have reversed the process by adhering too closely to the law of commerce: "give the public what it wants." Could it be achieved, this is no goal worth striving for. We theatre workers must seek to give the public much more than it knows it wants; only so can we as individual artists and the theatre as an institution move up and on.

Most of the dramatic critics in New York are sincere in their devotion to the theatre; most of them I believe would concur in theory with such a statement of principle. A dramatic criticism devoted to these ends, however, would have to do much more than the Broadway reviewers are able to do. For it would have to spend at least three-fourths of its time in constructive thought. It would become primarily concerned with avidly seeking out each feeble particle that exhibited intimations of creativeness and with nurturing it. The watering-can would be as fa-

miliar to its hand as the scythe. Even its destructiveness—
which would be necessary—would be predicated on a vision
of what might take place after the objects marked for destruction were removed. That kind of creative criticism was
the criticism of Bernard Shaw.

But Bernard Shaw, I am aware, did not write for a
daily paper. Midnight deadlines did not intrude to force
snap judgments from him. Perhaps it is the newspaper editors, who treat premières as "news" and require morning-
after reviews of their critics, who are frequently responsible for turning those aisle-seat-holders from dramatic
authorities into men who seem sometimes to be little
more than reporters. Certainly the astute writing of a
Brooks Atkinson in his "Sunday articles" indicates that,
given time for reflection, several of our critics can turn
out commentaries of high caliber.

Even when at their best, however, most of the New
York drama critics reveal a one-sided understanding of the
stage. Their appreciation of the art of playwriting, which
in some instances is quite keen, is seldom equaled by their
knowledge of the other ingredients of the theatre. Except
for two or three, their appraisals of acting, direction
and scene design reveal few well-established standards of
judgment.

I regret that my salute to revisited Broadway should
end on so choleric a note. Let me, therefore, append a
postscript. Since everything is relative, let me say that the
New York theatre—if one can except the commercialism
that pervades so much of its thought and motivates so
many of its activities—is clearly still the best in the country. The best of the dramatists who write for it and whose
work it welcomes are men of artistic talent and integrity.

The best of its actors, its directors, its designers are master craftsmen with a technical facility that is unsurpassed in the world today and among whose number are some that are more than expert: who are informed with passion and possessed of great artistry. The theatre of Eugene O'Neill and Robert Sherwood, of Norman Bel Geddes and Robert Edmond Jones, of Pauline Lord and Nazimova and Helen Hayes cannot be peevishly dismissed.

But again, since everything is relative, I can still say that Broadway should be a great deal better than it is. For, in the first place, one cannot except the commercialism that pervades it. In the second place, it does not cherish these best of its artists as it should; it does not afford them the constant opportunity to express their talent which they need to exercise and we long to receive. In the last place, Broadway is not America. Insulated against the rest of the country, the New York theatre stands in danger of creating its own set formulas, applicable only to itself. Its own values resting on an insubstantial urbanity and a false sense of superiority may disintegrate without the freshening wind from the prairies of middle America and the icy water of the Rockies' slopes to temper it. Broadway can be better than it is if it rediscovers these United States and makes itself one with America.

ADVANCE

CHAPTER TEN

Theatrical Ends

THE LAST STUB of the round-trip ticket has been yielded; the traveler has returned to the Broadway from whence he set out; his accounting is due. It must be abundantly clear that I have had great difficulty in setting limitations to my subject. Lines of the picture have kept constantly leading outside the frame, and to include them the frame has had to be taken down, knocked apart and enlarged time and again. Have I been wrong to set my course along so many channels to look for theatre? Would I have done better to stick resolutely to the Broadway line—"for after all, Broadway *is* the American theatre," many New Yorkers still insist? Or should I have kept to the little theatre movement? Or traced the theatre in education and nothing more? If I had done so, no doubt whichever subject I had chosen would have been more satisfactorily treated than by this "hit-the-highspots" method of including them all. But that field of my specialization would have inevitably become an end in itself, and I am more convinced than ever that none of the wandering threads of stage activity I have described *is* the end in itself. Some are the warp, some the woof, but it takes them all to make the American theatre pattern.

Frederic McConnell was repeating what several other workers had said when he remarked: "You make a mistake when you try to pigeon-hole us—when you talk about professional and non-professional theatres. It's all the same, really. We're all caught up in the same excitement. We're all modeling with the same clay. We all have budgets to meet and audiences to satisfy. We are all trying to be artists and business men and jugglers and jokesters rolled into one." There is some truth in that claim. So before we start to put the pieces of the puzzle together, let us give some thought to the theatre as a whole—to the problems common to it everywhere. Let us clarify its meaning and its purpose.

Disquisitions on the art of the theatre have been made by more learned and philosophic scholars and critics than I. It is not my purpose here to propose new definitions for it. I should like, however, to make one point clear. I do not see the necessity for the separation that exists in many people's minds between the conceptions of theatre as art and theatre as entertainment. Frequently one seems expected to make a choice as though they were mutually exclusive. In the sense that the experience of esthetic enjoyment is embraced in the idea of entertainment, it seems to me that all art is entertaining. The Elizabethans who stood in the pit to listen to Marlowe's "mighty line" were not there because they were art-lovers. They went to be entertained. Since the Greeks were a cultured people, ideas concerning the artistry of Aristophanes may have entered their heads as they watched *The Birds* and their enjoyment of *Oedipus* may have been accompanied by thoughts of Sophocles' art; but I doubt if even the theatre of ancient Greece was looked upon self-consciously by the people as art divorced from entertainment. Furthermore, I would not deny the appellation of "artist" to Charlie Chaplin or to Toto the Clown simply because they are masters of entertainment, any more than I would disallow the impersonators of Arlecchino and Brighella their place in the history of the art of the theatre because they performed a similar service on the street corners of Renaissance Italy.

That we must distinguish between theatrical art and entertainment seems to me to be a recent idea and primarily limited to the Anglo-Saxons, whose congenital distrust of art is well known. Americans, unlike most continental Europeans, seem to find it hard to believe that anything they can enjoy is art; conversely they imagine that all art, although no doubt good for them, must be tedious and difficult. In the theatre this attitude prevails to an even greater extent than among the other arts and is perhaps responsible for the glorification of safe mediocrity on our contemporary stage.

No, I am unwilling to separate the art of the theatre from entertainment. Although there may be too little of the former for the amount of the latter today, they are not mutually exclusive.

The sociological and artistic approaches to theatre, however, I find less easy to reconcile; their relationship nevertheless lies at the heart of an exposition of American dramatic activity. A good deal of this book has been concerned with work that seems a far cry from the art of the theatre. The farther one advances into cup-and-saucer, text-book and soap-box dramatics the more remote artistic impetus becomes and the more important are another set of values: social or psychological or both. In attending to much that I saw and heard about in this year of travel, I had to ask myself whether and to what extent it was appropriate to a study of the theatre. The question arises again now.

Much grade-school, high-school and college dramatics occur, as we have seen, for many other than artistic reasons. The same applies for folk-drama festivals in the corn and cotton belts, for fashionable little theatre productions, for labor plays in trade union halls. The purpose is not so much to further the cause of drama, to look upon the theatre as an end in itself, a mistress to be served and suffered for; as it is to encourage community spirit, to help develop personality, to create an awareness of social problems or engender class consciousness.

The Rockefeller Foundation, as I understand, holds its millions in trust—as far as the "humanities" are concerned —to use in broadening the base of culture in this country; to make it possible for an increasingly large number of Americans to experience the benefits that accrue from such contact with the arts as heretofore have been available only to privileged and monied persons. It has appreciated that, as Lewis Mumford says, "A community whose life is not irrigated by art and science, by religion and philosophy, day upon day, is a community that exists half alive. A personality who has not entered into this realm has not yet reached the human estate." Broadway has been little interested in such irrigation; so it has seemed to this Foundation, to some of the others and to many individuals that the non-professional theatre was the ditch through which the arid field might be watered. For it is part of the community in a way that the traveling road show out from Times Square can never be. Out of this point of view has come to many persons an abhorrence of the professional and a conviction that the amateur spirit is the only hope. Consequently, most educational theatre leaders, as we have seen, are preparing their charges to become educators like themselves, or occasionally to become leaders of groups of amateurs calling themselves little or community theatres. The majority of these organizations are proud of their amateurism and oppose any tendency to "go professional."

As this sociological approach to the stage which sees it as a means to other and (as it believes) greater ends gains ground, more and more people are involved in putting on plays for fun, for the educational or social or personal dividend accruing to the participants from such performances. It was devotion to this point of view which made one of its champions say to me, after we had witnessed a "festival" of badly-performed high-school one-act plays and I had regretted all absence of artistic merit: "My dear fellow, you miss the point. It doesn't matter whether these productions are good or bad; the important thing is that people are doing them."

When I came back to New York, I told one of the most exacting theatre artists of my acquaintance about the extent of this stage activity across the country and its motivations. He was considerably upset. "Surely all these people are not artists?" he inquired. "Oh, no," I responded, "And they do not claim to be." "Then they should be thrown out of the theatre," he replied. "The theatre must be peopled only with superior persons. I am convinced that that is the only way America can create a theatre worthy of her. By letting every soda-jerker and truck-driver or every lawyer and debutante who wants to people our stage, we shall only succeed in plunging it to unrecognizable depths. We must have sufficient respect for the stage to allow only the finest artists to work in it."

In his writing, *The Dramatic Imagination,* Robert Edmond Jones repeats this: "Exceptional people, distinguished people, superior people, people who can say, as the old Negro said, 'I got a-plenty music in me.' These are the actors the theatre needs."

Here are the two extremes: on the one hand faith in a democratic theatre wherein the more people having a hand the merrier; where the distinction between good and bad art is looked upon as unimportant; on the other hand insistence on an aristocratic theatre where the best must undisputed reign. Maxwell Anderson, in *Knickerbocker Holiday,* said: "A democracy is where you are governed by amateurs." He seemed to find it a pretty desirable situation in the long run. Those who demand democratization of the theatre would apparently like to make it a place where we are governed by amateurs too. Are the conditions desirable in politics equally desirable in the arts? That is the question. In attempting to "democratize," to broaden the base of culture, have we perhaps spread the product so thin that it has ceased to be culture?

I sat on the lawn outside Paul Green's house in Chapel Hill. The spring woods and fields stretched off in every direction beyond the low wall. That question was on my mind. "What good does it do the theatre," I asked, "for all these youngsters to put on plays so badly and drag all these audiences to see them? Doesn't it simply turn people against the stage in the long run and cause them to say, 'If that's a play, give me a movie any day?' This activity may be fine for the people involved (although if they do bad work, I'm not so sure) but what has it to do with the theatre?"

Green sat for a moment and looked out at the country-side still in the noonday Carolina sun.

"Well," he said slowly, "it's true that a lot of this stuff is bad—bad art, bad theatre. But look," and he raised his arm toward the field and the edge of the woods; "look at all those grasses and brambles; all that scrub underbrush and thicket. Most of it grows up a way, struggles along and dies. The leaves fall off and the stalks drop; they all become mold and go back into the ground to fertilize it. Next year where the soil is a little richer, one of those stalks may grow sturdier or a seed dropped there may strengthen into a tree.

"It seems to me that a lot of this dramatic activity is like that scrubby underbrush. It doesn't look like much, a lot of it dies away quickly; but it all helps to fertilize the ground. Our soil isn't very rich and we need all the manure we can get. Don't scoff at the fertilizer because it isn't a rose or an oak. Rather rejoice that because of it a rose may some day bloom more fully here or an oak grow sturdier."

That, I suppose, is part of the American dream, is the real reason for democracy. "Equal opportunities for all," we have said and although it has not worked out quite literally yet, we still believe in it. We have never claimed that each man would make the most of his chance if he got it, or that any two men would make the same; but that has not taken away from the power or validity of the idea, and we still believe that out of its application comes a higher state of society than if only the few have the opportunity.

This democratic philosophy does apply in the theatre. The man who contends that our theatre will be great only if superior people lead it is quite right. But the question is, from whence come these superior beings? We believe in this country that they come from the people, that they may be anywhere. In 1860 there was a superior man in an obscure law office in Springfield, Illinois. By the processes of democracy that country lawyer became the guide of America's destiny. By the processes of a democratic theatre a garment-worker may become our Duse or a truck-driver our Molière. A democratic theatre certainly does not deny the importance of a Duse and a Molière. When it fills the stage with garment-workers and truck-drivers it simply seeks to extend the opportunities of developing more of them. It argues that from a thousand plays presented on a thousand stages there is a stronger chance for something fine to emerge than from ten plays on ten stages.

By turning the sociological approach to theatre into the democratic approach, I have managed to argue the social into becoming the servant of the artistic. We encourage more theatres, more actors, more dramatists, more audience in order that we may have a better theatre. This seems to me of fundamental importance. For by having a greater theatre we strengthen the arts; by having greater arts we possess a richer culture; with an advancing culture we grow as a nation and a people.

The trouble with the strictly sociological approach to the stage as preached by so many educators, philanthropists, social workers, and their disciples is that the encouragement of *more* dramatic activity becomes an end in itself. Everywhere schools boast of the *number* of people to whom they are giving an education in theatre; but almost everywhere as the number increases the quality of preparation seems to deteriorate. Everywhere as granges and farm bureaus and university extensions carry forward the frontiers of drama, there is rejoicing that *more* people are able to see the light: the kind or color of the light seems unimportant. Everywhere the New Theatre League sends a mobile unit, it exults that *more* sharecroppers or trade unionists are experiencing theatre of their own devising and that more people who know nothing about it at all are putting on plays. In all of this sight is lost of the fact that the reason we must have more theatre is in order that we may enlarge the chances of having *better* theatre. A great deal of bad art does not produce a state of culture. We can tolerate the bad art only if we are determined that out of it may come some good art.

With this in mind let us re-examine the fields that have been explored in this report. While acknowledging the tremendous value of the theatre as a social agent, let us consider it now as an end in itself. I should by no means be construed as saying that the social, therapeutic uses of the stage are insignificant. I think I have given them sufficient emphasis throughout this book to indicate my understanding and appreciation of them. When a young college professor says, "The satisfaction and the joy of my work lies in the confidence I have that for a few years the young people who act on my boards will live fuller, richer lives and because of that, will ever after be keener, more sensitive men and women," I am strongly tempted to say, "That is enough. What better reason is there for the theatre to exist?" But while that may be enough at the time and place it was said, that is not enough for the theatre as a whole. So I leave to the sociologists and the psychologists and the authorities on adult education an assessment of the value of the stage from their points of view and return to the theatre itself.

The commercial theatre—oligarchic and plutocratic rather than democratic—is in a state of contraction. The non-professional theatre, looked at as a whole, is in a state of expansion. In the school system, there appears to be an increasing demand for teachers trained in dramatics. Among the colleges there are only a handful of major institutions where theatre work is not carried on. Community and little theatres number into the thousands, their workers into the hundreds of thousands. The New Theatre League cannot supply the demands of working class groups for leadership. The Negro stage surges forward to assert its self-determination.

The result of all this is the creation of an awareness of the theatre which as yet has not penetrated very deeply nor sufficiently widely but which is moving steadily. To the educational, the community, the labor stages, we are indebted for this—not to the commercial theatre. Gradually the level of theatrical literacy is being raised. These agencies, however, seem dedicated to banishing illiteracy and nothing more. It is much easier to teach people to read than to create a literature for them to devour after they have learned their letters. The educational and community theatre movement seems satisfied to cultivate (so to speak) the enjoyment of reading without making an effort to supply good books.

This point is one which seems to escape many workers

in the American theatre off Broadway. Children's theatres and school dramatics provide the ABC's of dramatic appreciation, the colleges proffer the lexicon, community theatres are set up like branch libraries, but the spirit of theatre to the tapping of which the alphabet and the lexicon and the five-foot-shelf of dramatic activity are supposedly dedicated—that spirit is lost in the shuffle.

Emerson said that "in our fine arts not imitation but creation is the aim." Where is creation in our theatre today? Where is the spirit? In the barns and playhouses of summer stock? No more; for there is no time to create, we are told, and not enough money (as though lack of creativeness has anything to do with poverty of the purse). In the little theatre movement? In the Civic and Community Players groups? Once in a blue moon. Much of the time they remind one, as somebody remarked, of the old ladies who set up their easels in the Louvre and make pallid water-color copies of the masters; but with this unfortunate difference: their copies are seldom of Giotto or Renoir; most of the time they set themselves down to follow the Landseers and Parrishes.

Is creation to be found in the educational theatre? Perhaps twice in the same blue moon. It may be that the academic atmosphere is the wrong place to look for creation. The theatrical educators themselves do not think so, however. They believe they are the chief progressive factor in the theatre today. They institute new courses—but they seldom teach anything new in them; they enroll more students but they develop in them little initiative; they seldom recognize creativeness when they stand face to face with it. They build fine buildings—the best new playhouses in the land—but they look backward for their models and allow them to follow the architectural mold of the turn of the century; and they think that buildings will fool you into believing that there is theatre there! They have thought to substitute material and academic progress for creation; but in art you cannot have the former without the latter.

Is creative theatre perhaps to be found off the beaten path, among the players at the crossroads or on labor's stages? The signs are more hopeful, possibly because ignorance of established models on the one hand, or a revolutionary instinct to discard the trappings of the stage of the status quo on the other, forces these theatres to fumble toward something new.

As the people's theatre—using the term in its broadest sense—expands, it seems to depend more and more on the contracting professional stage for its inspiration; but since there is less and less that is inspiring there, the theatre everywhere grows pale. It must be admitted, however, that occasional creative sparks are struck off on Broadway. From that standpoint, in fact, the artists on Broadway, in spite of everything, seem to have more to offer than anyone else. The rest of the country vicariously feeds upon the dishes they prepare for the Belshazzar feast in Shubert Alley. But there is handwriting on the wall above the banquet table, and the Belshazzars of the Sardi Building as well as the plain folk in the rest of the country had better read it with care.

It might be called the signs of the times. Headlines from Europe are there and unemployment figures from home; not unimportant among its hieroglyphics are dollar signs and other symbols of trade, labor and the markets; the hand that wrote in some of these latter stretches three

thousand miles across the continent from Hollywood's
coral strand. And as it writes it beckons. On the day I pen
this Orson Welles' first film is to have its première showing and the morning paper says that "Jed Harris flew yesterday to the Coast to negotiate a producer-director contract in pictures." One by one the master chefs are being
lured to the more immaculate kitchens of Hollywood
where the wages are high, where birds always sing in the
window-sill and everything is cooked by electricity.

What I am meaning to say is that Broadway is becoming more and more a means to an end—a motion picture
end. This season we have seen plays sold to Hollywood
for one and two hundred thousand dollars and more.[1]
When such stakes are involved, the pressure gets progres-
sively stronger. Plays with increasing frequency are written for their film possibilities rather than for their stage
significance. Picture companies are now becoming stage
producers on every hand. The practice of buying up all the
acting, writing and directorial talent in sight, which the
movies have been doing for years, shows no sign of
diminishing. The studios have a nose for talent and
whether they intend or are able to make adequate use
of it, they are determined that they shall possess it. If
the people's theatre seeks to continue to depend upon
Broadway for what little nourishment is there to be meted
out, it will soon find itself starving to death. Already the
dishes grow fewer and fewer and the cupboard begins
to look bare.

The people's theatre—which is to say, the American
theatre—is growing, expanding. But this is a hollow tri-

---

[1] *Lady in the Dark* is reported to have been bought by Hollywood
for $283,000, *The Man Who Came to Dinner* for $275,000.

umph for the stage if it gets no better. The mere spread of Christianity means nothing unless it changes lives. In fact, the spread has never been very great in eras when the church was not dynamic. The spread of theatre across America will be meaningless and will disappear as rapidly as it has sprung up unless it is a dynamic living force. To be alive any art must be creative. The people's theatre —all our theatre—must develop a new creativeness to match, to justify and to assure the perpetuation of its expansion. These last pages will be devoted to a search for that new creativeness and the means to its development.

CHAPTER ELEVEN

By Theatrical Means

We must do neither ourselves nor the theatre the injustice of approaching it as if we were so many Bunthornes with a poppy or a lily in our medieval hands. We must remember that most of the things it sets before us—and in which we are delighted to share—have no more relation to art than has the price of spinach in Siberia.

So speaks John Mason Brown, mercurial word-juggling sage of Broadway's own spinach patch. His admonition (in *The Art of Playgoing*) comes as a dash of cold water in the face of the would-be critic who is about to set himself earnestly to the task of making some considered statements on the artistic form of the theatre. "Fortunately the theatre we know as playgoers," waggles Mr. Brown with a spiral toss of his head, "is not as serious as are those who write about it." I must agree and also plead guilty. I have taken the theatre pretty seriously in this volume. Undaunted by my lecturer-critic-author friend, however, I shall continue to take the theatre seriously through these last few pages.

I think that while it may be true that those who write about it and some of those who write for it put on too grave and sober a mien, one of the troubles with the theatre is that it has not often enough done likewise when looking at itself; or it may be that the theatre never looks at itself. It certainly seems not to have taken stock of its assets and its liabilities. Its carefree cry when admonished to do so has always been: "The theatre can never die. It has lasted for twenty-five hundred years or more. Everything's going to be all right."

That is probably true. Probably the theatre *can* never die. It certainly has a hoary and venerable lineage, this "strange agglomeration of amphitheatres, chancels, platforms, wagons, inn-yards, bear-pits, tennis courts, royal ballrooms, picture frames. It has flourished by sunlight and candlelight. It has danced and strutted and sat still. This Dionysius has died a dozen deaths and won a dozen rebirths." [1] Everything *is* probably going to be all right— but not unless the theatre soon awakens to its present situation.

For in the days of the amphitheatre and the inn-yards and ballroom the stage was the sole custodian and dispenser of that curious escape from and extension of immediate living which men have kept coming to the theatre to experience. Today that is no longer quite true. When Paul Green, pacing his pine-paneled library said to me, "I have a strong belief that every man among us has, consciously or unconsciously, a hunger for the theatre," I was doubtful. I wanted to believe it, of course; and I do believe that every man feels a need to rise out of himself and away from his surroundings to be entertained and amused, and sometimes to be moved and exalted, and again sometimes to look at those surroundings in a new

[1] Kenneth Macgowan: *The Theatre of Tomorrow.*

light. But is it the theatre alone he craves? Do not today the motion picture and the radio and tomorrow perhaps television share with the theatre the task of satisfying the kind of hunger to which the stage used to minister single-handed?

Theatre workers continue to ply their art and craft today as though nothing had happened in the last twenty years. In 1921 radio was in its infancy and talking pictures and technicolor were only half-realized dreams. Today more than fifty million people go to the movies every week and the man-hours consumed weekly by the American public listening to the radio rises into the billions. Of course the theatre knows all this. But it is primarily aware of the economic factors which have dislocated its life. It has not assessed the artistic implications in the new alignment.

It must be admitted that the stage has had a few far-sighted critics who have thought about its reorientation. Twenty years ago in *The Theatre of Tomorrow*, Kenneth Macgowan was reflecting on the effect of the motion picture medium on theatrical art:

This is something not to be dismissed too lightly [he wrote]. Is the new theatre already regnant among us, already a thing of fixed and appropriate structure, as different from our theatre in its physical and spiritual qualities as our theatre is different from the Greek? Is the motion picture, with its silent actors [remember this was 1921], its silver screen and its darkened auditorium the next theatre?

In the course of his remarks, Mr. Macgowan came to conclusions which were pertinent: "The power of the screen to be literally exact, both pictorially and humanly, to give us the absolute and intimate actuality of our life is more than evident. The screen is inherently representative, second hand. . . . Photographs do not speak to us directly." Finally he wrote, "The screen can do everything the realistic theatre can do; it cannot compass all the possibilities of the imaginative theatre."

Allardyce Nicoll echoed the same idea in a thoughtful chapter in *Film and Theatre*.

> The film has such a hold over the world of reality, can achieve expression so vitally in terms of ordinary life, that the realistic play must surely come to seem trivial, false and inconsequential. . . . If we seek for and desire a theatre which shall possess qualities likely to live over generations, unquestionably we must decide that the naturalistic play . . . is not calculated to fulfill our highest wishes.

To these admonitions to reconsider its style and technique the theatre has paid no attention. Today it is more devoted to realism and farther away from "the imaginative theatre" than it was in 1921. Critics seldom change the forms of art no matter how wise their counsels may be. The artists themselves do that; but now even the artists themselves are beginning to talk about it. Now perhaps things will begin to change—for change they must. It is interesting to observe that the designers are the most vocal.[2]

Mordecai Gorelik and Robert Edmond Jones arrive at

[2] A great wave of writing is overtaking American stage designers. Setting aside their brushes, they are all seizing pens. Robert Edmond Jones and Mordecai Gorelik have each published books within a few months of each other. So has Aline Bernstein. Lee Simonson is preparing a volume and here am I, who have made some pretensions at being a designer, presenting this book. I suppose this is indicative of the state of the theatre: designers turn writers either because the stage does not stimulate the exertion of their talent or because it has no place for their talent, or both.

different ends and travel by different roads but they start off in agreement. Says Gorelik:

The theatre which once tried to seize life whole now tends to describe life in terms of anecdotes and vague generalities. The theatre which reproached its predecessor with intellectual bankruptcy today looks askance at new ideas and makes a virtue of drifting. . . . If the stage wants to go on serving its audiences it will have to build a dramatic form suited to our times.[3]

Mr. Jones writes:

Our present forms of drama and theatre are not adequate to express our newly-enlarged consciousness of life. . . . The theatre we knew, the theatre we grew up in has recently begun to show unmistakable symptoms of decline. It is dwindling and shrinking away and presently it will be forgotten. . . .

We seem to have lost the original immediate experience of the theatre. Familiarity has bred contempt. In the dramas of today one feels an odd secondary quality. They are, so to speak, accessories after the fact. Our playwrights give us schemes for drama, recipes for drama, designs for drama, definitions of drama. They explain drama with an elaborate, beguiling ingenuity. But in so doing they explain it away. . . . There is nothing wrong with this recipe-theatre of ours except that it isn't the real thing. There is no dramatic nourishment in it. We are hungry and we are given a cook-book to eat instead of a meal. We expect to go on a journey and we have to be satisfied with a map and a timetable.[4]

The contemporary stage's shackle to realism is one of the chief concerns of both of these men. In this they echo Mr. Macgowan's words of twenty years ago, and in this they are right. In its attempt to exist side by side with the

[3] *New Theatres for Old.*
[4] *The Dramatic Imagination.*

cinema, the theatre will play a losing game as long as it insists on being realistic. For, as Mr. Jones points out, "Nothing can be so photographic as a photograph, especially when that photograph moves and speaks."

Now the issue of the theatrical versus the cinematic medium is joined. It is an issue that somehow takes on more moment outside New York than when one is caught up in Broadway's swirl. For in Manhattan there is still an audience for the theatre. The managers and artists along Times Square do not seem to be as aware of the inroads of movies as is the man who lives for a time in those parts of the country where legitimate theatre is so infrequent that the cinema reigns all but undisputed. Much more often outside New York than in it does one hear people say, "After all, what has the theatre to offer that the movies cannot provide?"

Very well, what does the theatre offer? First and very obviously, the living presences of the actor and the spectator in the same place at the same time. No matter how perfectly the complexion of Vivien Leigh may be reproduced in technicolor; no matter how miraculously three-dimensional techniques may hereafter present the contours of her tip-tilted face to us, Vivien Leigh herself will always remain absent from the motion picture house. Only what Mr. Macgowan calls her "representation" will we see and hear.

The theatre today, however, does not capitalize on even this simple, obvious and fundamental advantage it has over the movies. It clings instead to a picture frame which is regularly of the same general proportions as the movie screen. It watches that its actors never step outside that frame. It devotes itself to perpetuating a half-understood convention derived from Stanislavski and Antoine that the actors should conduct themselves as though there were no audience anywhere within miles. For the sake of fidelity to representation, inarticulate speech and bad diction have been tolerated, almost encouraged. In short, the stage has done its best to destroy its primary resource: living communication.

This destruction we may lay at the door of a too-rigid adherence to realism. That realism may have been all right for a day that knew not the cinema and our theatre that "grew up on a photographic basis . . . would have continued to function contentedly on this basis for many years to come if motion pictures had not been invented." But they were invented and so the theatre must put its faith in a return to what Alexander Bakshy first called "presentationalism."

After all, the realistic stage we know today is less than one hundred years old. In every era of the theatre's greatness the strong interrelation of audience and performer has been manifest. Ironically, it is only in this day of the cinema that the theatre has attempted the objectivity of the camera, the assumption of representation and of a technique based on ignoring the presence of the audience.

The Greek Chorus and the very semi-circular form of the Attic theatre; the Elizabethan soliloquy and the fore-stage on which it was delivered; the French *tirade;* the nineteenth century "aside" and the apron from which it was uttered; all these theatrical and dramatic forms conspired to draw spectator and actor into closer direct living communication. But today our theatre has thrown all these bridges out. Playwrights keeping alive an outworn Ibsen technique, directors following in the wake of Stanislavski conspire to keep the stage "true to life," but only in the sense that they seek to reproduce its externals.

But are all the bridges gone? Has the theatre entirely abandoned that theatricality which is its essence? I have exaggerated in my generalization. Fortunately, there are exceptions, and for the most part the communicative bridges that remain are the most significant manifestations of our theatre today. Let us recall them.

The lights are lowered, the orchestra blares forth brightly; the house curtain rises revealing a second curtain that is now blue, now gold, now rose, as lights change upon it. The overture is over. The inner curtain parts; a line of smiling boys and girls dances toward you. When their toes touch the footlight trough, they stop; leaning over it, they address to you the lines of their opening lyric. As they sing they smile and look at you. You are sure that the third girl from the left end intends her smile especially for you. You grin back. The song is done; the line breaks into a dance—but as their feet twinkle in and out, their eyes and their smiles remain directed at you.

Now a specialty dancer comes out: the spotlight picks her up. The shimmering curtain closes behind her and the chorus disappears. As she dances, she too looks brightly at you and when she is through and the boys and girls come back to reprise their lyric, you feel that already you are part of the show and that you and the performers are all sharers in some delicious conspiracy to rob the day of its woe.

The curtains part again. In broad, bright colors you see depicted a hotel bedroom, or the beach at Cannes, or the top of a bus: it is no realistic reproduction, just the essential or most amusing details that make some witty comment in themselves on hotels or beaches or buses. It is a comedy scene and before it has progressed very far, you find the comedians down at the footlights too, throwing their lines in your face. You laugh and they seem to take fresh strength for more sallies. The give and take is complete: it is hard to say whether the comedian gives more than he gets or not; without your laughter, he'd have a hard time.

Now the scene is over. A treadmill starts to work. Off goes the set slithering sideways before your eyes. Another set comes on from the other side as stage lights dim. Now it is a garden or a street corner—but of course it isn't really, for in the garden the flowers are painted vivid and gay flat on the wall; the street corner is just a bright blue lamppost and the houses are quite obviously projected by light, for they have a curious unreality that stone and brick or their imitations would never present. On this street corner a boy and a girl meet. And now it appears to be raining, but that doesn't bother them, for although they wear green trench coats, she has no hat. Under the lamppost they stop and sing, holding on to each other and never minding the weather. Now they move down from the post and are again at the footlights. The light is blue all around them, but they absurdly enough are haloed in a pink glow that comes from somewhere behind you and over your head. They sing of their love in the rain; but as they do, they take you in on their secret; they look at each other and smile and then they look at you, too, and smile; and you are part of their love.

The musical comedy, the revue—in them are the sound and spicy ingredients of theatricality. Living communica-

tion is their forte. They are so completely of the theatre
that they can never be successfully transferred to the
screen. I have never seen a musical show in the movies
—no matter how trick its shots of dancing couples and
lines, how sumptuous its décor—that I didn't feel the complete inadequacy of canned chorus girls as a substitute
for live ones. Their smiles I knew were never for me;
the comic's jokes never made the camera laugh and
whether I roll in the aisle or not he will never know and
never care. Something very valuable has been lost.

Vaudeville, the minstrel show, musical comedies and revues can be numbered among America's outstanding theatrical achievements. All of them are "presentational;" all
are of the theatre theatrical; none of them can the movies
beat at their own game. Their success when well done at-
tests to the public's appreciation that in them the theatre
offers something that can be gotten nowhere else. *Hellzapoppin* does not run on into its fourth year by chance.

The theatre, however, is not all jugglers and singers
and dancers, black faces and clowns. Let us go to another
theatre. The lights have scarcely been dimmed before you
hear a voice coming to you over a loudspeaker. It addresses you directly in a tone that commands your attention, like some radio commentator addressing his unseen
listeners. The voice is telling you the subject of the play.
It is slum clearance or electric power or agriculture or socialized medicine. Now the curtain goes up. Before a setting that is scarcely more than skeletonized, actors portray
a scene; in spite of the unreal environment it seems to
be a slice of life. But just as you are about to settle back
to observe, a man rises from a seat three rows ahead
of you. He runs down the aisle and up a flight of steps

which you discover for the first time are connecting the stage with you. "Just a minute," he apologizes and enters into a colloquy with the unseen loudspeaker voice, or with one of the actors.

What was the point of the scene, he asks, as the setting dissolves and the actors disappear. The editorial voice explains. To illustrate, figures are offered in chart form, flashed on a screen that has been rapidly lowered. "I see," says the man from the audience. So the play continues. Now another slice of life. Now another interrupting question. You yourself begin to be roused to think. You have a question, too: "How did this situation come to pass?" Your interlocutor wonders also; he asks for you. The loudspeaker voice replies, "We'll show you." Again a screen is lowered. This time a series of film sequences and montages rapidly extend the locale and the time; you are carried swiftly into the background of the subject: Europe, Asia; 1840, 1888, 1905, 1921.

The play begins to have the excitement of a radio news broadcast or a newspaper "Extra;" and more so: for this is a *living* newspaper and there are things to see, real people to watch. Now the final scene is reached. The man from the audience who has given voice to your unspoken inquiries asks his last question. Now he turns to you with some of the actors and the loudspeaker to back him up. "You, there," they all say, addressing the audience directly: "You see how it is. Something must be done," together they editorialize. "What are you going to do about it?"

This "living newspaper" technique is based on the idea of living communication and for this reason it has a peculiar urgency which even a good documentary film never

quite possesses. It assails the audience with its direct contact between spectators and performers and practically
makes them all participants together. For the development
in America of this technique, which Mr. Gorelik allies to the
"epic" theatre as evolved earlier in the 1930s by Piscator
and Brecht in Germany, we have to thank the Federal
Theatre. Wrote John Mason Brown (now in another
mood and himself quite serious):

From the very beginning it was clear that the most vital
idea the Federal Theatre had as yet contributed to stagecraft
as we have known it in this country lay in these dramatizations
of current events. . . . Here is a performance which is part
lecture and part history; which utilizes lantern slides, motion
pictures and an amplifier to make its points; which resorts to
vignetted playlets as well as to statistics; which is as broadly
humorous in its stylized manner as it is indignant throughout;
and which, although it has little or nothing to do with the
theatre of entertainment as we ordinarily encounter it, is none
the less theatrically exciting even in its most irritatingly partisan
moments.

The living newspaper is essentially didactic, but the theatre need not be afraid to be big enough to include
didacticism.

In 1938 the Pulitzer Prize for drama was awarded to
Thornton Wilder for *Our Town,* a play which has had
immense and immediate popularity throughout the country. Its form was the culmination of a series of experiments that Mr. Wilder had been making for several years
in one-act plays to release the stage from the bondage of
representationalism. Do you recall the performance? As
you took your seat, you observed that the curtain was already raised; the stage had no scenery; the back brick

wall with its corrugation of radiators stood gaunt in the gloom. Then a man came out. He arranged a few tables and chairs, came over and leaned against the proscenium, lit his pipe and stood gazing at you.

As the lights began to dim, without moving he addressed you in a conversational tone: "This play is called *Our Town*. It was written by Thornton Wilder and produced by Jed Harris," he began. "The name of our town is Grover's Corners, New Hampshire," and walking about the stage he pointed out various imaginary spots: "Up here is Main Street. Cuttin' across it over there on the left is the railroad tracks." And now "Another day's begun" and the stage began to be peopled with Grover's Corners characters. At first you were a little self-conscious at all the lack of scenery, at the obvious pantomime—you who were used to three-walled rooms and plenty of pots and pans in a kitchen set; you were a little self-conscious at being addressed so directly and simply. But soon you began to throw that off.

Interrupting a scene between two neighboring housewives, the stage manager (he who first addressed you) came out to say "Thank you very much, ladies" and off they went. Then he introduced a college professor and a newspaper editor to give you "a little more information about our town." These men spoke directly to you and when they were finished two or three men and women arose in different parts of the theatre to ask questions. The effect of all this was to break down all psychological barriers between you and the people on the stage. By the second act this was so completely accomplished that you felt it quite natural for the stage manager to say:

Now I have to interrupt again here. You see, we want to know how all this began,—this wedding, this plan to spend a life together. . . . George and Emily are going to show you now the conversation they had when they first knew that —as the saying goes—they were meant for one another. But before they do that I want you to try and remember what it was like when you were very young, and particularly the days when you were first in love. . . . You're just a little bit crazy. Will you remember that, please?

By the close of the play as the stage manager said, "Eleven o'clock in Grover's Corners. . . . Tomorrow's going to be another day. You get a good rest, too. Good night," you felt that a common experience in which you had shared was ended. The closeness of the relationship between spectator and performer upon which the play so much depended and toward the development of which Mr. Wilder had so consciously fashioned his style, was of the essence of theatre as apart from cinema.[5]

I spoke just above of "a common experience" in the theatre. This is another unique possession of the stage with which the motion pictures as now presented do not compete. When we go to the movies, we go as solitary individuals; we establish no contact with the performers because it is impossible; we establish no contact with our fellow-spectators because film moments are robbed by their nature of immediacy and hence we share no common experience together. This is accentuated by the continuous performance practice which prevents a theatre-full of spectators from getting out of each moment the same measure

[5] Marc Blitzstein's *The Cradle Will Rock* and *No for an Answer* are representative of another aspect of "presentationalism," of drama combined with music which addresses itself with great effectiveness directly to its audience.

of empathic response. For the scene of highest emotional tension I who arrived at the beginning of the picture may be prepared; to the man on my left who entered the theatre but five minutes earlier, the scene has no impact for he has been insufficiently prepared. Consequently, we can share nothing. In the theatre, whether he is aware of it at the moment or not, each spectator is sharing experience not only with the actors but with every other member of the audience. This is a precious thing and is of the essence of play-going. It is something which screen, radio and television can never take away from the theatre.

When sound was added to films a movement was started to call them "talkies." The movement failed. The cinema remained in the vernacular of the millions who attended it "the movies." There is something revealing about this and about the persistence of the term *"motion* picture." It suggests that the essence of the screen lies in action—in movement, motion. Speed is inherent to the medium—infinitely more so than to the stage, as anyone knows who has seen the straight filming of a stage play. Such a performance seems incredibly slow. For the screen has accustomed our eye to travel with it at a speed near to the swiftness of thought. And our eye, receiving impressions more rapidly than our ear, can accomplish the feat. Too many words slow down this magic carpet ride, so language becomes subordinate to action.

But man has invented language solely in order to have symbols for his ideas, to become their embodiment, their perfect vehicle. Of course, there are other ways of conveying ideas through artistic media: a dancer may utter no word and yet tell you everything; so may a musician, a sculptor, a painter. But the theatre as we have known it ever since the morning of Aeschylus has been concerned to communicate through human speech. I do not speak derogatorily when I say that the cinema appears to be potentially an art form farther away from the theatre in its non-verbal address to us than it is to painting or to dance. It is simply to make clearer the difference and to establish what we may demand of each medium.

The expression of ideas through words is then another of the particular powers of the stage and one of which the stage in our modern day seldom takes adequate advantage. We cannot look to Hollywood in the immediate future for the promulgation of many strong and original ideas, any more than we can expect at any time that whatever ideas are presented there will be projected primarily through the medium of speech. We have seen time and again the cinema's emasculation of an idea; take *Golden Boy* of Clifford Odets as but one example or for that matter the unwillingness of Hollywood to turn any of his other plays into pictures. When an idea is presented as in *The Grapes of Wrath*, it is interesting to observe how—quite properly—words are subordinated in the film to visual impressions and to action. This perhaps helps to explain the inability (which I believe is fundamental and will persist) of the motion pictures to make satisfying screen versions of Shakespeare's plays or of any of the great classics. When action and photography do their best they are still not substitutes for the language of classic writers for the stage.

The theatre then must repossess words if it is to make the most of its resources and take an assertive stand in this cinematic day. It must do away with "the cult of understatement, in which the climax is reached in an eloquent gesture or a moment of meaningful silence." It must seize the classics with less fear and show the people that there is glory in language. It must encourage our native poets to write for it, and it must demand of its playwrights a virile and more vibrant prose. Toward the close of his brilliantly-written last chapter of *The Stage Is Set*, Lee Simonson says:

In the modern theatre, as in every other, the beginning is in the word. The actor cannot be reanimated until he is given the task of animating language so enriched in texture and so resonant with implications that it requires for its expression the entire range of modulations of which the human body and the human voice are capable. Only speech that soars can fill the undecorated forms of our most formal stage settings with enough significance to make them more than barren architecture and, at the same time, prevent our ambient patterns of color and light from becoming empty decoration.

There are artists of the theatre who are not unmindful of the word. The Mercury Theatre was founded by Orson Welles and John Houseman on the belief that the stage must reassert its power over words, music and light. *Julius Caesar, The Shoemaker's Holiday, Heartbreak House* were all plays to which the movies could never have done justice and they were presented with conscious emphasis on the dramatic power of words and by a technique that was eminently *theatrical*.

A few years ago we seemed to be witnessing a revival of poetry in the theatre. Within two seasons we had three major productions of *Hamlet:* by John Gielgud, Leslie Howard, Maurice Evans. The latter's success in other less well-known Shakespearean dramas indicated that there was an audience for Elizabethan verse. Maxwell Anderson's poetic plays were likewise enthusiastically received so that he seemed justified in writing, "Unless I am greatly mistaken many members of the theatre audience . . . are not only ready but impatient for plays which will take up again the consideration of man's place and destiny in prophetic rather than prosaic terms." T. S. Eliot contributed at about the same time his *Murder in the Cathedral* and O'Casey his *Within the Gates*.

But that poetic upsurge seems to have somewhat spent itself. This must not be allowed to occur. Rather must the stage with renewed determination lay hold on the poets in its dooryard and impress them into its service. For that is one of the few ways along which its salvation lies. One need not claim that Mr. Anderson is himself a great poet in order to agree with him when he says:

Those who have read their literary history carefully know that now is the time for our native amusements to be transformed into a national art of power and beauty. It needs the touch of a great poet to make the transformation, a poet comparable to Aeschylus in Greece or Marlowe in England. Without at least one such we shall never have a great theatre in this country, and he must come soon, for these chances don't endure forever.

I have said that too seldom does the theatre examine its assets. In this chapter I have attempted to suggest one or two of the more fundamental and obvious ones. I have hoped that by being brought face to face with these assets, artists of the stage may be encouraged to seek a theatrical reorientation based on them, to undertake further explorations uncovering other resources peculiar to their medium.

Enthusiasm for exploration and constructive self-examination seem to me to have largely gone out of the theatre. The restless pioneering which brought into being the new forms that characterized America's theatrical renaissance of twenty to twenty-five years ago—that spirit is manifest on Broadway only in those quixotic egocentrics, Saroyan and Welles. The latter is now more a man of the screen than the stage, and although the former has brought a new and precious magic into our theatre, it is not safe to be dependent upon the unpredictable output of a single artist. As this exploratory spirit disappears from Broadway, I should like to think that it is at work elsewhere. But it does not seem to be the case. That is my chief regret as I look at the theatre off Broadway. Nine-tenths of the college theatres, the community and little theatres are no more concerned than Broadway is in devising ways to strengthen the theatre artistically.

In marked contrast to this is Hollywood. I am convinced that the majority of theatre workers in America underestimate the brains and creativeness of Hollywood. It may be true that its results fall far short of the mark, and there seems to be no doubt that much of its brains and creativeness is wasted and lost. Nevertheless, in the studios of the motion picture companies there is a ferment of creative activity that is seldom to be seen around Times Square or in any other of our theatres. There is an understanding of that medium and its potentialities such as few stage artists possess about theirs. There is enthusiasm for exploration, constructive self-examination, a pioneer spirit which seeks—against the fearful odds that Hollywood imposes to impede its own progress—to improve and extend the possibilities of the screen.

The theatre must recapture these things for itself. It must clarify its own design, it must strike out toward new horizons. It must realize that in a machine age the handicraftsman's only hope of survival lies in the perfection of his product. It must realize the truth of Robert Edmond Jones' affirmation that "the only theatre worth saving, the only theatre worth having, is a theatre motion pictures cannot touch."

CHAPTER TWELVE

Give, Gamble or Be Taxed

IT IS ONLY LATTERLY, in our mercantile age and particularly in English-speaking lands, that the stage has been looked upon as a business and a source of revenue to private investors. Throughout its ancient and more or less honorable history, this art has in other times and places been grouped with the other arts as the object of public or private patronage. Up to the present time—which is to say, up until the beginning of the war in 1939 —most of the nations of Europe possessed theatres subsidized by the state. This was carried to its extreme in the Soviet Union where, with the abolition of practically all private property, every playhouse was owned by the government. From the Baltic to the Mediterranean the other European countries maintained at least one state theatre, which although dependent primarily upon popular support, yet was guaranteed and backed by the government.

This practice of theatrical patronage by the state fell into desuetude in England in the eighteenth century and until 1935 it was practically unknown in America. Instead of any of the arts receiving government support in this country they have been primarily depend-

361

ent upon individual capitalistic philanthropy. The rise of libraries, art museums, galleries and collections, orchestras, operas in America is linked with such names as Andrew Carnegie, Colonel Higginson, Joseph Widener, Andrew Mellon, Otto H. Kahn, Cyrus Curtis. These men and hundreds like them poured forth millions of dollars each year in support of the arts. Whether they knew much about it or not, American tycoons apparently felt that a gesture toward culture was obligatory upon them, and in the instances of men like Higginson and Kahn, who were genuine and discriminating art-lovers, great good was accomplished.

Curiously, however, in the distribution of this largesse the theatre never participated. Rich men from time to time put money into it, but not for the same purpose that they endowed libraries, museums or music. From these latter they expected and received no financial return. But the stage was looked upon as a sort of gambler's paradise, and when a capitalist put money into a play, it was with the idea that he might reasonably receive a great deal more than he had invested.

For the exclusion of the theatre from among the recipients of endowment it is hard to assign any other reason than that it was not commonly considered an art or as being cultural. Probably for too long a time and in too large a proportion of its exhibitions the theatre was *not* an art. Then, too, strong in the Puritan strain that clung to the British bourgeoisie into the eighteenth and nineteenth centuries was the feeling that the stage was the realm of the devil, a place of license and deceit. It could barely be tolerated, let alone publicly supported by benefactions. This attitude was carried to these shores and traces of it can be found still strong today in America.

Consequently it is easy to see how commercialism has risen in the theatre. It is not hard, also, to observe that the very grip of commercialism has been in part responsible for its not coming to be accepted as an art and worthy of the private subsidy the other arts have received. So a vicious circle has evolved.

The first break in the circle occurred when the educational institutions began to put money into theatres of their own. Gradually the conception grew in this field that dramatic literature was not the only aspect of the theatre that was cultural—that its transformation into the living performance might qualify too. So we can set up as a milestone in the theatre's struggle for respectability and subsistence the grants it has received from academic sources.

The next break came when the great foundations, notably The Rockefeller Foundation, The General Education Board, The Carnegie Corporation and The Rosenwald Fund (the latter particularly to aid Negro expression) began to subsidize theatrical projects. Most of these grants, it is true, were dictated by an interest in the stage's sociological and educational usefulness rather than by a Medicean desire to support the stage as an art. Probably for this reason, as I have already said, the Foundations' subsidies have been withheld from the professional theatre and devoted exclusively to assisting the amateur. Still, money has been given for propagating the theatre, and it must be set down as another step in the right direction.

In 1935 the United States government at last entered the picture and under the Works Progress Administration set aside funds to support the arts: painting, writing, music, theatre. But there was a catch, as everyone knew. The theatre was still to be subsidized not because of its cultural significance, but again for sociological reasons. In the great unemployment problem with which the New Deal sought to cope, stage artists figured along with everyone else. The purpose of the WPA was that of "giving people employment in their normal lines of endeavor who otherwise would be in distress." Consequently it decreed that unemployed artists should be put to work in their own professions; stages must be created for actors on relief and it was these stages that became the Federal Theatre.

It is obvious that from the beginning and because of the very circumstances which brought it into being, the Federal Theatre Project was not a national theatre in the best and established European sense. It was first, last and always an unemployment relief measure. Hallie Flanagan, who was appointed its Director, and a number of her colleagues believed, however, that out of the amorphous organization and in spite of the misdirection —from a purely theatre point of view—of its appropriations, a national government-supported theatre could develop. The progress that was made during the four years of its existence suggests that their dreams would not have been vain, had they not been snuffed out just as they began to be realized.

Mrs. Flanagan's own account of the work of Federal Theatre in her recently published *Arena* is so comprehensive and compelling that there is no need for me to do more than hastily summarize what seem to me to be its principal accomplishments and the reasons for its failure. Its first and I suppose most important accomplishment was that it did what it was set up to do; that is, it put unemployed stage artists to work at practicing their own craft and provided them with a livelihood which the professional stage denied them. More important from the point of view of creating a national theatre, however, was the awakening of thousands upon thousands of people to an awareness of theatre. Because of its popular prices and because of its units which went into out-of-the-way spots where drama had seldom been, a great new public which had never seen plays came into playhouses of the WPA. In four years well over thirty million people witnessed its productions.

Typical is the story I heard on the West Coast of *The Swing Mikado's* performances. It played in a theatre that seated sixteen hundred. By 8:10 every night throughout its run not more than two or three hundred tickets had been sold. In the next twenty minutes every seat in the house was bought. What did this mean? It meant that thirteen or fourteen hundred people came each evening to the theatre as they would go to a movie: an audience knowing so little about the theatre that it was not aware that it is customary to buy reserved seats in advance; which took it for granted that as when going to a movie all one did was arrive, put down one's money and walk in.

This creation of a people's theatre, the building of a truly popular audience for the stage was the Project's greatest achievement. As Mrs. Flanagan said, "Any theatre supported by taxes from all the people must be a people's theatre. . . . For the theatre has never been greater than its audience and in our own vast country the theatre should not consist exclusively of plays done in a few cities for a few people." In addition, it seems to me that in certain special fields it did more good than any agency that had preceded it. For instance it made possible children's theatres on a broader scale than had ever existed. This the commercial theatre has never touched and the non-professional stage has regularly considered a sideline. It also gave opportunity for the development of Negro drama beyond anything that had been theretofore possible. Because it was relieved of the onus of box-office commercialism, it was free to seek new forms: the living newspaper, some of Orson Welles' and John Houseman's productions on the New York project and certain dance-drama experiments were the most notable contributions.

Federal Theatre's inadequacies were in many instances the result of forces beyond its control. The limitations imposed by its being a relief agency have been already mentioned. The fact that its excellent work was localized in New York, Chicago, Los Angeles and San Francisco, so that not enough worth-while productions were available to the public elsewhere, was the result of a WPA regulation which prevented transporting relief workers from one region to another. Since the best caliber of unemployed artists were in these cities, it is natural that the best work would be done there. Mrs. Flanagan herself says, "Any future plan for either a regional or a nation-wide theatre under governmental or other auspices, taking cognizance of the fact that the greatest need for theatre exists where there are few theatre people available, should be set up under a plan which permits flexibility of movement of both personnel and equipment."

Red tape and bureaucracy, excessive length of time spent in preparation of productions, interference of WPA administrators not on the Project, who lacked interest in or sympathy for it seem to have materially hurt the Project. Whether a government theatre in a democracy would always be subject to these handicaps, one cannot say; it might. Its collapse was, of course, not the result of its failure, but the determination of legislators to abolish it. The stigma of "communistic" was attached to it, but it seems fairly evident that this was on the whole an unjustified charge. That the Project was socially conscious nobody can or would want to deny, but that is not at all the same thing as being communistic.

It would appear that Federal Theatre became a political scapegoat. Determined to curb the New Deal's relief program, Congress abolished this project, some of whose publicity had been unsavory, as a compromise measure. I believe, however, that there was one good reason why Federal Theatre was singled out to become the sacrificial lamb: it began to be recognized as the powerful instrument that the stage can always be when it is in the hands of showmen who have something to say. Some people inside and outside the government did not want this. If the Project had said nothing about anything, had produced nothing sensational in its four years, had reached the ears of only a few people instead of millions, paradoxically I doubt if it would have been abolished.

Its closing therefore strikes me as a sweeping gesture of censorship. By the simple expedient of cutting off its allowance, Congress silenced this theatre completely. Would this be the inevitable fate of any other national theatre in the United States which attempted to speak freely about the people's problems? I am inclined to believe that it might. Of course we could have a national

classic theatre, along the lines of the state repertory theatres abroad—which would say nothing about anything
strictly contemporary, and would be concerned with presenting only the "universal." It would have great educational and cultural value and would not be apt to be
censored. But it would tend to make the theatre a museum,
like the Comédie Française, if it were exclusively devoted
to the past. Nevertheless a national classic theatre would
certainly be better than nothing.

What about a national theatre that would not be dependent upon the government's pocketbook? Might such
a theatre have greater freedom and come closer to the
ideal? As a matter of fact, we possess such a one. For
with that in mind a group of public-spirited citizens with
the backing of President Roosevelt in 1935 obtained a
charter from Congress that brought into being "The
American National Theatre and Academy." Its purposes
were summarized at the time of its incorporation as: "(a)
to present theatrical productions of the highest type; (b)
to advance public interest in the drama; (c) to further the
study of the drama in universities and schools; (d) to
include a school of the theatre in all its branches."

The chief differences between this organization and the
Federal Theatre Project seem to have been that it was
not to depend on a government subsidy; it was not to be
limited to artists on relief but was to call upon the best
artists of the American theatre; it was to seek insofar
as possible, to be self-supporting. The most significant
difference, however, lies in the measure of accomplishment: in the fact that the Federal Theatre during the
four years of its existence employed over 12,000 persons,

gave 63,000 performances attended by over thirty million people; the American National Theatre and Academy in the six years since its inception has done nothing. Today its officers consist of Robert E. Sherwood, A. Conger Goodyear, Edith J. R. Isaacs, J. Howard Reber, Stanton Griffiths, Brooks Atkinson and a Board of Directors of sixteen other prominent social, business and theatrical leaders of New York and Philadelphia. Its original prospectus somewhat illiterately stated that after it was granted its charter, "a selection will gradually and carefully be made of a nation-wide committee of persons best qualified to represent the following:

   I. Educational Institutions
  II. Representative Citizens; Civic, Patrons of Art, Labor, or any persons who are otherwise qualified
 III. Representative members of the Professional Theatre."

It further claimed that "The American National Theatre and Academy should be a People's Project, organized and conducted in their interest free from commercialism as its basis." One looks in vain, however, for any nation-wide representation, for any spokesman of education or labor, for any signs that the American National Theatre and Academy is a "People's Project"—or any other kind of a project for that matter.

Has the narrowness of representation at its council-table offset the presence of such illustrious names and brains, and been a reason for its failure to accomplish anything important? I think very possibly so. A national theatre cannot be created by a small group of New Yorkers and Philadelphians; we are too large a country for that. It cannot be created by a group composed solely of high-bracket capitalists and commercial theatre magnates; we are too broad and various a country for that.

Such a group, however, should in six years have accomplished *something*, it seems to me. Has lack of funds impeded it? I do not think so, for the Directors represented and had access to great financial resources. Of course, the Federal Theatre in four years cost in excess of forty-six million dollars, in spite of the fact that the great majority of its employees were receiving only a relief wage; and any national theatre attempting to do an adequate job of serving the nation along all the lines which the Federal Theatre showed to be parts of the problem, would need to spend a sum going into seven or eight figures.

Has a real lack of purpose prevented the fruition of this project? I suspect that this is true. The idea of a national theatre is grand and appeals to any idealistic citizen who cares for the drama. Putting it into practice is another matter. It is no part-time job—as Mrs. Flanagan and her cohorts can testify. The Board of the American National Theatre will never be anything more than a name unless it amplifies its number to include all the kinds of people it claims to want; until it formulates a program; until it raises money to set it in motion; and until either it employs some full-time administrators to accomplish it, or some of its number give up every other interest for its sake.

There are those who believe that we can never have a national theatre in the United States by imposing it from above. Such persons claim that if it is to come into being at all it must rise out of the people themselves, must be a confederation of regional or local enterprises. To a partial extent, we also already have such an organization, the

National Theatre Conference. Certainly it has accomplished more than the National Theatre and Academy. Its membership consists of sixty-four leaders in thirty states. Its president is Paul Green and its executives include Barclay S. Leathem and Frederic McConnell from Ohio, Gilmor Brown from California, Burton James from Washington, Lester Lang from Texas and Lee Norvelle from Indiana.

The projects which the National Theatre Conference conducts show its interest in training theatrical leadership, in securing certain royalty advantages to community playhouses, in enlarging dramatic library facilities throughout the country, in assisting the army in setting up dramatic entertainment programs in military training camps, and in encouraging the writing and production of new plays outside of Broadway. The financing of the Conference and its projects is done by a grant from the Rockefeller Foundation which for the period from 1941 to 1945 amounts to $55,000. As an organization it does not concern itself in the actual production or presentation of plays in any locality as the Federal Theatre did and as the National Theatre and Academy proposed to do. It is a purely consultative body aiming to stimulate dramatic activity throughout the country.

The National Theatre Conference calls itself a "cooperative organization of directors of community and university theatres organized collectively to serve the noncommercial theatre." From this definitive statement it can be seen that actually it is not at all a national theatre, and that it does not claim to be. It has no direct power and practically no money. It is exactly what it calls itself—a "conference."

The importance and usefulness of the National Theatre Conference seem to me to be impaired by two things. In the first place, it is exclusive and undemocratic. Membership in the Conference is by invitation only and a kind of aristocracy of the non-commercial theatre has been set up. Secondly, by its exclusion of all workers in the professional theatre, of all New York producers, directors, actors, designers and critics, it has cut itself off from brains and talent which could contribute much to any truly "national theatre conference." Instead it seems to encourage that antagonism between the professional and non-professional stage which is of no use to either and only harms the cause of the American theatre as a whole.

In discussing the National Theatre Conference at this point, we have been led away from the question of theatrical economy which is the subject of this chapter. We have not finished with the matter of government subsidy. What of state and municipal theatres? Both of these are also not unknown. The state of Washington for three years had a theatre project financed in part from a Rockefeller Foundation grant, in part by funds of its own. Set up through the Department of Public Instruction, it operated as a repertory group presenting plays to school children. Thousands of boys and girls in seventy-nine high schools throughout the state saw, among other things, *The Comedy of Errors, No More Frontier,* a bill of three one-act plays, performed by professional actors under the direction of Burton James of the Seattle Repertory Playhouse. Obviously this was a small beginning for a state theatre, with its attack on only the children's theatre problem. Nevertheless it was a start along a necessary and fundamental line. It is regrettable that it was not so handled that when the Foundation funds were exhausted the state would have considered it worth while to finance the project entirely; but such was not the case, and the idea has been allowed to lapse.

Many states actually sustain state theatres through their indirect support of playhouses on the campuses of their state universities. Some of these university theatres through their extension work, through setting up children's programs, through sponsoring high school dramatics, through taking student plays on tour out through the state are indeed fulfilling many of the functions of a state theatre. In these centers the machinery for a state dramatic program potentially exists. Legislators would do well to ponder the possibilities of endowing these theatres with sufficient funds to enable them to expand their service, to procure professional leadership, to employ full-time acting companies; (into which incidentally could be absorbed the most talented students, whose futures present today such a problem to conscientious teachers). With half of the money they pour into buildings, states could establish theatres for themselves. Of course, a school theatre—in which the artists are young people preparing for a future somewhere else and wherein they will pass but a few short years and move on—in its nature is a way station and a means to an end. A state theatre is not a means to an end; it is an end in itself. The establishment of such an institution is a full-time job—not possible of creation by professors worn out by hours of teaching and academic duties; not possible by students with credits to gain in French or chemistry at the same time. It demands the concentrated and dedicated energies of whoever undertakes it. These theatres therefore should be the *products* of the university dramatic programs, growing out of the present set-ups and employing much of that talent that is present in every region if it is not allowed to slip away.

To what extent would such a program if set up become bureaucratic and be subjected to the same political censorship and control that we saw at work in Washington in 1939 when Federal Theatre became a political football? Only a naive and uninformed citizen believes that our educational systems are wholly exempt from politics. Nevertheless they seem to function with more integrity and freedom than many governmental agencies. Conceivably state theatres might be able to function satisfactorily as part of the educational program until such time as they were able to stand alone and command support from the public treasury for their own sakes. Bureaucracy in a state office should be appreciably less than in offices administering a theatre for forty-eight states.

We have seen occasional examples of municipally subsidized theatres: in Palo Alto, to a limited extent in Houston. To this list must be added Cleveland Heights, Ohio, where the Cain Park Theatre operates in the summer time in an outdoor playhouse built by the city fathers and managed by enterprising Dina Rees Evans. A series of nine plays and musical comedies are presented by a semi-professional company at a forty-cent top. Cleveland Heights resembles Palo Alto in being a fairly small suburban city with a homogeneous upper middle class population. Whether either of these theatres could operate with equal success or at all in a large city with complex social stratification is a question. Certainly it would be more difficult. Ralph Welles in Palo Alto believes any municipal theatre can succeed only on an amateur basis with participation as the keynote. This enters into the picture, I am convinced; and any municipal theatre should be concerned to foster activity in settlement houses, schools, churches: wherever citizens foregather for recreation. But this is not all. Equally important, perhaps more so, would be the establishment of a first-rate theatre company that could provide the best possible dramatic fare at prices everyone could afford.[1]

I have often heard it said that only that theatre can be healthy which can be self-supporting. If the stage cannot draw enough people to it to keep its doors open, it does not deserve to exist, I am told. As long as it depends upon patronage of any kind, it cannot be a virile and indispensable part of the American scene. Theoretically, I am inclined to believe this. Practically, however, the history of art disproves it. During the two periods when the arts were most virile and most indispensable to the people—the days of the Greek Republic and of the Renaissance—they were the objects of patronage.

Furthermore, the stage can only become indispensable if it is an habitual experience; it can only be virile if it is in touch with all the people. In a democracy that means that it cannot belong exclusively to the wealthy leisure class. It must be something everyone can afford. I have spoken of the relation of the theatre to the motion pictures from an artistic point of view. It is now necessary to consider the economic relationship. Any high school student of economics knows that by mass production the cost of the individual piece can be reduced. The shoe factory which turns out a thousand pairs of shoes a day

[1] This idea will be amplified in the following chapter.

can afford to sell each pair for less than the cobbler who fashions but one. The parallel is obvious. Hollywood can afford to sell each of ten thousand imprints of Laurence Olivier for infinitely less than the theatre can afford to sell the original Olivier.

Can the theatre meet this competition? If it cannot, what chances has it for survival? It seems to me that this is at the heart of the discussion not only of this chapter, but of this whole book. The answer is that the theatre *must* meet this competition, or it has *no* chance of survival. For if it does not meet it, it will become a rarer and more esoteric experience available to fewer and fewer people and will eventually disappear. Whether it would then come back reborn—as most people who have thought about this eventuality believe—or whether the movies plus radio plus television, dividing theatrical talent among them, would conspire voluntarily or involuntarily to take its place completely, I do not know. I do not think the theatre can afford to run the risk.

The stage in a democracy must be available to all the people. That means both geographically and economically. That means a popular-priced theatre. That means a box office that can sell its product for the same twenty-five cents or forty cents or seventy-five cents that the movie box office demands—and no more. How can it be done? Can the commercial theatre do it? Can anyone do it and keep the theatre self-supporting? Does it require a subsidy; which means, in other words, that the tax-payers or some other source must make up the loss?

It is conceivable that the commercial theatre can do it. This is not to say, however, that it will. So complete a readjustment of the economic structure would be required that the commercial theatre would practically cease to be commercial. Actors accustomed to $500-a-week salaries would have to take one hundred dollars; union labor's wage scales would have to be reduced; real estate brokers, managers, backers as well as authors and directors would all have to be content with but a pittance of their former returns. Of course the volume of business might rise in compensation. The Federal Theatre showed what a vast popular-price audience potentially exists. Then the number of plays that could be sustained might double, as well as the length of their runs.

A popular-price theatre is certainly essential to the future well-being of dramatic art in this country. There are many persons on Broadway who are well aware of this. Elmer Rice, for instance, says:

The managers contend that ticket prices cannot come down until costs come down. In this I think they are unrealistic and unimaginative. The way to reduce costs in any industry is to cut down the overhead by a great expansion of the market; and this can only be done by cutting radically the price of the product. As long as the theatre is a luxury trade run solely to satisfy the feeble demands of a few hundred thousand agency customers, it will continue to decline both as a business and as an art. . . .

The fact is that the theatre cannot hope to survive economically unless those who control its destinies band together in the foundation of a program of long-range planning that includes an enlightened and constructive labor policy; a full-time utilization of plant (that is to say, a remedy for the present wasteful idleness of theatre buildings); a reduction of costs, through careful budgeting, pooling of resources, standardization of equipment and other similar measures, which are commonplaces in any well-run large-scale business or industry; a thorough-going continued exploitation of product, after the first quick profits have been taken; most of all, the opening of vast new markets, by a study of the needs and the purchasing power of the millions who never enter the doors of a theatre.

It is the last item in this program that is the most important to those of us who still take the theatre seriously; because the theatre cannot flourish as an art if it is conditioned solely by the tastes of the well-to-do.

The Playwrights' Company, of which Mr. Rice is a member, has twice attempted to present plays at popular prices. Neither was marked with eminent success, partly because popular prices were established after the play had run as long as it could at a three-dollar top. To make such a scheme effective it must be geared from the start as a dollar-top production. The Mercury Theatre was a successful popular-price producing company; so was the ILGWU Labor Stage. In the fall of 1941, Robert Lewis and Elia Kazan will have inaugurated another such theatre.

These are hopeful signs. They suggest that it can be done—and on Broadway. However, the extent to which this movement will be successful will depend upon the degree of unanimity that can be achieved among all theatre workers, including most definitely the managers and their backers. Here is where the hitch may come. For the stage is notoriously unable to agree about anything. Successful producers and artists are unwilling to make sacrifices and without the co-operation of the successful ones nothing can be accomplished. There is no central authority within the professional theatre which all wings acknowledge. Without such an authority (which would have to be representative of all factions and groups) it seems unlikely that any-thing so far-reaching as a fundamental change in the whole commercial theatre's economy can ever be effected. Mr. Rice is correct in his diagnosis and in his suggested cure. But will Broadway do it?

If the commercial stage itself eventually creates a popular-price theatre and succeeds thereby in wooing back a popular democratic audience to its playhouses, I am inclined to wonder how long it will be before prices will rise again. I am inclined to believe that the commercial theatre has serious interest in the idea of popular prices only because it is failing as a business enterprise and not because it believes as Mr. Rice does in the democratic concept of a stage available to all the people. If the theatre should take an upswing as a result of lowering its prices, I am inclined to believe that costs would rise again. As long as the stage exists for private profit this seems to me inevitable. Therefore, I am forced to conclude that with the commercial stage alone will never rest the solution for the creation of a popular American theatre available to all the people everywhere.

It is as dangerous, however, to make any predictions of the future in this cataclysmic hour as it is difficult to main-tain a measure of perspective on the meaning and activity of the moment. To attempt any suggestions as to how the theatre may subsist in the next years seems more than futile. It is generally conceded that our own country will move forward after this present war into a state so differ-ent from anything we have known that even our most far-sighted economists, sociologists, and political thinkers can-not at this moment chart the way. Such vast issues are at stake that any attempt at a theatrical prognosis seems unimportant and well-nigh valueless. Nevertheless I feel bound to take some soundings and peer as far ahead as the gathering fog and my own feeble sight will allow.

It seems fairly likely to me that the theatre will survive this present crisis. Whether our national social and economic structure will come through seems more doubtful. In its relation to these altered social and economic forces the theatre will therefore be bound to reorient itself. I suspect that private subsidy of art, either for commercial or philanthropic ends, will diminish and that public or institutional control will grow. What forms this may take—whether the arts will become closer allied economically to the educational institutions (and so to the state), to the trade unions (and so to the people) or directly to the government (and so to a people's state)—I do not know; but I believe that we are about to see the end of the theatre as a private enterprise. Whether this is a welcome sign, I cannot say. Only the kind of society and government which is ours hereafter will determine whether the theatre gains. I am bound to hope, however, that a great theatrical resurgence on a sounder economic basis and for nobler ends may be upon us.

CHAPTER THIRTEEN

Broadway and Beyond

THERE IS an American theatre today; there will be one
tomorrow. It will have strength and validity and
beauty in proportion to its ability to reflect the positive
forces in the American scene, creatively to transmute them
into artistic forms which are essentially theatrical, to find
means of conveying them to the people of every region
within our land. This, in sum, is what I have been attempting to say in these past three chapters. It is a task
which must be the concern of every theatre worker: of the
star arriving in her limousine at the stage door on West
Forty-fifth Street, of the professor in his lecture hall, of
the little theatre director at his board meeting, of the
young worker in his mobile group at a strikers' meeting,
of every student of the theatre as he stands tremulous and
bright-eyed on his commencement platform. It is a responsibility which must be shared equally by all.

This year we have heard a great deal of talk about
national unity. We have come to realize that we must put
aside prejudice and bitterness and suspicion if we are to
face the future with constructive purpose and a determination to make our way of life survive. I believe that the
theatre too must unite for its own salvation.

All artists are inherently and perhaps necessarily individualists. Artists of the stage, however, must wed their individualism to a collective creativeness in which others share collaboratively. Every play that has ever been produced has called forth this combined individual-collective artistic effort. Because of the individualism, stage artists have frequently exhibited jealousy and egocentricity; simultaneously out of the collectivism has grown a familiarity with loyalty and a common language which draws together all people who really care for the stage.

During seven months, I visited theatres in thirty states. I went north, south, east, west; into towns and cities and out into open country. I expected to find the people very different: far Westerners, Yankees, deep Southerners, corn-belt Middle Westerners—each with a different temperament and outlook to which I would have to readjust myself. No such thing occurred. Instead, from one coast to the other I met the same people. Their ages varied; their coloring; now their r's blasted joyously forth, now were softened and slurred to a fuzz of sound; here we talked under a palm tree, there under the "El"; here we were all brought up on Broadway; there I was the only one of that dubious breed. But everywhere we talked the same language; everywhere we exchanged the same hopes and forebodings; everywhere I was at home—everywhere, that is, that the theatre was really cared for.

Unity, therefore, seems so easy of accomplishment. At the same time, it seems so hard. For almost everywhere, pricking through this common loyalty and enthusiasm, flashed a needle of jealousy; the non-professional theatre as a whole suspicious of the professional; Broadway contemptuous of the amateurs. On Broadway mutual antago-

nisms and distrust were rampant; even more so among
the non-professionals: the community, college, labor stages
all so frequently at loggerheads, each believing itself to be
Aesculapius. Barriers rose on every hand where no barriers
should be.

The professional and non-professional theatre both have
common problems to face. I have suggested some of them:
the need for more theatre, in order that we may increase
the chances for better theatre; the need for a new creativeness so that the stage may reassert its identity alongside
of the cinema and the radio; the need for new playwrights; the need for a revolution to the dictatorship of
the box office so that the theatre may be released to all
the people. These problems, artistic, social, economic are
before us all. They cannot be solved by the professional
theatre alone, nor by the non-professional.

One weakness of the Federal Theatre was its inability
to utilize on the one hand the best talent of the professional stage and on the other the already established
people's theatres in community centers. One weakness of
the National Theatre Conference is its unwillingness to
shake hands with the profession; one weakness of the
American National Theatre and Academy is its omission of
everyone *but* the profession from its councils. Until a
deeper rapport can be established, we can never have a real
American theatre.

Until the last very few years the most creative talents
for the stage have been concentrated in New York (except as Hollywood has lured them away). Even with the
rise in these last years of the theatre-off-Broadway, only
a very small number of first-rate artists in this field have
chosen to stay out of Manhattan. Even today if the lead-

ing lady in a little theatre performance in Kansas is made to believe she is a second Helen Hayes (as to be sure, she may be), she will hop on the first train and head for New York. The most talented boy in the university theatre will be encouraged—even by those who profess to have lost their faith in Broadway—to try his fortune along Times Square. Frederick Koch, most ardent regionalist of them all, will tell you within the first five minutes about every ex-Playmaker who has succeeded in the big city.

There has always been a "hot spot" like this and I suppose there always will be; in our grandfather's day it was Boston; before 1914 it was Paris; our grandchildren may hie themselves off to Detroit or Chicago or California. It may move geographically, but always there will be a cultural capital where the Bow Bells ring for eager young artists. Today it is New York. As long as it remains New York the first-rate talent will continue to draw toward it as toward a magnet. And as long as the first-rate talent is in New York, the theatre of the rest of the country will inevitably be second-rate.

While the theatre was growing and expanding on that little island, it was not so bad. Talent was welcomed and shared with the rest of the country through a prosperous road. But Broadway, as we have seen, is contracting and there is not room for half the talent that is there. Still the lure has not worn off; still the leading ladies from Kansas and the graduates of the drama schools come to New York. Three-fourths of them end up in Macy's or Woolworth's or trudging with the gait that becomes hypnotic in and out of Broadway's offices. I know a number of them: most of them have charm, some of them have talent. One-tenth do get a "break"—the Betty Fields, the

Jim Stewarts; so the rest hang on believing their turn will
come next—lost to Kansas, lost to Broadway, lost to themselves; Macy's the only gainer.

When I have met prospective recruits for Broadway's
army of "forgotten men" I have told them that story.
They have regularly countered, "We want to be in the
theatre; where else can we go? New York is the only
place; nowhere else is there any theatre in which we can
work professionally." My only reply is, "You must *make*
theatres elsewhere. We must all make theatres all over
America wherein you may work and to which our people
may come."

The longer and farther I traveled up and down the continent the more I came to realize the necessity for a geographical decentralization of the theatre. Our country is
too vast to allow the best of any one art to be concentrated at one pinpoint on the map. Gradually I came to
feel that my chief concern was to discover in what ways
this decentralization was being and could be accomplished.
What responsibility was the little theatre movement assuming in this task? the educational theatre? the professional theatre? The answers lie already recorded in the
pages that have preceded.

In general I feel that no one has assumed adequate
responsibility. That is why I have been frequently impatient and unkind. For I believe that a real decentralization
is imperative and it lies so nearly within our grasp. When
I have seen it elude us, it has dismayed and angered me.
On the one hand, I have seen people working with no
adequate conception of what the theatre is and should be.
They had become aware long before I did of the need
for decentralization, for bringing the stage close to the

people; but they had no stage to bring—a point which I was appalled to discover did not bother them. They had built up a remarkable sales organization and had no product—or only a very old second-hand product—to sell. These people seem to have thought the theatre could be saved by good wishes.

On the other hand I have found superior artists at work with no thought of or concern for the fact that they and their medium were a part of the complex cultural pattern of a vast democratic nation. Their provincialism is more marked in New York than elsewhere; the whole pressure of metropolitan life seems to bear down to disrupt their connections with the sweep of the American day.

The more I reflect, the more it seems to me that our theatre problem is one of distribution. It reminds me of the tragedy of dumping wheat into the river here while men and women are starving there. Nine-tenths of our college-age young people all across the country have never seen any other play than one done by their high school or college mates. For nine-tenths of America the art of the theatre is meaningless because it is outside their experience. But in New York nine-tenths of our artists are unemployed. Nine-tenths of the talent that might create an American theatre is wasting away. This waste must be coupled to this need if we are to avert a major cultural tragedy.

How can this theatrical redistribution occur? The first step toward its successful accomplishment is the lowering of the present barriers between the professional and the non-professional stage. New York, which cannot sustain all its first-class talent must yield some of it to the country and the country must wish to accept it.

Take the educational theatre. I have inveighed against the tendency of that movement to develop into a formula: teachers teaching teachers to teach. The longer this continues the farther from the reality of the theatrical experience will this movement go. Some time ago Allardyce Nicoll said, "The more the artist sneers at the University, the more the University will tend toward traditional and hidebound methods. Let the artist come into the University, let him take his place in the development of that cultured side of academic work which after all is its chief task."

The University must welcome the creative artist and the artist must welcome the University. I do not say that every playwright, actor, director, designer should become a teacher, could become a teacher. Many are temperamentally unsuited and hence undesirable. But there are many who would be a considerable source of inspiration and stimulation to those young people with whom they would come into contact. Occasionally such an artist might become a permanent neighbor as Paul Green has become at the University of North Carolina or like Maude Adams at Stephens College. Occasionally he might come for a year, as Mary Morris went to Carnegie Tech; or he might come as a guest for a six- or eight-week period as Elmer Rice, Arthur Sircom, Harley Granville-Barker, have done at Yale this past year. It might bring new zest to invite a single actor to perform with the students, as Fred Stone was invited to do at Rollins College; or a director to stage a particular play, as Theodore Komisarjevsky directed *The Cherry Orchard* last season at Yale; or a nucleus company for a festival as occurs at the University of Michigan each spring. Campuses close to metropolitan centers might be visited by artists who would accept regular part-time posts as Donald Oenslager has done for many years at Yale and as Otto Preminger did there in 1939-40.

These are all arrangements involving participation of first-rate professionals (and that does not necessarily mean "big names") in the non-professional field. What occurs in the educational theatre could conceivably occur in the community theatre on a more limited scale. Already Zollie Lerner has had guest professionals act on his community stage in Kansas City; Aline MacMahon, Irene Purcell and a number of professionals have appeared at the Dock Street Theatre in Charleston; Luise Rainer appeared in a Piscator production of *St. Joan* at the Washington Civic Theatre.

None of this can be accomplished without a desire from both sides. Actors' Equity Association and the other theatrical unions must encourage such a movement rather than hinder it. Professional artists must grow to look upon it as more than a means of making extra money when times are slack for them. The local artists and teachers must not eye their professional guests with jealousy and suspicion, but rather seek to acquaint them with the possibilities for sharing in the creation of a truly American theatre.

A second line along which a theatrical redistribution might occur, side by side with this increasing liaison between professional and non-professional artists, can arise from the professional theatre's own rediscovery of America. What I mean, I suppose, is either the revival of the road or of stock companies on a new basis and with a new purpose. Heretofore both have been commercial in aim, one the mere extension of Broadway.

I envisage, for instance, the establishment of professional repertory groups presenting a series of plays—perhaps only three or four at the start—at a popular price scale which can compete with movies. Such groups must be directed by first-class directors, be composed of first-class actors and present first-class dramas. They might begin by performing in a series of half a dozen cities; Broadway would not be their end although it might be their beginning. If and as such an idea gained support the companies could extend their tours and increase in number.

This adaptation of the traveling repertory company might not be different in caliber from the Lunts' presentation of *The Taming of the Shrew, Idiot's Delight, Amphitryon 38*, with a permanent group; from Katharine Cornell's *The Barretts of Wimpole Street, Candida* and *Romeo and Juliet* offered in repertory, from Eva Le Gallienne's tours. It would differ radically from them in that it would cost the public one-third as much; would treat New York as but one city among many—as it used to be considered a good many years ago. To insure a truly popular-price season and at the same time to guarantee the excellence of the talent municipal support might be required in each city to make up the difference between the cost of such a first-rate enterprise and the gross obtainable. I do not however regard that as undesirable.

Alternatively, I envisage the establishment of resident professional theatres on the order of the resident theatres of the smaller European cities, each with a permanent staff, directorate and acting company; each performing a series of the best plays also at popular prices. These companies might conceivably exchange productions, might even take their repertories to New York from time to time—much as the Boston Symphony and the Philadelphia Orchestras invade New York's Carnegie Hall, but yet retain their residence elsewhere. This is no new idea. Ten years ago Lee Simonson saw in such permanent resident theatres a solution for the theatre's ills. In *The Stage Is Set* he wrote:

It is not beyond the bounds of possibility that the general level of culture in this country may eventually rise to a point where a group of wealthy citizens will feel that it is no less important to provide their city with a theatre than with a museum or a concert hall. The American theatre may yet become as honorific an outlet for private benefactions as art, music and literature have been. . . . When the performance of plays is felt to be equally important, these cities will provide whatever endowment is needed in order to have permanent acting companies of first-rate players, as they do now to maintain first-rate players of violas, tubas, French horns, and kettle-drums; and they will be directed by leaders comparable to Golschmann, Gabrilowitsch, Goosens, Koussevitsky, Sokoloff, Stokowski, and Toscanini. . . .

The first step toward rehabilitating the theatre in this country will be made when the wealthiest citizens of such centers of wealth as Philadelphia, Chicago, Boston, Detroit, Cleveland, St. Louis, San Francisco, and at least ten other large cities decide to devote as much money and energy to building and running a theatre as they now do to running art museums and symphony orchestras. . . .

In the ten years since 1931 when Mr. Simonson thus prophesied, there has been no evidence that the "wealthiest citizens" have become aware of the chance that is theirs. Now I fear it is too late. The depression years have reduced the wealth of the wealthy and the present national emergency is bound to reduce it still further, so that I doubt if these resident theatres can be built in the way that the orchestras and the museums were built. Rather does it seem to me, writing a decade after Simonson, that it rests with the people, not with the Maecenases. The establishment of such theatres either traveling or resident, now rather depends upon one of these things. Either they must wait upon the development of public demand; or else all production costs must be able to be reduced to a point where such projects can be inaugurated without great demand, and count on creating their own demand; or, finally, they must wait upon the creation among local or state governments of sufficient appreciation of the importance of the project that subsidies may be forthcoming.

The third line that can lead toward a more complete and desirable decentralization of the American theatre rises out of the non-professional theatre itself. Its goal would be the establishment of companies either resident or itinerant, such as I have just described, offering plays at popular prices, having its origin not in the professional theatre but rather in those dramatic centers already existing off Broadway and by their geographical situation already part of a decentralized theatre. I envisage, in other words, the establishment of super-graduate groups rising out of university theatres, or of permanent professional companies rising from community playhouses to absorb the first-rate talent that each now so frequently loses to New York, and thus to provide first-rate dramatic fare to the immediate public.

We have seen the graduates of the Chekhov Theatre Studio form themselves into such a company and tour with eminent success; we have seen the Carolina Playmakers do this in the past and watch them contemplate such a step in the future. We have seen the Cleveland Play House and the Seattle Repertory Playhouse, the Erie Playhouse and the Hedgerow Theatre become such permanent professional groups in specific localities. To accomplish this no doubt financial assistance is necessary. The community theatre that truly serves the entire community deserves its full support and is entitled to municipal aid; that may be one direction for it to look.

Existing side by side with regional professional theatres such as I have just described, even as they exist side by side with Broadway, I envisage continuing educational and community theatre movements. They will have new or, at least, clearer definitions of purpose which should make them stronger.

The educational theatre will find itself charged with two responsibilities. The principal obligation resting on its shoulders will be the creation of a demand for theatre, and of an appreciation of it. It will bear in mind with Maxwell Anderson that "there is only one condition that makes possible a Bach, an Aeschylus, or a Michelangelo— it is a national interest in and enthusiasm for the art he practices." It will recognize with Anderson that a national art resembles a pyramid: at its apex the supreme artists, its base a great body of art-lovers. The height of the pyramid will be determined by the breadth of its base. "The national culture is the sum of personal culture."

The educational theatre will also be concerned to train leaders for the professional and the community theatres and for its own perpetuation. Recognizing that in each of these fields leadership must assume differing responsibilities even while concerned with the same essential, it will attempt to meet its manifold challenges thus. In the student headed for the professional stage it will encourage the maximum of initiative and creative endeavor. It will temper this with an insistence on the discipline of acquiring a solid grounding in dramatic techniques, going far beyond present efforts in both directions. Appreciating the importance in artistic training of actual experience as opposed to text-book theories and of a master-apprentice rather than a teacher-pupil relationship, the educational theatre will encourage a rapport with leading professional artists and a program based on actual doing. For, as Thomas Wood Stevens aptly remarks to his non-commercial colleagues, "We all know that we have too many theoretical producers, too many window-dressers, too many jugglers with colored lights. What we must strive for is a body of workers who know the center, who can pierce to the heart of the mystery, and who have the courage to apply the yardstick."

In preparing young men and women for community theatre leadership, our educational theatre must recognize that to a fundamental stage training must be added an understanding of the unique problems of that field, which are principally sociological. Proper community leadership cannot be maintained by a young man who knows everything about window-dressing and juggling with colored lights, as Mr. Stevens would put it, and nothing about handling people, about relating a recreational and cultural program to his community. There must be a new emphasis given to this part of a community playhouse director's preparation. This is where most educational theatres fail today, and in the day to come I envisage the social significance of this community field as becoming more and more important. To strengthen its training of such leaders, I urge a rapport with existing community theatres and their leaders, comparable to the liaison I have recommended with the professional stage. Actual field experience should become a part of this preparation in more places than it occurs today.

With the kind of expansion of the theatre that I look for, teaching will no longer become the refuge of the timorous as it so often is today. Instead only those persons will be encouraged to become teachers of drama who have a sincere conviction of the importance of the educational theatre—right down through the high school level—and who are temperamentally suited to teaching. These people will be attracted to teaching because they recognize the primary importance of bringing into being that body of cultured citizens, of art lovers, upon whom the whole theatrical structure is based. For without such a citizenship none of this expansion which seems to me essential to the stage's continuation will be possible.

What place will the community theatre have in this new alignment of dramatic forces? When the day comes that each region has its own resident or touring professional company to supplement a Broadway-inspired "road," it seems likely that the custodianship of the art of the theatre will be lifted from the community theatre's shoulders. It will then be left free to exploit more thoroughly the social and recreational purposes which are usually at the bottom of its existence in any case. I know of no little theatre, middle-class or proletarian, which has come into being as a result of the demand of people who wanted to see plays. Always it has been organized by those who wanted to put on plays, to act, to express themselves or put across some specific idea to others.

This is sufficiently important that it should not be lost sight of. Community theatres must extend their influence and encourage more and more participation; they must seek to increase their sociological and recreational value. At the same time, they must give up the idea that they are *the* theatre—as soon, that is, as there *is* real theatre in their community. In Cleveland we have seen this work out. As the Play House has become professional, groups like the Eldred Players, the Lakewood Little Theatre and dozens of others have sprung up as outlets for amateur talent. There is no reason to deplore the professionalization of the Play House, and every reason to welcome the other groups. The Play House attempts to serve one need, the little theatres another. Both are important but they must not be confused. The Play House could not do a good job if it tried to serve as a platform for every amateur who desired "self-expression"; the little theatres would err if they tried to go professional, beat the Play House at its own game, and restrict participation only to those who were specially talented.

In conclusion, let me go back to the idea that is behind decentralization of the theatre. It is not simply that I am seeking ways to relieve the unemployment along Broadway, nor that I wish to find subtle means of extending Broadway's influence; I think that should be plain. My concern is for the strength of our American culture, to which I believe the theatre is one contributor. And that American culture I find tied with invisible but unbreakable cords to the American people wherever they may dwell.

It is those dwelling places that make the difference. The spires and towers of our greatest city throw long shadows when I stand in its streets. But the shadows are really short. I have to go no farther than the sandy lowlands of New Jersey or the foothills of the Catskills to lose sight of them. The towers have shrunk and no longer obstruct the horizon; the country stretches out and a new definition of culture, a new conception of patriotism pervade me. Says Lewis Mumford: [1]

> Patriotism is a universal attribute of normal people. It is grounded in space and time; that is, in the actual soil and landscape of a region, and in the experience of life that, in retrospect, constitutes its people's history. The deepest source of this love of country is neither law nor property, although they play a part in qualifying it: the ultimate source is the land as land, the sky as sky, the people as people.
>
> —The red soil of the Shenandoahs in Virginia, with the apple trees whose boughs skirt the ground; the granite hills of Vermont with their white churches, stiff against the north wind, honest and unyielding as only fanatics are honest and unyielding; the undulating meadow land of Iowa, with curves as delicate as a pea's tendrils; or the hard primeval clarity and the enveloping loneliness of the desert, from the white alkali of Utah to the red canyons of Arizona.
>
> These are samples of our regions: samples of backgrounds, to be filled out with the stories that are told and the pictures painted, by the houses that are fabricated, by all that the hand of man has added.

[1] In *Faith for Living*.

A new sense of region, a new kind of patriotism; out of it a new grasp on the meaning of culture, its sources, its power; and out of them all a renewed faith in the transforming power of the artist, of this art—the theatre. This is what has come to me from the miles piled upon miles that I crossed through Virginia to Vermont, from Iowa to Utah to Arizona. Mumford can sum it up better than I. But I know now that New York is only one region; Broadway is only one region.

The myriad lights of the fabulous signs over Times Square chase one another in dizzying circles. The tentacles of subterranean transportation beneath the asphalt stretch uptown—"Broadway-Seventh Avenue"; to Columbus Circle; to Central Park where the dogwood blooms, where little boys skate shrilly on the cement; to Riverside Drive with the Palisades across, purple against the setting sun; to Harlem, dusky and throbbing; to the Bronx with its rows of façades—windows open, gramophones playing inside. The tentacles stretch downtown: to the "garment district" where boys with racks of dresses dart among the hooting taxis; to "the Village" with its screaming urchins, garbage cans, brash night clubs of a pseudo-Bohemia, to Wall Street, sheer and stark, to the Battery—water beyond. The tentacles stretch cross-town: "the Shuttle," "Lexington Avenue Express," "the East Side"; downtown: tenements, areaways, Italian pushcarts, washings on the housetop lines, housing projects, foreign tongues; midtown: skyscrapers, smooth, solid, beautiful; uptown: Park Avenue, spaniels on leashes, doormen, long town cars, awninged canopies; St. James', St. Thomas', St. Bartholomew's, St. John's, brownstone fronts, more areaways, tenements; people.

New York is not America? Nonsense. Of course New York is America. Just as London is England; just as Paris is France. But hawthorne hedges and thatched cottages and coal mines are also England? And poplars beside a canal and the Cathedral at Chartres and the turrets at Carcassonne are also France? Certainly. So New York is just one America; one part, one region. Broadway is the flowering of its theatrical culture: Broadway too is regional. But Broadway is not America. Virginia knows that; so does Vermont, and Iowa, and Utah, and Arizona. The American theatre is Broadway and is beyond Broadway.

Broadway will not disappear; at least not until New York blows away. It will beckon; it will be a mecca; it will remain the standard of reference; its nod of approval will set the stamp—all this will continue to be so, as long as New York is the first city of the country. But as the nation grows up, as each state and region awakens to fuller self-consciousness, as the migrations cease and roots begin to grow deep into the soil, there will spring forth on the way to Mecca a thousand oases.

That is what I mean by decentralization of the theatre. It does not wait upon the destruction of Broadway; it is something that grows up coincidentally. Side by side with whatever form or dimension Broadway may assume in the years to come, and growing out of any one or two of the lines I have already traced, I envisage regional theatres: resident in the larger centers, traveling to the crossroads. These will be professional theatres, for I believe the final responsibility for the creation and perpetuation of every art rests upon the artists of undivided minds and spirits.

Between these theatres and Broadway and among these theatres themselves, I see a constant interchange of ideas and talent, for regionalism must not become provincialism. As a truly American theatre thus begins to grow, a theatre stimulated and complemented by educational and community stages that possess a new-found power and purpose, I see constantly increasing opportunities for absorption of the talent that is wasting in Manhattan and is stifling on the threshold everywhere. I see playwrights, who today find no market for their labors and turn their talent to other ends, returning to the theatre, some to sing the special song of the region, others to voice the words that unite all regions. I see a gradually enlarging public whose appetite is whetted by what it feeds on.

I shall doubtless be accused by some of wasting time in conjuring up a Utopia. I admit that all manner of things stand between ourselves and a real American theatre. Lack of money, lack of enough great talent; above all, lack of popular desire prevent the immediate fulfillment of our dreams. But without goals we shall progress nowhere.

We are living in a chaotic day; we are part of a contracting civilization, I am told. We cannot expect an expanding art in a contracting age—history has shown us that. To this I reply: if our civilization is contracting, may not one reason be that our arts have lost their power? Is a contracting day the cause of a weakening culture? May it not in some measure be a result? Part of what we mean by an expanding age, by a renaissance is a flowering of the arts. Why then is it not doubly urgent to call for an expansion of the theatre in such a day? It is more than ever important to strengthen our arts or we will find ourselves with a bankrupt civilization, with little worth fighting to preserve.

In the spirit of Thomas Wolfe, I believe that "the true

discovery of America is before us." With him I believe that "the true fulfillment of our spirit, of our people, of our mighty and immortal land, is yet to come. I think the true discovery of our own democracy is still before us." It is in this faith and for this reason that our theatre must persist and grow strong. None of us knows what the America of tomorrow will be nor how best our stage can serve it. I only know that the theatre must be dedicated to democracy, must belong to the people. I only know that it must be unashamed to laugh and to cry, unafraid to look steadfastly at our life as it really is and as we may envision it. I only know it must demand the best of its artists, must be devoted to the fullest measure of creativeness. I know that only so can our theatre have any validity as an art, any meaning for us as a people, any share in the final accomplishment of our democracy.

Index